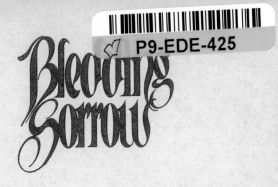

"FIERY...

More than enough to hold the readers' attention."
Library Journal

"ABSORBING...

A chilling novel, centered around an ancestral estate in England, a recurring family madness, a ghastly crime in the 17th century, reappearing spectres . . . rich prose and deftly maintained suspense."
The Milwaukee Journal

"EVOKES PAST AND PRESENT HORROR...

Yorkshire's desolate moors and an ancient grand house provide the setting for this tale of crossed love and brutal punishment reincarnated."
Booklist

A LOVE UNDYING

"If you like stories about ghosts haunting old English castles or estates you will love this book."
Best Sellers

Marilyn Harris
Bleeding Sorrow

AVON
PUBLISHERS OF BARD, CAMELOT AND DISCUS BOOKS

Poem on p. 408 from *The Complete Poems of Stevie Smith*.
© 1972 by Stevie Smith; © 1974 by James MacGibbon.
Reprinted by permission of James MacGibbon and Oxford
University Press, Inc.

AVON BOOKS
A division of
The Hearst Corporation
959 Eighth Avenue
New York, New York 10019

First Avon Printing, May, 1977

AVON TRADEMARK REG. U.S. PAT. OFF. AND IN
OTHER COUNTRIES, MARCA REGISTRADA,
HECHO EN U.S.A.

Printed in Canada

Whatever we see or feel or do, whatever action there is anywhere in the universe, while being the effect of past work on the one hand, becomes on the other, a cause in its turn and produces its own effect. Each one of us is the effect of an infinite past. The child is ushered into the world not as something flashing from the hands of Nature, as poets delight so much to depict, but he has the burden of an infinite past; for good or evil he comes to work out his own past deeds.

This is the law of Karma. Each of us is the Maker of his own fate. There is no other way to vindicate the Glory and the Liberty of the human soul and to reconcile the inequalities and the horrors of this world, than to place the whole burden upon the legitimate cause—our own independent actions.

—The Law of Karma
Vivekananda

Prologue

On the remote tract of England which stretches between the seacoast and the town of York lies the flatland known as the Yorkshire Plains.

The estate of Bledding Sorrow is situated in the East Riding of Yorkshire, midway between Driffield and the coast. Here the flat landscape changes, grows hilly with treacherous ascents and deep ravines, the earth in upheaval as it rushes to form the giant bluffs which lead down to the sea several miles away.

Bledding Sorrow stands elegantly on the side of such a bluff and is one of the authenticated haunted grounds of England. There still can be heard on certain nights the lady's screams echoing through the entrance front with its projecting bays. And on three occasions, recorded by the Investigative Society of Psychic Phenomena, in the small upper chamber where her final agony took place, blood has been seen to appear on the highly polished, though scarred and worn oak floor.

Because of this, in later years Bledding Sorrow was sometimes interpreted to be a corruption of the word "bleeding" by those who chose to romanticize the legend.

But of all the legends of England, the story of Bledding Sorrow needs no superfluous romanticizing. It stands alone, a grim account, still passed from cottage to cottage, whispered about, mused upon, dreaded, feared. . . .

The Legend

The story goes that from 1175 to 1599 the Bledding estate led a fairly placid life, maintained and cared for by a long, unbroken line of Bledding males who married, had children, and little by little increased the size of the estate and the ever-present sheep herds. Some married very well. The fifth heir, one Thomas Bledding, wandered as far as Shropshire in search of a wife, found, wooed, and won Eleanor Sorrow, the only daughter of a rich Shrewsbury farmer. The dowry was exceedingly generous, and the only condition of the union was that the name Sorrow be added to the title of the estate. Hence, Bledding Sorrow came into being.

These early Bledding males, by all historical accounts, appeared to be gentle, untutored men who were content in their ignorance and gradually increasing wealth, well-known and respected men in the Midlands who were born, procreated, and died, and who seemed to take little interest in anything beyond birth, procreation, and death.

Then, in 1599, the seventh heir to the estates, yet another Geoffrey Bledding, came to live in the old manor house. This seventh heir, as the villagers put it, swam in from a different sea. Although he reroofed the twelfth-century house and made it habitable, he was never happy there. A short, stocky, fair man with pale, almost feminine skin and dark blue eyes set wide apart, he had greater, more ambitious visions. He despised the crude country ways of his friends and neighbors and would actually pale and grow ill at the stench of sheep and stable.

Unable to find contentment in his earthly surroundings, he built a small chapel behind the manor house.

3

It still stands, although the interior suffers from decay and neglect. There Geoffrey Bledding made nightly visitations, appealing to any power greater than himself to lift him above the clay and dung that caked about his feet and held him prisoner on the bleak moors of Yorkshire. When no heavenly arms reached down in assistance, it was reported that he took to self-flagellation, standing naked before the small crude altar, inflicting unspeakable indignities on his body, emerging at dawn, scarred and weeping.

The servants, terrified by the sights and sounds of the night, fled the estate and refused to return, and ultimately Geoffrey Bledding was left alone in the old house to endure his agony, womanless, friendless, the sheep going unsheared and starving, the estate itself falling into a hideous state of neglect.

Twice, on the basis of his vast land holdings, he appealed to Elizabeth I for a title, and twice he was turned down. His outrageous bad fortune continued until all those who knew him considered him to be quite mad. He could be seen at night walking among the sheep, addressing them as though he were their lord. The green thickets around the old manor house grew higher as the man himself grew bearded and hoary and reclusive.

It was rumored about the village of Bledding that he was purposefully starving himself within the walls of the old house, and it would be only a matter of time until death triumphed and the Bledding estate would be up for public auction.

Then one sharp cold winter evening he emerged from the chapel. A farmer passing by in the lane saw Geoffrey Bledding through the night mist, but did not recognize him and went fleeing into the village crying, "Ghost!"

But it was not a ghost that the villagers saw as they crept up the lane, not a ghost insofar as a ghost represents the dead. Rather it was Geoffrey Bledding, an enraged, transformed, clean-shaven, erect Geoffrey

Bledding, announcing to the stars that he would create his own kingdom over which he would be king, that out of the dung and sheep dip would emerge the finest house and estate in all of England.

The ranting and raving went on for the better part of the night, the man himself treading erect up and down before the crumbling door of his house. At last the pledges and curses and avowals ended. This cessation of activity aroused the little knot of villagers from the ravine in which they had hidden. They looked up in time to see Bledding bow low from the waist as though thanking them for their time and attention and turn with a regal air and walk back into the confines of the house.

"Mad! Mad!" was the general opinion of the villagers, who muttered their way back down the lane to their cottages. But they were wrong, for that night signaled a new age at Bledding Sorrow. Within the year the construction of a new and elegant hall had begun. By some miraculous transformation Geoffrey Bledding had become a master overseer, not only restoring the estates to their previous good condition but showing safe and comfortable profits at every turn.

It was a magnificent Elizabethan house, an architectural triumph in spite of the obsessional nature of the man who ordered it built. The entrance front faced south, its symmetry retained by the device of putting the entrance door at the side of one of the projecting bays. Glittering mullioned windows laced back and forth across the imposing red-brick front. The eastern skyline of the hall was romantically irregular and showed how the front of the hall was built higher than the rear in order to accommodate the Long Gallery on the top floor. Stone quoins which have bravely resisted the ravages of an east coast climate set off the red brick of the hall. Above the entrance was the date 1603 with the initials of Geoffrey Bledding.

It was by far the most splendid hall in all the Midlands, set in formal gardens with topiary trees and roses and an incredible collection of life-sized statuary of working-class men and women all engaged in menial tasks, but all with their heads raised, looking up. And beyond the gardens were the thousands of profitable acres which now comprised the estates.

The decoration of the hall was completely unrestrained. The finest masons and wood-carvers were brought in to execute ornate and bogus family arms. The space between the formal south front and the wall was taken up with a bowling green and terrace. A charming cobblestone courtyard led to the gatehouse, which bore carvings of draped female figures and had beautifully proportioned angle turrets topped by domes. By late Tudor times the gatehouse no longer served any defensive purpose, but was designed solely as an imposing ornament to set off the hall. At Bledding Sorrow it accomplished this function triumphantly.

Throughout the hectic years of construction Geoffrey Bledding was a quiet, efficient, though possessed man. His shouted vows that cold winter night seemed to be coming true. He was creating a kingdom. His entire manner and demeanor had changed. He spoke little or not at all except to issue orders concerning the rake of a wall or the thickness of a beamed ceiling. He watched over every detail of his hall, and if his explicit demands were not obeyed, he could be a ruthless taskmaster. No social traffic passed beneath the ornate arch of the gatehouse, for he had no friends, only servants and hirelings, and he seemed to prefer it that way.

In 1608, when the last brick had been swept and the final richly carved door hinged into place, when the last army of artisans had been paid off and only silence echoed through the elegant rooms, Geoffrey Bledding appraised his kingdom and decided he needed a wife.

Of course, no local woman was good enough, and there was the distinct possibility that no local woman would have him in spite of his fine new hall, for the villagers were still convinced that his madness had not been cured, but had simply taken on a different face.

So it was that early one morning Geoffrey Bledding passed beneath the arch of his fine gatehouse in search of a wife. He was gone for more than a fortnight, and it was early in December when the villagers looked out of their windows and beheld the strangest of sights. There, riding on horseback down the lane, was Geoffrey Bledding. Attached to the horse was a crude harness, at the end of which was a cruder wooden cart. Scattered over the rough-hewn planks of the cart was a sparse bale of straw, and lying, apparently unconscious, on the straw was a woman, dressed wholly in black, her face veiled, only her hands being visible, pale, slender hands resting lifeless on the straw. Geoffrey Bledding had found a wife.

It was not until many years later that the lady's true origins were revealed. A diary belonging to Robert Dudley Leicester was discovered in which the whole story was told. Apparently the lady had been the illegitimate daughter of a lord. Queen Elizabeth, out of the goodness of her heart, had taken the young woman into her court as an underling attendant. Unfortunately the poor girl had caught the eye and temporary affection of Robert Leicester, the court's favorite. Enraged, Elizabeth had her spirited out of the palace and given to the stableboys for their own use.

While Leicester had been unable to spare her the hideous ordeal of degradation and humiliation, he was able to buy her ultimate freedom with fifty pounds and extracted a promise from the old stablemaster that he would find a safe place for her far away from London. The old man, a Yorkshireman by birth and a native of Bledding Village, made arrangements for Geoffrey Bledding to come for her. A late-night meeting was arranged, and Bledding came, impressed that the lady had at least a portion of titled blood in her veins, doubly impressed to be meeting Leicester himself and thinking somehow the favor would aid him in court.

Bledding took the lady back to East Yorkshire, and while was true that every month for almost a year a large sum of money arrived from Leicester, there were no royal favors forthcoming. And it was also true that Geoffrey Bledding brought home a totally silent, pitiably abused, and half-dead woman to serve as mistress of Bledding Sorrow.

A large, trustworthy female servant was assigned to nurse her back to health. And it was reported that even after the lady regained her strength, she never lifted her eyes and looked directly at anyone, as though her shame was a burden too heavy to be borne. She was never heard to speak a word, although she obeyed each and every command quite readily, such as the instruction from the female servant to lift her arm for the adjustment of a gown or raise her head so that the long pale blond hair might be brushed back and secured. As the gossips in the village told it, she was like a toy or a dead woman.

A few months after her arrival at Bledding Sorrow a late-night wedding ceremony was performed in the dank small chapel behind the elegant hall. The parish priest, though sworn to secrecy, later confided to intimates in the village that he had felt clearly God's disapproval over the recitation of the vows, that he would swear he had seen tears through the lady's veil, that her voice had been so low he had been unable to hear her pledge. He reported further that he had stayed at the wedding feast only long enough to witness Geoffrey Bledding order his bride to retire to the small upper bedchamber and, when she had hesitated for a moment, had seen him command two large male servants to escort her roughly up the broad oaken staircase. A few minutes later the master himself had followed.

The silence within the lady became deeper after that night. She was seen by no one except Geoffrey Bledding and the large womanservant, who served more in the capacity of jailor than attendant.

Around the small garden to the north of the hall

Geoffrey Bledding had erected a tall brick wall, completely enclosing and imprisoning anyone who walked there. But in truth, no one walked there at all. On occasion the lady sat on a small stone bench, placed in a direct ray of sun by the female attendant, who always stood a short distance away, watching. The lady left the garden only when the female attendant signaled that it was time to leave the garden. And as the days passed, her step became so faint that she could scarcely stand alone and walked only by leaning heavily on the arm of the attendant.

Shortly after Geoffrey Bledding had completed his fine new hall and had acquired a wife, he disappeared again one night and was absent from Bledding Sorrow for more than a week. Then one bright morning in early spring, when the snow was just melting, Bledding Village was again treated to a rare sight. The master of Bledding Sorrow had again returned, this time riding in utter splendor in the back of a gilded coach, quite the finest coach anyone in East Yorkshire had ever seen, a delicately carved, yet sturdy wonder with high spoked wheels which caught and reflected the sun as they swiftly turned down the village lane. Four royal purple plumes decorated the top of the vaulted carriage, and on either side of the two grand doors were tiny panels of mullioned windows with crimson velvet curtains which could be raised or lowered depending on the whim of the master.

Finer still than the coach itself were the four enormous white stallions which did not walk so much as they pranced, as though they were keenly aware of their own elegance, each magnificent beast lifting his feet high into the air before setting them down again on the rough earth. And more remarkable yet than the coach-and-four was the strange, tall, gaunt, black-haired and black-bearded coachman who held the taut reins in his massive hands and controlled the animals and the direction of the coach as though they were merely extensions of his own will.

It was a dazzling sight indeed for the villagers of Bledding, although in a way a predictable one. What was a king without a great hall and a mistress and a fine coach and coachman? The acquisitions of Geoffrey Bledding made sense. What did not make sense was the man himself.

For a while he seemed to enjoy his new toy. Every afternoon, through the large central arch of the gatehouse, Geoffrey Bledding could be seen, with the assistance of the female attendant, guiding the lady across the cobblestone courtyard toward the coach. Her step was becoming increasingly painful and weak, and at times they had to lift and support her, her head falling against her breast. While the coachman held the stallions steady, they placed the lady in the coach and drew back the crimson velvet curtains so that all could see her. Then they stood away as the coachman, looking neither to the right nor to the left, flicked the reins low across the broad white backs and with one surge, the coach moved forward.

The route was always the same, as though the coachman had been given explicit orders: thrice around the village square at a slow rate of speed, then five miles out from the village toward the seacoast on a straight and narrow road for the purpose of exercising the animals and with the hope, apparently, that everyone would see and admire the possessions of Geoffrey Bledding.

The ritual was performed daily. But it was such a sorrowful sight that the villagers could scarcely bear to watch the pale silent lady who never raised her eyes, who never moved. And instead of forming the envious audience that Geoffrey Bledding had hoped for, they took to staying inside their small shops and cottages until the terrible and cruel ordeal was over.

And in time Geoffrey lost interest in his new toy, and the daily coach ride was performed by rote, without the presence of his ever-watchful eye. Instead he turned his attention back to the enlargement of his estates,

buying up huge parcels of East Yorkshire land, journey-
ing great distances on horseback to inspect a new breed
of sheep, and on occasion going as far as London in
search of new and more expensive treasures for Bledding
Sorrow.

So while Geoffrey Bledding was gone a great deal of
the time, he still insisted that Bledding Sorrow be run
flawlessly and according to his orders. And it was,
armed now by several dozen servants who did their
master's bidding, not through any sense of loyalty, but
rather because the pay he gave them made them rich
in the eyes of the poor farmers surrounding the estates.
And, more important, because he terrified them. Shirk-
ers, poachers, those who disobeyed either the letter
or the spirit of his law were cruelly punished. Object
lessons were brutally performed whenever necessary.
Once a young male servant, caught poaching in the
distant corner of the estates, was dragged back to the
central courtyard, bound, his right hand placed on a
block and cut off, by Bledding himself, in full view of
all the servants.

Such a reign of terror served a purpose. The master
of Bledding Sorrow was not to be trifled with. In his
presence as well as in his absence, his kingdom was his
creation and was to be run according to his dictates.

So the coach rides continued, the coachman now
assisting the lady into the seat of the splendid carriage,
touching her arm ever so gently in spite of the obvious
strength and roughness of his hands as he lifted her
into the crimson velvet confines, carefully adjusting the
lap robe about her so that the ride would not bring on
an undue and dangerous chill.

In response to these kindnesses the lady began secret-
ly to raise her eyes on occasion and look silently into
the face of the coachman in unspoken gratitude for his
tender attention.

It was known throughout the hall that the coachman,
in spite of the fact that he had been bought and paid
for with a large sum of money, did not like the silent

coach rides around the empty village square. And with the master absent so much of the time, he took to skipping that part of the journey and instead would direct the four white stallions out into the lovely English countryside, urging them on at a gentle gait down little-traveled lanes and into broad meadows filled with wild flowers. On occasion he would stop the coach and assist the lady out, and they would walk together to the banks of a stream, speaking not at all, as though they both were aware of their positions and perhaps a little frightened of their feelings.

Throughout that spring and summer the coach rides continued, the lady growing stronger, walking unaided to the gatehouse arch to await the coach. Now she lifted her eyes to one and all and smiled at the servants and took greater pains with her dress and grooming. And on occasion the sound of her laughter, a rare sound for Bledding Sorrow, could be heard echoing through the upper chamber.

When Geoffrey Bledding came home from his many excursions, the laughter stopped and did not resume until he left again. It was rumored that he was seeing more than artisans in London, that he had only lately discovered that his great wealth would buy more than fine wood carvings and alabaster chimneypieces. So, during this time, the number and length of his stays at Bledding Sorrow were limited. His vast land holdings were in the hands of capable overseers. The hall itself was skillfully run by the servants, and there was nothing for him in the upper bedchamber but a wasted, used, and silent woman who had to be drugged thoroughly before he could even approach her bed. Why stay in Yorkshire when the coins in his pocket were plentiful enough to open up all the riches of London, when a man needed only a heavy purse to purchase any pleasure he desired?

During his long absences the estate functioned smoothly, all of his orders executed to the letter with the exception of the afternoon coach rides, which now, at midsummer, commenced early in the morning, the lady waiting at the gatehouse at dawn, in her hand a picnic basket filled with delicacies which she herself had prepared at midnight when cook was sleeping. And when the coach arrived, the coachman would gently assist her, their eyes meeting and, with no words spoken, revealing the anticipation of a glorious day.

They had several favorite spots. The large meadow filled with wild flowers at the end of a deserted lane was one. Another was a high bluff about ten miles from the village which overlooked all of the Yorkshire plains. There they would leave the coach-and-four and set off on foot for the edge of the bluff and gaze out and down at a panorama too dazzling to describe, of tiny green hedgerows and squares of golden grain and a high wide blue sky, flawless in every way.

They shared food and silences and stories, his of humble origin in the town of York, a large poor family of which he had never felt a part, of the time as a boy of twelve when he had felt his first real freedom driving a coach-and-four for the local blacksmith. And she listened and marveled at the fine cut of his jaw and the carefully trimmed Elizabethan beard, the way the dark wavy hair framed his pale, almost transparent skin, the depth of the eyes, the gauntness of both face and frame which belied the massive strength in his arms.

Finding nothing in either his manner or demeanor to frighten her, she in turn dared to reveal to him the outline of her degradation, how she had been forcibly taken by the stableboys, how, under threat of death, she had submitted to their cruelties, how she had lost consciousness only to awaken and discover that she had been sold to Geoffrey Bledding to serve as his mistress, how she had loathed every moment she had spent at Bledding Sorrow, how she feared her master, and how, on those occasions when he approached her bed, she fervently prayed for death.

So, saying all and, in the act of telling, reliving the

horrors of her life, she fell to weeping. And he, moved almost to tears himself by the sight, took her in his arms and held her and, with one enormous hand, pressed her head against his breast, as though he wanted to press her into his heart.

It was a love that had no alternative but to grow. She had never known such happiness. Touching him, tracing with her fingertip the outline of his cheek and jaw, caressing with a single finger the lips which would open to her were ecstasies she had never known before.

And he responded, as though he had stored up a lifetime of response for this one moment, a moment which did not include unbearable poverty, sick children, hunger, the stench of stable, the stinging burns of leather reins in the palms of his hands.

It was on a hot August evening that he first came to her fully. They had grown brave about keeping the coach out after dark. And why not? There was no one to issue countermanding orders. So they spent the day on the high bluffs overlooking the Yorkshire plains, a somnambulant interval of talk and naps and garlands of wild flowers and wine and cheese.

At dusk he playfully suggested that they climb to the bottom of the bluff, then climb back up again, just to see if they could do it. The descent was steep and the ascent even more grueling, and it was more than an hour later before they scrambled back up to the summit again, breathless, dirty, overheated in the extreme closeness of the warm August evening, but laughing at their triumph, as proud as though they had just scaled a mountain peak. Exhausted and overwarm, she loosened her garments and lay back on the soft grass to rest.

Then he was leaning over her, his face the brightest star, his features clearly visible even in darkness. There was only a moment's pause, as though they had reached a fork in the road and both required a moment to decide which path to take. Then she cupped both hands around that face she had come to love so well and guided him down.

It was a curious moment of passion, no immediate acceleration, but merely a quiet union, with breath held, as though they both were content simply to lie as one. Only later did he loosen her bodice further and caress her breasts, and the sensation of his hands and lips caused her to arch her body upward.

A few moments later he rolled to one side, relieving her of his weight. But she merely followed after him. They remained in each other's arms, unspeaking, for almost an hour. Then, as if by mutual consent, they rose, adjusted their garments, and discovered with great pride that their love had left scars. Around her shoulders and at the base of her throat were tiny purple bruises. And on his back were three small scratches, barely letting blood, but, all the same, she soothed them with her tongue.

It was after midnight when they returned to Bledding Sorrow. She waited outside the stables while he bedded down the stallions and secured the fine coach. Then, together, moving quite stealthily through the Great Hall in order not to disturb the sleeping servants, they made their way to her upper bedchamber. There, unencumbered by any garments, they tried again to feed a hunger so deep they both seemed to know it would never be satisfied completely, glorious explorations, still awake, though spent at dawn, lying quietly in each other's arms, staring up at the Tudor arches, listening carefully, as though it were the most sorrowful in the world, to the first morning crowing of a rooster.

Thus it was that they passed the summer, a splendid interval of days, hours, moments, as free and uninhibited as children, past agonies and past deprivations lifting visibly under the spell of their love.

It was safe to say that everyone within the confines of Bledding Sorrow knew what was going on. But what did it matter? They were paid handsomely to perform their duties, and their duties did not entail minding the coachman and the lady. And to those who preferred the sound of happiness to the sound of silence, the hum of human voices coming from the upper chamber was a relief from the tomblike atmosphere which usually pervaded the grand rooms and elegant staircases.

The idyll continued well into autumn. On one occasion Geoffrey Bledding returned, staying only long enough to strut about his estates and make everyone aware of his presence. And during this time the coachman and the lady played their original roles well. The old formality sprang up between them as once again the coach made its three dreary circles around the village square, journeyed the prescribed five miles out into the countryside, then returned promptly to the gatehouse, where the lady, veiled now to hide the new color in her cheeks, descended the coach and went directly to the upper chamber.

Then one day Geoffrey Bledding came home to stay.

It was rumored that someone had told him of the passionate liaison which had formed between his coachman and the lady. But if he knew, he gave no indication of it, and for a few days he performed as though nothing were out of the ordinary.

Then one night about a week later he ordered the large female servant to drug the lady, a habit of his when he intended to share her bed. And the lady, dreading the ordeal, but painfully aware of the need to keep up the appearance of normality, drank the warm liquid. But in truth, on this night the drug did not take effect. So alive was she with the remembrance of genuine passion and so in dread of the ordeal which was in store for her that as the hour of his coming drew near, she lay in the bed weeping, trying at the same time to brush away her tears, knowing that if he saw them, saw anything at all in her that was different, he would become suspect and all would be lost.

So it was that when she saw him standing obliquely in the shadows of the bedchamber, she threw her arm over her mouth and tried to stifle the scream with the

flesh of her arm. And when he fell on her, she closed
her eyes and tried to cancel all sensations with images
of the little south-facing dell atop the high bluff, surrounded by dense thickets of brambles and dogwood
and carpeted with primroses and wild violets and the
white stars of wild strawberries. Poised in such an
image and cradled in the residue of true passion, and
knowing full well that at that moment the coachman
was in the small walled garden enduring her agony
with her, and knowing equally as well that he would
come to her before the night was over to ease her
sorrow, knowing all this, somehow she endured the
rough hands, the unaccountable sensation that she was
being crushed to death.

When Geoffrey Bledding had done with her, he stood
beside the bed and looked mysteriously down on her,
as though in spite of all her efforts, he had discerned
something different about her. And when he started to
mount her again, as though to put her totally in his
power, she cried out, all reserves of self-control gone.
The discreet sounds of pretending ceased.

She looked up at him and must have seen that he
had discovered the truth, and once more she forestalled,
tried to castrate the accusation in his mind. In the
throes of her fear, she made the fatal mistake. She spoke.
He had never heard her speak before. She whispered,
"I—am not worthy of you."

Geoffrey Bledding knew in that moment that his wife
was betraying him. Suddenly he flew into a rage, called
forth in pitiable tones the long and honorable history
of the Bledding family, the cuckolded husband decrying
his humiliation, cursing her for the dishonor she had
brought to the name of Bledding.

The tirade lasted for more than an hour. Then
abruptly he fell silent. The Great Hall was quiet
throughout. The stillness shimmered in the firelight.
Outside a cold November wind occasionally rattled at
the window, but that was the only sound.

The servants, thinking that the worst was over, crept

quietly, wearily back to their beds. But it was not over. Shortly before midnight they were roused again, this time by the terrified screams of a woman. They gathered again quickly in the lower hall and stared fearfully up toward the small upper chamber. The cries continued, the lady alternately begging for help, then mercy, inhuman cries as those escaping from a torture chamber.

Paralyzed by their own fear, the servants continued to cower in the lower hall, eyes wide, mouths open, and when, a few moments later, they saw blood seeping through the cracks in the floor above, their own terror overtook them and sent them scrambling for safety inside the locked and bolted doors of their own quarters.

Shortly before dawn the cries ceased. The bravest of them all, a young stableboy of sixteen, crept up the steps. A few moments later he returned, unable to speak or utter words at all except for mindless mutterings. From his incoherent speech they were able to discern what had happened. Both the coachman and the lady were dead, brutally murdered, their bodies mutilated in unspeakable fashion, the specifics of which were never precisely known, for within the hour Geoffrey Bledding arrived on the scene, coming from the small chapel behind the old manor house, where he claimed he had been at prayer all night.

Quickly he took control of the situation. He ordered the servants back to their quarters and commanded two trusted male assistants to carry the bodies out to the small graveyard behind the chapel and bury them immediately. On threat of death, he made it clear that no one was to go near the burial plots.

For a few days he wore a proper face of grief, claiming that he would seek to the ends of the world, if necessary, to find the culprit who had committed this most heinous crime.

A few believed him. Most did not. But there was no proof. And without proof there was no solution. Who would challenge his word? Intimidated into silence, the servants kept their opinions to themselves and privately mourned the deaths of the coachman and the lady. What happened that cold November night in the small upper bedchamber remained a mystery and is still a mystery.

But it is known that it was the very next year that the hauntings first started, the lady's ungodly screams echoing through the empty upper corridors, mysterious spots of blood appearing on the worn oak floor of the upper bedchamber, dreadful specters and visions materializing without warning, sending all those unfortunate enough to witness them into spasms of terror.

The identity of the murderer was never discovered, and the hauntings have plagued Bledding Sorrow throughout its entire unhappy history and continue to plague it even now—mysterious stirrings in the quiet night, the lady's cries echoing through the entrance front with its projecting bays, the blood still appearing on the highly polished, though scarred and worn oak floor, the grim account of that night four hundred years ago, what little is known of it, still passed from family to family, from father to son, still capable of provoking terror, still eluding all answers, all solutions. . . .

The Present

⚜ 1 ⚜

Among the few features of twentieth-century England which retain an appearance but little modified by the lapse of centuries are the elegant, ornate, and usually unoccupied Great Houses, as they are indifferently called. If any mark of human occupation is found within them, it usually takes the form of a caretaker or warden or last and unfortunately penniless descendant.

Such was the case of Geoffrey Bledding, heir and present half owner, in awkward partnership with the National Trust, of that Elizabethan jewel of a house known as Bledding Sorrow.

In the mid-1960's tourists still flocked like pilgrims to London and heaped on her a richness of praise and left within the week, claiming that they had seen England, while less than three hours away by train, smaller splendors like Bledding Sorrow fell into hideous states of neglect and decay and would have perished altogether had it not been for the magnanimous offer from the National Trust to restore it, leave it in the hands of the present heir on the condition that he withdraw to an isolated wing and convert the remainder of the Great Hall into a kind of instant college for adult education, thereby supplying both a source of revenue as well as an outlet for the local societies of bird watchers, snake handlers, art historians, poets, and

21

amateur photographers who needed and were willing to pay for a pleasant place to go to pursue their talents.

Simple, yet complex, as full of exquisite wood carvings and fine plasterwork and legend as any Great House in England, Bledding Sorrow reluctantly opened her doors to the public in the spring of 1964. Ten years later it was something of a going concern, word of its legend having spread, amateur groups of all sorts coming from as far away as Wales and Scotland to live for a week in the refurbished upper-floor dormitories, explore its lovely grounds and gardens, listen at night in the hope that they, too, would hear the lady's screams of agony.

"A Country Retreat for the Pleasure and Expansion of the Mind," the brochure said, a brochure written and printed by Geoffrey Bledding himself, heir and apparently last descendant of the original Geoffrey Bledding, whose scrawled handwriting can still be seen on the first deed, dated 1177, in the Bledding Museum.

And it was indeed a lovely retreat from the rigors of urban 1974, a picturesque arrangement of fields and hedgerows where half a mile to the east across sloping meadows lay the small village of Bledding with its slated roofs, a town that had its heyday more than four hundred years ago and has been in a steady but graceful decline ever since.

Above the village rolled the endless hills and steep ravines, culminating in a dense woods which led to a high bluff known as Sutton Bank, a place for gliders and Sunday picnics now, but once, centuries ago, a last bulwark for lovers.

But without a doubt, the center of Bledding countryside was Bledding Sorrow itself. And the middle-aged man who sat behind the cluttered desk in the tiny cramped office off the Great Hall rarely took note of the loveliness around him. Overburdened as he now was with schedules and timetables, and incoming and outgoing students, and the endless feuds among the help in the kitchen, and the National Trust officer who periodically came snooping about, it was quite natural that he work late at night, ignoring the admonitions of the old crone named Caldy More, who had raised him and kept his house for him in the time when his house consisted of all of Bledding Sorrow and not just the obscure wing where on the third floor he kept his silent and invalid American wife.

In addition to the various groups of students who came to stay for a week, Bledding Sorrow was open daily from nine in the morning until noon for the benefit of any passing tourist, art historian, or Elizabethan architectural buff who perhaps had journeyed miles to see the hall, which was remarkable in that it had suffered so few alterations over the centuries.

These occasional visitors entered the hall by the main door in the south front. There they were greeted by one of the local ladies from Bledding Village, who took their twenty-five pence, sold them a guidebook for fifty pence, then escorted them on a guided tour past the Elizabethan chimneypiece, urging one and all not to touch the long oak draw table, directing the attention instead to the lantern which hung above it, a beautiful example of mid-Georgian metalwork.

Sometime later the guide concluded her tour in the Long Gallery, where, smiling, she pointed out the seventeenth-century oil of the Geoffrey Bledding who had inhabited the house at that time. Then, almost coyly, she asked the visitor to keep that "fine, strong face" in mind for a few moments as they walked back down the Long Gallery, through the Great Hall, and past the tiny cluttered office where the present Geoffrey Bledding was working.

Three, four, sometimes five times in a single morning Geoffrey Bledding was called on to look up and smile, displaying for the visitors the genealogical insistence of the slant of the Bledding eyes, the rake of the Bledding jaw.

He hated it. He found it humiliating and degrading. But he always performed for the simple reason that he had no choice. If he wanted to survive and inhabit Bledding Sorrow at all, it had to be on these terms. But still he hated it, and on an evening such as this in late May, when his house was already crowded with strangers, when at this very moment he heard the hideous laughter of the York Bird Watchers Society floating up from the basement dining room—once the massive laundry room and now a modern monstrosity of fake knotty-pine walls and nightmarish contemporary paintings done by the Manchester Art League several summers ago—at moments like this he closed the wide-set Bledding eyes and focused his blind gaze like a rifle on the farthest horizon he could find in total darkness.

It was true. He did resemble his ancestors, an incredible, almost ghostly resemblance. And on the surface of it he appeared to be a pleasant enough man. Of average build and height, with rapidly receding fair hair which lay about his head in unruly wisps, he appeared to be a strict proponent of English propriety. Thus the vague dislike that most people instantly felt for him was difficult to explain. He was keenly aware of this dislike and generally was capable of disregarding it. It was never easy for a man in his position, a man whose ancestry could be traced, in one unillustrious line, back to the twelfth century.

Because of this heritage there was a sense about him of genes gone awry. There was also about him an oppressive moralism, coupled with an incongruous air of apology. He had the annoying habit of never looking one straight in the eye. His visual contact landed somewhere above the hairline or the top of the skull, as though he were conversing with someone floating in air. There was never, except in quiet private moments such as these, an expression of honest anxiety in his face. But in the lightning-fast darts of his eyes and the almost constant wetting of his lips he gave the impression of incredible turbulence just beneath the surface of his painfully close-shaven English face.

All this and more combined to erect a considerable

barrier of sympathy. He smiled a bit too much at nothing in particular, as though pleasantness were a religion to be practiced at all costs.

He was a man of rigid habit. Late in April he took off his heavy brown-tweed suit and put on his dark green lightweight suit. He wore these clothes from the end of April to the end of August, changing his shirt once a week and his tie every other week.

He was not a particularly well-educated man. His degree in architectural archaeology was perfectly adequate. Nothing more. In other areas he was largely self-educated. He had been sole heir to Bledding Sorrow since the early forties, when both his parents had been killed in a London air raid. He had never mourned them and still did not miss them, for he had never known them, having been raised in good English tradition by the indomitable Caldy More.

He had left his island country only once in the early sixties, when he had journeyed to America on a lecture tour and had brought back an American wife, possibly the gravest mistake of his life.

Now he performed every duty with a fixed smile, as though he were serving a sentence. Bledding Sorrow, once his greatest love, had become an albatross around his neck, as had the American wife. Yet there was no way out. No way at all. Here, in his limited way, he must function, and do his penance, and learn to live with his obscure sense of defeat, a sense made doubly obscure by the fact that he had never had any real sensation of battle.

Before him on the desk in the dim light of the lamp —the electric bills were running far too high—he studied the schedule for the arrival of the Birmingham Art League tomorrow. There would just be time to bid the bird watchers good-bye, send the undersized and overworked staff scurrying to clean the dormitory rooms, and be standing at the gatehouse at noon. Another reception.

He had nothing very much against the students themselves. But he had the born Englishman's hatred of the invasion of his privacy. And his privacy had been brutally invaded for the last ten years. He lived in fear that some curiosity seeker, wandering too far into the upper corridors or peering over his private walled garden, would discover his wife, that tales would start even more insane and foolish than the legend itself, that the National Trust would ask questions, that the partnership would be dissolved and he would find himself penniless.

Still, while he hated his position, he knew better than anyone that he had earned a degree of respect in the Midlands with the skillful running of his "college." He enjoyed those occasions when visitors referred to him as "headmaster," more than enjoyed them, fed on them. He had no intention of losing his small but worthy kingdom, not for her or anyone else.

Now he looked up suddenly at the sound of footsteps outside his office door. A moment later the blue-eyed, gargoylelike head of Mrs. Hanson appeared in the cavity of the opened door. She was a curse of a woman, but leader of the Bird Watchers Society and prime instigator of a group called Friends of Bledding Sorrow, which regularly sent sizable checks to be used "as he saw fit." He now rose to greet her, coming around from behind his desk and taking her hand warmly.

His voice was firm, rather deep, retaining traces of the local accent. "Dear Mrs. Hanson." He smiled. "I do hope all has been pleasant for your during this stay."

The elderly woman adjusted the multistrands of pearls about her neck and beamed, as though Geoffrey Bledding were a welcome sight in an endless torrent of lesser mortals. "It has been perfect, Mr. Bledding," she said, "just perfect. Bledding Sorrow becomes more beautiful every time I see it. The only trouble is it's getting so popular. I'm afraid in the future we shall have to sign up months in advance."

He shook his head sadly. "We try to stay solvent, or it will be lost to all of us."

Mrs. Hanson looked inwardly shocked at such a thought.

Geoffrey took his cue. "You have helped us a great deal, Mrs. Hanson, and there is absolutely no way I can repay you for your continuing support."

The old woman gazed up at him as though she were gazing out to sea. She smiled coyly, as if a most pleasant thought had just occurred to her. "Several of the ladies are in the dining room having a late-night cup of tea. We'd be most honored if you would join us on this our last night."

He looked suddenly stricken. "What am I to do?" He gestured helplessly toward the desk behind him. "A mountain of paperwork, the endless tasks of a headmaster, and a charming invitation to join delightful ladies for tea." Still holding her hand, he looked down on her in mock pity. He repeated his initial question with varying emphasis. "What *am* I to do?"

There was a silence. Mrs. Hanson withdrew her hand and again adjusted the heavy pearls around her neck. Rather wistfully she sighed and said, "Once I had you all to myself, and now I am forced to share you." She shook her head. The little blue-dyed ringlets bounced around her parchmentlike forehead. "Well, sacrifice." She sighed again. "Bledding Sorrow comes first. Always Bledding Sorrow first."

He nodded in serious agreement, relieved to have escaped from the company of the hideous women.

She started to leave, but just outside the door she turned suddenly back. "Oh, I meant to ask you," she began, "about the coach. Was the last payment enough to cover the expense?"

He shifted his ground, feeling that perhaps he should have had tea with her. She was generous to a fault. "Yes, indeed." He smiled, somewhat guiltily. "The money was more than adequate. After careful investigation we located an independent coachman in Manchester. The chap owns his own coach, quite a modern wonder, capable of seating as many as forty-eight passengers. Through your generosity we were able to hire him for the summer." He stepped closer and again took her hand. "I believe, if I remember correctly, he is scheduled to arrive sometime this week."

"Splendid!" She beamed up at him, a plump, good-hearted vulture. "I think it's important that Bledding Sorrow students have the means at their disposal of getting around the countryside. We have so much to see here. Don't you agree?"

He agreed readily and with unfailing charm. It *would* be an asset for the college to have its own coach. The freedom would allow them to take students as far as the Wroxter Roman ruins, Shropshire, the Lake District. Bledding Sorrow's horizons would be vastly expanded, and it was hoped that Bledding Sorrow's purse would follow in like manner. And the acquisition of the coach and coachman had all been made possible through the generosity and dedication of Mrs. Hanson.

Still holding her hand, as though it might hurt him to let go, he looked down on her now as though meditating. "How can we ever thank you?" he mourned. "I'm just sorry you won't be here for the arrival of the coach."

She sighed modestly and shook her head. "Oh, I want no thanks or praise. Good works are their own reward. I just want to be absolutely certain that you have the necessary means at your disposal to do what has to be done."

He appeared to be near tears. "My dear Mrs. Hanson. If you speak like this, I shall have to reprimand you. You have done more than your share. Without you—" He broke off and gestured vaguely, almost helplessly in the air.

As though to ease his discomfort, she reached forward and dared to touch his shoulder.

Reflexively, he drew back. "Now, if you'll excuse me," he said, "I must get on with my work."

She nodded, somewhat flustered, still nervously fingering the pearls. "Good night, then, Mr. Bledding." She smiled sweetly. "If you change your mind, we'll be down in the dining room having a last fling."

Safe behind his desk again, he gestured apologetically at the mussed papers, indicating that as much as he would like to accept her invitation, it was clearly out of the question.

She bobbed her head in ready understanding, then left with a slight air of deference that he found pleasing.

Alone again, though still smiling, as though he had not yet shifted gears back to the privacy of his office, he picked up a stack of near invoices and stared blankly at them. In truth, he had forgotten about the arrival of the new coach this weekend. The arrangements had been made several months ago. Now, remembering, there were suddenly new problems. Where would he put the man? And what kind of man would he be?

It was a habit of Geoffrey Bledding's to choose his staff with care. Professional gossips and sensitive noses and prying eyes were out of the question. Yet he had hired the coachman sight unseen. He shook his head. The smile faded. He certainly needed no disrupting influences now.

Quickly he riffled through the mussed papers on his desk in search of the last correspondence with James Pask, the Manchester coachman who had agreed for quite a handsome sum to put himself and his coach at the disposal of Bledding Sorrow for the summer. Geoffrey remembered vaguely that the man had written and requested specific information concerning something. He couldn't remember what. Now he was unable to find the letter. Well, he could only hope for the best.

For a moment he stared blankly at the cluttered desk, taking mental inventory of the available rooms in the third-floor dormitory. There was a small cubby hole of a room near the grillwork barrier that blocked the private wing. It was a tawdry room, not fit for paying students. It would have to do. There was no place else.

The problem solved or at best postponed, he again scooped up the stack of invoices for food purchases. Monthly he did a balancing act with the books. The price of everything was soaring higher and higher, yet the rate of twenty pounds a week for room and board at Bledding remained fixed. It was an awesome task providing decent and adequate meals in such an arrangement. Again he regretted his decision not to have tea with Mrs. Hanson. He was completely indebted to her and to women like her who had adopted Bledding Sorrow as their favorite charity.

Slowly an unsmiling expression crossed his face. He leaned back in the chair as though it were a luxury he did not often permit himself. Carefully his eyes took inventory of the shabby, cramped office. In the heyday of Bledding Sorrow the room's only purpose had been to store cloaks and capes, boots, and rainwet outer garments. It was a room totally lacking in any sort of style or beauty.

He had tried to make it livable and failed. Windowless, its only decorations were two inexpensive prints, one by Turner, the other, Constable. There was a bookcase containing several thick volumes of British coach and rail timetables, a dusty collection of *British Country Life* and *Great Houses of England,* several college textbooks on architectural archaeology, and an assortment of back issues of the London Times. The only item in the room which might in all honesty be called attractive was the faded and relatively inexpensive Oriental rug on the floor, a gift to him from the restorers of Bledding Sorrow, who had found no value in it. And there was the desk, of course, and the small brass lamp and his own chair.

Looking about him, in an unexpected moment of personal inventory, he felt as though he were enduring a long fall, and that the beauty beyond the mean room, which was rightfully his, had for some reason been denied him and that he would forever be forced to operate in a colorless and meaningless vacuum.

The room became suddenly oppressive. He could still hear the females cackling in the dining room downstairs. His left hand trembled. There was tension building. Mysteriously, he felt the need to punish or be punished. He looked sharply up at the empty doorway. The current accounts of the entire world were inadequate. He was not prepared for every eventuality.

Suddenly he felt incredibly warm, perspiration dotting his forehead. He leaned back in the chair and tried to draw a deep breath. His eyes blurred; he looked toward the empty doorway. It was no longer empty. He started forward in his chair. He saw evolving out of the vacuum a single bright light coming from no visible source. Clutching the desk with both hands, he tried to steady himself, his nerves, but the light increased in intensity and whirling in the middle of the light was a black specter, merely a vapor at first, but slowly assuming the shape of a man, growing larger, still larger.

Geoffrey tried to draw back from the hideous vision. He threw his arms over his eyes as the light continued to increase, the figure of the man becoming clearer, a black cape rising before him now, held suspended by one bloodied hand, the hood, where a face should have been, empty, yet somehow retaining its shape.

Geoffrey's mouth opened in fear and he tried to cry out for help. But no sound would leave the cavity of his throat. And when a few moments later the specter, now hovering directly over the desk, reached out with that one bloody hand as though in anger to grasp Geoffrey about the throat, he fell backward in the chair, almost unconscious with terror, the pounding of his heart causing an ungodly racket beneath his chest, his head pressed rigidly against the chair, his eyes closed, his lips whispering frantically, "Please, God, please—"

The prayer ceased. He opened his eyes. The doorway was empty again, blessedly empty, the specter gone. He stared a moment longer, then slowly buried his head in his arms, still trembling, tormented as he had never been tormented before.

What it was or what had caused it to materialize, he had no idea. He must keep it a secret, though, must tell no one. Who would believe him? And a few moments later as his heart resumed its normal beating, he told himself that perhaps he'd only imagined it, the tormented wanderings of an overworked mind, a stray fragment of the foolish ghost story lodged in his subconscious.

He sat up now, more at ease, though still trembling. He gave one final prayer, "Please, God, never let it return."

Then suddenly he called out full-voiced for the one person who fully understood him. "Caldy More? Are you there?"

His voice echoed about the tiny room. He knew she was there. She was always there within earshot, waiting for his summons.

He called again, "Caldy More? Are you there?" using both her names, as he had always done since he was a boy, running them into one.

And within a few moments she appeared, as he knew she would, addressing him formally as Mr. Bledding, as she always did, as though she took secret delight in reminding him of his ordinary status compared to the other Great Houses in the region, proudly presided over by *Lord* Sykes, *Lord* Broyton.

Exactly how Caldy More herself had stood her master for so long was one of the local mysteries. Most probably it was because she had been with him for all his forty-three years, having joined the family when she was a girl of sixteen. Such dedication was its own reward. And punishment. Now, at sixty-two, she literally had no place else to go. Also it was suspected that her apparent delight in the domestic catastrophes that descended so frequently on Bledding Sorrow since the arrival ten years ago of the American wife kept her fascinated.

In this respect Caldy More was an incipient sadist, and Geoffrey Bledding knew it. But he needed her, now more than ever, and it was to their mutual advantage to tolerate each other.

Caldy More had two obsessions or, rather, two aspects of the same obsession. One was the care and feeding and general well-being of her master, Geoffrey Bledding. The other was to needle, preach, reprimand, snoop, pry, give advice, pass judgment, and generally insert herself into his life in the most unpleasant fashion possible. In neither field did she shirk her duty.

She resembled some hovering, overlarge bird, endlessly circling her prey, never quite closing in for the kill, for then the sport would be over. Taller than the average woman, approaching six feet, with a taut, muscular, almost masculine body, slightly graying and quite long salt-and-pepper hair, which she pulled back schoolgirl fashion, and a sharp angular face which had never known a makeup brush or night cream, she could be described with only the greatest of charity as a plain woman.

She would have interpreted that designation, as indeed she did, as a compliment. Frills were for lesser women with the curse of leisure time. Her favorite victims, other than Geoffrey Bledding himself, were the poor little sparrowlike local women who served as morning guides and the conglomerate of lesser humanity of both sexes who served loosely as the staff of Bledding Sorrow. In short, the most distasteful characteristic of all about her was that she acknowledged no bounds to her authority.

Periodically, every two or three months, she would drive Geoffrey Bledding into a rage and he would give her a tongue lashing for stirring up trouble among the kitchen staff, pitting one faction against the other, countermanding his orders, usurping his authority, and, at the pitch of battle, they both would somehow understand anew that they needed each other, that they could, in fact, destroy each other, and that it behooved them, as it were, to get on.

Thus repentance would move in, and Caldy More would limit herself to her only true domain, Geoffrey Bledding's private wing and his silent wife. And with crass arrogance, she would, for a few weeks, ignore the rest of the multitudinous activity of Bledding Sorrow, as though in his very act of scolding her Geoffrey Bledding had produced an incontrovertible piece of evidence regarding her superiority.

Now as he looked up to see her standing in the doorway, a faint impatient flush on her face, as though he had summoned her away from the most urgent of duties, although in truth he knew she had been sitting less than fifty feet away in the darkened Great Hall, a guardlike position which she assumed every night to look after the treasures there, he looked at her more closely in the dim light and, for one brief moment, tried to imagine what his life would be like if she were to die. The thought was beyond his imagining. He longed to tell her about the mysterious vision he had witnessed earlier. Again in thinking on it, he saw the specter as clearly as though it were before him, saw the bloodied hand reaching for him, the black cape, the faceless hood.

Suddenly the palms of his hands felt damp and cold as though something had touched him. He looked again at the stern-faced woman standing before him. Caldy More used to comfort him when he was a child, would scold him for his silliness, seeing spooks behind every door. But still there had been comfort even in the scolding, her good English common sense reminding him of the harmful nature of his imagination. And surely he had only imagined what he had seen earlier. There was no other way to account for it.

In spite of this logic, he shuddered involuntarily. He must, in the future, keep his imagination in check, must discipline his mind to concentrate only on the clear outline of reality. Now he rubbed his burning eyes and invited her to come in and sit down.

Immediately she objected. "It's late, Mr. Bledding, and there still are strangers milling about in the hall. I really should—"

Her imperious tone annoyed him. "They are not strangers, Caldy More," he said. "They are students, and they mean us no harm. Now, sit down, please."

She sniffed at the command, took a handkerchief from the sleeve of her plain, dark blue dress, patted her forehead as though summer heat were on her. Then reluctantly and at the last minute she did as she was told.

He waited for the endless straightening process to cease. And when the room was quiet save for the distant sound of old females laughing in the basement dining room, he looked up at a point slightly above her left ear. "I'm afraid I failed to tell you about the arrival this weekend of the new coach and coachman."

Again she contradicted him. "You told me."

"I did? When?"

"Several weeks ago. But I remembered." She looked sternly at him. "I don't always agree, but I always remember." There was a minute tilt at the corner of her eyelids when she disapproved of something. The tilt over the years had become a permanent part of her features. Now she went on. "I think it's a lot of foolishness if you ask me, but then you didn't ask me, did you, and it's not my money, so why should I object?"

He drew a deep breath at the innocently smiling and talking face and tried to explain. "It will be quite a benefit for our students," he said carefully. "It will enable us to take them anyplace in the region. It can only mean profit for us."

He saw in her gray eyes the hint that nothing he was saying was making a great deal of sense to her. He felt an emotion not absolutely connected with malice, but close to it. Rather sternly he now asked, "What, may I inquire, are your objections?"

She didn't answer right away, but amused herself with the folds of her dress. Finally she replied, as though what she was about to say would be massively irrefutable. "Another stranger," she said simply, "a permanent live-in stranger. Another set of eyes snooping where he has no business. Another curiosity to be satisfied." She looked at him, her head cocked to one side, as though she were about to drive the final nail into her argument. "I'll have to put him in the small room directly outside the private wing. You realize that, of course?"

He nodded, realizing all, even her unspoken implications.

She went on. "Sometimes it's difficult to keep her totally out of sight." She bowed her head as though overburdened. "I do the best I can under difficult circumstances. I'm sure you know that."

Again he nodded. Then abruptly he sat up as though to close a distasteful discussion. His tone sounded almost cheery. "You do a good job, Caldy More. I'm in your debt."

The admission seemed to please her. She stood up, as confident as though she had won a battle. "What you didn't tell me was his name, Mr. Bledding."

He looked blank, as though in that brief interval his mind had moved on to other matters.

"The coachman," she chided, "the name of the gentleman coming this weekend."

He thought for a moment, rustling through papers. Then, "Pask," he said. "James Pask, I believe."

She received this information with a slight air of disdain, as though already the man had somehow failed in her eyes. At the door she called back, "Will you lock up, or shall I?"

"I'll do it."

"Very good."

"One thing more, Caldy More."

Again she looked back, this time an air of genuine puzzlement on her face, as though up until this moment she had correctly guessed everything he had said. But this last detention apparently was a mystery.

Bledding contributed to her confusion by now, having won her attention, falling silent as though in truth he had dismissed her. His head was bowed as though he could not bring himself to continue or, more accurately, as though a fierce battle were being waged within him, a despair of sorts whose pains were made doubly worse by the other pains he took to conceal it.

She continued to watch him closely, an expression of bewilderment still on her face. Then suddenly that same expression changed rapidly into a kind of frozen revulsion, as though, at last, she was beginning to glimpse the outlines of his reasons for detaining her.

A bitterness crept across her face. "No, Mr. Bledding," she whispered. "Not tonight, please." And having so spoken, she turned quickly again, as though with greater determination to leave the small office before he could rouse himself and summon her back.

She was several steps out into the darkened hallway when again she heard him, his voice firm this time, as though leaving her no margin for argument.

"Caldy More!" In his tone was the centuries-old firmness which has always existed between master and servant. "I thank you," he called again, as though she had already obeyed him and was now standing before him, ready to do his bidding.

And within the moment she was, although she stayed in the shadows just inside the door, as though not wanting him to see the expression of revulsion on her face.

From that instant on, he did not once make eye contact with her. Slowly he reached into the pocket of his jacket and withdrew a small key. Equally as deliberating, as though he hoped that at some point his hand, working independently of his mind, would cease to obey, he bent over and inserted the key into the lock of the bottom drawer of his desk.

Silence. Caldy More's face was like that of a woman at a funeral.

A moment later Geoffrey Bledding withdrew a small bottle of white pills, shook three of them out, and placed them on the edge of the desk.

Caldy More gave the pills a sharp reproachful glance. Courage from somewhere surfaced. "She's quiet now," she pleaded. "Leave her be."

Still not looking at her, Geoffrey spoke sharply to the surface of the desk. "You have no right to speak like that."

Caldy More bowed her head.

In the silence he added, "What difference does it make? She knows nothing."

Again Caldy More stepped forward, anger replacing the revulsion on her face. "She knows more than you think, Mr. Bledding. You only see her after I have given her those," and she pointed sharply toward the pills on the corner of the desk.

But he merely shook his head and turned restlessly in the chair, still not looking at her, as though he could not bear her eyes. He said softly, almost apologetically, "I'll be up in about twenty minutes."

But still Caldy More protested. She went to the desk in an unprecedented outburst of pleading. "I'm only thinking of you, Mr. Bledding," she begged. "What you do to yourself. Let her be. Find another woman. One of the girls from the village." Her face brightened with the possibility. "I know several. I could—"

She broke off speaking for no reason. For several moments the tableau held, the woman bending over the desk, the man staring intently at the small white pills. The red in his cheeks deepened, and at last he whispered again, "I'll be up in twenty minutes."

She did not raise her head, but gave the smallest nod of assent, and then with an almost sullen movement she lifted the white pills from the corner of the desk and turned quickly as though she did not now want to see his face.

Five minutes passed, during which time the man behind the desk did not move. He remained staring fixedly at nothing in particular, listening to Caldy More's footsteps fade down the long darkened corridor, through the Great Hall, moving faintly now in the far distance to the locked door which led to the family wing.

Then he found himself smiling. He bent over again and took a small black case, rectangular in shape, about ten inches long, from the lower right-hand drawer, which was always kept locked. Carefully he inserted it into the pocket of his coat, then relocked the bottom drawer, tested it twice to make certain it was secure. He put the key back into his inner pocket and stood up to leave.

Suddenly, outside in the corridor, he heard the party of women just coming up from the basement dining room. As though in a state of panic, he quickly sat back down behind the desk and reached frantically for a sheaf of papers.

As the chattering, giggling women reached the office door, he gave the impression of a man buried in his work. He looked smilingly up at the sound of the first singsong female voice.

"We missed you, Mr. Bledding," it chirped. "We had reserved the seat of honor just for you."

He still felt as though his cheeks were red. He glanced toward the doorway now crowded with female faces in varying states of decay. He couldn't bear to look directly at them and again his vision moved up toward the top of the door. He smiled. "I do hope that Mrs. Hanson explained why I was unable to join you."

"Oh, indeed I did," the woman herself admitted. "But that doesn't prevent us from longing for your company."

He bobbed his head in mock modesty and again gestured helplessly toward his cluttered desk. "Bledding Sorrow comes first," he intoned.

Murmurs of sympathy floated up from the women, the overfed and shallow wives of prosperous shopkeepers on whom Geoffrey Bledding was wholly dependent. Again he could not bring himself to look directly at them. Now he focused on the papers in his hand; a few, he noticed, were upside down. But still he managed to smile and cordially ask the ladies if they had enjoyed their week's stay at Bledding Sorrow.

A general shrill and abrasive chorus indicated that they had. One, lost in shadows, asked timidly, "Will you be in the courtyard tomorrow to tell us good-bye, Mr. Bledding?"

With unfailing charm, he smiled. "I wouldn't dream of missing it."

There was a stiff pause, during which time his arm moved carefully down his side to confirm the security of the black case in his pocket. He felt somehow as though he were in a dream, facing squarely the hideous features of female demons who stood so sharply in the way of his fulfillment. Subtly he lifted the papers in his hand to signal that the pleasant interval must come to an end.

The women took the cue. They called out a chorus of good nights mingled with expressions of gratitude for his kindness to them. And he nodded his head throughout and smiled.

As they departed, he again became part of a tableau. When the last footstep had echoed on the central staircase which led up to the dormitory wing, he crumpled the sheets of paper in his clenched hand, and there was on his face now a certain expression of insolence, a dry knowingness beneath his mask of servitude. He threw the crumpled sheets across the desk and looked for a moment as though he might hurl himself after them.

But the disintegration lasted only a moment. Then he once again assumed the proper demeanor, a profoundly respectful obedience to the knowledge of who he was and what was expected of him.

Suddenly, in spite of his control, he found the atmosphere of the little office claustrophobic. He stood up and switched off the desk lamp and moved rapidly in semidarkness down the long corridor toward the glorious Elizabethan arch that served as the front door of Bledding Sorrow.

He started to lock and secure the door immediately, but then changed his mind. Instead he pushed it open and walked a few steps out into the cobblestone courtyard. A distant flash of lightning announced the approach of the nightly storm. At least he had that much to be grateful for. Thus far into the season the rains had confined themselves to evening. When they came during the day, the students complained endlessly, as though their twenty pounds a week had purchased for them the right to good weather. Looking up into the turbulent night sky, he realized that a coach would help enormously during inclement weather. If it was raining here, he could simply load the students aboard and have them driven someplace else. Yes, the coach had been a good idea, an excellent idea.

When he turned back toward Bledding Sorrow, his eye was attracted by the dim light coming from the small upper bedchamber on the third floor. He felt his heart miss a beat. He had rights. Even in this prison in which he was doomed to spend his life, he had rights.

On that note of self-comfort, he stepped toward the front door, ready to claim his rights. Suddenly, out of the stillness of the night, he heard something, a low moan at first, accelerating in pitch and tempo to a scream, a lady's scream, coming at him from all directions, still increasing in volume, the hideous sound threatening to split his eardrums.

Abruptly he bent over, both hands clamped over his ears in a futile attempt to shut out the horrible sound. But even with his ears blocked he could still hear it, a high-pitched, continuous scream of agony echoing about the empty courtyard.

His eyes rolled backward in their sockets as his torment increased. He was on his knees now, both arms pressed against the sides of his head. Would it never cease? And what was it, and why was it tormenting him?

No answers, just the never-ending scream, chilling his bones to the marrow, causing his face to contort in silent agony.

Then, as suddenly as it had started, it ceased, leaving him alone in a foolish kneeling position, gasping for breath, his watery eyes glancing fearfully about for some logical reason, some plausible explanation.

Nothing. He was alone in the deserted courtyard, shivering from a cold deeper and more penetrating than any cold he had ever felt before. He wrung his hands, unable to understand what was happening to him. Overworked? Perhaps, but it had never happened before. He recovered slowly, scolded himself for giving in to such foolishness, and eventually stood upright again, reason restored, though still glancing fearfully into the shadows.

It was some moments later when he finally reentered Bledding Sorrow, swung the great Elizabethan door into place, bolted and secured it, set the burglar alarm, and started once again down the corridor, through the Great Hall with its carvings and plasterwork, past the alabaster screen with its angels and crusading knights and Elizabethan ladies and the Twelve Apostles until finally he came to the locked door which led to the private wing.

He stood in the dark before the door fumbling in his pocket for the key. This door was always kept locked for the safety and protection of his wife. In fact, throughout the entire private wing there were only two access entrances to the outside world. One was the small door on the ground floor which led out of the makeshift kitchen directly into the totally enclosed and walled garden. And there was this door which he was now unlocking which gave general access to the rest of Bledding Sorrow. All other entrances and exits had been sealed and barred with grillwork barriers, thus converting the family wing into a virtual prison.

Not that he liked it that way. It was a matter of necessity. And not that there was that much of value in the family wing that needed such extreme security measures, for in truth there was nothing of value in the private wing. The rooms were mean quarters, sparsely furnished with items of no historic or artistic significance, every room bearing the makeshift scars of conversion; a lady's powder room, which now served as his kitchen; his own bedroom and parlor, which had once served as servant's quarters; and on up to the top of the hall where the stairs narrowed to permit the passage of only one, to the corridor which led to the upper bedchamber.

Suddenly he stumbled in the narrow passageway leading up. He reached out to the damp walls for support. As he struggled for balance, he glanced down toward the steps over which he had just traveled. Suddenly he pressed backward against the wall. He saw, or thought he saw, in the dim shadows of the narrow corridor the figure of a woman. She was dragging herself pitiably up the steps toward him, the hem of her long skirts soaked in blood, one hand extended as though she intended to reach out and touch him.

A single cry escaped his lips. He turned suddenly, facing the wall, grinding his forehead into rough plaster. What was happening to him? Was he losing his mind? He clung there a moment longer, and when he looked back, the specter was gone. The steps were merely steps again. A weak smile of relief crossed his lips. Perhaps it was his eyes, his vision failing. That was all. Nothing more. He must remember to make an appointment.

He smiled openly now in relief. He was becoming as silly and as overwrought as the young girls in the kitchen. He would have to watch that. *He* was the only cause of his own torment. All he had to do was control himself with a firm hand. Righting himself, he felt again in his pocket to confirm the presence of the black case. It was still there, and this knowledge forced him now to move with greater agility and speed.

At the top of the uppermost landing he stopped to catch his breath. He could remember as a boy running up and down the narrow steps with absolute ease. He was getting old. The realization turned sharply within him. Looking down the long corridor, he saw Caldy More standing outside the low doorway which led to the upper bedchamber. Even from that distance he could still see the expression of condemnation on her face.

As he drew near, he saw her straighten her shoulders, the expression on her face grim now and slightly pious. She spoke while he was still several feet away. "She was asleep," she hissed. "I had to awaken her to put her back to sleep." Her voice rose, anger building. "Does that make sense to you, Mr. Bledding? It doesn't make sense to me. Not a bit of sense." Then she moved suddenly forward as though to block his entrance into the room. "She knows," she warned sharply. "She is aware of everything that goes on. You don't think she knows, but she does. I can promise you that."

Now he stood confronting both the woman and the closed door. He inquired with an almost courtly politeness, "Did you give her the medicine?"

"The medicine!" scoffed the old woman. "Medicine, my eye." Then she said, almost entreating, "Deceive her! Deceive me! But don't deceive yourself. I beg you, Mr. Bledding. Please consider yourself."

The talking, pious face annoyed him. She was blocking his path as surely as the old hags had blocked it downstairs. For one terrible moment he felt as though he might strike her. His arm moved, lifted, the back of his hand ready to angle sharply down across the side of that condemning face.

She saw it, too, and stepped quickly away beyond his reach. And before he could say anything further, she hurried down the corridor toward her own room, where she slammed and locked the door behind her.

He continued to stand in the corridor for a moment, trying to rein in his anger. He would have to deal finally with the old woman one day. She was making a dangerous habit of overstepping her place, and that he could not abide. Of course, it was his unhappy lot to realize in the final moments of his anger that he needed her desperately, that he could trust no one else with the silent woman behind the closed door, that Caldy More knew far too much about him for him ever to release her to the freedom of the world outside Bledding Sorrow. Then, too, there was always the possibility that he would need her in other ways. No matter how hard he tried to resist it, he could not deny that he was worried, apprehensive, frightened. In unexpected moments he continued to hear the unearthly screams that he had heard earlier in the courtyard, his mind reverting effortlessly back to the black-caped specter which had evolved out of the empty doorway. And each time he thought on these things he felt a new disintegration, felt the blood in his veins grow cold. He felt like a man clinging to his sanity with tenuous fingertips. One slip and he would be gone.

He closed his eyes in fear over such an event. The chill was still there, plaguing him along with the terrible screams, the substance of the man whirling out of shadows.

Control. He must get control of himself. He must hold himself very rigid, must not allow anything to stand in his way of executing his duties as master of Bledding Sorrow.

So he roused himself out of his anger and brushed the memory of the confrontation from his mind like small flecks of fallen lint and turned his attention again to the closed door before him.

Inside his pocket his hand, trembling, found the black case and closed around it. He felt a deep silence within him. He moved forward, though still several feet away, so that he could face the door directly. His expression was strange, almost calm, as though what he was about to do had to be confirmed by some deep knowledge in his heart.

He remained staring at the closed door for several moments. His growing sense of excitement was good and natural; he always felt it increasing at this moment. What he was also aware of and what he loathed was his indistinct sense of guilt, his lack of sympathy.

She was his wife. He had no reason to feel guilt.

He stared at the closed door for several additional moments, the excitement building until it canceled completely the lack of guilt and sympathy.

Then he turned the doorknob and went in. . . .

ᕦ𝟐ᕤ

Occasionally, in spite of the white pills, there were cries.

This was why Caldy More, immediately on entering her room, went straight to her bed, lay down, and drew the pillow up around her ears. Not that she had any genuine sense of compassion for the wife. Still, there was a limit to what a decent Christian woman would be a part of.

Her face, half hidden in the pillow, tried to express a noble ignorance. She was only hired help. Nothing more. What went on anyplace in Bledding Sorrow was not her business. She knew this was true, for he certainly reminded her of it often enough.

Now she stared at the ceiling, loosed one side of the pillow so that her right ear could listen. Nothing. Yet. Quickly she turned her back to the wall, the long straggly salt-and-pepper hair pressed tightly over her face.

Oh, dear God! If only he had listened to her ten years ago. She had warned him. Hadn't she warned him time and time again? She had even told him that the trip to America would be useless and a waste of money. If she remembered correctly, and she was certain that she remembered correctly, she had even warned him of the dangers of scheming American women. "No prize greater than an Englishman," she had said. Yes! Her very words.

Again she turned uncomfortably on the bed, suffering from a trivial upset stomach, brought on, no doubt, by the events of the late evening and the sure knowledge of what was going on next door. She stared sideways at the room and softly shook her head. But no.

He hadn't listened to her then any more than he had listened to her a few minutes ago outside in the corridor. He never listened to anyone or heard anything except what he wanted to hear. And unfortunately he had listened closely and had heard clearly the repeated and flattering invitations from Joel Kromer, the English history professor at the small women's college in upper Vermont and longtime admirer of Bledding Sorrow Hall. Kromer had been the one, the distant but constant voice of flattery who had begged, pleaded, entreated Geoffrey Bledding to come to America to deliver an eight-week series of lectures on the Elizabethans.

Her face grew grim remembering how Mr. Bledding had responded to that bit of nonsense, ultimately dropping everything and fleeing across the water at great expense and small remuneration, his ego fanned. And Caldy More knew better than anyone that Geoffrey Bledding had an ego that loved and needed to be fanned.

In her very limited circle of friends Caldy More was renowned for her charity. But she had felt little or no charity at all when his letters had started arriving, singing the praises of Kromer's daughter, a second-year student at the college, a remarkable young woman, or so he had claimed, a budding poet, a keenly perceptive and sensitive soul in her deep love for England and all things English.

At that very moment Caldy More had seen the legendary handwriting on the wall. And when, less than three months later, Geoffrey Bledding had returned to Bledding Sorrow with an American wife thirteen years his junior, Caldy More had come as near to quitting the services of Bledding Sorrow as she ever had before in her life.

Now she shuddered on the bed. A painful cramp was forming in the small of her back, a knot growing tighter. She stretched quickly in an attempt to dispel it. How could she relax under the circumstances? How many years had it been since she had felt and enjoyed total relaxation? She was not a stupid woman and she had excellent eyesight. From the beginning she had been able to see what was going to happen. And it *had* happened exactly as she had predicted.

The young woman, Ann by name, although Caldy More had never addressed her by her name, had arrived, more a child than an adult. A pale, fair female, lacking in every way the good solid English sturdiness of local women, she had tried pitifully to insert herself into all aspects of Geoffrey Bledding's life, as though the hasty marriage vows had given her direct access to his soul. In the mid-sixties, when the restoration of the hall had commenced, she had followed the workmen and artisans around, suggesting this change here and that change there, as though her opinions were actually important and mattered.

Now, for the first time since Caldy More had taken to her bed, she gave the faintest smile. The American woman had had a will in those days, and frequently late at night she had heard the master's and mistress' voices raised in anger at each other.

Again she slowly, carefully lowered the pillow to see if she could hear anything yet. She listened a moment. The smile faded. The mouth remained clamped shut. Nothing. So far nothing. Half closing her eyes, she tried to envision what was taking place only a few yards away in the small upper bedchamber. Suddenly she closed her eyes, pressed them shut. She wished, she really wished, God forgive her, that the young woman would die and thus put them all out of their misery. As though inwardly shocked by her own thoughts, she rolled onto her back again, but kept the pillow clamped firmly in place over her ears.

In a surge of Christian compassion, she remembered the one occasion on which she had felt minor sympathy for the young woman. It had been again in the mid-sixties, when the restoration of the hall had been in full swing and the Vermont professor and his wife had planned to journey to England to visit their only child in her new life. Tragically, the plane had crashed while taking off in New York, killing them both.

That had been the end. For all of them. Certainly the beginning of the end. In her deep and mindless grief the young woman had totally withdrawn. Apparently she had lost interest in everything and had retreated into a deep silence, and shortly after that she seemed incapable of answering even the simplest and most direct question.

It was also true and very embarrassing that twice she had tried to run away. Once she had made it as far as Bledding Village, where Dr. Axtell had spotted her on the motorway and had brought her back. And three weeks later she had made it as far as London, where the police had found her wandering senselessly about Soho. And again she had been returned to Bledding Sorrow. And it was shortly after the London escapade that Dr. Axtell, at Geoffrey Bledding's request, had commenced prescribing the white pills, mild sedatives, he had said, to help her through this difficult period of unbearable grief. Over the years the dosage had increased. And was still increasing.

Caldy More continued to lie with her eyes closed, remembering too much, remembering all. Without warning, from those pouched, invincible eyes sprang moisture. Such an effect of sadness was in no way intended, but sprang merely from the sure and certain knowledge that the young woman would be better off dead. Indeed, over the years she gave increasingly the appearance of one dead. And now, with the exception of the late-night visitations such as the one taking place at this very moment, she was Caldy More's problem. Caldy More was the one who had to keep her out of sight of all visitors and students. Caldy More was the one who had to administer the white pills daily at the first sign of rebellion. Caldy More was the one who had to see that she was washed and dressed and placed in the small walled garden so she could have the benefit of sun on her pale face. Caldy More was the one who had to endure the blankness in the dark eyes which lay buried in shadows. And Caldy More was the one who had to survive her silences, her spells of gazing emptily at the sky, her occasional whispered requests for pencil and paper and the strewn and wadded gibberish which she later had to pick up from the garden path. Caldy More had to endure it all with the patience of a saint and the fortitude of Christ Himself. With no thanks and little pay, she had to endure it all.

Suddenly these thoughts and memories draped themselves like black banners in her mind and caused her to toss on her bed. And in her small agony she grew careless and allowed the pillow to fall away from her ears. And in that moment she heard clearly, coming from the small bedchamber next door, a sharp plaintive cry, followed immediately by another cry, followed thereafter by a series of low, pitiful moans.

Suddenly she thrust her hands over her ears and shut her eyes and ground her teeth together, and behind the barrier of clamped jaws and pinched eyes she prayed fiercely, "God, Jesus Christ, merciful Saviour in heaven, take her!"

❧ 3 ❧

On the following magnificent rain-washed cool May morning Ann Kromer Bledding sat in the small walled garden of Bledding Sorrow Hall having her fingernails clipped.

In actual years she was thirty, but she looked much younger, almost childlike, irrefutably innocent, her face and general manner the result of that peculiar mixed mercy which the aging process bestows on the mentally ill.

In another way, it might be said that she had the wrong face for her age. Small-featured, delicate as a cameo, she reflected none of the scope or breadth of the twentieth century. More likely you would be able to find her face in the workshops of the great sixteenth-century French painters or the eighteenth-century English painters of rural idylls. Her dark blue eyes and whiteness of skin only enhanced the delicacy of her features.

She was not in a good pure sense of the word pretty. Even in her healthier Vermont school days her most agreeable assets had been her almost poignant sensitivity and a kind of charming, cheerful optimism that one day the demons in her head could be talked away and replaced with the favoring warmth of surprise and conjecture.

But she'd never been able to do this, and throughout her young life she had been plagued by a progression of minor mental problems, periods of withdrawal followed by fits of depression, hallucinations so vivid and real that they terrified her, particularly when she realized at a very early age that no one else saw them.

She had been hospitalized twice, once at twelve and

again at sixteen, in a discreet private clinic for the mentally disturbed. There, under the watchful and fatherly eyes of a kind psychiatrist, she'd learned, not the source and cause of her distress, but merely how to conceal it. Madness was an embarrassment, a hardship on those who loved her. If she had any feeling for them at all, she must learn to keep her fantasies to herself.

So she sent her agony underground, kept her visions a secret, forced herself into human society with a gaiety she did not feel, and knew, deep within her soul, that it was only a matter of time until the sickness would overwhelm and devour her.

In those earlier days her two greatest loves had been her father and England. And since the two had been inseparably intertwined, both in the classroom and at home, she had, at twenty, met and fallen in love with Geoffrey Bledding within a month. Her father had been able to think of nothing better for her than marriage to this Englishman, whom he admired and respected so much, and though there was something in it which her own heart could not approve of, something of foreboding, a fulfilling of a destiny that was not truly hers, it had been done, the ceremony performed, her fate sealed.

Of course, she had suspected that she was not actually in love with the flesh-and-blood man as much as she was in love with an abstract personification of England. Still, his arrival on the quiet dull campus had been exciting and romantic. So it was only natural that the shy, dreamily inclined, totally protected and sheltered young girl should find the visiting Englishman attractive enough to marry and so join her life to his.

Unfortunately England had received her doubtingly, if not coolly, and nothing beyond the merest commonplace had been talked almost all the time. The Englishman who had been so cordial and expansive in America had turned suddenly measured and remote, denying her access into every area of his life. Left to her own devices, she had returned to her poetry, but the

penciled marks which she put on paper had been little
more than memorandums.

Then for too long she had remembered the day, the
hour, the instant when the news of the plane crash
had reached her. At the very moment when she had
been considering escaping back to warm parental arms,
there were suddenly no arms to receive her. With all
avenues of escape cut off, she still had felt the necessity
for movement. Her mind was already growing quite sick
from rejection and loss and loneliness. Perhaps other
airs would soothe, heal.

Unfortunately both escape attempts had failed. On
being driven by the police to the door of Bledding Sorrow for the second time, she had leaned back in the
corner of the car, accepting almost calmly the certain
knowledge that she would not leave again, the closing,
sealing terror of an ill-disposed mind.

That had been more than ten years ago. Her fears,
confirmed as they had been by the deep sleeps which
seemed to grow longer every day, her moments of rebellion growing fewer, her complete isolation from all
human traffic except for Caldy More, all this caused the
worn-out past to sink blessedly away. And in the rapidity of half a moment's thought she could dismiss all
aspects of the world as it existed beyond the walled
confines of her small garden. Although she felt dead,
she also felt safe, and safety was a condition much to
be desired.

Now she sat in the garden, a docile, quite pale child,
having her fingernails clipped. In spite of its beauty,
the morning was not right. She liked right mornings.
So often the afternoons and evenings faded into a blur
of drowsy heavy nothingness that she always looked forward to the crystalline rightness of morning.

But this morning was wrong, terribly wrong. She
sought in her mind for some way to demonstrate the
rightness of morning and could find none and shivered
slightly on the cold stone bench while Caldy More held
her hand in her lap and clipped her nails.

From the beginning, everything had been wrong. Caldy More had been late in unlocking her bedroom door and then had appeared so rushed and angry that she had scarcely given Ann time to dress properly. In her haste she'd left off undergarments altogether and had roughly thrust her arms and head into the gray smock dress and had almost dragged her, barefoot, hair uncombed, down the narrow steps to the small sitting room where Geoffrey Bledding was waiting.

Then there had been a harsh exchange between Caldy More and Bledding which Ann had not understood. Therefore she had taken no part in it. As well as Ann could make out, he was angry because of a scratch on his face. Then Caldy More had said it was not her responsibility and had shoved Ann close to the angry man's face. Terrified, Ann had run away to a corner of the room because the man frightened her and because it was none of her concern.

Now she sat on the stone bench, trying to make sense out of it, trying very hard to understand why they were angry and what she could do about it and what would happen if she couldn't do anything about it.

Suddenly Caldy More ordered, "Stop fidgeting!" and grasped her wrist even tighter and separated her fingers roughly and in her haste cut the nail so close to the quick that Ann closed her eyes. When she reopened them, the garden wall looked liquid, as though she were seeing it underwater. Idle fingers of hair brushed her cheeks. She tried to concentrate on the top of the garden wall, where, occasionally, the large white tomcat from the kitchen came for a morning visit. She hoped he did not come while Caldy More was still here. She liked her visits with the cat to be private. She was sorry that Caldy More was angry, sorry, too, that the man had scratched his face. But she had had nothing to do with any of it.

She looked up then at Caldy More with an intense earnestness and supplication. Tears had sprung in her eyes. Her mind and tongue struggled to produce words and failed.

Apparently Caldy More saw the expression on the entreating, confused face and sat now like a woman beneath a breaking dam. She turned away as though she could not bear to look at the face. The clipping became gentler as though she was newly aware of the helplessness of her mute charge.

Caldy More said softly, "Never you mind, now." Then more gruffly she added, "If it had been me, I'd a done worse than scratch his face." Carefully she turned her attention back to the job at hand and quickly completed the clipping. Without another word she stood up from the stone bench and went back into the small kitchen, locking the door behind her, pausing long enough to stare back at the young woman sitting alone now in the garden.

Ann could still see her through the curtained glass of the door. Slowly she licked the blood from the butchered fingernail, waiting for the old woman to go away. Not that she didn't like Caldy More, but she liked better the silence of the garden when it was empty. None of her friends would come as long as Caldy More was there. And she had friends, several of them, some light and graceful like the rose people who lived in the throats of the dark crimson roses growing by the opposite wall, and others repulsive and odious like the young woman with the absurd face and short ragged hair who lived under the very stone bench on which she was sitting. She disliked the young woman and had tried to figure out for ever so long precisely how she got into the garden each morning. But she had never been able to solve the mystery, and on certain mornings the young woman just appeared beside her, wearing a gray shapeless smock dress, her eyes almost totally lost in shadows of illness, whispering into Ann's ear and filling her head with terrifying stories of how she was a prisoner, watched over by a black witch who had butchered her hair to make her look ugly. The young woman always had such an aura of pain and brutality about her that she frightened Ann.

Now suddenly she stood up as though the woman were at that very moment beside her. The abruptness of movement caused her to gasp. Her body this morning was wracked by subtle discomforts. Moving more slowly, she walked away from the stone bench. But the discomfort merely went with her. She felt battered, unspecified aches which seemed to increase with every step. Slowly she leaned against the trunk of a near tree. One hand moved tentatively down to her legs as though in an attempt to localize and identify the discomfort. But there was nothing.

She pushed away from the tree and for a moment almost lost her balance. Her bare feet struggled on the moss-covered stones of the path. Her arms reached out for support that wasn't there. Suddenly she had no more strength for standing erect and fell lightly onto the moist dirt skirting the path. She lay still for a moment, one hand idly fingering small stones. The fall did not alarm her. She frequently fell and had learned over the years to spare herself serious injury by simply giving in to the fall.

Now she stared out from her sideward vision of the world. The roses and larkspur and poppies formed a gigantic and multicolored forest about her. The splendid sight took her mind off the discomfort of her body, and she raised slightly up, half in fear, half in expectation to see if the horrible woman was standing by the stone bench.

She wasn't. The garden was empty except for a snail shell, which she now studied closely, marveling at its brilliant and encircled construction, wondering vaguely what had become of the snail that had inhabited it. She decided, still lying in the path, that before the heavy sleep came this day, she would write a poem about the snail shell. She must not make it a more decided subject of misery by a melancholy tone herself. She must not appear to think the snail a misfortune. With all the spirit she could command, she would describe him first as something strange and then, in a few words, say that if his consent and approbation could be obtained, she would describe exactly how it felt to carry around such a splendid shell on such a small back.

Suddenly and very softly she groaned. She knew there would be no poem. Of late, when Caldy More had very kindly brought her pencil and paper, the pencil had refused to make contact with the paper. No matter how hard she had pressed downward, the pencil had always slid along several inches in the air above the paper, refusing to make any contact at all.

Now slowly she replaced the snail shell in the dirt where she had found it. It occurred to her that the snail might come back looking for his home and it had to be in the same place where he had left it. She didn't want to cause him any undue pain and worry. It had to be in the same place, the exact same place.

Rising carefully now so as not to reawaken the discomfort in her body, unaware of the clinging dirt on the side of her face, she crawled on hands and knees the short distance to where the rose people lived in the centers of the crimson roses. The white cat had not come as yet, so she had a few minutes to spend with the rose people.

Raising up on her knees, she buried her face in the broadest crimson rose she could find. At the bottom of the blood-red well she saw a tiny face staring at her. She had never seen the rose people whole, only their faces. The rest of their bodies appeared to be caught and imprisoned in the throat of the rose.

She tried now to form words of greeting. Her short jagged hair fell over her face. She closed her eyes in an attempt to send the burning, aching sensations away. But every movement that she made on this wrong morning caused her to wince, and the tiny smiling face at the center of the rose refused to speak to her, as though taking dark delight in her discomfort.

Again she looked quickly over her shoulder to see

if the stone-bench woman was watching her. For one terrible moment she thought she saw a corpse. But it was merely the woman asleep. While Ann had been talking to the snail, the woman obviously had appeared and fallen asleep. Her immediate instinct was to run to the far wall and hide behind the lilac bushes. The lilac bushes were her fortress in spring and summer.

But she was incapable this morning of running anywhere, and the best she could do was drag herself past the roses, past the man in the honeysuckle who always shouted at her about the black path which stretched across the ocean just waiting to take her home. She didn't trust the man in the honeysuckle. She had climbed the wall once and had taken that black path across miles of water where sharks had nipped at her heels, where the winds had blown so cold and fiercely, where the storms had raged with such power that they had shaken the narrow black path and the cold waves had washed over her. And just when she thought she had seen land, she had seen instead a most hideous sight, had seen human bodies being burned alive. So terrified was she of the sight that she had turned and had run back across the ocean, the black path quickly crumbling behind her, the sharks biting closer and closer until at last she had reached the small walled garden, where she had cried out her despair and had vowed never to leave its safety again.

She sat immobile now in the garden path, her arms wrapped tightly about her, rocking softly back and forth. Carefully she looked toward the honeysuckle bush. But the honeysuckle man was asleep. Blessedly asleep and still.

Slowly she looked up at the sun in the high blue sky. Even the sun was wrong, terribly wrong, as wrong as she had ever remembered it. Nothing was clear. She could *feel* presences rather than see them, as though everything were out of sight, dreaming in an immense nightmare.

It was only a short distance to the fortress of lilacs.

She could make it if she tried. The garden was not her friend this morning. There were enemies everywhere, shadows growing uncannily large. No one was inclined to speak to her or to offer consolation or to ask questions. But all seemed to be watching her in the heavy and oppressive silence.

Now she crouched in the garden path, looking up now and then at the sun, staring with dark eyes wherein the pupils seemed to have melted away into a bleak white void. Although she was shivering, still she laboriously dragged herself along the path, heading for the lilac fortress.

Suddenly the night's horror rose vividly before her mind. Behind her the stone-bench woman was awake now and calling out to her exactly what had happened, what had happened before and what would happen again. The path grew narrow as she scrambled forward into the safety of the lilac bushes. She had to be careful not to move too rapidly or she would fall and not be able to right herself. Now there was a drumming inside her head which would not cease.

The green lilac leaves turned into a spiral. They twisted about her face as though they meant to ensnare her. She was now nearly blind with fear. Enemies everywhere. The morning was wrong. Strange that the drumming had increased even inside the lilac fortress. Perhaps her head would explode. Why was the lilac bush trying to strangle her?

Now she pressed against the base of the red brick wall, her arms covering her face as though for protection against blows, her bare legs, dirt-covered, curled tightly beneath her. Wherever her eyes looked, she saw nothing but threats.

Suddenly something soft and white fell against her. She had long expected it, the arrival of the white kitchen cat come for his morning visit. She lifted her head, her hand reaching out to touch the cat which crouched before her. Yet she felt nothing. Instead the cat turned suddenly dark. He lay crumpled on the ground before her, his eyes lifeless in the cool dirt. She bent close to him, concerned, when, without warning, out of the still, furred form a vapor began to appear, merely a wisp of smoke at first, then gradually assuming the shape of a lady.

Ann had never seen such a specter before and pressed even closer to the base of the wall, watching, horrified, as the shape grew, increasing in size and dimension until it resembled a full-grown woman who writhed beneath the lilac bushes, her arms, moist red, reaching out toward Ann as though entreating, the folds of her curious garments red with blood, her face twisted in pain, one hand continuously reaching toward her legs, which lay hidden out of sight beneath the soiled garment of her skirt.

Ann felt as though she were swaying high up in the air instead of pushing close to earth. This was a new demon, one she had never seen before, brought on by the wrong morning and the constant drumming at the base of her skull.

Now she closed her eyes and begged softly for the lady to go away. But instead she felt a curious current of fire, like an impulse, an unloosening of passion, as though her blood were in flames. And when she opened her eyes to see where the heat was coming from, she saw instead the lady lying in the path, moving now, dragging herself pitiably forward.

Ann pushed backward against the wall. The figure was drawing nearer. The drumming increased to a deafening pitch. The base of the wall which had once protected her now imprisoned her. There was no way out and around the bloodied entreating hand, which was only inches away from her face.

Suddenly Ann saw the ghostly figure try to rise. But she seemed unable to stand, some hideous mutilation beneath her skirts preventing her from standing erect. She fell sideward once again and in clear agony began to scream at Ann, begging her to run away, to leave this place, this garden, these people.

Suddenly, in an attempt to escape, Ann gave one enormous wrenching backward and struck her head against the wall. Then all became quiet. The specter faded, though agony still glinted in her eyes, but it was mostly now as if shining from behind a veil of tears.

Ann lay in the dirt at the base of the brick wall, panting slightly, a heavy curtain of silence hanging over her, loose strands of hair plastered across her cheeks, the gray smock dress covered with dirt. Breathing through her nose, her jaws clenched with fear, she began to burrow into the earth, burrowed deeper and deeper into the dirt, a self-burial, a missed heartbeat, a shrug of eternity. . . .

❧ 4 ❧

Geoffrey Bledding sat behind his desk, weary from the events of the night, and felt suddenly unable to face his future, which was only a form of terrible emptiness.

He had passed a restless night, awake more than asleep, any disturbance, no matter how small, causing alarm, causing him to sit rigidly up in bed, searching out the shadows for what he feared most, the return of the specters.

Now he rested his head in his hands. What was happening to him? What was he allowing to happen to him? There were no ghosts, not here or anywhere else. Why such tawdry nonsense should interest others, he had no idea.

Still he felt weakened, vulnerable somehow. Hallucination or not, what he had seen had taken a terrible toll, the constant tremors in his hands, the dull but omnipresent pain at the base of his skull, the shortness of breath, the constant anxiety that they would again appear and he would be helpless before them.

Suddenly he groaned softly. Oh, dear God, what was he to do? He waited a moment as though fervently hoping for an answer. Receiving none, he slowly straightened his shoulders, scolding himself for giving in to such self-induced torment. Still the despair remained, the realization that at any moment the specters could again descend on him, send him hurtling through a black abyss, perhaps from which there would be no return.

He clasped his hands together in an attempt to still their trembling and now tried to focus his attention on the work before him.

Scattered about him on the desk was the daily

disaster known as the morning mail. Every envelope contained a pressure; bills due and past due, requests for special privileges, absurd requests ranging from the warning from the Birmingham Art League, which was due at noon, that some of their members were over seventy and could not manipulate the climb to the third-floor dormitory to the letter from the Manchester Herpetologists requesting special accommodations for two crates of adders which they planned to study during their late-summer stay at Bledding Sorrow.

And there were other insanities as well; applications for work from local ladies who seemed only to want short hours and handsome pay. And a very angry letter from the Manchester coachman who was due to arrive on Friday and demanded again to know the precise measurements of the gatehouse arch, as he had no intention of scraping his new coach.

Also there were more than a dozen requests for brochures from England and America. This was good. At least their reputation was spreading. But a spreading reputation meant additional duties, more strangers demanding service of all kinds, a greater invasion of his privacy, more curious eyes, more human bodies, more intrusions.

He leaned forward on his desk now and inadvertently rubbed his face. His hand caught on the small plaster which covered the scratch along the side of his jaw. For a moment the tips of his fingers hovered over the plaster as though they were eyes. The scratch was still raw, slightly throbbing. He hadn't expected her to resist. It had been months since she had resisted. Martin Axtell had warned him of the body's ability to build up an immunity to any and all sedatives, thereby requiring the necessity to increase the dosage continuously. Then there was nothing to it. They would simply have to increase the dosage.

He patted the plaster gently and resolved in his mind to find a free interval out of this hectic day to phone

Martin Axtell. The man was a friend and ally. He would help. He understood the situation at Bledding Sorrow all too well, having looked after the American woman since her first illness. Yes, Martin knew better than anyone the necessity for keeping her quiet and peaceful.

This resolve brought a temporary ease to his mind. But it didn't last long. Outside in the hall, just coming down the steps, he now heard the giggling chatter of the departing bird watchers. He wished too late that he had remembered to close the office door. But he hadn't, and now the female parade was upon him, a chattering, grinning gallery of aging harridans with hair too white, too red, too black, a loathsome commonness about them all and yet a certain boldness in their withered eyes and red-lipped smiles.

Now one peered into the office with dark-shadowed eyes and a vague wistful stance. "You'll be coming to the gatehouse, of course," she pronounced, "to bid us good-bye. You promised. Remember, Mr. Bledding?"

He smiled. "I wouldn't dream of not coming."

Then another appeared. "Mrs. Hanson thinks we should stay for a few extra days so that we can be here to see the new coach. After all, it was our support that—"

"And I'm truly grateful," he interrupted. "But I'm afraid that your rooms are booked." He rose from his chair as though to speed them on their way.

Both women disappeared from his sight and said something to the ladies behind them. Then one of them stepped forward again, blocking the office door, her face suddenly still as though she were about to deliver a speech. "The ladies have asked me to thank you for your gracious hospitality," she began.

It *was* a speech. He flushed slightly in the embarrassing moment and felt a fresh throbbing in the scratch on the side of his jaw. The woman droned endlessly on, rhapsodizing about the glory and beauty of Bledding

Sorrow, telling him how their summer stay here was a high point in their otherwise routine lives.

And Geoffrey Bledding stood behind his desk and closed his eyes as if he hoped to obliterate both the woman and the speech.

Finally he heard Mrs. Hanson's dominating voice cut through the effusiveness. "Enough, ladies," she suggested. "We've taken up a sufficient amount of Mr. Bledding's time. On to your cars now. Hurry, hurry!" And the ladies obeyed, each stopping at the door long enough to wave at him.

A few moments later only Mrs. Hanson remained. Now she stood in the door staring at him seriously, as though she saw something she didn't quite approve of. "Are you quite well this morning, Mr. Bledding?" she inquired primly.

He assured her that he was, and in order to scatter the focus in her eyes, he moved quickly around the desk, took her arm, and began to steer her toward the sunlight of the open front door. He seized the opportunity to thank her again for her generosity in all matters.

But as they walked out the door and into the courtyard, he noticed that a sullen little line had set about her mouth, and her eyes had never wandered very far from the plaster on the side of his jaw. He knew she would not be mollified. And indeed, midway across the courtyard, she stopped and looked directly at him. "Your American wife, Mr. Bledding," she began, pursing her lips as though the better to approach a disagreeable subject. "Is she—I mean, is she—"

"Yes," he replied sadly but firmly. "She's still ill, but doing nicely, thank you."

She shook her head as though in deep commiseration for this one shabby area in his otherwise spotless life. "A man of your great responsibilities and duties," she mourned, "to have the additional burden of a—"

He could not stand her pity and quickly cut her off.

"Yes, well. . . ." And as his voice trailed away, he managed to fix the smile on his face.

She stood then, leaning forward as though she wished to be kissed lightly on the cheek. He could not bring himself to do so and instead grasped her shoulders and told her again, "Farewell until next summer, Mrs. Hanson," wondering all the time how she had managed to find out about his wife. Someone had been talking; the kitchen help, the chambermaids, Caldy More, someone.

The high sunny day sank into a black gloom as he watched the ladies pile into the small cars, each jockeying for window seats, each determined to wave the last good-bye. Suddenly he felt peculiar, felt as though there were threats all about him, not just the visible ones in the gossipy women who were now leaving. There was something else, something moving in the air, coming closer to him. Yes, he was certain of it. There! Listen! A fluttering like wings. Abruptly he looked over his shoulder. Nothing, only the sun-glazed cobblestones of the courtyard.

Then what? And where? Rapidly now he turned in all directions, his eyes frantically seeking out each shadow, scanning quickly the broad red brick exterior of Bledding Sorrow.

He was breathing quite heavily now, out of fear, like a man possessed. The sensation of a foreign presence increased. He was not alone, yet he couldn't see. Dear God, how could he possibly do battle with something he couldn't see? At that moment, although he was standing in a patch of brilliant sunlight, he shivered. An incredible chill was creeping over him, source unknown, face unknown, cause unknown, everything unknown.

Suddenly he looked up at the third floor, saw one of the young serving girls staring down at him, her mouth open, as though frightened and alarmed by the peculiar behavior of the master of Bledding Sorrow.

He stared back at her for a moment, acutely aware

of how foolish he must have appeared to her. Then again he laced himself rigidly into the proper stance, the proper demeanor for a headmaster, head erect, shoulders back, and hoped that the violent trembling which was now sweeping over his entire body was not visible from the third-floor window.

He held the position throughout the endless process of motors turning over, cars angling backward and out the narrow gatehouse arch and onto the dangerously steep road which led down to the village and the motorway beyond. He was certain that tongues would clack all the way home as they speculated on the reason for the plaster on his face and the greater mystery of the invisible American wife.

There would have to be an accounting. As he watched the last car turn out into the narrow road, he vowed that there would be an accounting. Someone had talked out of turn, and he couldn't, he wouldn't abide that. A man was entitled to a basic privacy. It was out of the kindness of his heart that he kept the woman here in the safe confines of Bledding Sorrow instead of banishing her to an institution, where she undoubtedly belonged. If his reward for such kindness was backstairs gossip which endangered the entire institution of Bledding Sorrow, then he would ferret out the gossiper and send her packing. He had enough to contend with without having to deal with enemies from within.

The courtyard was empty now. But he continued to stand, a solitary figure, his head slightly bowed under the awesome weight of his duty and position. The insane wife had to be kept a secret. For the sake of his life and livelihood, the wife had to be kept a secret.

He turned and looked back at Bledding Sorrow, as though the imprint of scandal had suddenly appeared in broad letters across the front of the projecting bays. Suddenly, out of the reflection from one of the glittering mullioned windows, he saw something moving toward him. He held his position, confident that in broad daylight he had nothing to fear. But he was wrong, for out of the glare caused by sun on glass he saw the specter again, the black-caped man, featureless, moving steadily toward him, an aura of pain and outrage about him, speed increasing, something terribly wrong with him, that one bloodied hand extended again toward Geoffrey's throat.

In a spasm of new torment, Geoffrey fell back, almost losing his balance, running wildly now toward the safety of the gatehouse arch. Once he looked back in dread over his shoulder. The specter was still pursuing him, coming closer, closer. His head spinning, Geoffrey stopped and clutched at the brick wall for support, glancing a second time over his shoulder, feeling that he had to escape, that if the specter ever caught up with him, all would be lost.

But this time when he looked back, there was nothing there. The courtyard was empty, the sun dancing in harmless reflection off the mullioned windows, the passage of a heavy cloud overhead obscuring for a moment the normal brilliance of the sun.

So that's what had happened, merely the passing of a cloud over the face of the sun, causing a natural distortion in light and darkness. He laughed openly in relief, the torment once again becoming merely a memory. He was not a man given to hallucination. There was a reason for everything.

Now, once again, he glanced back at the front of Bledding Sorrow. Seeing nothing but the elegance of Elizabethan architecture, he walked hesitantly, still shaken, through the arched front door.

Inside the darkened hallway he almost collided with a young chambermaid struggling under the weight of an armload of clean linen. Those eyes and gently curving lips smiled at him and seemed to say:

You have a mad wife. Your wife is quite mad.

He brushed past her and moved rapidly through the length of the Great Hall, heading toward his private quarters and the one woman who had intimate knowledge of the mad wife to share with others.

If Caldy More had talked, Caldy More would have to be punished. And if Caldy More had not talked, then there was a serious leak in his household that would have to be found out and plugged.

Either way there were new and foreboding problems in Bledding Sorrow this morning. And so intent was he on solving them that he walked directly past his office door, where at that moment the phone was ringing. . . .

❦❦ 5 ❦❦

Her own tea canister being empty and the young woman safely deposited in the garden for her morning air, Caldy More had slipped through the front corridor at the very moment when Mr. Bledding was telling the ladies good-bye.

And now she sat at one of the long tables in the basement dining room consoling herself with a steaming cup of tea and enduring the company of Mavis Bonebrake, the London import who had served for the past two summers as chief cook for Bledding Sorrow Adult College.

A gross, fat woman with frizzy red hair which stuck out over her head, she was certainly not Caldy More's choice of an ideal companion. But at times Caldy More found her diverting and amusing, particularly when she started talking about the countless men who had shared her London flat over the last thirty years and how she had scrupulously avoided the snare of the altar with all of them.

At fifty-seven Mavis Bonebrake was a crude, plainspoken woman who had the unusual ability to shock, repulse, and amuse simultaneously. It seemed that one of her many lovers had been Italian, and he had been the one who had taught her how to cook and season, an art apparently beyond the reach and comprehension of the average Englishwoman. The other males who had shared her bed—and Caldy More could only wonder at the masculine desperation which would lead a man to Mrs. Bonebrake's bed—ranged from a policeman to a cabbie to a Covent Garden fruit merchant to several self-confessed hoodlums to the original Mr. Bonebrake, who had died of a heart attack on their

71

honeymoon to Blackpool, "the best pecker of them all," according to Mrs. Bonebrake herself, who could become positively misty-eyed at the remembrance of her first love.

No! She was not Caldy More's type of woman, but at least she was not insane and could talk. Oh, dear, how she could talk! Now she sat opposite Caldy More at the long dining table, scratching openly at one enormous breast, drawing a long breath of fatigue.

"Lunch will be catch-as-catch-can," she warned, stirring endless spoonfuls of brown sugar into her tea. "Just the staff, you know. I'll be damned if I'll cook meat and cabbage just for the staff."

Caldy More nodded. At least they had one thing in common. They both were overworked and underpaid. Mrs. Bonebrake completed the scratching and leaned back in the narrow chair in order to adjust a strap inside her white uniform. When that was completed, she leaned forward again, resting a dimpled arm on the table, her ruddy face grinning. "Those bird watchers were for the birds if you ask me." She grinned, sharing a poor joke which had undoubtedly originated in the kitchen and had run rampant through the staff for the past week.

Caldy More gave her a genteel and slightly condescending smile. "They are paying students, Mrs. Bonebrake, and without them you wouldn't be here."

The woman's red eyebrows arched high. "Oh? Indeed. Wouldn't I? People always have to eat. And it was their grand manners I objected to more than anything. Common women they was, at home down on their knees scrubbing their men's piss from round the loo same as meself. But here, my gawd, curling their little pinky away from their teacups like they was the Queen's handmaidens." She shook her several chins. "It's the show I hate, Caldy More, the show and pretense that sticks in me craw."

She signaled her contempt with a sharp explosion of air and took a noisy swig from her teacup. "If the truth were known," she whispered, leaning close across the table, "they probably peel and boil the same spuds as I do and spread their legs for their mates the same as me." Again she sniffed her contempt. "Like I say, it's just their airs I can't stand. Just their airs, that's all."

Caldy More made it a point to ignore the vulgarism of "spread legs." Still she took a certain delight in informing the woman, "Well, the Birmingham Art League arrives in a few hours, and then it will be back to work. You are not paid to express an opinion of the students. You are paid to cook three square."

And in her turn Mrs. Bonebrake apparently chose to let the scolding pass and concentrated instead on the nature of the incoming party. "Painters, you say?" she asked, and again the red eyebrows lifted higher. "My gawd a mercy, I hope they don't leave us any more gifties like the group last summer." She motioned with her spoon toward the large contemporary paintings which hung slightly askew on the knotty-pine walls. "You see that one, Caldy More?" And she singled out the largest painting of all, an enormous canvas filled with small, irregular-shaped brown objects against a light blue background. "Well"—she grinned slyly—"us in the kitchen has given that one a very special title." She leaned back in mock grandeur. "We call it 'Mr. Bledding's Morning Stool.'"

Caldy More grinned, then laughed aloud in spite of herself. "Shame on you, Mrs. Bonebrake," she scolded, pressing the napkin lightly against her lips.

"Well, it's true, ain't it?" exclaimed the large woman. "Look at it," she ordered. "Now, don't that look like someone's turds?"

"Hush, now," Caldy More warned, though still grinning in spite of herself. If only Mrs. Bonebrake were not so coarse, she would not be impossible to like. Caldy More suddenly had a dazzling and heavenly vision, that she would somehow lead Mrs. Bonebrake out of her coarseness and into a saintly refinement. It would certainly give her something to do this summer and help take her mind off the poor creature now wandering about in the walled garden.

To this end, Caldy More slowly leaned forward, her voice deep and rather firm, certain questions necessary to the woman's salvation forming in her mind. "Mrs. Bonebrake," she began, almost sweetly, "what precisely is it that you do in London during the winter?"

Mrs. Bonebrake drained her teacup in one long swallow, wiped her lips with the back of her hand, belched, and said, "Fuck." Again she rubbed her breast in a curious manner and leaned back in the chair, her round face beaming. "I go out of my way to find as many good mates as I can. People look at me and can't believe that I'm going on sixty. But I am. And when I tell them that the secret of my longevity and good health is a nice thick stand-up pecker, still they don't believe me."

All the color seemed to have drained out of Caldy More's face. The line of interrogation which was ultimately to have led to the salvation of Mrs. Bonebrake's soul quickly faded from her mind. Now she sat transfixed and horrified as the woman went breathlessly on, explaining the health properties in a good pecker.

"You see, Caldy More," the woman whispered, as though lowering her voice out of reverence for her subject matter, "a man and a woman is like a violin and a bow. One's absolutely no good without the other, but when that bow presses against that violin, and that violin tips upward against that bow, then they make beautiful music." She sat back as though pleased with the poetic nature of what she was saying. "It's the same for men and women. There's got to be a lot of tipping and tilting and pressing and pushing, but, my gawd, is it ever worth it!" Her face glowed with ecstasy, the wide grin on her face now fixed as though for all time.

Caldy More concealed her face in her upturned teacup, but she could do nothing to conceal the heat rising mercilessly on either side of her face.

In a rush of warm affection, Mrs. Bonebrake made her an offer. "I tell you what," she said, still whispering, "you come visit me in London next winter, and I'll find a pecker as big as an ax handle, and then you'll understand about the violin and the bow. Hear, now?"

Caldy More heard. She stared at her own reflection in the teacup and felt her heart race at the suggested horror. It wasn't that she was a virgin. As a young girl of fifteen she had had a man once, a despicable, drunken, overheated sheep farmer who had forced her into the grotesqueness of sexual coupling, a brutal, terrifying interlude, totally painful and humiliating. "No, thank you, Mrs. Bonebrake," she said primly, returning the cup to its saucer with slightly trembling hands. The woman was beyond salvation.

With the immediate intention of leaving such a shameful presence, she stood up rather quickly. The chair scraped across the concrete floor and threatened to fall backward.

Mrs. Bonebrake, apparently unaware of anything amiss, rose, too. "No rest for the wicked is what I always say," she intoned. "You to your crazy woman and I to my spuds."

Suddenly Caldy More stopped cold in her efforts to readjust the chair. What was the woman talking about? And if she knew, how did she know?

The urgent questions in her mind were beginning to evolve into words when suddenly Mrs. Bonebrake apparently saw the stricken face opposite her. "Never you mind, dearie." She smiled, leaning over and patting Caldy More on the hand. "The secret will go with me to me grave. But if I'm a good girl and make you a nice rice pudding every Friday, will you let me see her one day? I'd give me arm and leg to catch a glimpse of her. I really would."

Still shocked that such a matter would be openly discussed in the public dining room, Caldy More did well to hold onto the back of the chair, as though she now were the one who needed the balance. At the last minute her innate sense of authority took over. She drew herself up to full height, which was considerable, and tried to wither the woman with a glance. "I haven't the faintest idea what you are talking about, Mrs. Bonebrake. I really haven't. Now, I thank you for the tea, and if you will excuse me, I'll—"

But the massive woman merely moved up to the end of the table with her, talking full-voiced every step of the way. "You don't have to pretend with me, dearie. I know. I really do." Then she was standing before Caldy More, blocking her path to the door, a strange glittering light in her eyes. "You see, I was living with a chap several years back, a fine upstanding man he was, a policeman—" Her eyes grew wide and she became secretive, as though she were coming to the heart of her story. "The very same bobby who escorted the young lady back here after her runaway to London. Of course a Scotland Yarder was with them, too, but me bobby did most of the work."

Caldy More felt slightly nauseated. She remembered the day.

The gross woman went on, undaunted. "It was me bobby who told me all about this place and Mr. Geoffrey Bledding himself and his insane little piece of an American wife. I tell you, it fascinated me. It really did. And when I saw that advert in the *Daily Mail* for a cook at Bledding Sorrow, I said to meself, 'Mavis, that's for you.' "

She straightened up as though everything had been explained, and now everything was all right. Again she leaned close. "You see, Caldy More, people interest me, all sorts of people, and it's kind of romantic, if you know what I mean." She hesitated a moment, then rushed on. "But never you mind. Like I said, I'll take the secret with me to me grave." She leaned still closer, anchoring Caldy More with one beefy hand. "Do you think I could get one tiny peek at her? Just one? I mean, where's the harm?"

Caldy More pulled away in disgust. "Good morning,

Mrs. Bonebrake," she said archly. "There's work to be done." But on her face was an expression of defeat, as though someone had just proved her wrong, that there was no accounting for the twists and whimsies of fate.

The happy triumphant look on Mr. Bonebrake's face followed her as far as the stairs which led up into the central corridor. Then, as though to add to Caldy More's obvious discomfort, Mrs. Bonebrake called after her, "I'm a good woman with a secret, Caldy More. No need to worry about me. When it comes to secrets, me eyes are blind and me tongue is cut out."

Caldy More dug into the steep incline of stairs, muttering, "Would that they were." She took the steps staring fixedly at the worn oak treads. Clearly this meant trouble. In all the years that Bledding Sorrow had been opened to the public, the staff, out of necessity, had been large and ever changing. She was certain that in the past there had been those who had known about Mrs. Bledding or at least suspected her invisible presence. But in all those years no one had mentioned her openly, in broad daylight, as it were. One and all had had the good sense and decency to ignore the young woman, never, certainly never making blatant and crass inquiry about her.

Now, for the first time, the subject was being bandied about as easily, as casually as though the young woman were a legitimate member of the family. It wouldn't do. It wouldn't do at all. Still, what was the solution? Mrs. Bonebrake was a despicable woman, but an adequate cook, and they were hard to come by. Mr. Bledding had searched high and low for one. He couldn't afford to let her go now, not at the beginning of the summer season. So where was the answer?

It was with this burden that Caldy More reached the top of the steps, slightly breathless from the climb and the cross she was bearing. Suddenly, from around the corner, she saw Gerry, one of the young local girls hired to come in once a week to help change linens in the upstairs dormitory rooms. The girl was carrying an enormous stack of clean towels, and her usual blank and empty face appeared to be twisted in the agony of indecision.

When she saw Caldy More, she rushed toward her. "Oh, Caldy More," she gasped, "thank God."

As she lurched forward, Caldy More was afraid the clean linens would topple to the floor. As she reached out to assist, the young girl explained, "It's the telephone, ma'am, the one in Mr. Bledding's office? Well, it was ringing its head off. Every time I'd pass the door there it would be ringing and ringing and—"

Caldy More was in no mood for the girl's wide-eyed exaggeration. "Leave it alone, Gerry," she scolded. "It's none of your concern." She was in the process of pushing on through the narrow corridor when once again the girl stopped her.

"Well, I couldn't just let it ring, Caldy More," she whined. "It might have been something important. One never knows."

Truly angry now, Caldy More released on the young girl all the fury which rightfully belonged to Mrs. Bone-brake. "You were hired to change bed linens, Gerry," she scolded. "You are never, under any circumstances, to go into Mr. Bledding's office, is that clear?"

Under the storm of wrath, the girl clouded up and appeared to be on the verge of tears. "Well, where I live, people answer the telephone," she whimpered.

Suspecting the worst, Caldy More asked, with a great show of patience, "And *did* you answer the phone, Gerry?"

Embarrassed, the girl nodded.

"And who was it, may I ask?"

Again the young blank eyes grew cloudy. "Who *is* it, you mean," she corrected. "Some gentleman," she went on, "quite urgent he is, wanting to speak to someone in authority." She gave a weak smile. "Well, like I told him, that certainly ain't me, so I told him to hang on and I'd go see if—"

Suddenly, at that very moment, there came from

the distant recesses of Bledding Sorrow a woman's scream, a prolonged, single-pitched siren of terror. It lasted only a moment, but in echo it seemed to reverberate endlessly about the narrow, gloomy passage.

The young girl gave a sharp gasp and stood staring at Caldy More, her wide-open gray eyes full of fear. "My gawd," she whispered, "what—was that?"

Caldy More herself was not faring so well. She felt as though everything were over and dead, killed in the agony of that one scream, leaving her alone among the living.

The girl continued to look at her, the terror in her eyes increasing. She hugged the stack of towels to her as though for protection against that which she could not see or understand. "Was—was it—the ghost, Caldy More?" she whispered.

Quickly the old woman snapped at her, "Nonsense!" Stirred finally to a semblance of reason, Caldy More cut her off, afraid that the foolish ghost story would be reborn and move like a forest fire through the largely young and ignorant staff. "Get on with your work now," she commanded, nodding her head toward the staircase which led to the dormitory rooms.

But the girl would not be put off. "What *was* it?" she begged, apparently refusing to move a step until she had a good, reasonable explanation.

Hurriedly Caldy More rummaged through her mind for ways in which she could put the girl at ease. "An animal, perhaps," she said lightly, "or wind. Yes, wind. Occasionally the faintest of winds coming around the bays can cause a whistling sound."

"That weren't no whistling," the girl said soberly, shaking her head.

Caldy More, annoyed by the waste of time when obviously she was needed elsewhere in the hall, dismissed the girl soundly and firmly. "No need to worry about it," she said crossly. "Now, move along and get your work done, or I'll give you the sack. You don't want that, do you?"

Reluctantly the girl began to do as she was told. But she looked back once, her eyes still wide. "That weren't no wind, Caldy More," she insisted again, "and you know it as well as me."

"Run along now," Caldy More ordered again.

Finally the girl obeyed. "Don't forget the gentleman on the telephone," she said, still whispering.

Caldy More nodded and held her position in the corridor until the girl had disappeared up the stairs. Then she moved rapidly toward the central hall and Mr. Bledding's office. All she could do was take things one at a time. Never before had she heard the young woman scream like that. Usually she was quite placid and peaceful in the mornings. Obviously someone had frightened her, and since Mr. Bledding was nowhere to be seen, she put two and two together and again cursed the fact that fate had dropped her down into this madhouse with apparently no avenue of escape. She was certain that others working throughout the hall had heard the scream. The staff would be buzzing with curiosity. And Mr. Bledding's generally well-kept little secret was on the verge of being revealed for all the world to see.

Caldy More moved rapidly down the hall. Either way Mr. Bledding wouldn't like it. The thought of his problems increasing brought a curious peace to her mind. She was well in control again as she entered the office and moved toward the phone, which was lying off the hook on the desk. Scooping up the receiver, she shouted into it as though she had to project her voice over the distance. "Hello. Who is there?" she called.

There was no reply.

"Hello, hello, is anybody there?"

At that moment a man's voice, deep and far away, filled her ear. "What in hell took you so long?" he demanded. "I've been hanging on here for half my life."

She lowered the receiver and looked at it, a hint of defiance in her eyes. But there was a certain expression of eager anxiety for further information in her face, and she lifted the receiver again to her ear. "Who is speaking, may I ask?" she demanded primly.

"I'd like to ask the same question," parroted the male voice at the other end of the line.

She hesitated for a moment, as though she were engaged in a battle to be won. Finally, "Caldy More," she answered forcibly.

There was a pause, then a faintly arrogant male voice replied, "I would like to speak to Mr. Geoffrey Bledding, please."

"Mr. Bledding is unable to come to the phone at this moment. May I help you?"

There was another pause, as though the man were thoroughly put out with this new information. "Mr. Bledding also seems unable to answer his correspondence," the man criticized. "What kind of place is he running up there?"

Caldy More became livid. God alone knew what was going on in the rest of the hall, and here she stood trying to converse with some inpudent bastard. In this frame of mind she concluded the conversation. "We are very busy here this morning," she snapped. "If you care to identify yourself and state your business, fine. Otherwise I am going to hang up now."

And the man's voice came back equally as angry and stern. "Well, you tell Mr. Geoffrey Bledding that this is James Pask speaking. Tell him further that I intend to arrive tomorrow and that if that bloody gatehouse arch isn't wide enough, I intend to bring my own crowbar and do the widening myself, do you hear? And tell him further that I—"

Then suddenly again there came from the recesses of the private wing the hideous sound of a woman's agony, different from the first time, when the tone had been clearly a scream. This sound was like nothing that Caldy More had ever heard, a slow, bewildering moan which did not stop short but seemed to roll endlessly from room to room, a monstrous sound darkly etched on the air and unceasing.

Caldy More's hand which held the phone began to shake. The sound had not come from the young wife. She was certain of that. Then what? Slowly, as in a trance, she placed the receiver back on the hook, cutting off the angry male voice on the other end of the line.

She stood thus for several seconds, locked in incomprehension. She was unable to do anything but stare down at the telephone, as though the hideous wail had originated in the instrument. At some point the sound had ceased, but she could still hear it in memory. She looked up once, so quickly that for a moment all objects in the tiny cramped office blurred and refused to come into focus.

Something was wrong. Then she started forward, moving rapidly through the Great Hall, breaking finally into a run as she approached the locked door which led to the private wing, certain that something dreadful was happening and that she, Caldy More, was needed to set it right again. . . .

6

Throughout all the trials and horrors of her long illness Ann Bledding had learned how to cope with almost everything. That is to say, she had learned how to cope so long as the specters appeared before her at the same time every day. Routine, the curse of normal people, is the greatest of blessings to the mentally disturbed. Within the safe confines of routine they know precisely when and where the greatest battles have to be fought, when and where their guard must be securely in place, and when and where it behooves them to become speechless, feelingless, and blind.

Safe within such a routine, and with the help of an increasing amount of daily sedatives, Ann was normally a quiet child, completely controllable.

In mornings she was accustomed to dealing with the flower people, the rose family, the honeysuckle man, even the stone-bench woman. It was true that on this morning she had had a new vision, the pitiful image of the injured woman who had begged Ann for help. But she had dealt with that simply by burrowing deeper into the lilac fortress and covering herself with dirt.

What she had not expected and what she was totally unprepared for was the sudden and terrifying appearance of the man. The man did not belong in her morning garden, had never appeared there before. The man was a nighttime horror. He was supposed to appear only in her upper bedchamber after Caldy More had given her a cup of hot tea and put her to bed. Then she was ready to face the man when her brain was sleepy and her eyes heavy and her limbs as relaxed and indifferent as though they belonged to someone else.

But when he appeared without warning in the morning garden, trampling over the ghost woman, causing her to cry out in even greater agony, and when he glanced down at Ann through the protection of her lilac fortress, the raw scratch clearly visible on the side of his jaw, and when he reached roughly down through the bushes and tried to drag her forcibly out onto the garden path, she had no choice but to scream. Even the stone-bench woman ran in fear back to the grassy incline and hid her face.

Horror-stricken, Ann screamed as the hand loosed one sharp blow against her head. And when the man moved on again, not another sound escaped her.

With her arms thrown over her head for protection she watched him as he walked angrily back to the kitchen door. Her scream had been natural. What was unnatural was her now quite distinct sense of regret. It was as if she had misbehaved, when she was quite sure she had done her best.

She continued to stare sideways at the kitchen door until he disappeared. Then she turned and looked back at the woman still lying in the path, as though in the hope that the specter might provide her with an answer.

But it did not. The madness was floating in the air. The ghost woman was wailing now, a slow bewildering moan which did not stop short, but seemed to roll endlessly, an unearthly sound etched on the wind. . . .

∽◦(7)◦∼

The exchange which took place inside the massive door of the private wing was brief, brittle, and to the point. The two had almost collided in their urgency, the one to escape and the other to see if and how she could be of help. They had known each other too long to mince words or otherwise clutter their innermost thoughts and feelings.

Geoffrey Bledding led off, standing safely in shadows with a direct accusation. "She was unattended."

Caddy More closed the door and countered with an accusation of her own. "Obviously you frightened her. She is not accustomed to seeing you in the morning."

"She is my wife."

"She is no one's wife, Mr. Bledding. You should know that better than anyone."

"Do you often leave her unattended?"

"When I have other duties, yes, and when I know she is calm and won't be disturbed."

"There has been talk—"

"I know. What's more, I know the source."

"Not yourself, I hope. I trust—"

"Of course not." She straightened herself as though to lend authority to what she was about to say. "Mrs. Bonebrake," she said, grimly. "In the kitchen."

He looked puzzled. "How would she know any—"

"She knew the policeman who brought Mrs. Bledding home. The second time. Of course, it happened years ago, but a woman like that has a good memory, if nothing else. Obviously she remembers."

He looked about at the floor, slowly shaking his head. "What do you suggest?"

"It's not my domain, Mr. Bledding, as you so frequently remind me. You must make the decision. It's your responsibility."

He glanced up at her now. "The drug will have to be increased. I'll phone Martin Axtell."

"And what about Mrs. Bonebrake?"

"You see to it that she stops talking."

Her anger flared. "Now, how in the name of God am I to do that? She is not my responsi—"

Suddenly he glared at her as though she had instantaneously pushed him beyond the point of control. "I must have help, Caldy More," he shouted. "I cannot handle this situation alone. Too much is expected of me as it is. I must have help."

Caldy More retreated before his rage. Repentant, almost martyred, with eyes down, she asked, "What do you want me to do?"

"You make it clear to her that what goes on in this part of Bledding Sorrow is none of her concern. You make it clear to her that at the risk of losing her employment she is to say nothing more about anything that is not of direct concern to her."

Caldy More shook her head. "She is a stubborn, gross, vulgar woman."

"And you must make it clear to her that in addition, she is to learn to be a silent woman."

Now she looked up at him. "Why was she screaming?"

He turned away from the direct and obviously painful question. Revulsion showed clearly in his face. "She resembled an animal," he muttered, "covering herself with dirt. In the bushes I found her. Like an animal." He shuddered and shielded his eyes as though to block the vision from his mind.

"She's a child, Mr. Bledding. Children enjoy playing in the dirt."

"She's a grown woman."

Their eyes met and held for a long moment. He straightened his head and swept a hand through the thinning blond hair. "Did you hear the scream?"

She nodded gravely. "I suspect that everybody, including the deaf and the dead, heard it. And the rest of it as well."

He looked quizzically at her. "What do you mean, the rest of it?"

Caldy More hesitated a moment, unable to describe the second sound she had heard. Finally she shook her head vaguely as though she didn't want to speak about it. "Well, she's quiet now. Where have you left her?"

Another look passed between them. "In the garden," he replied, still shaking his head, as though he were unable or unwilling to believe the horrors which had ensnared him. "Will you see to her?" he asked almost timidly.

"I always do, don't I?"

And with that it seemed for a moment that the conversation was closed. Deftly they exchanged positions, he moving closer to the door as though ready to leave and she taking his place in the shadows of the small corridor. As though in afterthought, she called out a warning to him. "I suspect there will be new talk about the ghosts now."

The subject was clearly distasteful to him. He looked over his shoulder at her, his brow creased in bewilderment. "For God's sake, why?"

"I was with one of the young maids, Gerry. She was terrified, seemed more than willing to attribute it to the ghost."

Again he looked defeated. "Oh, my God."

Caldy More seemed pleased now, satisfied that she in some small way had contributed to his anxiety. "Don't worry, Mr. Bledding," she called out cheerily. "It will run its course. It always has. Might be good for business. People love a good ghost story."

His hair was still ruffled by the passage of his hand through it. He looked as though he had been in wind. It gave him a kind of wildness which the fixity of his stare at her aggravated. He looked slightly crazed himself. "There are no ghosts in Bledding Sorrow," he warned. "The Trust does not approve of such foolishness, and you know it. It attracts the wrong people for the wrong reasons. You must put a stop to it as soon as possible."

Her eyes grew wide and slightly indignant at another such command. "*I* must put a stop to it," she repeated. "And how do I go about that?"

"By immediately dismissing the individual who speaks of such foolishness."

"Do I have that authority, Mr. Bledding?"

He hesitated a moment, then as though again roundly defeated, muttered, "Yes."

Pleased beyond words, Caldy More drew herself up to new heights. "Very well, Mr. Bledding. I'll do the best I can. In the meantime, you leave her to me." She began to feel in a better humor with the gift of new and awesome authority. She was two or three more steps down the narrow corridor when she stopped again and looked back, surprised to find him still standing before the closed door. "Oh, yes, one more thing," she said lightly. "You had a phone call, Mr. Bledding. I took it. If you ask me, you have made another serious mistake in hiring that man. He was angry and impudent beyond words, even dared to threaten—"

Again that fixed stare had descended on his face, as though he were listening but not hearing anything she was saying. Slowly he shook himself out of his lethargy and appeared to be trying to bring her into focus. "What—man?" he faltered. "What are you talking about?"

"The coachman," she explained patiently. "The one you hired. From Manchester, I believe. Due tomorrow, or so he said."

Still the news did not seem to penetrate the maze of his assorted worries. He continued to look about the corridor as though seeing nothing. Then, in a sudden burst of anger, he shouted, "Damn the man!"

With that he flung open the door and slammed it behind him, causing the corridor to reverberate even in his absence.

Caldy More waited a moment, her eyes focused sharply on the lock mechanism. No. He had forgotten to lock it. The man was growing careless. She stepped forward, a pleased expression on her face. Quickly she withdrew her own key from her pocket and turned the bolt.

A careless man was a dangerous man, and a dangerous man was a desperate one. So! She was sorely needed after all. What would he and the mad wife and, for that matter, all of Bledding Sorrow do without her? She smiled.

The question required no answer. . . .

⌬ 8 ⌬

Dr. Martin Axtell dug his heels into the steep incline which led up to Bledding Sorrow, cursing the treacherous ascent and the number of times he was forced to make it. Still, he was pleased. It meant another chance to see Geoffrey Bledding. True, the man called him only when he needed him. But Martin was smart enough to know that need was the foundation and bulwark of any relationship. And on that he would gamble and be patient.

He was a large, comfortable, slightly effeminate man, musty, with white hair, who intensely disliked suffering and sick people. He always looked as though he were playing the role of an English country squire. He had fled London and his failing medical practice there more than twenty years ago and had retreated to Yorkshire, where failure did not seem to sit so heavily on a man's head.

His had been a life with only one tragedy; the simultaneous death of his mother and father in an auto accident in the early thirties. Now, though approaching mid-sixty, but still vital and in excellent health, he passed his days solving minor medical problems; cuts, scraped elbows, farming accidents. The more complicated diagnosis he always sent to the large hospital in York. His favorite pastimes were eating and the sport of shooting small game in the remote corners of Geoffrey Bledding's estate, and in return he felt a kind of obligation to come running whenever the poor man called for help.

In truth, it was no obligation at all. He liked Geoffrey Bledding immensely. The man was trying to make the best of a bad situation, and there was no accounting for the curses that God rakishly visited on mankind.

Now, growing quite breathless from the incline, he slowed his pace and walked leisurely along the narrow road which led to Bledding Sorrow, enjoying the peace of dusk, the various and lovely odors of early English summer evenings, leaning heavily now and then on the ornate hand-carved Chinese walking stick, which he used, or so he claimed, only for balance. The woman could wait. She wasn't going anywhere, and it might be well for Geoffrey to understand fully how much he was dependent on Martin's medical sense and goodwill.

He walked with his eyes cast down, fearful of losing his footing in the road, telling himself that he had simply been born in the wrong time, possibly even the wrong place. Now that age was overtaking him, the rest of the world was enjoying freedom and personal liberties that had been sternly denied to him as a young man. How much he had sacrificed to avoid the absurd criticisms and judgments which generally had been leveled by the most narrow and antiquated minds. And how much, he, Martin Axtell, had had to suffer all his life.

Now he looked up for the first time, knowing that at this precise point on the road he would get his first uncluttered and incredibly lovely view of Bledding Sorrow, silhouetted at dusk against a crystalline blue-black backdrop, its sturdy but delicate Elizabethan outline of turrets and towers standing like a monument to a more graceful, more sensitive age.

He stopped, literally overcome by the sight. Oh, my God, how he would love to be the master of such a hall or perhaps even co-master in affectionate and conjugal bliss with Geoffrey Bledding. He smiled warmly at the thought. What revelries they would hold, inviting young men from as far away as London, shy, magnificent young men, who perhaps at first would murmur excuses, but ultimately would bow slightly and accompany them without a word on gloriously sensual adventures.

So intense was his vision that he had to reach out for

the pasture fence in order that his rapidly accelerating heart might subside. Thinking on such splendors left him feeling utterly empty. Clear images of male physiognomy appeared before him. He was afraid to envisage himself approaching them. Yet he did. And in the image of the act itself he could not breathe.

Panting quite heavily now as one who has not breathed for several moments, he pushed on up the road, as if by escaping from that particular section of pasture fence, he would also leave behind his visions which tortured him so.

Well, no matter. Geoffrey would cheer him up. And he, in turn, would bring Geoffrey a portion of good cheer by presenting to him the large bottle of white pills which he carried in his pocket, a common enough drug, Chlorpromazine, the same sedative he had always used on the madwoman; only in the beginning he had prescribed a mere ten milligrams three times a day. Now the pills he carried in his pocket contained fifteen hundred milligrams with the instruction to be administered "whenever needed." It was a dangerous dosage; he knew that as well. Whenever he remembered to do so, he always checked the woman for visual impairment and change in skin pigmentation. So far, nothing. And it was true that she was a constant source of mortification to Geoffrey Bledding. The man was a saint to endure her, and the least that he, Martin Axtell, could do was assist him with that endurance.

Now he squared his shoulders, smoothed down the shirtfront over his protruding belly, brushed his hand lightly over the fly of his trousers and the limp organ beneath, adjusting the worn tweed jacket, gestures of preparation for his meeting with Geoffrey Bledding.

The discouragement and despair which he had felt earlier in his walk was gone. A man learned to content himself with small pleasures. He would invite Geoffrey for dinner the following evening and would prepare for him the succulent pheasant he had bagged that very morning. They would have wine and eat the pheasant *au naturel,* gorging themselves on the tender pieces of fowl, then licking their fingers like children.

Totally absorbed in the vision, he looked with eyes of amazement through the gatehouse arch as though beyond lay paradise itself. Then abruptly there was another small depression as he glanced about the courtyard at the number of automobiles parked there in a hideous state of disorder. Who was it now? Oh, yes, he remembered. The Birmingham Art League. In fact he had heard them arriving that very afternoon while he had been talking to Geoffrey over the telephone. The poor man had scarcely been able to make himself heard for the chattering, giggling females in the background.

He shuddered at the thought and mourned the loss of his childish enthusiasm for the projected dinner party. It had been a sad day for Bledding Sorrow when the National Trust had inserted its greedy head into Geoffrey Bledding's life. Now the poor man was forced to endure not only the mad wife but hordes of crowding, screaming common men and women of every description. It was humiliating and incredibly degrading.

Martin's throat went dry. He wanted so desperately to take Geoffrey in his arms and comfort him with assurances that he, too, knew all too well the agonies of survival.

Now, as he glanced distastefully about at the clutter of automobiles, he took the final steps to the elegant front door, thinking again how different life would be if he and Geoffrey were co-masters, alone, of Bledding Sorrow.

He hunched his shoulders in an attempt to recover from the dazzling vision; his lower lip drooped a little. Then he lifted the ornately carved walking stick into the air and knocked it four times, with great authority, against the closed front door. . . .

ᴖᴖᴖ 9 ᴖᴖᴖ

Caldy More sat in a straight-backed chair outside the locked upper bedchamber, busying herself with a small basket of mending. Beneath her breath she cursed the dim light, cursed everything, for that matter, the fact that she had to mend the heavy brown work stockings, the fact that she had to sit like a jailor outside the locked door, the fact that the entire hall was alive with movement as the new students explored and probed into every corner of Bledding Sorrow.

Twice she had heard scuffling at the locked door two flights down. Twice she had heard them try to force the door open as though enraged that this wing, the family wing, was closed to them. And at least three or four times, down this same corridor in the opposite direction, she had heard them, footsteps drawing close.

Suddenly she sat up straight. There they were again. She held her breath and kept her eyes riveted on the grillwork barrier and the heavy dark blue velour drapes.

Then she heard one of them musing aloud. "What do you suppose is behind this, Bessie?"

And the reply, "I haven't the foggiest. Try it and see if it opens."

Caldy More sat like a statue, listening, watching.

The second female mourned, "Locked tight, it is. And look, even the drapes are nailed down."

"Curious. We must remember to ask Mr. Bledding."

"A charming man, really. Don't you think so? He'll tell us."

And the voices faded away. But Caldy More knew from experience that their appetites to know had been whetted and they would continue to make assaults on the family's privacy, and for this reason the young woman must be guarded and kept utterly quiet.

She knew further that there must not be another incident such as the scream earlier that morning. The young woman was becoming unpredictable. It had long been clear to Caldy More that the girl's silent meekness ran contrary to her nature and that she was therefore playing a part. Further, Caldy More had only recently decided that the silent Mrs. Bledding was laboring under a sense of injustice and very interesting to a shrewd observer, doing singularly little to conceal it.

Hence the reason for Dr. Axtell's late-night visit. The medication had to be increased until they could trust her again. It was either that or place her in an institution, which, out of respect for his family name, Geoffrey Bledding seemed unwilling to do.

So it was that, occupied by such thoughts, Caldy More thrust the needle back and forth through the heavy knit fabric, closing up the heel of her stocking. She looked up again, listening. The rest of humanity seemed very remote in the dimness of the corridor. The sounds of distant female laughter seemed only to heighten her loneliness. She was meant for better things than standing watch over a madwoman. And there was Mrs. Bonebrake, with whom she had yet to contend. And there was her new authority to dismiss anyone who was found guilty of reawakening the foolishness about ghosts.

She shook her head. There was so much for which she was responsible. Not that she couldn't handle it. But she didn't have to like it. Suddenly the needle froze midway through the knit stocking. Her head jerked upward, one ear cocked toward the faint noise coming from the locked door two flights down. Someone was coming. She stood up as though ready to do battle with the intruders.

A moment later she heard the familiar voices of Mr. Bledding and Martin Axtell. Well, at last. It took him long enough. As she heard their steps on the stairs, she hastily slipped the basket of mending beneath the chair and arranged her face, with knitted brows, into the face of a person not to be trifled with. She looked up as the two men stepped into the passage. Mr. Bledding was in the lead, advancing gravely, almost mysteriously. They looked as though they were performing a rite or walking in a procession. Martin Axtell looked a little unsteady on his feet, as though the climb had winded him.

Caldy More knew all too well about Martin Axtell. There wasn't a mother in Bledding Village who would dare send her young sons to Dr. Axtell. The women went on occasion and in emergencies, knowing they would be safe. But not the men.

Still, she couldn't be too harsh in her judgment of the old queen. He had certainly come to their aid often enough, although she suspected that his largesse was based on a simple desire to get close to Mr. Bledding or, more accurately, Mr. Bledding's bed. Off and on over the past ten years she had speculated on whether or not the two men had ever had intimate relations. It was true that Mr. Bledding spent at least one evening every week at Martin Axtell's large comfortable stone house in the village. But for the rest of it, she doubted it seriously. Mr. Bledding was many things, but he was not *that*.

Now as the two men drew near her, she felt a slight flush on her face, punishment, no doubt, for her thoughts. Mr. Bledding said nothing, but merely pointed out for Martin Axtell the grillwork barrier and heavy drapes, clearly indicating the presence of the students beyond, and perhaps even eavesdroppers, and therefore the need for silence.

Axtell nodded solemnly, clamping a hand over his mouth, though one little finger arched demurely outward. When they reached the door, they both stood as though for a moment's breathing space. Mr. Bledding nodded his head to Caldy More and gave vent to a little sigh through his nose, as much as to say, "We're here now. Unlock the door."

Caldy More took the key ring from her pocket, found the appropriate key, but hesitated a moment longer. In that instant she was suddenly and overwhelmingly aware of the enormous amount of trust which they both placed in Martin Axtell. The man was the only other human being besides themselves who had access to the private wing, who was ushered immediately and without question to the locked upper bedchamber. He knew all their secrets. Indeed he was a part of them, and perhaps that fact alone kept them all safe.

Then she saw Mr. Bledding again, more urgently nodding his head, commanding her to unlock the door and not waste any more time. She acknowledged Martin with a scant bob of her head, then bent low over the keyhole. A moment later she pushed open the door, and they all filed silently inside.

The upper bedchamber was in fact two small rooms joined at the center by a splendid Elizabethan arch. The first, or outer, room had initially been intended as a dressing chamber. Now it was merely an empty room with a moderately vaulted ceiling of cracked plaster through which rain from the roof had seeped and caused damage.

The second room was the bedchamber and it contained one single iron-frame bed, two nondescript chairs of questionable origin, a small bedside table, and a single closet, which was kept locked at all times, the key in the possession of Caldy More.

All three paused for a moment in the first room as though to prepare themselves for the ordeal. Caldy More carefully locked and bolted the door behind them. The two men exchanged curious glances. Martin Axtell half opened his pocket and lightly touched the bottle of pills with his fingertips as though he wanted to make certain he could withdraw them at a moment's notice. Mr. Bledding motioned him forward, indicating clearly that he was to lead the way. For a second Dr. Axtell sniffed about as though to scent out the best approach. Then slowly he stepped forward, clearly taking the lead.

"I'll go in alone," he suggested. "You two wait here. I know how to handle her."

Immediately Caldy More objected, "No, I—"

But Geoffrey, apparently relieved, interrupted with, "Let him be. He knows what he's doing."

Still not satisfied, Caldy More felt compelled to offer an explanation. "She's becoming more and more rebellious, Dr. Axtell. She can scarcely be trusted alone now at any given point of the day. With my other duties I am unable to stand constant guard over her." She glanced up at the dim bare bulb overhead, as though entreating God to understand. Then she looked back at Dr. Axtell. "Obviously she has built up an immunity to the present dosage. We don't like to ask this, but you must help us by making her peaceful again. She must not be allowed to interfere with the smooth running of Bledding Sorrow."

Thus she concluded her speech, pleased to see that obviously Mr. Bledding had approved of everything she had said. Having had her say, she stepped back from the archway, clearing a path for Dr. Axtell. She watched, slightly annoyed, as the large man straightened himself, adjusted his jacket and tie, as though such male vanities would make the least bit of difference to the wretched creature in the small upper chamber.

As Martin Axtell stepped into the sickroom, Mr. Bledding retreated to the outer door, as though longing to escape to a safer place. He grasped the doorknob, and for a moment Caldy More thought he was on the verge of leaving altogether. But obviously he changed his mind and now stood rigidly facing the closed door, his back turned on the activity that was taking place in the bedchamber.

In truth, for a few minutes Caldy More wasn't certain that anything at all was taking place. The room was utterly quiet. She considered peering through the archway, but decided against it. In all honesty, she, too, had little appetite for the sight and sound and torment of the young woman.

Then a few moments later she heard a soft moan, heard Martin Axtell mumble something. Both sounds were short-lived and quickly replaced again by a consummate silence.

As the waiting increased, so did the tension. Mr. Bledding began to pace in the far corner of the antechamber, a restless, anxious gait, his face down, his hands locked tightly behind him. Caldy More now stood at the door, still torn between wanting to see and not wanting to see anything, everything.

About ten minutes later Martin Axtell emerged, his normally ruddy face drained of all color. He began to wag his head back and forth.

He whispered hoarsely, "She should be in an institution."

Geoffrey Bledding's response was strong and immediate. "No!"

Martin tried to reason with him. "You can't continue to look after her yourself or even ask Caldy More here to do it. She needs constant care."

Geoffrey turned angrily on the man. "I said no. She will stay here, where she belongs. It's a waste of time to talk about it. You know as well as I that there is no money for a private sanatorium, and I will not place her in a public hospital." He looked sternly at the old doctor. "The matter is closed. Is that clear?"

Dr. Axtell shrugged as though he had no desire to make his friend angry. "As you say," he conceded. Then he handed the bottle of pills to Geoffrey. "At least be aware of the fact that you can give her no more than three of those in one day, or she will become totally immobile. The effect of one, for a while, should last for twenty-four hours. Not that she will sleep all that time. But on awakening, she should be pliable and calm."

And having so spoken, and as though there were no further reason for his presence in the disagreeable room, he strode purposefully toward the outer door and stood impatiently as though waiting for Caldy More to step forward and unlock it.

Without a backward look both men left the room, left Caldy More holding the door for them, left her watching them as they moved down the corridor, an expression of disgust clearly stamped on her face as she heard Martin Axtell describe the succulent young fowl in his freezer, seeing the large man's hand resting lightly around Mr. Bledding's waist, and seeing Mr. Bledding himself lean into the man's offer of comfort.

She held her position by the small upper chamber until she heard the door two flights down open, then close, then lock.

Then, silence. Suddenly she felt indescribably weary. The dimness of the tiny passage seemed alive. She felt as though eyes were watching her. The silence had become so great that she could hear her own pulse in her left temple; her head, with the slightest of movement, followed its rhythm, with regret, with dread, with resignation.

She looked slowly back toward the inner bedchamber. A sound of deep breathing began to rise in her ears. Nothing there now. Literally nothing there. Now.

Wearily she closed and locked the door and stood for a moment in the dim corridor. She felt dull and evil, malicious. Everything was going around in circles. For fear of fainting, although she was not a fainting woman, she hurried into her own room a short distance away.

She sat on the edge of her bed in her own room, her hands pressed so tightly against her face that tears came to her eyes. . . .

❦ 10 ❧

At nine o'clock in the morning on a cool Friday at the beginning of June the handsome purple-and-bronze coach was approaching Manchester at full speed.

It was still so foggy that it was almost impossible to distinguish anything twenty paces from the right or left of the coach windows. All of the passengers were old people, senior citizens from Manchester, returning from an exhausting twenty-four hours in Edinburgh, most of them poor and on pensions, and for whom the outing had been an annual holiday. All, of course, were tired and shivering; their eyes were glazed after the night's journey, their faces as pale and blank as the fog.

The driver of the coach was a man in his late thirties with straight black, rather long hair, turning gray at the temples, and intensely deep brown eyes. He had a slender, almost aquiline nose and high cheekbones. His lips were thin and parted under the duress of driving the coach, and his chin was adorned with a neatly clipped and very becoming Elizabethan beard. The high and well-shaped forehead enhanced the beard and the handsome gauntness of the lower part of his face.

What was particularly striking about him was the transparency of his complexion, a characteristic of many Englishmen, but so fine and rare on this particular face that in the areas of the temples the traceries of blood vessels were actually visible. This delicacy of complexion gave him a look of gentleness in spite of his tall frame and at the same time an almost painfully sensitive expression out of keeping with the occasionally coarse and insolent breed of men who drove coaches for a living. He was plainly dressed in a dark olive-green suit with the light touch of blue shirt and matching tie.

He had not felt the damp night at all under the labor of driving, while he knew that his shivering passengers would never get warm no matter how high he turned up the heater. His eyes continuously searched the rearview mirror, constantly checking on his ancient charges, longing for a way to make them more comfortable, to remove somehow the glazed, distant looks from their eyes.

Now he gripped the wheel and thought it was criminal the way the coaching firm took their money and then sent them on such an impossible journey. "Twenty-four Glorious Hours in Edinburgh." Glorious hours, my ass, he thought. Twenty-four hours in Edinburgh for anyone over sixty was like merely the first act of *Henry V* or a scant fifteen minutes with a lovely woman, wholly incomplete and totally unsatisfying.

Then again, as he cast his eyes over the rearview mirror, this was precisely the expression he found on the old faces. Wholly incomplete and totally unsatisfying.

And this was exactly the reason why he was no longer with the Burton-English Coaching Firm, why last year he had finally saved enough to purchase his own coach, and free-lance, as it were, among the hordes of tourists as well as local people who longed for new visions, new worlds.

Now softly into his thoughts he heard a voice behind him, an old woman with tightly bandaged ankles. "Jamie, it's chilly. More heat?"

He glanced over his shoulder, then sent his eyes immediately back to the road. "Sorry, luv," he replied. "It's up as high as it'll go." He thought a moment, then added, "I can give you music, though. The radio?"

The old woman shook her head. "It's not music you'll be getting at all. Just more bad news, prices rising so that I can't even afford a cod."

Her neighbor stirred and agreed with her. "Ain't that

the truth? Starving out most of the time is what we're doing. What's the end of it?"

Then a few moments later the old ladies had fallen easily into talk. And the coachman was pleased. Talk might warm them or at least help them forget about the thinness of their blood and rising prices. Now if only he could stir some life into the other forty-three passengers, who sat like corpses behind him.

Well, as far as he was concerned, this was the last run. Of course, he knew that the poor abandoned souls would continue to sign on for a variety of tours to a variety of places, always hoping they could find a new life or, rather, new impetus for life among strangers and always returning, looking more dead than when they had left. But at least he, Jamie Pask, would not have to take their money, then witness their despair.

Now he grasped the enormous wheel and maneuvered the coach expertly onto the circle which led to the main motorway, the last leg of the trip back to Manchester. There he would kiss the old folks good-bye, clean up his coach, then take off for his new job at Bledding Sorrow in Yorkshire.

As he angled carefully into the long line of oncoming autos, he felt again that curious twinge of anxiety which had plagued him from the beginning of his correspondence with Bledding Sorrow. True, the pay would be good. He would perhaps have greater freedom and leisure to read, to pursue his own studies, which ranged widely from the recent progress in British archaeology to the legends and ghost stories of England to romantic novels and the wildest of American Westerns.

According to Mr. Bledding's secretary, he would have to make no more than one trip a day, locally in the region to such places as Castle Howard, Harewood House, the various abbeys, and other Great Houses. And indeed this should give him at least half of every day free.

Still, there was a cloud hanging over the arrangement. He couldn't say what, was unable even to see the vague outlines of his anxiety. But it was there. Every time he thought about it he wished that instead of heading for Yorkshire, he had taken his bright new coach and gone straight into London, where at the beginning of the tourist season he would have had more tours than he could have handled, thus enabling him to slip away in October to Hastings and a long quiet winter holiday.

Now, as the traffic increased around him, he noticed in the rearview mirror that the passengers were beginning to stir, rousing their stiff bones in the narrow cubicles of seats, nodding self-consciously one to the other, readjusting bridges and wigs, pulling down corsets.

At times like this Jamie saw old age as a punishment. They all looked as though they were being punished, as though, as one neared the end, God raised a particularly stern head.

He found it within himself to dislike such a God, and, giving vent to the slight anger within him, he pulled out and around a slow-moving caravan. He took the turn much too fast and for his own punishment had to endure the honking of a large lorry loaded with potatoes and heading for Manchester.

He waved his apology. Normally he was a very good and careful driver. It was an enormous responsibility, the charge of forty-five lives, and he took that responsibility with utter seriousness.

Now someone at the back of the coach had started a song, a hymn, a low, toneless humming which he only faintly recognized as "Sweet Hour of Prayer." Softly other voices joined in the mournful dirge, contributing to his bleak mood and ever-increasing anxiety.

Well, if it made them happy and helped keep them warm, no harm. He had no right to impose his mood on others.

As he approached a fairly clear stretch of the motorway, he took one hand off the wheel and felt inside his coat pocket for the brochure and copy of his contract from Bledding Sorrow. It was all there, the signed agreement, the directions, although he knew the way, knew the area well, the description of the hall and the organization of the adult college in partnership with the National Trust. Unquestionably it was a good job, an opportunity he could never have taken advantage of if he had stayed with the coaching firm.

Then what was the problem? Perhaps his worry had something to do with the fact that Mr. Geoffrey Bledding had never personally answered any of his letters. And from the chaos and confusion of his phone call to Bledding Sorrow yesterday morning, he had good reason to doubt the efficiency of the organization. And again that single resounding question echoed through his mind. What had he gotten himself into?

There was no answer, only the roar and confusion of increasing traffic and the quiet hymn being sung at the back of the coach. He looked at his watch. No need to hurry. It was only half past nine. His coach would be on schedule, as his coach was always on schedule. In a way he dreaded saying good-bye to his passengers. It was peculiar how total strangers suddenly became family, perhaps to take the place of the one he didn't have.

He smiled softly at the broad expanse of windshield. One day he would marry if he could find a woman who did not demand everything of him. He was a man who needed privacy and solitude, twin gifts that most women were loath to give.

The hymn coming from the back of the coach was beginning to produce a melancholy. He eased the coach over into the slow lane and allowed his eyes to scan affectionately his beloved England. In his darkest and most bereft moments, while out of the habit of honesty having to admit that he wasn't much, he could always manage to lift his head a bit higher in the comforting realization that he was an Englishman.

His people had come from Northumbria, near the

Scottish border, a fiercely proud breed of men who had been trying for three hundred years to migrate southward to the warmth and economic promise of London. Jamie's mother and father had made it as far as Manchester, where consumption had taken his mother and alcohol had taken his father, leaving Jamie to be raised by a fierce-eyed Methodist grandmother who had taught him the simple, important lessons, frequently with the aid of a rod, to do the best you can, to do unto others, and to be satisfied with who you are. He had learned all the lessons well except for the last one. And a God-given gift or curse of intelligence had made that lesson impossible to comprehend.

And James Pask was intelligent. But his real intelligence belonged to a rare kind. It was not in the least analytical or problem-solving. Nor did it manifest itself in the form of any particular vivacity or wit. It was rather an uncanny ability to classify other people's worth; to understand them, in the fullest sense of that word. And to understand himself as well. Nothing was real for him until he had turned it into feeling. And this gift-curse frequently made him restless, made him seek broad and new horizons such as the venture last year of going into business for himself, to take the chance of a summer's employment at a remote Elizabethan hall buried in Yorkshire, working for a man he had never met, under conditions that were completely strange to him, moving out of his two-room flat at the edge of Manchester, packing all his earthly belongings into two suitcases, telling his landlady good-bye, visiting his grandmother's grave a final time, and heading straight into—

What?

Suddenly he felt his spirits dip menacingly, as though he were not going on to a mere job, but rather confronting in all its bewilderment a preordained destiny, as though his entire life had been constructed for this moment, a helpless sense of being unable to turn back, a realization of bridges burned, of circumstances closing in, of only one path remaining open to him and that path leading inexorably to the Yorkshire plains.

He stared fixedly a moment longer at the gray concrete rushing at him. Then he cursed softly under his breath, cursed the excess of his imagination.

Then, out of habit, he thought of the ancient monarch King Henry V, his beloved Henry. Well, what the hell. As Henry would have said, "Follow your spirit, and upon this charge cry 'God for Harry, England, and Saint George!'"

Abruptly, and for no reason that was discernible to the passengers on the coach, James Pask laughed aloud. He threw back his head and reached for the microphone and shouted into it, full-voiced, "Ladies and gentlemen, we are approaching Manchester. Let's look alert and tell them where we have been. All together now, in perfect chorus, gents leading, ladies following, 'You take the high road and I'll take the low. . . .'"

And as his voice, raised in song, filled the coach, the old people stirred themselves out of the lethargy produced by the hymn and their various pains. Their glazed eyes cleared and sparkled as they joined in the singing.

The handsome purple-and-bronze coach fairly exploded with glorious sounds of life as it hurtled down the motorway and into Manchester. . . .

❦ 11 ❧

Geoffrey Bledding had scheduled a late-afternoon staff meeting to be held in the small reception room off the Great Hall. On the agenda for the meeting was a discussion of all incoming groups for the summer semester, the imminent arrival of the new coach and coachman, the necessity for cutting down waste in the kitchen, and the National Trust's suggestion to raise the weekly tuition from twenty pounds to twenty-two pounds.

To be present at the meeting was the warden himself, Geoffrey Bledding, the deputy warden tutor, a bookish, horn-rimmed, prematurely wizened little man named Arthur Firth, a classmate of Geoffrey's from the University of York. Arthur Firth was a quasi-scholar who knew a little bit about a great many subjects and therefore was qualified to lecture the comparatively uneducated students of Bledding Sorrow on almost any subject ranging from genealogy to bookbinding.

Geoffrey liked him, not particularly for the job he did, but because he said nothing outside of his lectures, asked no questions, and kept to himself in small Feather Cottage at the edge of Bledding Village, where he lived in quiet seclusion with a black woman.

And Mr. Bledding's part-time secretary was to be there, a plain-looking young woman of local origin named Stella Trinder, who had taken shorthand and typing by correspondence and who was held a prisoner in Bledding Village by a ninety-two-year-old mother who refused to live or die.

And, of course, Caldy More would be there, bearing no official title but feeling the need to have a hand in the running of everything. Geoffrey sometimes wondered why he even permitted her to attend.

Generally her only contribution was to cause a squabble of some sort. He knew her to be deeply skeptical of the democratic process of general staff meetings. Caldy More's idea of good efficient government in any form was a firm hand and a firm voice, preferably her own.

Also to be present at the meeting was the domestic bursar, a fancy title which translated into cook and was represented by the gross but necessary personage of Mavis Bonebrake. Her assistant was to be there as well, a pleasant, grandmotherly woman from the village named Mrs. Prosser, a totally mute woman whose cancerous voice box had been removed surgically some years ago.

Now, as Geoffrey locked his office door, he thought that it was wrong of him to be so hard on Caldy More. For all her faults, she performed distasteful duties for him. In the remote regions of the private wing she went through hell for him. Like last evening. He shuddered, remembering, and moved quickly toward the tasteful and elegant surroundings of the reception room.

As he walked down the corridor, he looked to either side at the day's efforts of the Birmingham Art League, watercolors which had been propped against the wall for the purpose of display. Earlier that morning he had seen the ladies scattered throughout the pasture. Their common subject had been the gatehouse. Almost to the painting, the results of their efforts, he thought, smiling faintly to himself, resembled nothing so much as two giant red ice cream cones connected in the center by a wad of chewing gum through which someone had poked a hole.

Hideous, really hideous, and again he was overcome by the mediocrity of human effort. Well, no matter. He would revive his spirits later that evening in the company of Martin Axtell over a good dinner and good wine. He wondered briefly, as he always wondered before an evening with Martin, if this would be the night that the man made an open sexual move toward him. He hoped not. He greatly enjoyed the courtship air of their friendship. Then, too, homosexual liaisons did not interest him. Nor did commitments, literal or figurative. He'd learned his lesson with the American wife. Commitments too easily became nooses. And there was no room around his neck for more.

Still, he was fond of Martin Axtell and in a very real way indebted to him. The increased drug was working. According to Caldy More, the woman had slept until noon, then had been totally obedient and docile. Perhaps later tonight when he returned, refreshed, from Martin Axtell's, he would visit the upper bedchamber. He preferred her obedient and docile and had come to look forward to his late-night visits to her room.

Thinking on such matters, his step accelerated as he turned the corner into the Great Hall. Staring down on him in the dim light, he saw his sixteenth-century ancestor. For a moment their eyes met. For Geoffrey it was like looking into a mirror. Of course the clothes were different, his ancestor's hair slightly thicker, but for the most part it was the same face. The recognition gave him a surge of pleasure. An awareness of continuity of line was good, gave a man a sense of belonging, a right to be.

So engrossed was he in the painted face staring back at him that he failed at first to hear the subtle disturbance in the far corner of the room, no more than a rustling at first, a mere suggestion that perhaps he wasn't alone.

The room, an interior one, was naturally dark, so when he at last turned toward the faint disturbance, he saw nothing. Then slowly the rustling increased, accompanied now by most pitiful moans, a soul in great agony. Quickly he stepped away from the painting, now focusing all his attention on the increasing disturbance. Then without warning it evolved, horribly, quickly before his eyes, the image of the woman again, with blood-red skirts, dragging her body across the floor, her head alternately falling down between her shoulders as though in complete exhaustion, then lifting, displaying as though for Geoffrey's benefit the pain on her face, the drops of red where tears should be, her eyes glinting in rage from out of the shadows.

No hallucination this time, no reflection of sun on glass, merely the undeniable reality of the mutilated woman, dragging herself ever closer to where Geoffrey stood, paralyzed by his fear and torment, now unable to move, unable to speak, locked in position beneath the painting by the chill in his blood, the rapid beat of his heart.

Still closer she came, her agony increasing as she dragged the deadweight of her body after her, her eyes focused in clear hatred on Geoffrey. When she was less than five feet away, she raised a trembling hand and pointed directly at him, as though accusing him, a vengeful gesture, the blood on her hand freshly gleaming.

Slowly, in horror, Geoffrey began to shake his head back and forth, denying all. He whispered a tormented "Leave me be," then, unable to endure the hideous sight a moment longer, he ran from the room, took refuge behind the door, fearing that he was on the verge of losing consciousness.

A moment later, when he dared look back into the Great Hall, the specter was gone, although from where he stood he thought he could still see drops of fresh blood on the carpet, and on the wall above he saw his ancestor staring down on him, a benign, almost satisfied smile on his face.

A surge of impending doom overtook him. He was cursed, Bledding Sorrow was cursed. There was no way out. The specters were now appearing with greater regularity. The best he could hope for was to cling to his sanity as long as possible and to resist, as best he could, whatever forces were invading him, moving over him, occupying his very soul.

Still shaking, he considered prayer and dismissed it.

He was beyond help. God did not move in this realm any longer. Despairing and tormented, he realized that he was alone in a death battle with unknown forces.

Quickly now he averted his eyes from the sixteenth-century face and walked rigidly past the Elizabethan carvings of angels and knights and Twelve Apostles.

He paused a moment outside the reception room for the purpose of putting his thoughts in order.

He felt exhausted, felt the presence of threats and hazards behind every door, evolving out of every shadow. Inside his head he felt a dull pain. He closed his eyes, longing for a moment to take refuge in self-imposed blindness. But without warning, in memory, he saw her again, the mutilated woman pointing her finger at him, and quickly he opened his eyes, moaning softly, clinging to a near table for support until the trembling passed.

He felt haggard, worn out somehow, weary from trying to understand, and understanding nothing. And the worst of it was there was no one he could go to for assistance or even comfort. Whatever was happening to him, he must deal with it alone, always alone, the predominant condition of his life. Alone.

Suddenly he gave a tormented wrenching upward, lifted his head to the glorious plasterwork ceiling. But in his despairing state he saw nothing of glory, looked only with dread-filled eyes on every suspect shadow, every unidentifiable reflection of light. Then, affixing the ever-present smile on his face and smoothing back the blond thinning hair, he went in.

The reception room, once used as a small family sitting room, reflected the fashionable taste for the Oriental in the mid-eighteenth century. The walls were covered in lacquer panels which had been imported as conventional screens and adapted to this use. They showed scenes and festivals of Chinese life. The elegant chimneypiece was also of the eighteenth century, but was a comparatively recent addition to the room. The mahogany chairs and tables were in Chippendale's

Chinese style, and the early-nineteenth-century chandelier came from London.

It was a pleasant, though slightly garish room, used and enjoyed by both guests and staff for small meetings as well as a convenient place to wait before dinner.

Now, as Geoffrey Bledding entered the room, he saw all his staff gathered about the table, the tutor, Arthur Firth, hidden behind the morning *Times,* Mrs. Bonebrake chatting softly with the young secretary, Stella Trinder, and Mrs. Prosser, smiling at no one in particular, sitting alone at the end of the table. Caldy More was not yet present. He felt a sudden surge of anxiety. Her absence could mean any number of things, few of them good.

Everyone looked up and smiled at him, all except Arthur Firth, who remained buried behind his newspaper. Geoffrey took his seat at the head of the table, trying to avoid direct eye contact with anyone. He reached inside his coat pocket for the small note pad on which he had scribbled the agenda for the meeting. And while his eyes appeared to be searching for something near the top of the ceiling where the walls intersected, he apologized eagerly, almost obsequiously to his staff for calling them together.

"I know you all are very busy and I don't intend to keep you very long. I simply felt there were a few matters which ought to be gone over with you."

Out of the corner of his eye he saw Mrs. Bonebrake whisper something to Stella Trinder. He disliked the large woman, now more than ever, since he had learned that she had been discussing matters which were clearly none of her concern. Now he sought purposely to embarrass her. "Mrs. Bonebrake," he began, his tone imperious, "this is a staff meeting. Anything said here is for the benefit of the entire group."

Mrs. Bonebrake seemed petrified. Then gradually the fear left her face and was replaced by a kind of mock seriousness. "I was just exchanging a private word here with Stella, Mr. Bledding," she replied, her round brown eyes fixing him with an expression as severe as his own.

A frenzied smile strayed on his chalk-white face. He gazed mutely at the surface of the table, then repeated himself as though for the benefit of a slow-witted child. "I said that everything discussed here is for all to hear, Mrs. Bonebrake."

The woman tugged at a strap inside her dress and looked like a person who was trying very hard to get something straight. "You want to hear what I just said to Stella. Is that correct, Mr. Bledding?"

The mock innocence on her face clearly signaled who had the upper hand. And when, after a few seconds, Geoffrey Bledding refused to confirm or deny precisely what it was that he had meant, Mrs. Bonebrake drew a deep breath, lifted her chins, and said full-voiced, "Stella here and me was talking about female problems. You know, the monthly cycles? I just told her that the cramps seem to get better, the older one gets." She settled back into the chair now as though still utterly bewildered by his interest in such a subject.

The effect on the others gathered around the table of such a taboo subject was instantaneous. The newspaper behind which Arthur Firth was hiding jiggled as though the man were laughing. Stella herself, an overly large, almost masculine-appearing girl, looked mortified beyond words. She bowed her short-cropped brown hair and stared rigidly at her hands, which were clasped in her lap. Even Mrs. Prosser seemed unable to look anyone directly in the face. Instead she fell into a close study of one of the nearby ornate Chinese screens.

Now, with an extraordinary air of dignity, as though he were trying to compensate for his foolishness, Geoffrey Bledding quickly cleared his throat and reminded them that time was passing.

"It is, indeed," concurred Mrs. Bonebrake, who had an unmistakable air of victory on her face. "And I should be in the kitchen this very minute. My gawd, this new group," she went on uninvited, "you know, the artists, so called"—and she winked massively at Stella, who still sat with her head bowed as though at prayer—"well, they eat like they've been working in the hop fields instead of sitting around on their fannies dabbling with their little paint pots. Never seen such appetites in me life." She giggled suddenly and leaned close to Mrs. Prosser as though to share a joke. "If you ask me, they carry their main pots around with them." And she made a massive curved gesture over her stomach to indicate a huge belly.

Clearly Geoffrey Bledding had seen and heard enough. "That will do, Mrs. Bonebrake," he said with unsmiling sharpness. "They are our students, our guests, as it were, and I will not have you treat them with anything but complete respect. Is that clear?"

There was silence then. Apparently Mrs. Bonebrake resigned herself to the reprimand. Bledding watched her closely for a moment. He sensed that she was calculating, that she had gone out of her way to embarrass him and impede the progress of the meeting. How foolish of him. He had played right into her hands.

Now Arthur Firth meticulously folded the newspaper and addressed a direct question to the chair at the head of the table. "What exactly is the point of this meeting, Geoffrey? It's late and I must get home." The man was small of build, wiry, totally bald at mid-forty, a hard little knob of a man.

Geoffrey looked down at him and wondered briefly how he managed to keep the black woman happy. Now he stared at a spot just over his colleague's right ear. "The purpose of the meeting, Arthur, is to apprise you of the other groups which will be coming in during the summer so that you may prepare comprehensive lectures. Also to let the rest of the staff know the size and needs of those groups so that Bledding Sorrow can function as smoothly, as professionally as possible." Now he turned his attention to the note pad before him. "If any of you care to write the information down, feel free to do so."

No one did. Instead they all gazed rather blankly as he read from his note pad. "Now, from June twenty-first through June twenty-seventh we shall host the workshop on Facing Retirement. Arthur, I suggest that you concentrate on such points as finance, housing, health, diet, opportunities for voluntary and part-time work." He looked sternly toward Mrs. Bonebrake. "And since most of the students will be sixty-five years and over, I suggest you choose your menus accordingly."

"According to what?" queried Mrs. Bonebrake, still wide-eyed and innocent.

"To the dietary needs of a person over sixty-five," snapped Geoffrey, as though he could scarcely bear to look in the woman's general direction.

"Well, that's no bloody help," the woman responded. "I've known mates seventy-two years old who could eat a cow and others who—"

"Do the best you can, Mrs. Bonebrake."

"I always do, Mr. Bledding," she purred.

There was another moment's silence while the tension built. In the interim Geoffrey let his mind wander to the private wing and the absence of Caldy More. It wasn't like her. She always insisted on being in on everything. If anything interfered with his evening with Martin. . . .

"Do go on, Geoffrey," Arthur Firth was now saying. "It *is* late."

"Of course," Geoffrey conceded, forcing his attention back to the note pad in his hand. "Then from June twenty-eighth to July third we shall have a group entitled Discover Your Ancestors."

Mrs. Bonebrake snickered, "Who wants to?"

Geoffrey ignored her and went on. "They will bring their own lecturer, Arthur, the past chairman of the Society of Genealogists. But I would appreciate it if you would stand by and be willing to help. It *is* a large group."

Arthur nodded, his eyes closed. He looked as though

he could just barely wait to flee the room as well as his boredom.

"Then," Geoffrey went on, trying to ignore the look, "on July sixth the Transport Restoration Society arrives. They will be here through July thirteenth and will need the lecture room almost every night and of course will put to great use our new coach and coachman for the purposes of visiting the—"

"The new what?" piped up Mrs. Bonebrake, as though his words had just reached her ears.

Again, as though exercising the last measure of his patience, Geoffrey Bledding briefly explained. "We have acquired, through the generosity of the Friends of Bledding Sorrow, the services of a coach and coachman."

"Well, ain't that something!" exclaimed Mrs. Bonebrake. "Real class is what I'd call it. Wouldn't you, Stella? Real class."

Stella still had not recovered from her earlier mortification and continued to sit with her head down. Now, to make matters worse, Mrs. Bonebrake leaned close to her ear and whispered for the benefit of all, "Did you hear that, Stella? A coachman. Perhaps an eligible male. That would suit you well enough, wouldn't it?"

The shy girl actually groaned in her embarrassment, as though she were in pain.

For the first time Geoffrey Bledding came close to losing his temper completely. "That is enough, Mrs. Bonebrake," he commanded.

But Mrs. Bonebrake merely smiled. "Not for Stella, it ain't. She ain't never had none at all. I always believe in encouraging romance whenever possible, don't you, Mr. Bledding?"

Geoffrey could feel the heat of rage rising in his face. Again he suspected that the woman was purposefully baiting him. It occurred to him to dismiss her then and there and give the job to the blessedly silent Mrs. Prosser. But reason and good sense intervened. Mrs. Prosser could never handle the job alone. And if Bledding Sorrow Adult College was to survive, Bledding Sorrow needed a cook.

Wearily now he passed a hand over his forehead. Why was it that all avenues of his life started and ended with the primary question of survival?

No answers, merely the upturned and bored eyes of his staff. He realized belatedly why he missed Caldy More, why now he needed her. She could handle Mrs. Bonebrake.

Laboring now as though with great effort, he forced his attention back to the note pad. "Following the Transport people," he began in a dull voice, "we have the Poetry Society from York. Byron will be their central discussion, Arthur, so be prepared."

Now he moved rapidly down the list, giving no one a chance to reply or respond. "Then there is the Commonsense Psychology group, the meeting on Propaganda, the Tree and Natural Environment people, and near the end of August we will host the Manchester Herpetologists."

Finally he put down the pad. "The last group," he said quietly to Arthur Firth, "will require accommodations for two crates of adders, their central study for the week. I would suggest the crypt beneath the basement for safety's sake."

Mrs. Bonebrake gasped. "I won't have no bloody snakes next to me kitchen, you hear?"

"They won't be next to your kitchen, Mrs. Bonebrake," he snapped. "They will be no place near your kitchen." He made no attempt to mask his disgust for the woman, and while she was still muttering about her fear of snakes, he vowed to himself that within the week he would place several new adverts in the London papers. If anyone showed up who could boil water without scorching it, he would hire her on the spot.

"Then that's it?" Arthur Firth asked impatiently, half rising from his chair.

It wasn't, but Geoffrey was as weary of them as they obviously were of him. "I'll have Stella type up a com-

plete listing for all of you," he said. "I want no excuse
for lack of preparation. Is that clear?"

The little group, including Stella, who was gradually
recovering from her earlier embarrassment, nodded.
Then, as though to punish them for their lack of interest and attention, Geoffrey added, "We will have to
have another meeting tomorrow for the purposes of
completing the agenda."

A distinct groan passed up and down the table. They
looked sullen, but obedient. Bledding didn't give a damn
about their sullenness. It was their continued obedience
that was of primary importance.

Now he was as eager as they were to depart the
garish Chinese reception room. Martin Axtell would
be waiting for him, gin in hand, ready and willing to
commiserate, to sympathize, to comfort. And Geoffrey
Bledding needed understanding as much as anyone.
On that note of self-pity he stood up, pocketed the note
pad, clearly indicating that the meeting was over.

Suddenly, halfway out of the chair, he stopped, head
lifted. There was a tremendous commotion coming from
the courtyard. He looked now in that general direction,
confusion mounting in his face. "What in the—" There
was a deep roar and screeching as of air brakes, of
gears being ground, and the continuous wail of a horn
which sounded more like a broken siren spreading
alarm.

Apparently all the others, in the process of rising
from their chairs, heard it as well. They stared in bewilderment at one another. Even Mrs. Bonebrake
seemed puzzled, though not speechless. "My gawd,"
she murmured, "sounds like Judgment Day, it does."

Still the din rose, the continuous wail of one predominant horn, but joined now by a tinny, irregular
chorus of smaller ones.

Arthur Firth peered over the thick lenses of his
glasses, as though personally affronted by the ungodly
noise. "What in the hell is—" and then stopped, apparently realizing that communication was hopeless.

At that moment Caldy More appeared in the doorway. She looked as though she had been running, but since Geoffrey, in all their years together, had never seen her run, he couldn't be sure. There was a breathless rigidity about her face, as though the one aim of her existence was to keep her head while all about her others were losing theirs. "Mr. Bledding," she began, and paused to wait out a particularly discordant crescendo of horns. As she waited, she pressed one hand against her breast as though to still a rapidly accelerating heart.

At the first opportunity she tried again. "Mr. Bledding, I think you had—" But again her last words were totally obliterated in the screeching, bleeping, tooting, wailing, whining cacophony which was coming, or so it seemed, from the courtyard. Through the new din she stood rather forlornly, as though she might be held accountable for the obvious disintegration of what was normally a placid country setting.

Then Geoffrey Bledding was moving toward the door, his face looking suddenly scraggy under the duress of the noise as well as the mystery. The others followed after him, their bodies leaning slightly forward, as though their ears were leading them.

As he passed Caldy More, she tried again to say something to him, but he caught only fragments of words. "Outside" and "he" and "traffic."

Finally she, too, apparently gave up all hope of communication and fell in at the front of the little parade, sternly leading one and all down the corridor, past the gaping, puzzled faces of the Birmingham Art League, and out into the early dusk, where the sight that greeted them resembled Trafalgar at high noon.

Geoffrey Bledding stopped for a moment just outside the front door. There, beyond the cobblestone courtyard, wedged half in, half out of the narrow gatehouse arch, he saw an enormous purple-and-bronze coach. The protruding rear end of the coach, which obviously had been unable to squeeze through the arch, was now blocking traffic on both sides of the county road which ran steeply in front of Bledding Sorrow. At least thirty vehicles were lined up in both directions including bulky farm machinery, small lorries, private autos. Even another tourist coach had been hopelessly bottle-necked. Unlike most civilized Englishmen, all were using their horns, and a few drivers had stepped, outraged, from their blocked vehicles and were now trying uselessly to shout above the din.

The angle at which the diminishing sun struck the broad expanse of the coach's windshield prohibited Geoffrey from seeing clearly the face of the coachman who was causing such chaos.

Now, as Bledding walked forward a few yards, trying to see around the blaze of sun, he felt outraged. Surely all this might have been avoided. There was a high pasture directly above Bledding Sorrow with a broad open gate. Why couldn't the man simply have pulled in there? Why was it that some people considered it their duty to complicate life and make it even more miserable than it already was? It was a favorite device of the working classes to go out of their way to upset the carefully oiled machinery of civilized existence.

Thus armed with one tenet of his basic philosophy, Geoffrey approached the front of the coach and discovered, on closer examination, that he could not possibly squeeze between the wall of the gatehouse and the door of the coach. That passageway had now been reduced to only inches. He turned back and looked over his shoulder to see if any help would be forthcoming. He might have known. He noticed that the others, including Caldy More, were huddled together near the front door as though for protection against the continuing din, leaving him alone to deal with the coach, the coachman, and countless irate drivers.

Now he looked cautiously around, assured of his complete solitude in the matter, and then carefully stepped up to the front of the massive coach. At this close angle he saw, sitting quite relaxed behind the wheel, a tall, gauntly handsome man with dark hair and a trim Elizabethan beard. The man sat askance, one leg propped up against a small protrusion at the front of the coach, coatless, sleeves rolled up, and tie askew. One hand was resting on his hip while the other hand was pressing relentlessly, palm down, against the horn. He appeared, although Geoffrey couldn't be certain, to be smiling, as though he were accustomed to passing objective and therefore comic judgment from his high seat behind the wheel of his coach.

Standing this close to the actual source of the ungodly racket, Geoffrey could only raise his hand and sternly motion for the man to do the most obvious thing, to back out. There was a brief cessation of noise from the other horns, as though the drivers, seeing the arrival of the master of the hall on the chaotic scene, knew that the matter would soon be put to rights and that they would be on their way again.

But apparently the coachman had not understood precisely what it was that Geoffrey wanted him to do. He continued to sit behind the wheel, a calm expression on his face, as though he were actually enjoying the turmoil he had created.

Again Geoffrey raised his hand and waved it rather wildly through the air, clearly indicating that since obviously the coach could not come forward, it had no choice but to go backward.

Now, as though in answer to the second gesture, the coachman merely touched his hand to his forehead, as though he were cordially returning a greeting under the best of circumstances.

Through the large glass Geoffrey saw clearly what could be interpreted only as an insolent expression on the strong face. The man *was* enjoying the turmoil.

Again, and rather helplessly, Geoffrey glanced around. He understood all too clearly what was happening. The coachman was reprimanding him for the unanswered letters, the repeated queries about the width and height of the gatehouse arch. Now the gallery of faces lined up by the front door all stared back with suppressed exclamations, and he noticed numerous curious faces staring out of the third-floor dormitory rooms. The scene was becoming a carnival.

The hand of the coachman had never left the surface of the horn, and he continued to gaze down at Geoffrey with maddening calm. Several other drivers, blocked in the road, were now shouting instructions at him. All the horns had resumed their various angry tones. Suddenly Geoffrey had had enough. He shouted back at Caldy More, "Call the police!"

But Caldy More merely stared back at him, apparently unable to hear his command.

At that moment he saw, striding down the road, a burly man in gray sweat-streaked work clothes, a giant of a man, apparently the driver of the large transport lorry. He watched apprehensively as the man jumped the fence in one fluid leap which belied his size and marched angrily forward until he stood only inches away from Geoffrey. The man's fury seemed to border on madness. "What's the fucking matter?" he shouted.

Geoffrey stepped away from the man's odor, the brutish, primitive strength in his bull neck, freckle-covered face, and long stringy red hair. It seemed a stupid question. In all honesty, he felt no need to answer. Instead he simply gestured again to the coach, the narrow gatehouse, and the blocked traffic.

The large man surveyed the scene, his eyes darting impatiently from problem to problem. Then he stepped up to the front of the coach as though he intended single-handedly to push it back through the gatehouse and out onto the road.

But to Geoffrey's surprise, the honking suddenly ceased, the coachman shoved the gears into reverse, and slowly the coach lumbered backward. As soon as it had cleared the arch, the burly man ran out onto the road and skillfully directed the first four cars to pull out and into a holding position along the shoulder. The deep ravine on the opposite side of the road made the job treacherous, but the man was always there, urging each car forward, then sharply holding up his hand to stop it. This accomplished, the coach then was free to manipulate the narrow curve onto the main road. It was a moment of some suspense as all watched the giant back tires roll perilously close to the edge of the ravine. But the large man was always there, running to the back of the coach, then up to the front, constantly giving directions, coaxing, urging, waving his hand forward, then stabbing it suddenly in the air as the enormous tires rolled only inches from the edge of the cliff.

Finally, when it was in a relatively safe position, half on, half off the road, the red-haired giant took his place in the center of the blocked road and began skillfully waving the automobiles forward, again shoving his palm forward when he wanted one to stop, impatiently motioning them forward when he wanted them to advance.

In less than twenty minutes the area had been cleared, the noise subsided, and all that remained was a smell of dust, burning rubber, and petrol.

Geoffrey watched it all from the gatehouse arch. He felt helpless, womanlike, emasculated. The bastard had gone out of his way to embarrass him. Now he found he was unable to turn around and face the gallery of faces at the front door. A thin line of perspiration dotted his upper lip and he fixed his eyes on the two men standing alone now in the middle of the road.

The coachman had abandoned his coach and had joined the lorry driver. They stood in the road, apparently exchanging pleasantries, the red-haired man gesturing broadly as though re-creating the scene, the coachman throwing back his head and laughing heartily, the two men clearly understanding each other, obviously of the same temperament and class.

Instinctively Geoffrey withdrew into the shadow of the arch and watched them. The coachman was tall, with strong features. Geoffrey saw him glance now and then in his direction, his face full of pride and in-

subordination, stroking the affectation of the Elizabethan beard.

Both men knew that Geoffrey was standing there. He
was certain of it. Truly they were prime examples of
the most crassly arrogant and ignorant working class,
men who had scrambled for second-rate positions of
small and insignificant responsibility and who now
felt it incumbent on themselves to flaunt, exploit, be-
little, and ignore the very virtues, grace, and breeding
of the ascendant British Empire.

Thinking on all this and fairly shaking now with rage
and humiliation, Geoffrey tried to turn away to show
them his backside, the only view of which they were
worthy. This was what he should have done and he
knew it, but instead he continued to stand and watch
in some fascination the appalling cordiality taking place
in the center of the road.

Finally the large red-haired man slapped a broad
hand across the coachman's back and thrust the other
hand forward, inviting a warm handshake. And the
coachman responded with an eager thrust of his own
hand and shouted after him some invitation as the large
man strode down the road to his waiting lorry. A few
moments later, as the lorry rumbled past him, the
coachman stepped back and again the two men exchanged a warm and respectful salute one to the other.

Then there were only two left in the heavy evening
silence; the coachman standing alone in the middle of
the road, arms hanging at his side, a strand of loose
black hair curving down over his forehead, his eyes
fixed on Geoffrey Bledding, who still stood in the
shadow of the gatehouse arch.

For a moment there seemed to be an unspoken communication going on between the two men. Geoffrey
made out clearly the tall, lean figure and behind him
the purple-and-bronze coach perched precariously on
the side of the road. But it was difficult to see beyond
that since shadows were falling, the sun fading from
the sky. Geoffrey advanced a few feet and then stopped

with a sudden dread. Beyond the figure of the coachman he could make out something moving like fog; a black hole in the middle of fog.

Perhaps it was only his still-ragged nerves from the disordered scene of a few minutes earlier or a residue of dust still in the air from the rapidly departing vehicles. But he had a strong and incredibly powerful premonition that some ghastly sight lay beyond the coach. He did not know what. He didn't want to know. But he felt strongly the desire to be rid of the coachman, somehow to avoid contact with him altogether, to destroy the man's contract, give him two weeks pay, and send him on his way.

He saw him as a new source of disruption, and more, saw him now as an actual threat. The man meant to bring him down, as surely as the specters which of late had been tormenting him.

There was no air in his lungs, as though he had forgotten to breathe for several moments. With a sudden gasp he felt a wave of dizziness wash over him. His physical discomfort was very real, mirroring the subtle but steady mental disintegration. His eyes showed a peculiar brilliance as he glanced all about him and saw nothing but enemies.

And now, as the man approached, Geoffrey continued to feel obscurely debased. He had, with an acute unexpectedness, a clear glimpse of what the man's presence in Bledding Sorrow could mean. More intrusions, greater loss of privacy, an increased need for total vigilance.

The abstract idea of total seclusion was appealing, but its practice seemed as far removed and as fanciful as the shadows now being cast by the evening sun that framed the arch on whose threshold he and his new tormentor now paused a second.

In spite of the man's obvious arrogance and recent insubordination, he stood erect a few feet before Geoffrey, head back, smiling confidently. His voice was firm and filled with pride as he announced, "James Pask, sir. Coachman. At your service. . . ."

⌘ 12 ⌘

When Jamie at last found himself settled in the cramped room at the end of the third-floor dormitory corridor—the ceiling was so low near the eaves that he had to stoop to fill the bureau with his clothes—it was already past midnight; black beyond the slit of a window, still and crisp. He could see a faint mist in the distance along what appeared to be woods. Obviously his room was in the back of the hall. In truth, for one of the few times in his entire life he had lost all sense of direction. Following the woman named Caldy More through the labyrinth of rooms and corridors had left him hopelessly confused. Now he simply wanted space in which to move and fresh air.

He decided to walk and wondered only after the decision had been made whether or not the master of Bledding Sorrow had strong feelings one way or the other about nocturnal wanderings. He'd had the sense earlier in the basement dining room that Bledding Sorrow was operated and run by a velvet glove inside of which was a tightly clenched fist. The ladies, from Birmingham, he had learned, had fallen obediently into line at the serving counter, picking up tray, silverware, and foodstuffs, and at the end of the meal they had filed back up, depositing silverware in specially marked bins, scraping their plates themselves into an appointed receptacle, and at last filing out, as though the entire event had been a ritual rather than a meal.

Thinking again on the stifling regimentation, Jamie sat for a moment on the edge of the narrow and slightly concave bed. His eyes scanned its length. Obviously too short for his six-foot, two-inch frame.

Again he felt a slight depression of spirit. The scope

127

of the room would have been better suited for a midget. Sparsely and meanly furnished, it resembled a cell more than a room.

To make matters worse, the woman named Caldy More, a cold fish if he'd ever met one, had pointed out the loo, a good fifty feet down the corridor, an obstacle course which he would have to run through all the hazards of females whose rooms lined the corridor on either side.

Now he rested his head in his hands and smoothed back the long black hair. Well, it was simply a matter of making certain assessments. The cold fish, Caldy More, undoubtedly wielded great but unofficial power. And the man himself, Geoffrey Bledding? He'd met his type before, landed gentry, untitled, once sheep and land rich, now a closetful of skeletons and debit accounts and psychic wounds of inferiority festering for years, centuries perhaps.

And there were the other staff members, and he'd met them all, although now their faces and names blurred into a muddled gallery of rather ordinary folk who enjoyed the prestige of being employed by the local Great House. Some had eyed him with greater skepticism than others. Some had appeared highly amused by the coach incident in the courtyard, others outraged.

Perhaps he shouldn't have done it, make such a spectacle on his first day. But he had tried countless times to find out about the accommodations for his coach, and when he had seen the narrow gatehouse arch, he had felt an incredible desire to create a scene of havoc.

Softly he smiled, remembering how successful he had been. Then abruptly he looked up. Suddenly the cramped room seemed stifling. He had to move about, to stretch his legs after the confinement of the long drive to Bledding Sorrow. If he was seen and questioned about his midnight walk, he would simply say that he was checking on the security of his coach, a dubious security, as Geoffrey Bledding had finally given him instructions to park it in the high cow pasture about a quarter of a mile up the road. He disliked the thought of his handsome coach sitting in a field of cow dung. True, Bledding had said he would turn his mind to a more satisfactory location later, but Jamie doubted seriously if that moment would ever come.

Now he grabbed his jacket and left the confinement of the room for the semidarkness of the corridor outside. As he quietly closed the door behind him, he stood for a moment, assessing his location. A few yards on his right he saw a curious barrier of grillwork and heavy drapes. "The family wing," had been Caldy More's brief and rather curt explanation. Now he stared at it for a moment, wondering about the "family" on the other side, curious about the sort of woman who would join her life with Bledding's.

Well, it was none of his concern, and as he walked down the corridor in the opposite direction, he decided that he would be much better off this summer if he simply did his job, read his books, and kept to himself. There was a feel, a sense to the place that he couldn't understand, clearly an environment which was being exploited.

Now he felt it keenly as he turned down the broad oaken steps which led to the ground floor, a resentment coming, as it were, from the walls themselves, as though the hall were a living presence, angry at the use to which it was now being put. Such an assessment was not merely the whimsical wanderings of an overactive imagination. Jamie had felt it often in other Great Houses, a stillness, almost a brooding, as though the plasterwork, wood carvings, paintings, statuary resented their fall, deeply resented the prying common eyes of the public.

Then he was moving with greater speed down the corridor and through the Great Hall, vowing to himself that tomorrow in daylight he would explore the large rooms at greater length, perhaps even take advantage of one of the morning tours for a concise account of where he was and where he would be for the next three months.

Ahead by only a few yards he saw the front door. He approached it almost running, as though the sense and feel of the hall were about to overtake him. Out at last into the cool night air, he slowed his pace and tried to get control of his splintered feelings. He found a path which apparently led around to the back of the hall and took it, hoping to keep out of sight of any students returning late from the village. It was well that he did, for no sooner had he turned the corner than he heard footsteps crossing the cobblestone courtyard, heard women laughing and chattering, clearly warning him that others besides himself were still up and about.

He couldn't quite account for his antisocial behavior. Normally he was as open and friendly as the next person, but tonight, for some reason, he wanted solitude, more than wanted it, craved the comfort of privacy.

As he turned the corner at the rear of the hall, he found himself facing what appeared to be a splendid formal promenade, flanked on both sides by topiary trees. While he could not clearly see, his nose told him there were gardens, large gardens, nearby. He took the central path and went on his way with earnestness. If he checked on his coach at all, he would do it later.

A few steps down the promenade and he felt again a curious sensation. Some residue of fatigue now made him feel that the trees, the flowers, all the inanimate things around him were watching him. The night became solid eyes, the path had ears, the trunks of the trees were recording his movements. Perhaps he shouldn't be here. And yet why not? Surely the gardens were open to the public.

He came to where the path forked, two small avenues moving around an enormous stone-winged figure of some sort. Jamie stared up at it. Even in the faint light he could see the green corrosion which marred the beauty of the statue. He noticed the tip of one wing had been broken off. Still a little nervous, he walked on past the statue, rather like a man going through a jungle known for its vicious beasts. He expected to be pounced on.

He followed the promenade to its natural end, about seventy-five yards from the hall itself. There, in an arbor of low-hanging trees, he found a carved stone bench. He hesitated, then sat, withdrawing from his pocket cigarettes and matches. Only a moment. One cigarette to steady his nerves. Then he would check on his coach and return to his room.

The mist which he had seen from his window was still about, thicker here near the beginning of woods, not so much as to obscure all, but sufficient to give what he saw a dreamlike quality.

To be without the customary confidence of his personality was almost to be naked. He had not expected to feel so wholly disoriented. He inhaled deeply and let the smoke slip out slowly between his lips. He tried to relax, stretched out his legs, and told himself that he had a right to be here, that the uneasiness would pass.

He told himself all this, but continued to look around as though something were threatening him. His breath actually slowed as he looked rapidly over his shoulder into a black denseness of foliage.

Suddenly he sat up and ground out the cigarette beneath his shoe. His eyes made a quick survey of the back of Bledding Sorrow, dark for the most part except for the dim glow cast by the night lights and the brighter glows coming from a few of the third-floor dormitory rooms. He determined the location of his own room, there on the left at the point where the totally darkened family wing commenced. In spite of his attempts to keep his mind and eye busy, he continued to feel an unprecedented unrest.

Finally he rose, out of sorts with himself, tired beyond words. It had been a long day. What he needed was a lager and lime, a quick glass before he started the perilous journey back up to that cramped cell on the third floor. It was hopeless, though. The pub in the village was undoubtedly closed by now. He made a mental note to pick up several cans of ginger beer and keep them in his room. They would be better than nothing.

On that small note of self-comfort, he began to make his way back up the promenade, noticing for the first time other pieces of life-size statuary scattered throughout the gardens. He could see them only in outline, in various positions, men, apparently, with spades and hoes, and there a woman, peasant-looking figures.

At the moment of his turning away he thought he saw, out of the corner of his eye, faint movement. Quickly he swiveled his head back in the direction of the statues. His eyes struggled to bring the night into a clear perspective. He waited a moment, still searching. And several minutes later, during which he had not so much as moved a muscle, and convinced by now that his eyes had deceived him, he began once again to move slowly, cautiously up the promenade.

Then suddenly he saw it again, more clearly this time, a figure, no, two, standing like statues among the statuary. Quickly he fell back behind one of the large topiary trees, not moving. He listened carefully, trying to catch the sound of their voices.

But there was nothing to be heard except for the rush and pulse of his own blood and his own restrained breathing. Then carefully he looked out and around the topiary tree. He could still see them, two figures, one tall, bending protectively over the smaller figure— a man and a woman was his guess—strangely dressed, the woman in a long garment of some sort, a shawl over her head.

They appeared to be in close and intimate conversation. Jamie felt keenly the absurdity of his position, spying on them from behind the tree. Who they were was no great question; members of the staff, perhaps students, a couple from Bledding Village who had wandered up under the cover of night to enjoy the grounds and gardens of Bledding Sorrow.

Thus reassured by such commonsense conjecture, he considered stepping out into the path, greeting them quickly, then just as quickly bidding them good night and taking his leave.

But something prevented him from doing this, some new intensity which seemed to be passing back and forth between the couple. They were moving toward him now, walking in close unity, the woman, her shawled head bowed, as though she were distressed, perhaps weeping. They were less than ten feet away now, their specific features still lost in the mists and dark night.

He held his ground for the simple reason that he didn't know what else to do. Surely the slightest movement on his part would draw their attention to him. He didn't particularly relish his role of eavesdropper and spy. For this reason alone it was too late to reveal himself, either to advance or to pull back, so he had no choice but to wait and hope they would not discover him.

Now the woman *was* weeping. He saw it clearly, saw her bow her head into her hands and cover her face, the shawl, in the process, falling back and catching on her shoulders.

Quickly the man stepped forward and took her in his arms. She seemed to press against him. She lifted her face and they kissed tenderly. She seemed to wish to be kissed and the man drew her yet closer as though he wished to pull her into him.

Jamie found himself most suddenly embarrassed. He found it only slightly unusual that thus far no words had been spoken at all. But on the other hand, perhaps it wasn't so unusual. Their obvious and deeply felt mutual desire apparently canceled the need for words.

In the press of the embrace, he saw the shawl fall from her shoulders and onto the path. Unnoticed by either the man or the woman, he saw the man's hand flatten, caress, move in a circle over her back, saw her arch upward toward his touch, their lips still pressed tightly together, the rest of their bodies now straining for similar union. He could watch no longer. He felt vulgar, more than embarrassed, felt as though he were actually trespassing on an intensely private human moment, of which he longed to be a part, but knew he had no rightful place.

And at the very moment when he was considering withdrawing in spite of the consequences, he saw the man bend over and gently scoop the woman up in his arms, her curious long garments caught in the press of their bodies. She lay back as though she had fainted, her head rolling softly against his chest. Then he carried her off into the night, down the promenade, toward the carved bench on which Jamie had recently sat.

He continued to stand behind the tree fortress as if paralyzed. His own loneliness, the deep alien feelings swept over him. The pair had touched him deeply, the urgency of their need for each other, the woman's unexplained sadness.

He glanced a second time into the darkness at the far end of the promenade. All was silence there now. Briefly he wondered again about the identity of the pair. No matter. Whoever they were, they were most fortunate.

Then he chose for his exit the avenue that led down the back of the topiary trees. He still remembered as he hurried through the darkness, their passion, their mutual need, the closeness of their embrace. And all these thoughts, coupled with his earlier feelings of lostness and disorientation, now blended into an indistinguishable loneliness. As he walked rapidly toward the back of Bledding Sorrow, he thought, *I belong nowhere, to no one.* The thought was an old friend, almost a constant companion, but coming as it did now, under these circumstances, it seemed something hard and pitiless against which anything human would inevitably be broken.

The back of the hall now loomed large before him. Still glancing now and then at the cavity at the end of the promenade, he increased his step until he was trotting, as though he wanted to outrun the feelings which were relentlessly pursuing him.

In spite of his haste, he noticed that the path which led to the gardens completely encircled the hall. Instead of returning in the direction in which he had come, he decided to take the left path. Obviously the distances were the same, and he was suddenly tired of night, of hiding, of bearing silent witness to the raptures of others.

Now, as he kept close to the red brick hall, he saw through the half windows of the basement dining room the tables below, saw a half dozen ladies sipping tea and chatting late, apparently enjoying their week's freedom from domestic chores.

So absorbed was he in staring down into the basement that he reached the end of the hall and turned the corner and almost collided with a solid expanse of red brick wall. He stepped back a moment, trying to assess the curious barrier. It jutted out from the private wing for a distance of about sixty feet and appeared impenetrable. Using his own height as a yardstick, he estimated the height of the wall to be about eight feet tall. By stretching he could almost touch the top. Apparently it was a walled rectangle, perhaps a private garden.

At any rate, it was a damned nuisance now, forming a complete barrier to his passage, forcing him back in the direction in which he had come. Well, there was nothing to do but retrace his steps the length of the hall and return on the other side.

The half-light spilling out from the basement windows made the path look as if it were lined with gravestones. He walked rapidly now, his thoughts moving ahead to a hot shower. He had had his walk, enough fresh air, and a bonus besides. The world would look better in sunlight. It always did, all mysteries solved, all doubts laid to rest.

He never lifted his eyes off the ground as he walked except once, as he passed the central path which led beyond the winged figure and to the carved stone bench. He stared blankly into the night, then slowly closed his eyes. There was probably nothing more moving in a man's life than the accidental discovery of the depths of his own loneliness.

Now his steps struck the ground as though he were trying to jar himself out of his depression. Nothing to do but surrender to sleep and hope for its absence on awakening.

But as he approached the front of the hall, he heard footsteps on the cobblestones of the courtyard. Quickly he drew back. A moment later he saw the hunched figure of a man and instantly recognized Geoffrey Bledding. He was walking, head down, apparently lost in thought, moving rapidly, as though he were late, toward the front door.

Jamie watched him as long as he could, then fell back as he heard the massive door swing open and shut. He leaned against the side of the hall, wanting to give the man plenty of time to disappear. Of all the people in the world whom he did not want to meet this night, Geoffrey Bledding headed the list. So he held his position in shadows and waited perhaps fifteen minutes, feeling certain that by now the man had had time to clear the corridor.

Then Jamie emerged into the courtyard, still keeping close to the hall. Quietly he pulled open the front door and just as quietly closed it. The warmth felt good after the cool night air. He looked down the long hall as though it were a minefield through which he had to pass. At the far end he saw a faint spill of light coming from Bledding's office. Damn! The man was still about.

Then suddenly, at that moment, the office light was switched off. Quickly Jamie fell back into a small alcove and watched as the man emerged from the office. He appeared to be carrying a black case of some sort, which he shoved under his arm as he closed and locked the office door. He paused a moment, seemed to glance furtively in Jamie's direction, then walked rapidly the length of the corridor in the opposite direction, heading toward the private wing.

When Jamie was fairly certain that the passage was clear, he darted out and around the alcove, moving toward the staircase. There was something uncomfortable about the silence around him, the same discomfort he had felt in the garden, the feeling that in spite of the emptiness, he was not alone, that someone was watching him, following his every move. This inexplicable feeling resulted in a strange excitement that ironed out every shade of reason and made every shadow, every sound equally significant and aggressive.

He took the stairs two at a time, his disgust at his own foolishness reaching enormous proportions. He was becoming as silly as a schoolboy. At this rate he wouldn't last the summer. He would have to get himself in check.

As he reached the third-floor landing, he searched in both directions for additional obstacles. The corridor was blessedly empty. He walked the length of the hall and turned the corner and saw the door to his own room, like a safe harbor. He felt like a man fleeing from a calamity, felt a bit mad, as though in the last hour he had suffered a permanent loss of his reason.

It was from the depths of this disintegration that he heard or thought he heard voices. Quickly he lifted his head, his hand frozen en route to grasp the doorknob. Real or imaginary? He listened more closely. There! He heard them again, hushed, muted voices coming from somewhere beyond the iron grillwork barrier.

After the sensations of the evening the voices did not particularly surprise him. He walked toward the iron barrier as though he had expected to hear them, in fact was meant to hear them.

One voice belonged to a woman, an old woman, her tone crackling with age and what sounded like anger, certainly protest. Jamie leaned closer to the barrier, heard clearly the words, "Not tonight, not again, I beg you."

He shut his eyes and heard a man, this voice rigid as though someone had challenged its authority. He couldn't make out the actual words, heard only a low angry hum, rising, then falling into some mysterious protection, as though the man knew that someone might be listening.

The woman protested again, a plea this time, then ceasing, as though crushed. A few seconds later Jamie heard a door open, then close, more than close, slam shut as though someone in anger had turned his back on the muted discussion.

Then all was silent. He heard or thought he heard another door, farther down, open and close. But he couldn't be certain, and obviously the argument was over, won by one party or the other, the matter closed.

Still leaning against the grillwork barrier, his ears straining for more, Jamie felt suddenly heavy and rancorous, as if he had been or was being wronged in some way.

And when, a few moments later, he heard, coming from the far recesses beyond the grillwork barrier, a cry that hung in the air like death itself, he felt himself become a motionless object, his forehead pressed against the ironwork barrier.

There were no further cries, only now and then a soft moaning which might have been the wind. Before returning to his room, he tried to hear again in memory the frail mournful sound he had heard but once. It was as if he were trying to engrave its features in his memory so as to be able to recognize it if he should hear it again.

He kept saying to himself, *Something is wrong, I*

must do something. I must act. And a kind of anger at his own weakness swept over him, a determination to make some gesture that would show he was more than a pawn to his own feelings.

But it took all the will and discipline at his command to walk the few feet back to his room, to close the door and lock it, to lean against it, and shut his ears to the soft moans which might have been the wind of a windless night. . . .

❦ 13 ❧

She had no one.

Friends from home had written to her for a while, but then all letters had ceased. Now her garden friends had disappeared as well. The white kitchen cat and even the rose people, who had come to her aid in times of difficulty, had not put in an appearance for several days.

The dull fluttering, like a trapped insect in her head, came early in the morning now and persisted throughout the afternoon and into the evening. Voices tapped on her ear, like wool on wool. On one or two occasions she had been unable to determine whether she was sitting up or lying down. Her muscles felt uniformly heavy and without sensation.

In spite of all this, now and then her mind still worked, and that was perhaps the greatest tragedy. She preferred the long intervals of nothing, of simply being vaguely aware of Caldy More guiding her arms into the gray smock dress, the faint pressure against her head which signaled that her hair was being brushed, the firm arm around her shoulders, the faint scent of lavender and body odor which meant that Caldy More was taking her someplace. And as long as her mind accepted all this without struggle or question, she was placid.

The long intervals of sleep helped, and it seemed as though now she was sleepy all the time. Some mornings she would awaken, open her eyes to the plain drab walls of the upper bedchamber, find nothing there of substance that interested her, and thereupon would immediately close her eyes and fall back into sleep. And on those days she would not even bother to dress. When she opened her eyes again, it would be dark outside the window, and Caldy More would be bending over her, scolding her, as her mother used to scold her, then propping her up in the narrow bed and coaxing her to eat at least part of the soup and half a biscuit. Ann could never tell which was which. They tasted the same. And there were always the white pills and the cup of hot tea which Caldy More insisted that she drain to the bottom.

She knew she was ill and perhaps getting worse, and only now and then did the nature of her illness puzzle her. But she had begun to sense a new tenderness in Caldy More, the kind of pity that healthy people feel for sick ones, and it was on the basis of that new kindness that Ann knew she was sick and getting worse.

So while the new moments of immobility increased, there were other moments, hideous moments, when unexpectedly a light would flash before her eyes, when without warning the fog would lift, when she would open her eyes and they would stay open, when she would remember clearly names, faces, events, sensations as though she were just experiencing them. Then her mind was sharp and alert and would send frantic signals to the rest of her body.

Tonight her mind was awake, had stayed awake all through the feeding process. Her taste buds reacted violently to the bitter pills, causing her to spit them out, forcing Caldy More to get angry with her as she inserted two additional pills down her throat, holding her head at that sharp angle, forcing her to swallow.

And even as Caldy More helped her up the stairs to the bedchamber, her body fell fast asleep, so deeply asleep that Ann stumbled twice and Caldy More had to carry her the last few feet. And yet throughout all this the mind, the damnable mind, stayed awake, still alert, screaming things at her, the most insane suggestions, that she should try to escape, that she should refuse to be obedient and docile, that shortly there would be a point of convergence between her sleeping body and what was left of her active mind, and that when that happened, she would be forced into a totally imprisoned life, no more trips to the garden, only the unbearable punishment of nonsound, nonsight, nonfeeling.

All the way up the steps the mind screamed these unspeakable threats at her while her body slumped weakly against Caldy More. And in defense against the battle which was raging inside her, Ann tried to moisten her lips in order to speak and ask for help. But her lips tasted dry and dusty and the tongue simply rolled to one side of her mouth, as though in alliance with her useless body, and she did well simply to draw breath while her head hung limply from her shoulders, her eyes taking dull note of the familiar, highly polished wooden planks beneath her feet.

Terrified, though with no avenue of escape for her terror, wishing only that her mind would put itself out of its misery, she wept silently all the way up the stairs, her mouth working uselessly against the screams of the mind, trying to convey something, anything to Caldy More, and failing.

Inside the room Caldy More placed her on the bed, saw the fresh tears, and quietly knelt before her. The old woman looked at her for a moment with such a twisted expression that Ann was certain the woman herself was not feeling well.

Then quickly she hurled herself into the preparation for bed, as though not wanting to look at Ann anymore. She undressed her and went to the closet. On the bed, shivering in her nakedness, Ann caught a glimpse of the docile sleeping body. No wonder it did not obey the mind. It was not her body, but rather that of a starving child. This thought caused new terror, the suspicion that she had lost her body someplace, that someone had stolen it from her and replaced it with a skeleton scarcely covered with flesh.

But still the mind screamed at her, told her this *was* her body or what was left of it, that when she shortly died, the worms would be cheated, for there was no flesh for them to eat.

Then Caldy More came back, slipped the nightdress over her head, and covered the body that did not belong to her and guided her back and down onto the pillow. Again the dried lips begged Caldy More to give her something to put the mind to sleep. But still the tongue refused to work and she saw Caldy More's face hovering over her, looking down on her through narrowed eyes, the lenses of her spectacles as thick as magnifying glasses.

A few moments later Caldy More moved away; the open mouth formed one ring of the circumference while the rest of the face started a slow, stately revolution around the room, finally disappearing altogether from Ann's view, leaving her motionless on the bed, legs extended, arms heavy at her sides, securely anchored by a light coverlet which felt as though it were pressing her into the coiled mattress springs.

Then suddenly, without warning, the mind grew quiet. No sound, nothing. She lay on the bed, gasping for breath, her head making faint motions on the pillow as though she were suffering from a high fever. Still she waited, listening. The mind could not always be trusted. Sometimes it fell silent simply to renew its energy for a greater assault.

But now there was only calm around her, a suspicious calm, as though elsewhere something were going on, like the eye of a hurricane, as though all sources of energy had been drawn in a different direction. It was a sensation so glorious that Ann dreaded its departure. But for now she was almost happy, almost expectant, as though something were forming in the room, a promise of some sort, a message of hope which most certainly needed deciphering, but which still had brightly invaded the dark atmosphere of the room.

Suddenly the spot of the far arch on which Ann had chosen to rest her vision blurred. The architecture changed, became liquid, the red brick tones became more vivid. In the center of the arch there suddenly appeared an explosion of colors out of which in rapid sequence came images of chalets, cloisters, bastions, pavilions, carriages, four handsome white stallions, dungeon gates, iron hoops, golden panes of window glass, variegated mosaics, a thousand images rapidly passing and fading one into the other, none lingering long enough for a clear and concise view, but all evolving quickly before her eyes.

Then, without warning, close to each other, emerging from between the images, she saw clearly the figure of a man and a woman. Ann watched, amazed, as the couple stepped out of the twirling images and stood only a few feet from where she lay on the bed.

They took no note of her, but she took careful note of them. The woman was small and fair and dressed in a long gown of some sort; a lace shawl rested lightly on her shoulders. The man was tall and gauntly handsome in a black jacket, his face lean and adorned with a trim Elizabethan beard. They looked deeply into each other's eyes as though seeing all of the universe or all of the universe that they cared to see.

Then, with no words spoken, as though to postpone their desire for another moment would be more than either of them could bear, the man reached out and drew the woman close to him, so close that for a moment Ann thought they had blended into one. Their mouths met, and after the kiss he covered her cheeks, her eyes with kisses, his hand caressing her hair, and finally he buried his face in her neck.

Ann closed her eyes and could feel the passion as clearly as though it had been directed at her. And when she opened her eyes, they were gone. The arch was just an arch again, the explosion of colors and images no longer visible against the curved expanse of dull red brick. But still she felt her heart trembling. Her lips pressed open in a soft smile. She discovered that by closing her eyes again, she could still see the couple in her mind's eye, could feel acutely the depth of their love.

She did not question the vision. While she did not know its source or the reason that it had appeared to her on this particular evening, both questions seemed insignificant.

Softly she turned her head on the pillow. How glorious it had been. And if it wasn't for her in this lifetime, perhaps the next. She could wait, would be willing to wait as long as the promise was there.

She shifted a little to relieve the pressure of her numb body. Sleep was coming and it would be sweet this night, for if the mind started screaming at her again, she would simply blot it out with the warm cherished memory of the vision, of the man and woman in close embrace, their priceless, healing love.

It was with her eyes closed, still enraptured with the vision, that she heard another movement in the room. Her head tried to lift from the pillow, sensing a threat. In desperate haste, she ordered her hands upward in feeble protection. But she was too late. She saw the man standing at the foot of the bed, no vision this time, but the man himself, his bland pale face clearly discernible in the dim light.

Already the lovely memory was beginning to fade as though a new dusk were falling. She didn't want to lose it so soon, but obviously it had not been strong enough to direct her eyes away from the man standing over her now. Perhaps if she tried again, shut her eyes this time, remembered clearly the sequence of events, the dazzling rainbow of colors and images out of which the couple had evolved.

But still it was not enough. At the same moment she closed her eyes she felt a cool rush of air as though someone had just removed the coverlet from her bed. Her hands tried to grasp for it, but they merely flailed at the air. Through partially closed eyes she still saw him standing at the foot of the bed, looking down on her as though she were refuse to be discarded.

As two hands moved over her breasts, there was nothing she could do about it. The mind told her to keep silent in order to endure. Even as she felt the nightdress being lifted, pushed back until it covered her face, the mind continued to warn her against outcries, told her it was best to keep silent.

Through a screen of muslin she saw the man, blurred now, saw him step closer to the foot of the bed, heard the rapid increase in his breathing, felt only the slightest pressure as his hands manipulated her legs. She shuddered. She would forever live in the upper bedchamber, be dressed and cared for and guided about as though she were a child, and at night forever endure the visitations from the man.

She listened and waited with a feeling of childlike shame for what was about to happen. The veil of muslin obscured her face; her head pressed rigidly back against the pillow as though in defiance of her humiliation.

The rate of his breathing was still increasing. In the last interim of nonfeeling she saw herself standing by a window. It was raining. A familiar, soft and loving voice was asking her if this was really what she wanted and did she know that she would be far away from family and friends, that she would be entering a life and a world totally different from her own. And she, still standing at the window, had answered, "Yes."

Suddenly she screamed, merely a reflex against the thrusting assault on her body. The invasion had been launched. There were no further screams, for a hand reached up and forcibly stuffed the muslin into her mouth. Her breath caught in her throat. She heard her own muffled moans. Her legs on the bed were no longer subject to her will. They felt heavy and useless.

Periodically the man's hand covered her face as though he wished to stop the moans. Once she heard clearly the ticking of his watch. The pressure increased until she felt as though she were being cut in half. From close beside her ear, where his hand held her forehead rigid, came the sound of ticking blending with distant, but familiar voices.

He's a remarkable gentleman. I think she'll be quite happy, don't you?

Something was burning inside her. She felt as though she were on fire.

Your father is so pleased, Ann. In fact, he couldn't be more pleased. You have made him so happy.

She felt her dead legs being adjusted again. A sharp pain began in her lower left side and climbed to above her rib cage.

You must promise to write and describe in detail all the beauty that you will find there. Mistress of Bledding Sorrow! How romantic!

Now strong hands were pressing against her pelvis, lifting it, her monstrous, deformed limbs defying gravity.

You are the luckiest girl in the world, Ann. Everyone on campus is so jealous.

Her breath, insucking against the horror, dragged the muslin into the cavity of her throat. She felt as though she were suffocating.

You're a lovely bride, and he's such a handsome groom. Remember to be a good wife.

Her body's suffering was intense now, her spine twisted and bent in a futile effort to avoid the repeated thrusts.

We'll all come and visit you, Ann, and revel in your newfound glory.

Then she was no longer capable of enduring the prolonged assault. The muslin slipped deeper down her throat. His hand pressed relentlessly against her abdomen. Additional pain spread throughout the cavity of the womb. The man's shapeless figure now bent over her, scolding her as though she weren't cooperating. A fist delivered a dull blow to the side of her head. In the moment before she lost consciousness she heard a chorus of distant voices: *We envy you, Ann. We envy you. Farewell....*

ᴄᴏ❨ 14 ❩ᴏᴈ

In view of her vast personal experience—she had had her first sexual encounter at the age of ten—Mavis Bonebrake considered herself to be a prime authority on the subject of men.

Now, as she stood behind the serving counter in the basement dining room, she looked out over the gray bobbing heads of the Birmingham Art League to the far table where James Pask sat alone, stirring cream into his tea.

Incredibly she felt her heart miss a beat. She smiled. The realization that she was still capable of being aroused was a good one. Not bad, not half bad for a fat old woman her age.

She smiled again, musing, all the while deftly lifting soft eggs onto pieces of fried toast. My gawd, the old biddies were hungry this morning. They kept coming back to the serving counter, their pinched and wrinkled faces revealing the sad consequences of their pious lives.

"Pious, hell," she snorted under her breath, but still loud enough for Gerry, the young serving girl working next to her, to hear.

"Did you say something, Mrs. Bonebrake?" she asked, her pencil-thin eyebrows arching high in question.

"Not a thing," came the reply, at least until the old lady of the moment had picked up a plate of eggs and toast and moved on.

Then, relishing a moment of minor wickedness, Mavis leaned close to Gerry. "What do they look like to you?" she asked sweetly.

"Who?"

Mavis Bonebrake opened her eyes wide and spoke in tones of mock grandeur. "The Birmingham Art League, that's who."

Gerry giggled. She was empty-headed and harmless and altogether tolerable, a perfect blank slate against which Mavis could bounce her little volleys of blue humor. Now, concerning the matter of resemblance and the Birmingham Art League, she looked gloriously, gratifyingly confused.

Mavis was only too happy to fill the vacuum for her. "Prunes," she whispered. "Look at them! They all look like they came out of the same box of prunes."

Again Gerry giggled and blushed and kept her eyes down as another gray-headed prune passed by the serving counter.

Suddenly, and with just a hint of mischief and clearly within earshot of the passing old lady, Mavis said, full-voiced, a single word. "Fornication!"

Just one word. But the old lady and several of those around her froze, as though in that instant their muscles had mysteriously solidified.

"I beg your pardon," the old lady said rather sternly to the two women behind the serving counter.

Again Mavis smiled sweetly. "I was having a little conversation with my young friend here. That's all. Cheerio!" And with a slight wave of her hand she motioned for the line to keep moving. The ladies continued to gather up their eggs and toast, all the while keeping a wary eye on the area behind the counter in general and on Mavis Bonebrake in particular.

In the meantime, Gerry, blush red, fled the area. A moment later Mavis heard her back in the kitchen, giggling openly, sharing the prank with the kitchen help.

Satisfied that she had made a point, Mavis served alone, studying the pinched old women with a sense of increasing horror. How they had cheated themselves! In Mavis' opinion sex was downright necessary, indeed, medicinal. Look at her. She had never had a serious illness in her entire life. She was fit and hale, perhaps a little overfed, but men liked that, liked to be able to get their hands on something. She had always had a man or men in her life, someone to keep her bed warm, to lift her spirits as well as her skirts after a hard day's work.

That was the trouble with Bledding Sorrow. Thus far she had been unable to find a man, and she needed a man as fish need water, as birds need air, in order, quite simply, to function and survive.

Again she looked quickly across the crowded dining room toward James Pask. He sat in the farthest chair, his tall lanky frame hunched over his cup of tea, still stirring as though he had hypnotized himself. He looked tired, she thought, looked totally removed from the clattering, chattering atmosphere of the dining room.

He *was* a good-looking bastard, she decided again, narrowing her eyes shrewdly in the manner of a connoisseur. A sense of gentleness, of vulnerability in a large man always struck her as an extremely attractive combination. And there was something about his gaunt and sensitive face, the trim Elizabethan beard, the deep brown eyes, and fine skin that most definitely appealed.

At last the old ladies appeared to be filling up. The serving counter was empty. Most of them now sat sipping coffee or tea, dunking hard crusts of toast into their cups to soften them out of consideration for their bridgework and false teeth.

Mavis Bonebrake glanced toward the kitchen. The girls there were still giggling. The counter should be cleared, but there was time. For now, she thought, she would fix herself a cup of tea and take it to the far table where the man sat, looking quite tired and alone. Perhaps she could cheer him up, and again as she quickly assessed his dark good looks, she was absolutely certain that he could cheer her up.

As she poured herself a cup of tea, she tried to imagine him naked. And succeeded! The vision literally caused her hand to shake, scattering dark granules of sugar about the counter. Dear gawd in heaven, what an image! Broad shoulders, a fine mat of black hair on his chest, tapering hips, well hung, a masculine machine designed for the gratification and pleasure of females.

Her tea prepared, she stepped back out of sight behind the small expanse of wall which separated the serving counter from the door which led out into the dining room. Hell, she didn't look like much; grease-splattered from sausage, slightly sweaty from the heat of the kitchen, her hair matted and pulled back in a bun, no makeup, not a sign of makeup. She turned toward the wall and lifted an arm. She wasn't even absolutely certain how she smelled. Then she was. The strong scent of body odor, coupled with a downward glance over her protruding stomach and bulbous breasts, caused a slight sinking in her spirits. She was outclassed, clearly outclassed. Once, thirty years ago, she might have been attractive to him. But since the Italian had taught her how to cook, she had had to satisfy herself with males as misshapen as herself.

Well, what the hell. It wouldn't hurt to be nice to him. He looked as though he could do with a spot of kindness. After all, they were prisoners here together, at least for the duration of the summer. She would have to turn her sexual pursuits elsewhere, perhaps the local publican, a mountain of a man with one eye missing, who last week had looked with obvious appreciation on her protruding and generous breasts.

You can't please them all, she decided, with a visible lift in her spirits. Thus resigned, she gathered up her teacup and waddled almost majestically out into the dining room, bobbing her head on either side to the old ladies, pausing once to accept graciously a compliment regarding her cooking, stopping at last at the far table opposite the coachman, where she saw him, still sitting, with his head in his hands now, as though he were asleep or brooding.

"Penny," she said brightly, placing the tea on the

table and easing her ample bulk into the chair opposite him.

He looked sharply up as though under attack. His eyes had been closed and now she saw them struggle for a moment in an attempt to bring her into focus. "I—beg your pardon," he said rather vaguely, as though it had been a long journey back from where he had been to where he sat.

She shrugged and smiled. "Penny for your thoughts," she repeated, "although if you're like me, I wouldn't sell some of my thoughts for all the tea in China."

For the first time he smiled. My gawd, did he smile! A most pleasant crinkling spread out on either side of his mustache, revealing even white teeth, the light spreading as far as his eyes, where from those brown depths she saw microscopic lights shining. The warmth covered his entire face, a genuine response as though he were grateful to her for pulling him back from some hostile territory.

"Mavis Bonebrake," she said, wiping her hand down the side of her white uniform, then extending it across the table. "I owe you two apologies," she went on. "I didn't stop and greet you yesterday after your arrival, which I thought was splendid, and apparently," she added, surveying the lone teacup before him, "I did not cook anything for breakfast that pleased you."

He hesitated only a moment, then reached slowly out and returned her handshake. His hand was large and strong. She felt calluses on his palm, but his grip was excellent, clearly the touch of a true man.

"James Pask," he said, smiling, returning the introduction, although it was unnecessary. She knew who he was. Apparently he chose to let slide her mention of the traffic jam and concentrated on the subject of breakfast. "I'm not much of a morning eater," he explained, "although I do like a bowl of porridge now and then."

She responded immediately. "Then I shall fix it for you in the morning," she said firmly.

"Oh, don't go to any trouble."

"No trouble," she said, closing the subject. "I have a bowl myself every morning," she lied. "It will be just as easy to fix two as one."

He appeared to accept her offer begrudgingly, as though he didn't want to cause anyone extra work. Yes, she liked him, she liked him immensely and longed to ask pertinent questions regarding his marital state, but restrained herself for a few moments, at least until a civil interval of time had passed.

Now instead she settled on a subject which she was certain was very close to his heart. "That's just about the most handsome coach I've ever seen in my life," she said, emphasizing the key words, instantly pleased with the reaction on his face. She might be old and flabby, but she hadn't lost her touch. She could still put a man at ease.

He leaned back in the chair for the first time since he had been in the dining room. "It's not quite paid for," he said, "but it took me five years of hard work to get possession of it. And it *is* a good coach, quite comfortable, I can promise you that."

She murmured that she didn't need his promise, but would willingly accept his word, and added further that she hoped before the summer was over, she would get a chance to ride in it.

He assured her that she would and for a moment the talk died and they were held suspended by the silence, drinking their tea, glancing now and then at the ladies who were beginning to leave the dining room.

"Are you taking a tour out today?" Mavis asked.

He shook his head. "I believe Mr. Bledding told me the first trip is Sunday. Fountains Abbey." He bobbed his head toward the departing art league. "They want to paint it."

She saw or thought she saw a twinkle in his eye. She murmured beneath her breath, "God help Fountains," and was instantly gratified by the light of humor in his face. They might never be bedmates, but there wasn't a reason in the world why they couldn't become good friends.

She settled back into her chair, taking her teacup with her, basking slightly in the knowledge that she had found such an attractive new friend. "Are you all moved in and settled?" she asked. "Where did they put you?"

He appeared for a moment to go tensely polite. "The third floor," he replied, not looking at her. "It's a small room, but I think it will be adequate."

"The third floor?" she repeated. "You're up with the old ladies. Which end?"

Obviously he had to stop and think for a moment. "West end, I believe. Near a grillwork barrier of some sort."

"My gawd," she exclaimed, sitting up in mock horror. "You're right outside the family wing. Strictly off limits, you know. Be careful you don't bump into the ghosts up there."

Slowly he looked at her, piercing her now with an intense stare. She was amazed at how quickly his expression could change, one moment relaxed and smiling, the next taut. "Ghosts?" he repeated.

He seemed interested and she decided to capitalize on that interest. She leaned close over the table and kept her voice low, some latent dramatic instinct telling her that ghost stories were best whispered. "Oh, several hundred years ago, it was, about 1600, I believe—" She was delighted by the interest which continued to wash across his face. "The lord of the manor, another Geoffrey Bledding, caught his lady in bed with a servant."

She paused for dramatic effect. "'Tis said," she went on after the proper moments had elapsed, "that a person can still hear her up there on cold windy nights, crying out in agony, pleading for mercy, praying to God Himself."

She watched his face closely, felt clearly the intensity of his concentration. He looked so seriously back at her, his handsome features appearing fixed, as though frozen. Almost apologetically he murmured, "I —did hear—something."

Suddenly she laughed aloud, then quickly looked about as though to check the rapidly emptying dining room. In the moment, she weighed the wisdom of telling him about the mad wife. Obviously he didn't know, hadn't heard. Now she leaned even farther across the table, lifting one hand to her mouth as though to catch and contain the words as she spoke them. "No doubt you did hear something." She smiled. "But I don't think it was the ghost."

Fed by his interest, she went on. "You'll know it soon enough anyway, so you might as well hear it from me. The present Mr. Geoffrey Bledding," she began, relishing the story, "has an American wife. Quite mad, she is, mad as the March Hare actually. I've heard he keeps her under lock and key so she won't disturb the students. She ran away once several years ago, clear to London she made it A friend of mine, a policeman, helped bring her back to Bledding Sorrow." Her voice lifted on a note of pride. She was pleased to give him such firsthand information.

But within the moment, she saw clearly that her pleasure did not extend to James Pask. He looked stricken, as though, first, he did not believe her, and second, if he did believe her, he found the information intolerable.

She saw a tiny light in his eye, something singularly like a flash of defiance. "It's true," she insisted. "Every word of it gospel." She renewed her efforts to convince him of the validity of her story. "A few days ago," she went on, her hand still cupped around her mouth, "before you arrived, we all heard screaming that would wake the dead. Oh, it didn't last long, but it clearly weren't no ghost." She sat back, planting her folded hands before her on the table with a heavy stroke. "It was the mad wife, that's who it was." She shook her head and shuddered slightly, hearing the sound over again in her head. "It was a cry that would wake the dead," she repeated meditatively. She drew herself up. "Once you've heard something like that, you're not likely to forget it."

She saw James Pask eye her, as if calculating her words. He still seemed unable or unwilling to believe. "What I heard—" he began, then faltered, then finally stopped altogether. He seemed in a way not to want to talk about it. Now she saw him glance about the dining room as though looking for a tactful way out.

Never one to hold a man beyond his desire to be held, Mavis stood up rather abruptly, stared down on him a moment while a group of ladies passed by close enough to hear. As soon as it was safe to speak, she bent over for a brief departing lecture. "The present Mr. Bledding"—and she curled her lip around the name, overpronouncing each syllable—"does not like us to mention either the mad wife or the ghosts. Everyone who works here gets along just fine if they go conveniently blind, deaf, and a little dumb. So whether you choose to believe it or not, mum's the word."

She began backing away from the table and the intensity of his eyes. She smiled down on him. "You're such a nice addition to the staff, I'd hate to see you get sacked. So whatever it was you heard up there last night, just pretend you never heard a thing."

He didn't nod, apparently refusing in any way to acknowledge her final warning. She was greatly impressed by his look of almost total exhaustion, as though he were too tired to argue or pursue the discussion any further.

She reached over now and scooped up both their teacups, her eyes falling on his hand which rested on the table curled into a tight fist.

"And relax," she whispered kindly. "You'll do fine, just fine. And if you ever get lonely, I've got a whole kitchen out there of twittering, giggling, overripe, and unplucked females. Take your pick, you hear?"

Incredibly she saw him blush slightly and lower his head, although a faint smile played about his lips.

Leave them laughing, she thought, *that's the best way.* She took in again his pensive, downturned face, the clean, broad slope of his forehead, his fine narrow nose, the soft dark hair nestling at his temples and the nape of his neck. *My gawd,* she prayed silently, *if only I were one of the giggling, unplucked kitchen females.*

Now he looked directly at her. "Thank you," he said quietly.

"For what?" she asked, surprised.

"For talking to me, for taking the time."

She laughed and shrugged. "We'll share a bowl of porridge in the morning, agreed?"

"Agreed."

She winked at him in parting and turned toward the kitchen. Well, it wasn't as good as sharing his bed, but at least it was a start. She had a fine new face now which she could remember on those cold winter nights when her beery, misshapen mates mounted her and made love. She would simply close her eyes and fill the void with the fine, darkly handsome features of James Pask. Oh, Lord a mighty, how she cursed age and ugliness. Here she was, an inflated old hag with fine visions of naked limbs intertwined, of lustful appetites that would make a sixteen-year-old blush. No justice, less mercy.

Inside the serving area she stole a backward look at the man still sitting alone at the far table. There was something about him that worried her, a gloomy foreboding, a cross that had to be borne, a vulnerability, a man, she suspected, destined for sudden falls that could bring disaster.

Abruptly a loud uproar of laughter drew her attention toward the kitchen. She sighed heavily and began stacking the soiled dishes before her. When the cat's away, the mice will. . . .

"Gerry!" she shouted, full-voiced and stern. "And all the rest of you. Get your fancy asses in here and tend to this mess." She scolded the girls one at a time as they came through the kitchen door and expertly dispatched them to the various tasks that needed doing.

As the flurry of activity increased around her, she looked out once again for a final look at the handsome coachman.

But he was gone. By leaning quickly out and over the serving counter, she caught a fleeting glimpse of him as he disappeared up the steps.

She stood a moment longer, brooding on both his presence and now his sudden absence. He was a queer one, really. She'd have to keep her eye on him, watch out for him, look over him, as it were.

Having now poured a second cup of tea for herself, she reached beneath the counter and pulled out a covered plate. On it rested an enormous cold meat pie.

Then she began to eat, and without any grace whatsoever. . . .

❦ 15 ❧

Jamie took the stairs two at a time, eager to be out of the stuffy dining room, though having no definite destination.

The woman had been kind enough, and he was grateful to her for that. Regarding her story of the mad wife, well, he would take that with a grain of salt. Still, in a way he had longed to share with her his curious experiences of the night before. And perhaps one day he would. But not now.

As he reached the landing of the central corridor, he saw in both directions a milling mass of human obstacles. The Birmingham Art League, all forty-five strong, were gathering up their canvases from the night before, rearranging their paints, every movement, no matter how insignificant, requiring endless commentary one to the other.

At the end of the corridor, near the front door, he saw a small group of tourists waiting patiently under the guardianship of their guide for the corridor to clear. It occurred to him that he might join them. He remembered thinking last night that he wanted to know more about Bledding Sorrow, its history, treasures, uniqueness. Now that he was Bledding Sorrow's official coachman, he considered it his duty to know as much as possible about the hall. In the past he always enjoyed delivering impromptu lectures to the passengers on his coach; it pleased him, knowing that he had somehow added a new dimension to their excursion.

Still, he could not quite bring himself to join the group. Clearly the restless night had taken a toll. He felt the dull beginnings of a headache. There would be time later for guided tours. For now he simply wanted the luxury of freedom to explore the hall on his own perhaps, to check on his coach, to shore up in the brightness of morning the undermining that had occurred the night before.

So he held his position out of the flow of traffic for a moment, content merely to watch the pageant of humanity, extremely pleased that he had nothing to do with it, owed it no responsibility.

At that moment, looking up, he noticed a young girl making her way slowly, apologetically through the stooping, bending women. She appeared very prim, old beyond her years with her light brown hair cut short, almost masculine, colorless lips, and quite large silver-rimmed glasses. She bobbed her head politely to everyone and seemed to be making her way toward the small alcove where he stood.

As she drew near, he noticed that her face was quite flushed, as though she felt a kind of embarrassment at simply being alive. She walked directly past him, then stopped abruptly and turned back.

She stood about five feet away, her eyes behind the glasses making one single contact with his face, then appearing to take permanent refuge in the vague area around his shoes. "Are—are you Mr. Pask?" she asked, her voice scarcely audible.

He said that he was and wished he could do something to put her at ease.

Then she looked at him again, a swift sideways and upward glance. "I'm Stella Trinder," she whispered, as though she wished he would keep the news a secret. "I'm Mr. Bledding's secretary," she went on. "He asked me to find you and bring you to his office. He wants to see you right away."

Jamie nodded, silently cursing the message, but feeling sympathy for the messenger. The girl looked as though someone had permanently intimidated her. He tried to put her at ease with a poor joke. "I'll go willingly." He smiled. "No handcuffs are necessary."

His attempt at humor, admittedly weak, was lost on

her. She gave him an imperceptible nod and hurriedly moved away. She led the way back down the crowded corridor, almost like a furtive animal.

In front of Bledding's office he made it a point to thank her warmly, and seeing closely the distraught reddened face, he lightly touched her shoulder, an impersonal yet warm gesture which he hoped would put her at ease.

Unfortunately it had just the opposite effect. She drew suddenly back and stared at him with profound suspicion. Her hand moved tremblingly up to the high collar of her dark dress. She took another step backward, then fled across the hall and disappeared behind a door marked LADIES.

Jamie stood a moment longer, appalled by her shyness, and vowed to himself to go out of his way to be very kind to Stella Trinder. Obviously she needed kindness as acutely as she needed oxygen.

While he was still gazing at the door marked LADIES he heard Bledding call out to him. "Mr. Pask? Is that you? Please come in."

The voice sounded cordial enough, and before he turned, Jamie made another silent vow, that in the interest of peace and, he hoped, a pleasant summer he would try to understand this man who would be his employer for the next three months.

Apparently Geoffrey Bledding had made the same silent vow, for he rose hospitably as Jamie entered the small office and extended his hand over the desk in a warm greeting. "Mr. Pask." He smiled. "I trust you got settled in and slept well?"

Jamie shook the hand extended to him and answered yes to both questions. The man did seem changed somehow. His eager, ever-moving face bore no resemblance to the sullen man who had stood in the shadows of the gatehouse arch. Suddenly Jamie felt as though he owed Bledding an apology. If the positions had been reversed, if he, Jamie, had been master of the hall and forced to witness such an impudent disturbance, he, too, might have appeared sullen.

The handshake over, Jamie began, "Mr. Bledding, I'm sorry about yester—"

"No need, no need." Bledding dismissed the apology with a wave of his hand, sat down behind his desk, and motioned for Jamie to take a chair. He looked at him now or appeared to look at him and smiled openly. "I deserved it. I should have answered your letters." He shook his head and one hand fingered a small plaster on his lower left jaw. A shaving accident, Jamie assumed. "We get so busy around here, Mr. Pask," he went on. "I have repeatedly asked the National Trust for a larger secretarial staff, but as you know, we are forced to operate on the proverbial shoestring."

He shrugged and leaned back in the chair, his eyes moving now in the area around the top of Jamie's head. "So," he went on, still smiling, "sometimes letters don't get answered." He laid a finger on his mouth and gave a profoundly unambiguous wink. "I'm just sorry our Trust representative was not here yesterday to witness the furor. It might have served as a marvelous object lesson."

Jamie smiled and nodded in agreement. Perhaps he had judged the man too hastily. "At any rate," he said, "I *am* sorry about the traffic pileup and any other inconven—"

But again the man would hear nothing of it. Instead at this moment he seemed most concerned about the coach. "Do you think it will be all right in the high pasture?"

"I don't know why not," Jamie replied. "Perhaps some of the ladies might object to traipsing through the cow dung, but when we get ready to load, I think I can pull close enough to the gatehouse."

Geoffrey nodded. "I'd be most grateful."

There was a silence then as Jamie tried to make out in which direction they were heading. Bledding now seemed to be waiting for him to speak. His hand continually fingered the small plaster on his face, and his eyes seemed to have gone temporarily blank. He muttered, "So much to do, so much to remember—" And his voice shook slightly as though it were aware that the mind had drifted.

Jamie felt sorry for him. He looked like a man in over his head, not really designed by heritage or nature to be warden of an adult college. He would have been more at ease several centuries ago in the role of country squire.

Still the mind had not made connection, and on the pale face Jamie now saw a rise in color. He moved quickly to aid him in his obvious confusion. "Do you have a schedule for me?" he asked quietly.

The light of relief flooded Bledding's expression. Quickly he reached into the top drawer and withdrew a sheet of paper. He handed it across the desk to Jamie. "As you can see," he began, back on the track again, "it's a light schedule thus far simply because all of our summer groups do not know as yet about our new acquisition of coach and coachman. We're trying to get a letter out now, informing them, asking them if there are any special trips they wish to make." He rested his elbows on the table, his fingers kneading the skin on his forehead. He spoke now around the barrier of his hands. "So while the schedule appears light, I can't absolutely assure you that it will remain that way."

Jamie nodded. "I like to keep busy. That's what I'm being paid for." His eye ran quickly down the typed page. There were fewer than fifteen planned excursions to predictable points of interest in the Yorkshire area. Taken altogether, they scarcely amounted to a summer's work. He folded the page and put it inside his coat pocket. "I'll feel guilty about picking up my paycheck." He smiled.

Geoffrey sat up in his chair and folded his hands before him on the desk. "No need," he assured him, "but I was wondering if in your spare time you would be willing to help us out in small ways. Nothing very big, you understand."

Jamie waited, slightly on guard, yet still eager to maintain his new rapport with his employer. "In what ways?" he asked.

"Oh, small ways," Geoffrey repeated. "Sometimes our students need help getting their luggage up to the third-floor rooms. That's quite a climb, as you so well know, and occasionally, like now, our students are elderly and need—"

It *was* a small thing, and Jamie readily agreed. "I'd be happy to," he said. "Anything else?"

"Well, I don't want to press you," Geoffrey said, still cordial. "And I'm well aware that none of this is in your contract, and you have every right to say no."

Jamie tried again to put him at ease. The man seemed so nervous, so eager not to overstep his boundaries. "I doubt if I'll say no." He smiled. "The schedule *is* very light so far. What is it?"

Nervously Geoffrey riffled through the mussed papers on his desk, apparently not really looking for anything, but at least the small action relieved him of the necessity of looking at Jamie. "The gardens," he said, nodding his head gravely. "We're very proud of our gardens. Peter Endicott is in charge, but he's a very old man and deaf as a post. If you could find it in your schedule to give him a hand now and then, I'd be most appreciative."

Gardener! Jamie hadn't counted on that. Oh, well, the fresh air and exercise would be good for him, help postpone the coachman's chronic ailment of poor circulation. It took him only a moment to nod in agreement. "I'd be glad to help if I can." He smiled.

"Marvelous!" Again relief flooded Bledding's face. He seemed most anxious to please. "Then it's settled," he concluded. "I hope we haven't asked too much of you."

"You haven't," Jamie assured him.

The man stood up then, clearly signaling that the

meeting was over. As he came out from behind the desk, he added, "Oh, yes, most important. You will be paid every two weeks, if that's agreeable. My secretary, whom I believe you met, will issue the checks, so please see her."

The discussion of payment obviously was distasteful to him. Again Jamie nodded quickly. "That will be fine."

The man drew a deep breath, gave one swift look up, like a frightened penitent. "Well, then, can you think of anything else?"

For a moment Jamie couldn't. Then he added, "I'd like very much to see around the hall, if I may, learn something of the place, in case I'm asked questions by any of the students." He pointed toward the corridor outside the door. "Should I simply fall in with one of the morning tours?"

Quickly Geoffrey shook his head. "Oh, my, no! Those dear ladies, I'm afraid, are fountains of misinformation." A minute passed, his hand smoothing his hair as if he were searching for the solution at the top of his skull. "I tell you what," he said finally, "I'll see if I can arrange for Caldy More to show you around this afternoon. I believe you met her yesterday. She knows more about Bledding Sorrow and everything in it than I do. Quite a proprietary air, she has, but I think she'll give you a good tour."

At the door now Jamie said, "I'm grateful. What time?"

The direct question seemed to throw him for a moment. Again he covered his face with his hands as though trying to hide his confusion. "It's hard to say. She has so many duties. Why don't we say around two."

Jamie nodded in agreement. "Shall I meet her here?"

A silence. More confusion. Finally he replied rather vaguely, "Yes, I suppose so." His face was working as if he wanted to say more, but could not. He sat now on the edge of the desk as though the short meeting had completely exhausted him.

Jamie watched him a moment longer, his sympathy for the man increasing. He did have a most difficult job. "Then, this afternoon," Jamie concluded.

Geoffrey looked up at him. Still his eyes refused to make direct contact, but he smiled warmly enough and said, "Welcome to Bledding Sorrow, Mr. Pask. I'm certain you will be a valuable addition to our staff." He tried to say something else, but failed, and in the awkward silence Jamie acknowledged the welcome with a bob of his head and left the office.

Outside in the corridor he was pleased to see that most of the human traffic had cleared. The last members of the Birmingham Art League were now struggling through the front door, juggling their equipment, on their way to their painting assignments for the morning. His eyes fell on the door marked LADIES. He wondered if Stella Trinder was still crouched in a stall. He hoped not. He looked up now in time to see a thin, bespectacled, short, and slightly choleric man just entering the front door. The man was book-ladened, dressed in winter tweeds. He looked furtive for some reason, as though he were being followed. As he passed by Jamie in the hall, he gave him a scant nod of his head, then quickly slipped into Geoffrey Bledding's office.

Before the door was closed, Jamie heard Geoffrey's voice, "Good morning, Arthur. I see you've been doing your homework."

And he heard the other man say, "The adders, Geoffrey, are going to be a problem. The crypt is too—"

Then the door was closed, and Jamie was left alone, his eyes focused foolishly on the ladies' room across the corridor. Another young woman scurried by him, carrying a stack of linens in her arms. She did not so much as look up. Down the hall he saw two elderly women wielding enormous brooms, making their way down the corridor, moving toward him. From the downstairs dining room he heard the clatter of dishes as breakfast was cleared away and preparations were started for lunch.

Everyone appeared busy. So busy. Suddenly he felt quite self-conscious in his idleness. Obviously the best way to fit in was to give the appearance at least of being busy. With that thought in mind, he headed toward the front door. What was the old gardener's name? Endicott? Deaf as a post. No matter. Perhaps he had a job that needed doing.

Retracing his steps of the night before, he walked rapidly around the red brick hall to the rear, reveling in the bright, warm, sun-drenched morning. To his mild surprise, he discovered that he felt relatively good. The amicable meeting with Geoffrey Bledding had lifted his spirits and helped to dispel the old cook's tale of ghosts and mad wives. Even his own experiences of the night before faded rapidly under the dazzling glare of morning sun. He smiled as he walked, remembering the lovers he had discovered in the garden. It might be fun to try to discover who they were. Not that he would ever reveal their secret. Rather, he just wanted to be pleased for them.

A few moments later, at the rear of the hall, he found himself facing the same long promenade that he had discovered the night before. But now he saw more or, rather, saw clearly that beyond the straight gravel path lined on both sides with meticulously trimmed trees were two additional avenues of statuary, life-size figures of men and women from an earlier century, dressed in peasant clothes, the women with baskets of fruits and vegetables, the men carrying or leaning on various garden tools—spades, hoes, rakes—a charming panorama of frozen figures representing the plenty of harvest and hard work.

Then, beyond the twin avenue of statues, he saw a breathtaking Garden of Eden, flowers of all sorts, descriptions, and colors stretching as far in either direction as he could see, to the very fringes of the woods, a continuous carpet of color and life and incredible odors.

The flower beds nearest him were studded gold and pale yellow with celandines and primroses and marigolds and banked by the white of densely blossoming sloe. And beyond these were beds of purple iris and larkspur and clusters of moschatel and wood sorrel. Higher up the gently sloping ground he saw the white heads of anemones mixed with lily-of-the-valley and bridal veil and blending finally with vivid explosions of English roses, velvet suns of red, pink, orange, yellow.

For a moment the sight, quite literally, took his breath away. Peter Endicott might be deaf as a post, but clearly he was an artist. Now, as Jamie walked slowly down the path, he reveled in the beauty around him, heard a woodpecker drumming in the branches of a near tree, and bullfinches whistled gently over his head. Now that he was listening, he heard willow warblers singing in every bush and treetop.

At the center of the promenade he stopped. Curious. This one winged statue seemed out of place, a Greek misfit in a garden of English peasants. He circled the statue, his eyes wandering down the path to the stone bench at the far end. For a moment he almost thought he saw them again, the lovers, but it was merely the uncanny shadows caused by the sun and the densely woven canopy of trees.

In the blaze of morning sun he found his eyes watering. Blurred, the statue and all those around him seemed to shimmer. Quickly he lowered his head in order to rest his eyes. It was while his head was down, his eyes closed, that he first heard a voice.

Quickly he looked up, looked suspiciously for a moment at the statue itself. But it was a distant voice, someone speaking at a point removed from where he stood.

Shading his eyes with his hand, he glanced toward the rear of the hall, his eyes moving slowly across the expanse of red brick, stopping finally on the high red brick wall, the sealed enclosure on the left wing of the house, which he had noticed the night before.

That was where the voice was coming from, and now he moved toward it, cutting directly through the gardens, ignoring the dampness gathering on his shoes from the heavy morning dew.

It was impossible to say what was drawing him forward. For a moment he clearly felt a force greater than himself, something gently but firmly urging him onward, one step after another, toward the mysterious voice. Once he tried to draw back and alter his destination. Whatever it was that was going on behind the wall, it was none of his concern.

But the force of his reason was meager and inadequate compared to the force that was drawing him forward. He had never felt such a sensation before in his life and could not now understand it, much less articulate it. All he knew was that there was something beyond that wall, that he must go to it and must finally deal with it. As he drew near, the voice grew louder, then suddenly ceased. He stood still a few yards from the wall, listening, feeling as stealthy and intrusive as the night before.

A moment later he heard a door slam. Apparently the voice was gone. Still he held his position, listening. Then he heard a faint scratching, a muffled, weak sound as though someone were walking slowly across gravel.

Quickly he moved to a position directly beneath the wall. He wasn't at all certain what he was looking for or what he expected to find. He felt a suppressed intensity as he continued to hear the muffled sound coming from inside the wall. If it was a footstep, it was clearly that of an older person, for he heard the movement stop now and then, as though the person tired easily or was in fear of losing balance.

He followed the curious sound to the far end of the wall, where suddenly it ceased altogether. He thought once he heard a soft moan, but he couldn't be certain. He considered calling over the wall, but decided against it, and now spied at the end of the wall near the beginning of rank woods a large copper beech tree, its trunk gnarled but sturdy and growing quite close to the wall, its upper foliage thick and spreading shade over the bottom of the garden.

He hesitated only a moment. He was not by nature a spy. Duty and agreeable conformity raised their stern heads. And so did the awareness that if discovered, he could legitimately say he was looking for the old gardener, Peter Endicott. He took off his coat and loosened his tie and looked sharply back over his shoulder. Only the statues were watching him. He was in no real danger of being discovered since the heavy foliage would give him adequate concealment. It would be a simple matter to scale the tree. In fact, on closer examination, the tree looked as though it had been created to be climbed.

With only a minimum of effort, he made an easy job of it, certain branches appearing just as he needed them, and within moments his hands grasped the wall and he dragged himself forward and up until he was perching on top. From behind a safe concealment of coppery leaves he looked down.

It *was* a garden, smaller and not as well cared for as the larger gardens flanking the promenade. The flowers and shrubs grew next to the wall on three sides. Then there was a gravel path skirting the flowers and in the exact center a small square of grass. The side of the hall formed the fourth wall, sealing the garden with only one access door in or out.

He settled himself more comfortably on top of the wall, catching his breath, feeling slightly bewildered. From where he sat he could see no sign of life.

Then he did.

For one incredible moment he thought it was another statue. But the position of the figure bore no resemblance to the statues in the outer gardens. It was a young woman, sitting cross-legged on the gravel path directly beneath him.

Jamie's immediate instinct was to draw back, but then his curiosity held him fast. The woman, scarcely more than a girl, sat in a childlike position, legs crossed. Her gray smock dress looked mussed and filthy, unrelieved in its severity. Her face was down; he could see only the top of her short fair hair. In her lap she held a notebook opened to a blank page. In her right hand she grasped a pencil and moved the pencil across the blank page in the awkward, tentative, labored manner of a child just learning to write. There was something intensely tender in her effort and something equally mysterious. From his sharp downward angle Jamie could see that the pencil was not making contact with the paper. The young woman was writing on air, the tip of the pencil hovering about an inch from the surface of the paper.

Suddenly something stirred within him, a depth of feeling and compassion that threatened to overwhelm him. All his life he had been attracted to the helpless, the mute, the victims. As a child this vulnerability had manifested itself in a constant parade of homeless, abandoned animals, dogs and cats of every description, which his grandmother had systematically discarded as rapidly as he had brought them home.

The longing to comfort, to give aid had never been completely satisfied. It was a feeling not unlike actual pain, a sharp turning in the pit of his stomach, a shortness of breath, an incredible urge to embrace, protect, comfort.

Now he felt this same feeling, only more pronounced, more acute than he had ever felt it before. The pitiable image of the young woman was overpowering, her obvious helplessness, her clear distress almost more than he could bear.

Now he moved forward slightly on the top of the wall, parting the heavy foliage to where he could see her better. There was something else about her, a vacancy, an emptiness. Suddenly he remembered the old cook's tale concerning the mad wife. He looked down again on her. Part of her short-cut hair fell forward in her effort and half covered her cheek. The skin below it seemed very pale, a thin nose, knitted brows, the mouth he could not see at all. It annoyed him strangely that he had to see her at such a downward angle.

But still he was unable to do anything but stare, fascinated by this unexpected encounter. He felt mildly depressed, felt an equally strong feeling, perhaps paternal, a certainty of the innocence of this creature, of her being driven into madness and thus outcast, imprisoned in her garden with what must surely be for her appalling loneliness. He could not imagine what, besides total despair, could drive her to this secluded place, to pass the morning in total isolation, writing on the air with a pencil gripped between trembling fingers.

A sweeping simplicity marked the moment. The sight of her moved him in a way that he had never been moved before, a feeling which perhaps had its closest parallel to his past experiences with the dying and injured animals which he frequently saw beside the road. To the annoyance of his passengers, he always stopped and waited with the animal, mostly dogs, until help or death arrived.

Now he inched forward to the very edge of the wall, a spot almost directly above her, and at that moment she raised her head and looked past him skyward, and there he saw all the sadness, all the pain that would have provoked sympathy from a stone. As her eyes swept the sky as though entreating it, he saw a wild shyness in her face. The slight wind ruffled her hair, obscuring for a moment the look of bewilderment in her eyes.

Suddenly, still looking up, she closed her eyes, more than closed them, pressed them shut as though to cancel the most hideous of images. The notebook and pencil fell to her lap. She wrapped her pitifully thin arms around her body and began to rock quietly back and forth in a childlike self-soothing motion.

Again Jamie found the sight of the young woman, so frail and alone, almost too much to bear. As much for his own benefit as hers, he parted the tree foliage and leaned over and whispered, "Don't, please."

She looked up at once, so quickly that any attempt to reconceal himself was in vain. He was detected. And when the young woman scrambled weakly to her feet, gathering up the notebook and pencil, and stared wildly up at him on his ledge, he had no choice but to bob his head and smile politely. She said nothing, but fixed him with a look of shock and bewilderment, perhaps not untinged with shame. He saw now that she had fine eyes, blue eyes.

They stood thus for several seconds, as though locked in a mutual incomprehension. She seemed so small and terrified, standing down there, clutching the empty notebook to her, as if, should he make one move toward her, she would faint from terror.

Finally, although he doubted seriously if it would do any good, he came to his sense of what was proper. He smiled again. "My name is James Pask," he said gently, "and I don't usually climb trees, but—"

She continued to back away from him, viewing him now as though he were a specter, a vision of some sort, and from the spreading fear on her face he could only assume that he wasn't a very pleasant vision.

She turned then and tried to run a few steps farther away from him, her bare feet struggling with the rough gravel, some inner weakness causing her to waver unsteadily.

He did not want to raise his voice, but he longed to put her at ease, at least to try to convince her that he meant her no harm. Suddenly he saw her stumble and fall on the grassy area near the center of the garden. She went down in a small heap, the notebook and pencil falling to one side, her arms struggling to right her body, but buckling each time she tried to raise up, her fear still consuming her, her face, what he could see of it, half hidden in the grass, totally without color.

Her collapse reduced Jamie to silence. He would not try to speak to her again. He was only causing greater pain. From where he sat he could see the slight heave of her shoulders as she tried to digest her fear. Her strange weakness puzzled him. The simple mechanics of coordination seemed beyond her. It was as though she were physically crippled in some way and, once having fallen, was now forced to lie still until someone came for her.

He continued to watch her struggle until he could bear it no longer. Following fast on the heels of his compassion and pity was a growing sense of anger, that a human being in her condition should be left alone and unattended. Now, as he looked back down, he saw her lying quite still, one weak hand kneading the grass as though she were embarrassed and humiliated by her condition and wanting to signal to him somehow that she was still alive, that perhaps within the moment she would arise and be a human being again.

But there was no further movement. For a few seconds Jamie held his position on the wall, a mute party to her agony.

Then, at the very moment that he raised his knee in order to brace himself for the leap downward, he heard a disturbance at the rear door, a lock mechanism being opened. He realized with a rapid increase in rage that the young woman had been locked out, her access to the hall cut off. Obviously she had been placed in the garden and was forced to remain there until someone came for her.

Now he did not move except to lower the branch of the tree slowly, thus ensuring his concealment from whoever was on the other side of the door. A moment later he saw the tall angular woman named Caldy More step out into the garden. He saw her slip a large ring of keys back into the pocket of her dress, then look quickly about as though she were searching for something. As she spied the crumpled figure of the young woman in the center of the garden, a quick look of anger, perhaps impatience, crossed her face.

She strode rapidly across the lawn, and while she was

still several feet away, she started scolding, her voice low but distinct. "I don't know what you think you are doing, Mrs. Bledding, but this is not your bed. I should think you would see enough of that. Look at you! Your clothes are—"

She did not finish the sentence, but reached down and grabbed the young woman beneath her arms and jerked her onto her feet. The head bobbed weakly, fell backward, then forward, and the young woman herself, erect for only a moment, slipped back down onto her knees, her hands curled limply in her lap.

The tall woman stared down on her, her stern face a curious mixture of anger and pity. "Look at you," she scolded. Then slowly she knelt in front of the young woman and almost tenderly lifted her face. She seemed to stare for a long minute at the blue eyes, hollow-circled, at the tears silently streaming. Her hand passed lightly over the ruffled hair. He face contorted, then slowly, tenderly, she enclosed the young woman in an embrace, drew her close to her own strong body, pressed her head against her breast, and held her as she would hold an injured child.

The unexpected moment produced a stinging in Jamie's eyes. He stared down on the two women, feeling clearly his role of trespasser. He felt baffled, obscurely wronged. He should never have climbed the wall. What he had seen, what he was seeing now made no sense. That normal activity was being conducted elsewhere in Bledding Sorrow seemed incredible.

He lowered his eyes in an attempt to clear them, then again he looked slowly down on the two women. Caldy More was now rising to her feet, taking the young woman with her, speaking softly to her, urging her to try to stand. And from the incredible strain of effort on the young woman's face Jamie saw clearly that she was capable of understanding, if not response.

Once she was up, her legs threatened to buckle again. Quickly Caldy More reached around her shoulders and supported her and tried to lead her forward, moving slowly toward the rear door. But once, then twice, the young woman stopped, turned weakly back toward the spot where she had fallen.

Caldy More, her display of tenderness apparently fading rapidly, looked back toward the same spot to where the notebook and pencil still lay on the grass. "I'll get them for you later," she scolded. "Now you're soaking wet, and we must—"

But obviously the young woman would not be put off. With an unexpected flare of will, she pulled loose from Caldy More and took a step, then two, toward the notebook. Suddenly her knees buckled again, and she fell forward, face down, a stunning blow, moaning slightly, more in frustration, it seemed to Jamie, than in pain.

Clearly angry, Caldy More walked back and grabbed up the notebook and pencil and with her free hand bodily jerked the woman up again. There was a long silence as the struggle continued, the laborious passage to the rear door, the young woman leaning heavily on Caldy More for support, trying now and then to lift her head and walk erect and failing, crumpling as though the last vestiges of her strength were rapidly fading.

When they reached the rear of the hall, Caldy More had to release her in order to open the door. In that moment, now using the building for support, the young woman turned slowly back and looked in the direction of the copper beech tree at the end of the garden, a strange, glistening look, so direct that Jamie feared she might call out to him. She remained looking up toward the tree until Caldy More turned her around and guided her through the door and into the dark interior of the hall. A moment later he heard the door close, then lock. Then the garden was empty and all was silent around him.

He was left sitting on the wall in an absurdly foolish position. His amazement was natural. What was unnatural was his now quite distinct sense of anger. It was as if he had shown a callous lack of sympathy when he was quite sure he had done his best. He stared at the closed locked door for several moments. What he had seen he would not soon forget. In fact, his mind was already turning, working, devising a plan of some sort. He knew he would be back on the wall the following morning, that somehow he must convince the young woman that he meant her no harm, and that in this vital matter he must not fail.

Up until now his future at Bledding Sorrow had seemed vague. Now suddenly he felt as though he were on a fixed voyage to a known place. He waited a moment longer, looked sharply in all directions, then climbed quickly down from his perch. The remembered images that passed before his eyes as he stood at the base of the tree were many and vivid. If the young woman were truly ill, Caldy More would not have treated her so roughly. If she were truly mad, Caldy More could not have communicated with her. And if she were truly free, she would not have been locked in the garden with all access doors bolted.

Then what was her crime, her offense? What had happened to her to produce the obvious and debilitating weakness? And perhaps the most puzzling question of all, why had the sight of her had such a profound effect on Jamie? And he could not deny that he had been affected by all that he had seen and heard. Even as he pulled on his jacket and straightened his tie, he saw only the young woman's face, saw the pencil moving through the air above the empty page, saw the terror as she had looked up at him, the frustration and despair as she had tried to run away, and saw finally her curious backward look at him.

Now he walked rapidly around the hall, again craving solitude. What he had seen was puzzling and bewildering, but most of all, what he had seen was wrong. If the woman was ill, then she needed medical attention. If she was being punished, then the punishment had gone on long enough. If she was merely lonely, then she needed comfort and solace.

As his splintered thoughts rose and fell inside his head, he increased his step until he was running. He passed through the open front door and the long central corridor, climbed the stairs to the third floor, went into the little cramped room, closed the door, and sat down on the edge of the bed.

He felt as though he were being torn in half. His mind, his reason, marched steadily in one direction, informing him over and over again that it was none of his business, none of his concern. His heart and emotions marched just as steadily in the opposite direction, telling him he had no choice, that regardless of what he *should* do or *might* do, he would continue to seek out the perch on top of the garden wall, he would persist until he knew all about the young woman, not merely her identity but her entire nature and personality and ultimately her soul.

He shook his head and buried his face in his hands. Something mysterious was moving over him, like a magnetic field, drawing him back to the garden. No, he mustn't. Not now. Then when? Later. Perhaps later. Surely later.

The struggle was so intense that perspiration dotted his forehead. His mouth felt dry, his head bursting.

He sat there for a long time. The box filled with his books was beneath the bed. He leaned over and pulled it out quickly; quickly he reached inside and, without looking, lifted one out.

But even as he tried to escape into the printed page, he thought he heard someone weeping. . . .

❧❦ 16 ❧❦

"Something must be done," warned Caldy More from the office door. She shook her head with sudden vehemence. "The drug is too strong. Something must be done."

Geoffrey Bledding looked up from the papers on his desk. For a moment he seemed to be forcing himself to look away from the bearer of bad tidings. Then suddenly he stood up, his face white with anger. "For God sake," he exploded. "What is it that you expect of me? A few days ago it was too weak. Now it's too strong. What in the—"

Voices passed by in the hall outside the door, females, strangers.

He waited a moment, his anger not dissipated, merely held in check. Then he ordered sternly, "Close the door."

Caldy More, with her customary estimation of her own dignity, waited a moment, then reluctantly stepped inside the office and closed the door behind her. Now she gave him a long reproachful look. "There is absolutely no need for you to vent your spleen on me, Mr. Bledding. You have put me in charge of a most difficult task. I feel it my duty to report to you when that—"

Then he retreated. He waved aside her lecture and sat wearily on the edge of the chair. With his head down, eyes closed, he asked, "What's the problem?"

Caldy More smiled at her master's weakness. In spite of her private sense of amusement, she thought there was something pitiful about him. He was one of life's victims, as surely as his drugged wife in the upper bedchamber, one more wretch caught in the vast movements of time, stranded now for eternity, a member of the landed gentry, with no land.

Now pleased by the clarity and precision of her thoughts and doubly pleased with the bowed, defeated man before her, she straightened her shoulders and delivered herself of the facts of the case. "The problem, Mr. Bledding," she began, "is that she is now almost totally helpless, incapable of movement without my constant assistance. She's scarcely human. What small responses I've been able to elicit from her in the past are now completely gone. I find the responsibility awesome, to say nothing of the work involved. In short, I need help, or the woman should be placed in hospital."

"No!" The response was strong and immediate. He looked up only briefly at her, then turned away, the subject clearly closed.

But Caldy More had other plans. She knew instinctively that the one shouldering the responsibility had the loudest voice. "Then I must inform you, sir, that I refuse to be held accountable for anything that might happen."

Again he looked at her, a terrible expression on his face. "What's that supposed to mean? What's likely to happen?"

She shrugged. "I don't know, and I'm not saying. I found her this morning face down in the garden. She must have fallen. She was incapable of rising without my assistance."

"So?"

"She was weeping, sir."

"She always cries."

"No, not always. Only lately. I'm afraid that she might try—"

"What?"

This exchange suddenly struck Caldy More as bizarre. Almost in spite of herself she softened. "She's a human being, Mr. Bledding. Granted it was a mistake for her to come here in the first place, but that was your doing. Still, she's—"

"She's my wife," he interrupted sternly. "I'm doing what I think is best for her."

Caldy More glared at him across the desk, saw clearly his meanness, his condescension, his stupidity. "You know that's not true, sir," she said, her voice cold. "You wouldn't treat a mongrel the way you're treating her. So why pre—"

"Then what in the name of God do you suggest?" He whirled on her again, half rose from his chair, and leaned heavily on the desk. "You come in here with vague threats and admonitions, interrupt my work, and do nothing but preach to me. Then what do you suggest?"

With the grim sense of a bulldog about to sink its teeth into an intruder, Caldy More said, "I need help with her."

"Then get it."

"How? Do I have permission to hire a girl?"

"No."

"Then what?"

Again he sank wearily back into the chair, shaking his head. "There's no one we can trust," he lamented. "I don't want the talk to start again. I don't want people snooping about, asking questions. I don't want—"

"Then send her to hospital. It's where she belongs."

"No!"

As again he shook his head adamantly, she noticed a peculiar color rising in his cheeks. No, of course, he didn't want to send her to the hospital. How long, she wondered, had the Bledding family struggled to keep up the façade of gentility? She knew his weakness, as his father's before him. At least that disturbed man had had the good sense to indulge his appetites in London, miles away from the clacking tongues and prying eyes of Yorkshire.

Finally, as though with a sense of compassion, he said, "I'll talk to Martin Axtell again. Perhaps the medicine can be—"

"Reduced?" She shook her head. "Now I'm not certain it would help. Somewhere behind all the drugs she still has a will. I don't think you want any more outbursts such as the one we had a few days ago. Everyone heard it and now, as you know, everyone is talking."

He looked at her with heavy, pleading eyes, as though she were his tormentor and he was begging for mercy. "Then what, Caldy More? Precisely what is it that you want me to do?"

She had no solution and even if she did, she wasn't certain she would give it to him. There was something about his misery that she found enormously satisfying. Now she lifted her hands in a gesture of resignation. "I've reported the situation to you. That's all I can do. Beyond that, I am simply an employee. I will continue to try to do the best job I can. But the circumstances are getting more difficult. She is requiring more and more of my attention, and I fear that she may—"

"What? May take her life?"

Caldy More nodded.

"Then simply remove all objects of that nature—"

"I did that some time ago."

"Then what?"

Caldy More hesitated a moment, finding the young woman's deepening despair a difficult subject to put into words. "The will, I suppose," she said vaguely. "Can one die when one simply loses the will to—"

He dismissed this theory with a shake of his head. "She's not aware of enough to—"

"She's aware of everything, Mr. Bledding." She paused a moment, then repeated the last word, "Everything." She felt a sharp surge of anger at his blank, almost senseless expression. She repeated still a third time, "Everything!"

For a second they held each other locked in a gaze of mutual intensity, the knowledge of the secret late-night abuses rising between them.

Geoffrey Bledding looked away first. He lowered his head and folded his hands before him on the desk, as though at prayer. His eyes were nearly closed, but his face was stern and relentless. "Do the best you can, Caldy More," he muttered. "I've never asked more of you, and I'll never ask less." Then, in a major but safe concession, he added, "If her father were still alive, I'd send her home."

"If her family were still alive, she would have left here of her own accord years ago," Caldy More said.

He raised his eyes to her. He seemed to be looking for a little softness, a little weakness in her. While his eyes were searching, her face remained fixed. "I'll leave you alone now," she said, "but don't be surprised at anything that happens."

Some moments passed before he grasped the full meaning of that last oblique warning. Now, as he saw her turning toward the door, he shouted at her, "Then for God sake, tell me what I'm supposed to do."

Suddenly, outside the door, there came a soft knock. Caldy More's eyes sharpened as though she wanted to see through the door. For a moment the tableau inside the office held as both tried to assess who it was and how much of their conversation had been overheard.

Bledding rose slowly to his feet. His voice was faint as though he had suddenly suffered a lack of oxygen. "Who is it?" he called.

For a moment there was no reply. Then, "It's me, sir. James Pask. It's two o'clock. I was wondering if Caldy More was—"

Caldy More looked sharply toward the desk. On her face was an enormous questioning expression. Bledding motioned quickly for her to come nearer. "It's the new coachman," he said, keeping his voice down. "He wants to know about the hall. I told him that you would—"

But already Caldy More was shaking her head, anger rising. "I can't," she protested. "I must get back upstairs. I didn't give her any medicine at noon and she's—"

"Please," he begged. "It'll take only a few minutes. He's—"

"And in the meantime, what if she—"

"Give me the key. I'll go look in on her."

There was a silence between them. Almost instinctively Caldy More clutched at the pocket of her dress where she kept the key ring. "She'd be better off alone," she said firmly.

Again the voice came from outside the door. "If it's inconvenient, I can come back another—"

"No, wait, Mr. Pask," Geoffrey called through the door. "We'll be right with you." Then he looked back at Caldy More in dismay, like a man who had been irreparably injured. "She's my wife. Give me the key."

"No," she repeated. She drew herself up. "I'll take your Mr. Pask around, but you stay away from her. She's not accustomed to seeing you in daylight. I shouldn't have thought that you would have so soon forgotten what happened the last time."

He stared at her; one hand moved reflexively up to the small plaster on his jaw.

For a moment she was afraid that he would order her to hand over the key. But instead he sat down again behind the desk, again defeated, again without any solution whatever to his despair.

Caldy More accepted his surrender and seized the opportunity. "If I am to join the ranks of tour guides," she said with emphasis, "I now more than ever relinquish all responsibility for her. I will, as you say, continue to do the best I can, but I refuse to be held accountable. Is that clear?" She paused cunningly. "I have the strongest feeling that something is about to happen." Then, sensing that her oblique approach might be lost on him, she added quickly, almost lightly, "Did you know, Mr. Bledding, that I pray nightly for her death?"

With that, she swung open the office door with such force that it bounced loudly against the wall behind it. Without looking, she called out, full-voiced, "This way, Mr. Pask, if you're—"

She almost collided with the tall man, so surprised was she to find him standing directly outside the door, as though he had been listening. . . .

✦ 17 ✦

The tour was totally unnecessary, considering the fact that when Jamie had come down for lunch, he had spied, directly outside the dining room, a small stand filled with elaborate guidebooks on Bledding Sorrow Hall. He had deposited his fifty pence in the metal box, then had slipped one of the brochures into his pocket. It was complete with color photographs and clear instructions, and he could guide himself about the Elizabethan hall anytime he wished.

But still he kept his two o'clock appointment with the dry, lean woman. Now he wanted more from her than a guided tour. He wanted, first, her approval, then her trust, and finally her confidence. As keeper of the keys to the garden where he had witnessed the incredibly moving incident of the morning, he felt in the long run Caldy More could be a valuable ally.

This feeling had been confirmed as he had stood outside the office door and had heard voices raised in anger, had heard Bledding shouting, "Then tell me what I'm supposed to do," and had heard clearly a moment later Caldy More say, almost pleased, "I pray nightly for her death." The office door had then swung open before he had had a chance to move back.

In the first minute of his confrontation with Caldy More he had seen an accusation in her eyes. But now, midway through the tour, the old woman seemed to be softening under his barrage of questions, his obvious interest, and the fact that he seemed impressed with her vast knowledge of every detail, no matter how small.

Now, as they entered the Queen's state bedroom on the second floor, Caldy More pointed out the amazing complexity of the plasterwork on the ceiling; fronds of honeysuckle intertwined around the frieze and across the ceiling, some hanging free.

"Clearly the work of the finest artisans," Caldy More said, pointing with pride up toward the ceiling.

Jamie agreed with a respectful and awed silence. His eyes scanned the complicated design incorporating a series of leaf-and-flower patterns, among them the oak, holly, thistle, and pomegranate. Under her guidance he observed the chimneypiece flanked by a pair of Corinthian columns, its overmantel divided into three panels by more columns.

"You will notice," she instructed, hand raised, "that the allegorical figures are Patience, Truth, Constancy, and there, the one who rewards these virtues, Victory."

He noticed and said nothing, letting his silence pass for speechlessness at the exquisite beauty before him.

"And there," she went on, clearly pleased, "in the frieze above you will notice that the artist carved the antithesis to these same virtues: Tribulation, Fraud, and Danger. The date of the completion of the work is carved there." And she pointed toward the base of the frieze. "You can just make it out if you look closely. Twelfth July, 1610."

He followed her instructions and bent close. Seeing the faint scratchings, he murmured, "Really incredible."

Again she looked pleased, though still slightly suspicious. Now, as he continued to survey the grand room, he was aware of her watching him, as though awaiting his comments. He obliged. "It's hard to believe," he began, his eyes sweeping across the splendor, "that anyone ever lived in such a room. Can you imagine awakening every morning to such as this?" And he gestured broadly toward the ornate plaster-work ceiling.

"Well, I can assure you they *were* lived in," she said with all the authority at her command.

"Oh, I'm not doubting your word, Caldy More," he soothed. "It's just that most of us get by on so much less." He still felt that she was holding him at arm's length. "You and me, for instance," he added, smiling warmly, "or at least certainly you. Then, as now, there are always those priceless people who somehow hold it all together and make it work so that a select few can enjoy such as this."

He saw just a glimmer of interest in her stern face, neither approval nor disapproval, merely the faintest desire to hear more.

She walked away from him then to the door and stared out into the corridor for a long moment and finally glanced back at him, a strange, penetrating look, so direct that he felt a warmth on his face. She asked, "Are you ready to move on?"

He nodded and followed after her into the corridor, still trying to interpret the curious look she had given him. She would not be easy; he knew that. She reminded him of the sort of woman who perhaps had made it this far on her singular ability to keep her mouth shut and trust no one. When he asked her where they were headed next, she merely shook her head, mumbled something he couldn't catch, and went on walking as steadily as before.

And he followed after her, remembering again the scene in the garden, more determined than ever to try to win at least a small portion of her trust.

They were descending the oak staircase now, apparently heading toward the Grand Dining Room. He decided to try again while there was still time, for he had the feeling that she might terminate the tour at any moment.

"Caldy More," he called out, laughing. "Could we slow down?"

"I have no time to waste, Mr. Pask," she called over her shoulder. "Some of us at Bledding Sorrow have a great deal to do, and this is not actually my job. I'm doing it only as a favor to Mr. Bledding."

He caught up with her at the bottom of the steps. "And I'm most grateful," he said, "and in return I hope you'll let me do something for you, help you out in some way."

She looked up at him, her face as stern as ever. "I need no help, Mr. Pask, only time in which to execute my duties properly."

Suddenly he became annoyed with her imperious, slightly martyred air. He stepped away. "Then I have no desire to detain you further." He withdrew from his pocket the guidebook and held it up for her inspection. "I can see myself through. I simply thought it would be helpful to have your personal commentary. But I can see that I'm being far too demanding, so—"

"Nonsense!" Her eyes flashed around at him then, as though he were a stubborn child. "That guidebook tells less than half of what's in this hall," she criticized. "I've begged Mr. Bledding to let me write a more complete and accurate account, but—"

As her voice drifted off, Jamie found himself warmed to interest again. He walked with her down the long corridor leading to the dining room and was pleased to notice that this time she had set a slower pace. She seemed to be treating him now with a culpable forbearance.

"May I ask questions, Caldy More?" He smiled, playing the role of the child because it seemed to be the one she preferred him to play. Again he recalled the scene in the garden, her treatment of and attitude toward the young woman, clearly a relationship of child and mistress.

Now, in answer to his question, she nodded, the slightly vexed expression fading from her face. "I did not mean to be rude a moment ago, Mr. Pask," she murmured, her pace slowing more than ever. "It's just that it's difficult for a person to be in two or three places at once, and it seems as though my responsibilities require me to do exactly that."

"How long have you been at Bledding Sorrow?" he asked, trying to make his voice light, his manner casual.

She laughed softly, "Forever. Simply forever, Mr. Pask."

He looked perplexed and hoped that she would interpret his expression as an invitation to talk further.

She did. Directly outside the door of the dining room she stopped altogether, folded her arms over her chest, and looked at him, an expression which seemed to say there was a very good chance that he would not believe what she was going to tell him.

"I came to Bledding Sorrow, Mr. Pask, as a girl of sixteen. I am now sixty-two. It's the only employment I have ever known. I knew the present Mr. Bledding's grandfather as well as his father. I have served the family in every capacity from upstairs maid to part-time cook to nursery maid to nanny. There is not a corner of the hall or, for that matter, the entire estate that I do not know as intimately as I know the back of my hand." For the purposes of demonstration she held up a hand. Her eyes seemed unnaturally bright.

Slowly Jamie shook his head. "Then you've given them your life," he said in amazement.

She nodded broadly. "More than that, Mr. Pask," she went on, leaning slightly against the wall behind her, as though merely talking about it made her weary. "More than that," she repeated, her voice falling.

He stepped closer to her, no longer trying to manipulate or impress her, but now sincerely moved by the degree and depth of her devotion. "I hope you have been justly rewarded," he said, "but I'm afraid I suspect otherwise."

She moved a hand lightly across her forehead as though enjoying her moment of weakness. "I've been provided for," she said, not looking at him, "a roof over my head, food to eat, clothes to wear."

"But what of your own life? Have you never wanted to marry?"

She shook her head. Her long oval face was set with two stormy black eyes, and for a moment her whole frame seemed wrought by some consuming fever. "Marry?" She laughed bitterly. "Now, who would I marry? A farmer? A laborer? A peddler? A poacher?" She laughed again, a poverty-stricken sound. "I'm afraid that for a Yorkshire lady the choices are few, Mr. Pask."

While he disagreed with her, he held his tongue. It wasn't that the choices were few. Rather, it was because over the years in her servitude to the Bledding family she had nailed herself to that blank wall which stretches between the two worlds of the master and the servant. Unable by birth to enter the master's world and incapable by taste of going back to her own world, she had been forced to pass her life in a vacuum.

Again he felt a surge of genuine compassion for her, a sympathy of the truest sort based on understanding. He, too, lived in the same vacuum. Finally he concluded softly, "Well, it's as I said, Caldy More. There have always been those, like yourself, who somehow hold it together and make it work for the enjoyment of others."

Then for some reason—perhaps it was because he had caught a clear glimpse of the barren empty stretches that composed her entire life—he now had no desire to add to her burdens in any way. He almost blessed this opportunity to make peace with his conscience for trying to manipulate her. He stepped forward and placed his hand on her arm. "I've taken up enough of your time, Caldy More. I'm sorry to have added to your labors. Please let me know if I can help in any way." He smiled in an attempt to lighten both their moods. "My schedule is easy. Mr. Bledding has asked me to make myself useful. I'd like to help."

He saw her look down at his hand on her arm, as though the sensation of a human touch was a totally new experience for her. Then slowly she glanced up at him. She seemed flustered, seemed unable to remember what it was she was going to say to him. Finally she stammered, "What about—the dining—there are several others, if you're interested."

He stepped back. "I don't want to take—"

"Nonsense!" she countered, a portion of her old authority returning. "Of course I have the time. And

I think it's important that you know about the hall. You may be in a position of having to answer students' questions, and I'd like you to have accurate answers." She pushed away from the wall and her moment of weakness and led the way into the Grand Dining Room, calling back as cheerily as he had ever heard her, "I want you to see these excellent Gainsboroughs, and we also have some magnificent Chippendale—"

The Gainsboroughs and Chippendale were fine, but Jamie was more impressed by her new mood. No longer reserved or restrained, she showed him the various objects in the room with a new lightheartedness, inviting him to touch, feel, explore to his heart's content, no longer a contest measuring her strength with his, but a new relaxation as though she had searched him for threats and hazards and had found none.

The tour ran on until almost four o'clock and was concluded in the foyer outside the Grand Salon, only a few feet from the door which led to the family wing. In the distance he heard the Birmingham Art League traipsing down the staircase on its way to the basement dining room and afternoon tea. Caldy More withdrew the ring of keys from her pocket, almost regretfully eyeing the locked door which led to the private wing.

Jamie said sincerely, "I can't thank you enough for your time, for sharing with me what you know."

Her eyes flashed around at him and she ducked her head. "It's here to share," she countered, almost dismissing his expression of gratitude. She did not move, but continued to focus on the keys in her hand, sorting through them in an idle nervous gesture. "If anyone asks me, Mr. Pask, I would say, offhand, that in my opinion you will be a most valuable addition to the staff. Most of our employees couldn't care less that they are surrounded by priceless treasures of all sorts." She dared to look up at him for a moment, then quickly sent her eyes back down to the keys. "It's refreshing to find someone so aware of where he is."

Again he smiled. It was as though he could see the

years tumbling off her, see her mind and spirit stepping back to that shy, hesitant, blushing, though still willful young girl of sixteen. Her voice, when lowered and restrained, was extraordinarily soft and musical.

Now she was silent. He hesitated a moment, then spoke. "For your troubles, Caldy More, and your kindness, would you share a cup of tea with me? I hear the ladies going down, and my nose tells me there are scones somewhere fresh from the oven. I'd be most—"

He broke off as suddenly she looked quickly around at the locked door behind her. It was as if her sharper ears had heard a sound. But before he could ask her what was wrong, he too heard a low faint scratching.

By then she had already acted. Sifting again through the keys, she walked swiftly over to the locked door and, without another word, unlocked it and then disappeared behind it; in the moment before the door swung shut, in the spill of light from the foyer in which they were standing, he saw or thought he saw a huddled form in the shadows, one arm reaching up.

Then the door was closed, locked. Jamie stood alone and dumbfounded. A voice, clearly Caldy More's, grew louder beyond the door. Certain words reached his ear with astonishing clarity. He heard her say, "You shouldn't be here. How in the name of God did you get out? Come along, now. No trouble, please," and the sound of a faint struggle. A few moments later there was an urgent low command and a soft whimper as from an animal. Then silence.

He waited a minute, until he was certain they had gone, then he stepped back from the door, though still staring intently at it, as though he longed to see through it.

So engrossed was he with the incident and his apparent close proximity to the young woman herself that he failed to hear the footsteps approaching from behind.

"Are you lost, Mr. Pask?"

He whirled around at the sound of Geoffrey Bledding's voice and confronted the man, avoiding his eyes. "No, sir. I just left Caldy More. The tour was most satisfactory. I —was—"

Bledding nodded and smiled, seemed aware of his confusion and seemed curiously eager to put him at ease. "I told you she knows more about the hall than I do." He smiled. "Now I'm afraid that her other duties are calling. You see, in addition to being a very effective tour guide, she also serves me in a private capacity."

Jamie nodded, still unsettled by the man's sudden appearance. "I understand," he murmured, and tried to step around the man. "If you'll excuse me, I'll—"

Again Bledding smiled warmly. "Of course. I do believe they are serving tea in the dining room. Please help yourself. You must come to look on Bledding Sorrow as your home."

Still moving away, Jamie assured him that he would and thanked him again for his kindness.

"One thing more, Mr. Pask." Again the man stopped him, his hand extended. "I've asked Peter Endicott to meet you in the garden around five thirty, if that's convenient. Now, remember, the man is deaf as a post, so you may have to shout."

There was a long silence. Geoffrey Bledding moved forward, as though he wanted to see clearly the whole of Jamie's face. His expression was almost calm, as though what he was about to say was of the utmost importance. "Mr. Pask," he began, "your duties this summer will take you to the dining room, my office, your room on the third floor, and the public gardens. A simple route. No need to deviate. Is that clear?"

Jamie nodded.

"Then, do go have your cup of tea." And with that the man turned toward the door, withdrew keys from his pocket, unlocked it, and disappeared.

And it *was* clear. Jamie had heard and understood all too well. In effect, what the man had told him was stay away from this door, this part of the hall.

He continued to stand a moment longer, his hands shoved into his pockets, staring at the door as though at any moment it might swing open in revelation. But of course he knew it wouldn't, and there was always the possibility that whatever was going on behind the door was none of his business, absolutely none of his concern. Like the native-born Englishman that he was, he had a deep respect for an individual's right to privacy, the freedom to conduct his life in any way that he saw fit, providing, of course, that in the process the same rights of others were not infringed on.

Perhaps he had been merely melodramatic from the beginning. That the young woman was suffering intensely was clear, but how was it his concern and what could he possibly do about it? Two very simple questions with no answers.

He looked at the door a moment longer, on the verge of putting everything out of his mind. He was an employee, nothing more. He had been hired to perform a service, not to play Sherlock Holmes.

While he was not altogether satisfied with this rationale, it seemed to make sense. The young woman, whoever she was, was already lost. That he wanted very much to catch another glimpse of her was beside the point. That he was also incapable of blotting from his mind the scene that he had witnessed earlier in the garden was beside the point. For now a good bracing cup of hot tea would put him in fine fettle for his meeting with the deaf gardener.

The terrible thing was that even as he turned his back on the door and walked away through the labyrinth of rooms back to the central corridor, he could still see her.

Yet something else had also changed. It was some moments before Jamie realized what it was. From the upper recesses of the hall, so faint he could scarcely hear it, there came the sound of a woman's cry. There was no one else in the corridor to hear it, so for a moment he wasn't sure whether or not he had imagined it.

But the sound of it or, rather, the echo of the sound was so piercing in his ear that he forgot about the cup of tea and took the steps three at a time, intent only on reaching the privacy of his room. His sense of order had been profoundly disturbed. The great immutable rural Yorkshire peace was a fantasy. He had never felt such discontent, a restless questioning amounting almost to a continuous agony.

At the third-floor landing he broke into a run as though he were attempting to outrace the splintered feelings, the sense of malevolence, the now suspect stillness.

Inside his room he closed and bolted the door and leaned against it. Even as he turned away to his bed, the plaintive cry came again. And he hurled himself full length on the bed and buried his head beneath the pillow.

But still he did not guess. . . .

⨾ꞈⳐ⟨ 18 ⟩Ⳑꞈ⨾

Nor did Ann—but in this case how could she?—guess what had happened when the voices inside her head grew to such inordinate proportions that in order to escape them, she feebly left her bed and found the door unlocked and ran stumbling down the hall, then the steps, tripping on the long white muslin gown, her hands pressed tightly over her ears, falling painfully now and then as the voices increased, filling her head with thoughts, images, visions, each more fearful than the one before, of human butchery and cruelty, of imprisonment and death. And one voice predominant above all others, a woman's voice, the same woman she'd seen in the garden, pitiably dragging herself along the garden path. But this time the woman had appeared to her as in a fog, only her head and upper torso visible, the rest of her, the actual source and cause of her agony, obscured in swirling mists. This same woman had banished all the other specters, had started, softly at first, merely pleading with Ann, urging her to flee. And ultimately the gentle pleadings had given way to a kind of hysteria, shrieking at her then, commanding her to escape, to find the downstairs door beyond which at this very moment stood a man who could help her.

So desperate was the woman that Ann had obeyed, had no choice but to obey. But just as she had reached the door and the promise of help, the spectral woman had disappeared into the swirling mists. And lacking direction then and, in a way, confidence, Ann had fallen and had remained fallen.

Caldy More found her and, scolding, helped her back upstairs and did not seem to hear her when Ann begged openly, though incoherently, for the pills which would put her to sleep, silence at least for the time being the hideous voices inside her head.

Instead she now felt herself being placed on the bed again, felt her arms being pulled gently over her head, heard someone's continuous apology as her wrists were secured to the iron bedstead with long strips of muslin. Thus she lay in full view of the two figures at the bedroom door.

Suddenly a phantom's dark figure appeared before her. It was moaning as though in acute pain. She tried not to look at it, but gazed instead toward those two surprised pairs of eyes at the door.

"It was locked," a voice insisted. "I know it was locked. I have no idea how she got out."

"It must not happen again."

"How do you plan to prevent it?"

"Martin Axtell is coming tonight."

Then the pain-ridden phantom closed in on her. The air felt hot on her face. There was thunder in the night or in her head.

In shock and terror, she lost consciousness. . . .

❦ 19 ❧

The mulch was damp and dark and rich-looking. Jamie spaded it this way and that around the rose bushes, enjoying the sound and feel of it, clearly enjoying the warmth of sun on his back and his close proximity to the walled private garden. Now and then his hand trembled with eagerness as he lightly touched the pocket of his shirt, wherein lay his plan.

Pressing his lips together, he took a deep breath through his nostrils and sank the spade into the mound of mulch which Peter Endicott had deposited near the rose gardens. From where he stood it was less than twenty yards to the wall. The spade rested against the earth as he turned quickly over his shoulder and surveyed the gardens. Empty. The old man was nowhere in sight. He had grumbled continuously at Jamie for missing the five-thirty appointment the previous day. Hunchbacked and hairless, he then had dragged the plastic bags filled with mulch to the garden path, had brusquely tossed the shovel in Jamie's direction, and had limped off toward the far woods, a bottle protruding from the rear pocket of his soiled, dirt-encrusted trousers. Now, Jamie hoped, he was deep in the woods and deeper into his bottle.

Working more rapidly now, he spread the mulch around the bushes and patted it into place, listening for the first sound of life behind the wall. He felt again the folded piece of paper in his pocket, newly aware of the enormous chance he was taking, not at all certain that the plan would work, even less certain that his idea of the night before was even worthy of the name plan.

Still, he had to try. In spite of the morning with the brightness of sun and the excitement of the moment at hand, he still felt a degree of bewilderment and confusion. Why he was here and what he was doing and what he hoped to accomplish remained enormous question marks. All he knew was that he *had* to be here, that there was no place else in the world where he belonged, and that beyond the garden wall was a source of agony and unhappiness that could not be ignored, that, indeed, demanded his attention.

Again he felt a curious sense of company, of not being alone, of spirits which he could not see, of eyes watching, ears listening, certain wills more powerful than anything he had ever experienced in his life directing him, guiding him, forcing him to fulfill a destiny that was his yet not his.

These thoughts and feelings continued to assault his conscious mind. And while he could not understand them, he also knew that he could not dismiss them. Then, moving more slowly, he lifted another spadeful of mulch, deposited it, then sent the spade back for more, a faint rhythm creeping into his actions, listening, always listening.

Then he heard it, the sound of the back door being opened. He raised up from his labors, frozen now, his eyes riveted on the earth at his feet, looking at but not seeing his mud-covered shoes.

There were no voices, at least none that he heard, although he was aware of movement behind the wall, the sound of steps on gravel revealing the passage of feet.

In the fundamental silence of the morning he was still plagued with doubts and certain misgivings, futile exercises really, like a man halfway across a tightrope wondering if he has done the right thing. That there would be a price to pay he had no doubt. What he couldn't glimpse clearly was the outline of that price.

Now he heard a voice behind the wall, someone giving instructions over and over again, in a slow aggravating way, setting limitations, mild threats.

Then it was over. The voice faded and was replaced

by the firm tread of footsteps on gravel, the springs of a door squeaked open, then shut. Then a heavier inner door was closed. He even heard the metallic scrape of a lock and key.

He stood foolishly staring at earth, pleased by the new silence, yet unable to move. He waited a moment, then lifted his head, his eyes falling easily on the copper beech tree at the end of the wall.

By all his reckoning, it was time now for him to advance. The folded piece of paper was still in his pocket, the outer gardens were empty, the walled garden clearly occupied, its prisoner having been punctually deposited within the confinement.

Then he forced himself forward, moving quickly but stealthily to the wall, then feeling his way down it as though he were a blind man, coming at last to the trunk of the copper beech. The atmosphere through which he moved seemed to announce a far deeper reality than the one he had sensed before, as though the very morning air, the sky, the wall were urging him on.

At the trunk of the tree he stopped, again looked quickly about, then reached up for the low branch that enabled him to get a foothold on the tree itself. As his hands grasped the top of the wall, he paused again, listening, before he dared to emerge headfirst into the view from the garden.

And then he saw her.

It was a sight similar in nature to the first time except now she was not sitting in the garden path, but rather on the stone bench a short distance away, like a small girl, her feet drawn up from the morning's chill, her head turned away from him and lightly resting on her shoulder. He noticed that her eyes were open, yet fixed on a spot near the center of the grass, one hand resting limply in her lap, the other weakly supporting the angle of her body.

Jamie eased himself up onto the wall, always keeping well behind the safe protection of branches, but totally unable to take his eyes off her. There rose in him an inextinguishable desire to protect. So sharply did it come upon him that ultimately he tore his eyes away from her for fear that he would immediately leap to the ground and go to her side, not considering the consequences either to her or to himself.

He felt himself, under the second impact of the sight of her, like a man drowning. He needed help. There was no possible way that he could reach her, signal her, and, more remote still, communicate with her. If his plan was to work at all, she would have to move, would have to drag herself from the stone bench and walk the length of the garden to the spot where he had first seen her.

But now, as he studied her, she gave no indication of movement. The stillness about her was even deeper today than the day before. In fact in the few minutes that he had been watching her, he had noticed that even her eyes had failed to blink. Her gaze, so rigidly fixed on nothing, was set, as though for all time.

Then she moved.

He sat up, newly alert, as he saw her slowly lower her feet to the ground. Bare feet they were again, as the day before, small, white, childlike feet, toes slightly pointed in their long descent from the bench to earth, feet firmly clasped together until they touched the ground, then tentatively spreading as though struggling to provide a base of support.

She sat now with both palms pressed against the bench, as though lacking all confidence in her ability to support herself. Her head fell forward; one hand moved up in a light gesture across her forehead as though she were dizzy and struggling to remain in an upright position.

He watched with held breath, continuing to fight the incredible urge to go to her side, to assist her with whatever weakness was undermining her. Now, through the russet-colored leaves, he saw her start to stand; her head and shoulders moved forward, but the rest of the body seemed to refuse to follow. She wavered for a moment in a half-raised position, her hands reaching out on either side for something of support. Then, as though she had no choice, she sat weakly back down on the bench and covered her face with her hands, her body curled in on itself in a position of utter despair.

Jamie was silent, watching. She seemed worse today, seemed weaker. Then the battle was on again. He could see clearly the strain of effort on her face as again she pushed herself forward off the bench, the hands grasping at nothing, at anything, the feet spread wide now in a broad base of support until finally, triumphantly she stood erect, not quite erect, but at least upright.

Now slowly, painfully she commenced the simple process of walking as though she were an infant just learning to master the feat. Her head was continuously down as though it was necessary for her to check each step for barriers and obstacles. Exerting what was clearly a maximum effort, she made her way to the garden path, then stopped.

She looked slowly toward the back door as though fearful that she was being watched. She held her position a moment longer, her right hand pressed against her side directly beneath her breast, as though she were experiencing a mild discomfort and was forced to wait it out before she dared to attempt the hazard of further movement.

Silently Jamie urged her on, knew without knowing how he knew that she was coming toward him if only her will and stamina held out. As he watched her, he remembered, irrelevantly, the time he had been in the hospital about six years ago with pneumonia. He remembered the sensation of being sedated, of trying to lift himself from his bed so he could go to the bathroom and avoid the indignities of the bedpan. In his drugged state the world then had suddenly gone topsyturvy. Now, as he watched the young woman, he recalled those sensations clearly.

Drugged? Perhaps. But why? And by whom? Now, as he looked back down on her, she stood at the edge of the garden path, alert and tense, yet pitifully weak. She appeared to be tearful now, like a child in pain, her hands moving slowly through the air in front of her, the body following reluctantly, her feet never clearing the ground, but rather propelling her forward in a shuffling movement.

Jamie's face grew dark, his eyes glazed in compassion for the silent, suffering, and struggling woman. Time was slipping by. It was midmorning. He heard the sounds of light traffic coming from the road in front of Bledding Sorrow, occasionally heard a distant voice, heard all this but was scarcely aware of anything except the solitary battle being waged in the garden below.

Near the end of the wall where the path turned and led to the copper beech, she stopped again. She was so close now he could see perspiration on her forehead. The morning was growing hot. He could hear her breathing. The gray smock dress, hideously oversized, hung limply down about her thin body. Her hands, trembling, reached out on either side, as though she were incapable of going another step.

So great was his sympathy for her that he whispered aloud, "Please come closer." The words were no louder than an exhalation of breath. But he had reason to believe that she had heard them.

Her arms, reaching out on either side, suddenly froze. If she hadn't in fact heard his whispered command to come closer, she now clearly sensed him. Her face lifted. She looked so small standing beneath him, no less than ten feet away.

He grew brave and moved closer to the edge of the wall. "This way," he whispered. "It's not far. Please—"

Never had she looked so terrorized as now when her eyes darted, unseeing, to the top of the copper beech.

Fearful that he was causing her greater alarm, he saw no alternative but to speak aloud, to try to put her at ease and coax her forward the few remaining feet to the spot directly beneath the wall where he sat.

There was a considerable pause, then he whispered, "Can you see me? Here on the wall. Near the tree."

Again she raised her face and appeared to be gazing through and beyond the tree. He had a good look at her now. A beautiful face with delicate features, but it had grown like a mask, as though all inner fire had been quenched. The skin was white and smooth, the hair fair but unkempt. She evidently wanted very much to see who had spoken, and yet she seemed unable to move.

"This way," he whispered again. "Remember? I was here yesterday. You saw me. I didn't hurt you then, did I? I won't hurt you now."

Then, to his surprise and extreme pleasure, she was moving again, torturously dragging herself down the path until she stopped directly beneath him. As though following his orders, he watched as she slipped to her knees on the rough gravel, then readjusted herself in a sitting position, identical to the one she had assumed the day before.

Once she was settled on the path, he saw her fold her hands neatly and place them in her lap, watched as she pulled the gray smock dress down over her legs and feet until at last she sat quietly beneath him. A portion of her fear seemed to have diminished. No longer visibly alarmed, she now appeared merely obedient, as though she were accustomed to following orders. Suddenly she looked as though a feeling of great weariness were creeping over her, as though the short walk had left her bereft of strength. Her head fell forward.

"No!" he warned strongly, daring to raise his voice. "You mustn't sleep now. Look at me. Look directly above you."

Then she was doing it, her head lifting, her brow creased as she searched through the leaves and found him. Their eyes met. Too late to go back the same way. In the sight of her face, upturned toward him, he felt like a man released from every bond. He smiled. "Will you talk with me for a while?"

She continued to look at him, bewilderment on her face. He did not want to force his presence on her, but he felt certain that their time was limited. He was still uncertain how much she would understand, but decided to speak to her as though she were perfectly capable of complete comprehension. Buoyed by the fact that she did not now seem afraid and that she had not yet averted her face, he asked softly, "What's your name?"

She did not move. The shadows on her face remained unaltered.

He waited a moment, then said, "My name is James. James Pask. Can you remember that?"

A sudden sharp wind took a wisp of her hair and blew it forward. Still she sat beneath him, looking up, unresponsive, unmoving. For some reason he thought of the wheels in a clockwork which had been wound too tight and now, for all eternity, had been stopped.

He looked quickly toward the back door to reassure himself that they were still alone. Then carefully he reached into his pocket and withdrew the folded piece of paper. He stared at it a moment, then gazed back down on the small, blank, upturned face beneath him. He said softly, "I brought you something. Can you catch it?" And with that, he dropped the small white square of paper and watched intently as it fluttered down, landing only inches from where she sat.

For the first time she looked away from him as she, too, watched the progress of the folded paper. She continued to stare at it for several moments after it had touched ground.

"Go on," he urged softly. "Pick it up. It's for you."

Hesitantly at first, then almost docilely she obeyed, one thin hand starting forward, pausing a moment, then going the full distance, touching the paper first, then finally lifting it, returning it to her lap.

Jamie sat on the wall, his legs beginning to cramp at the awkward angle of his position, yet totally fascinated by the small, obedient figure beneath him. In a curious way, he disliked her readiness to obey, yet for the moment, at least, he would have to exploit it. He still had a great desire to reach down and lift her up, to feed her from his own strength.

But he contented himself with staring down on her, softly urging her now to "Open it. It's for you. I copied it just for you. Last night."

Slowly, though predictably, her hands followed his instructions. Thrice folded, the sheet of paper began to enlarge in her lap. He could still see that her hands were trembling and noticed now for the first time red raw chafed places about her wrists, as though she had recently been bound.

Strange that in such a quiet moment he felt an incredible surge of anger. Still there was the visible certainty before his eyes.

He saw now that the piece of paper was opened in her lap. She seemed to be staring at it. Whether or not she was reading it was impossible to tell. Her hair continued to blow lightly over her face, and he saw again how beautiful she was, how beautiful and dreamlike the play of wind in her hair, how beautiful the fall of the thin gray dress over her young limbs.

"Can you read it?" he asked gently. "Shall I repeat the words and you can follow them on the page?"

Without waiting for a reply which he felt certain would never come, he began quoting the passages he had found in one of his books the night before, seeing her in them, wanting somehow to share them with her, wanting her to see what happened when pen touched paper instead of merely floating above it, as hers had done the day before.

He kept his voice low and even as he spoke; he concentrated on how the wind streamed through the loose hair beside her pale cheek. He spoke slowly and watched closely to see what, if any, effect the poem had on her:

> She dwelt among the untrodden ways,
> Beside the springs of Dove,
> A maid whom there were none to praise
> And very few to love.

Her breathing seemed to have increased. Feebly she lifted one hand to her forehead as though experiencing an increase in suffering.

Still he spoke on, moving word by word through the simple verse:

> A violet by a mossy stone
> Half hidden from the eye!—
> Fair as a star, when only one
> Is shining in the sky.

Suddenly she bowed her head low. He heard a curious sharp intake of breath. The paper rested in her lap, its corner lightly lifted by the breeze.

There was a long silence. He had hoped she might look up at him. But she remained staring downward, her face hidden.

"Do you understand the words?" he asked gently.

Slowly she nodded. A new tension seemed to be building within her. One hand reached out flat against the earth as though it had threatened to rise up against her. Something was pulling within her. Then he heard the softest of sobs, saw tears on her face. Her eyes lifted to him. Though wet and sorrowful, they shone with a light he had never seen before. As though with the greatest of efforts, her lips moved, came together, formed one brief, scarcely audible word.

"Poem," she said.

He had brought himself perilously near to tears. He nodded and repeated, "Poem."

Then she looked back down at the paper, carefully lifted it, and in a childlike gesture gently pressed it against her cheek, rocking slowly back and forth.

He averted his face for a moment. When he looked

back down, she appeared to be studying the words again. Still he fought off the strong urge to jump down to her side. Instead he whispered, "Please tell me your name. We can talk like this again, but I must know your name. I'll bring you another poem tomorrow if you like."

Again she looked up at him, and again their eyes met. In a thin but clear voice she murmured, "Ann."

A simple name, simply spoken, yet the word mattered less than the depth of feeling behind it, and this one seemed to come out of her whole being. For a long moment she continued to stare at him, something of the helpless outrage in her soul reflected in her eyes. Then, with an acute abruptness, she lowered her head again, as though not wanting him to see too much.

He hesitated one last second. His greatest enemy was time. The luxury of a prolonged interval alone with her was out of the question. He knew that she was closely watched and guarded. Yet so many questions remained in his head. "Ann," he called softly down, "do you come here every morning?"

But she did not answer and he saw that she had slipped into some kind of reverie, a trance. Although she still held the piece of paper in her hand, her eyes, the bulk of her attention seemed to be concentrated on the base of the wall directly beneath his perch.

He spoke again, more urgently this time. "Ann, listen to me." His voice was rising in an attempt to jar her out of the isolation to which she was clinging. "I must know if you come here every morning. I must know if it's the same time. Otherwise how can I—"

But she had drifted off far beyond his reach. From where he sat he saw her eyes glazed, her mouth slightly open, a hollowness that could not be penetrated.

With deep remorse he let her go. She looked exhausted as though their brief meeting had drained her completely. Once she shifted ever so slightly on the path, but the movement was not significant, and nothing altered on her face.

He watched her thus for what seemed hours, but what was in reality only ten or fifteen minutes. He found continuous pleasure even in her silent company. All further questions would have to wait. But he was a patient man and the summer loomed large ahead of him. He wasn't going anywhere and neither was she; of that he was absolutely certain.

Still, something in him faltered now and then, rage perhaps or more truly outrage that a human being could be reduced to such a pitiful state. Perhaps Caldy More had been right. Better death. Far better, death.

Yet something within her persisted in spite of what was being done to her, and he would gamble on that tiny spark of life, court it as assiduously as he had ever courted anything in his life, try with all the effort and will at his command to feed it and thus resurrect her, bring her back from the cold, silent, withdrawn world in which she presently existed.

Suddenly he heard a sound. He looked up toward the back door and saw the set face of Caldy More. She stood for a moment, holding the door ajar, surveying the small garden.

Trapped! Quickly he considered and dismissed the idea of jumping down from the wall. By his action he would only call attention to himself and thus be discovered. He tried quietly to rearrange the branches for greater protection. But he feared it was useless. Anyone with competent vision who cared to look up would effortlessly see him.

Caldy More still stood at the back door, one hand raised, shading her eyes against the blaze of sun. A moment later she lowered her hand, apparently having found what she was looking for, her vision resting now on the small, seated figure at the end of the garden.

There was nothing he could do but hold his position and hope that her attention, focused on the young woman, would prohibit her from looking up.

Now she was closing the door behind her, moving slowly down the path, stopping now to examine a tall delphinium, as though she were enjoying a brief respite from her duties, in no particular hurry.

Suddenly he saw movement directly beneath him, saw Ann stir herself out of her lethargy and look slowly over her shoulder in the direction of Caldy More. Then she looked quickly up at him where he sat atop the wall. She stared at him for a moment, terrified, as though she perceived his potential danger. Then she was on her knees, struggling even more than ever under the duress of speed for balance, making visibly difficult efforts to control herself, still grasping the piece of paper in her hand, thus denying herself one limb of support, scrambling now on all fours, animallike, in an obvious attempt to head off Caldy More.

She made it as far as the end of the path, where suddenly the gray smock dress tripped her, caught under one knee, and sent her sprawling into the rough gravel.

Caldy More rushed to her side, lifted her up into a sitting position. "No need to hurry," she scolded.

She examined the palm of one hand, brushed away the dirt and sand, then reached for the other hand. As she opened it, the piece of paper, wadded now, fell out onto the grass.

Ann looked at her, the terror in her eyes increasing.

"And what have we here?" Caldy More asked, still in the manner of humoring the girl.

As Caldy More picked up the paper and smoothed it out, Jamie saw Ann bow her head, as though forcing herself not to look back at him.

Caldy More read in silence, then looked sharply at her. "Where did you get this?" she demanded.

The young woman did not move or respond in any way.

"You didn't write this," Caldy More persisted, her voice growing hard. "Now, where did you get it?"

When the girl refused to answer, Caldy More looked sharply around the garden, her eyes scanning the lower part of the brick wall, but staying safely away from the upper part.

Jamie continued to hold his breath, afraid even to breathe, lest he be heard.

Still Caldy More questioned her. "Look at me," she ordered now, and when the girl refused to obey, Caldy More jerked her hands down and held them rigidly by the wrists.

Jamie felt himself inching involuntarily forward on the wall. Again he stopped. He could not. He could not. . . .

Caldy More then stood up. Again she quickly surveyed the interior of the garden, alarm spreading over her face, her eyes still lingering on the lower part of the wall, as though it had never occurred to her that someone might scale it.

At Caldy More's feet Ann shivered visibly in the heat. She tried once to rise, but Caldy More merely pushed her back down. "You are going nowhere," she scolded, "until you tell me where you got this. I have all the time in the world, and so do you." The old woman straightened up, still holding the paper in her hand. She looked about. "I'll sit here on the bench in the shade, and you stay there. In the sun. When you feel like talking, I'll be here to listen."

Slowly she made her way to the stone bench about ten feet away from where Ann sat on the grass in the blaze of high sun approaching noon.

Jamie watched as her head sank even lower, saw her still shivering in spite of the heat.

Something howled within him. He watched Caldy More as she settled herself comfortably on the bench in the shade, still examining the piece of paper, as though it were a threat, as though she had perhaps failed to see and recognize an important clue concerning its source. Only occasionally did she glance down at the suffering young woman and even then her face was void of any trace of pity. Twice she asked in a dull monotone, "Where did you get this?" and twice receiving no answer, she merely settled herself in a new position on the stone bench, clearly signaling that she was prepared to wait as long as was necessary.

The noon sun rose higher, dissipating the coolness of morning. Jamie's eyes, fixed so intently, began to see the scene shimmering under a mirage of heat waves. Never once did the young woman protest her punishment. Never once did she make any move to disobey the stern-faced woman who sat in the shade watching. But he noticed that as her discomfort increased, she became restless. He saw her lift a hand and feebly brush away an insect drawn close by the smell of sweat.

Still minutes passed. The moisture on the gray dress spread into a dark circle which extended over the thin back and disappeared beneath her arms. The heat, while not very great in the comfort of shade, was incredibly harsh on a pale fair complexion in unrelieved exposure.

"Are you ready to tell me where you got this?" Caldy More demanded again. "Your lunch is waiting and the kitchen is cool. When you are ready—"

But the young woman was weaving now as though drunk. She fell forward, braced herself, tried again to straighten up, then fell finally to one side, face up, her arms limp, eyes closed, her face glistening with moisture.

Suddenly he saw Caldy More sit up as though to get a better look at the still figure before her. She stared for a moment as though her will had been thwarted in some way. "Well, the matter isn't closed," she said angrily. "Don't think for a moment that it is."

Then she strode forward, bent over, and with the violence of determined unforgiveness, she jerked the young woman upward, supported the limp body against her own, awkwardly dragging her toward the back door, talking all the time, scolding her for not being capable of walking, shouting at her once, "Stand up!" grasping her again about the waist, then both of them disappeared into the hall.

Jamie stared straight ahead as he saw the back door close. He had a desire to cry out. Yet curiously he felt paralyzed both physically and psychologically. His most powerful, yet also his most despicable argument was that he had failed to go to her aid because to do so would have been to destroy all hope of future contact with her. But this did nothing to still his almost unbearable sense of guilt.

Then he forced himself to climb down from his perch, welcoming the agony of cramped muscles, the tendons in his legs objecting to the sudden activity, a burst of punishment like a criminal receiving justice.

He knew clearly what he had just witnessed, and he knew with equal clarity that he would return the following morning and the morning thereafter and the morning thereafter, not because he particularly wanted to but because he had no choice.

As he looked back at the garden wall, he had to muster all his willpower to suppress the desire to scale the red bricks again. But the garden was quiet now. The private agony had been moved to some place blessedly beyond his realm of sight and sound. But it would be back and he would nevertheless wait and go on waiting.

As he turned from his place in the shade near the base of the garden wall, he thought he saw movement out of the corner of his eye. There it was, about twenty feet away near the edge of the woods. Swiveling his head quickly about, he perceived a bright glow, an illumination stronger than the sun, though falling in shadows.

Jamie pushed backward against the wall, his eyes burning from the powerful illumination. Suddenly, out of the center of the brightness, stepped a man. Jamie tried to turn away but could not, held in some fascination and considerable fear over what he was seeing.

The specter wore a black cape, its hood raised, but nothing was visible inside the hood, a terrifying vacuum. Yet the vision was communicating with him, sending a discernible message with his hand, which he now held upright, as though forbidding Jamie to come closer. Again he lifted that one white hand in Jamie's direction, now more urgent, moving it rigidly back and forth through the air, as though urging him away. He made this gesture three times in all. Then suddenly the wind increased, causing the black cape to flutter. The illumination began to fade, the specter growing smaller until at last he disappeared, leaving Jamie staring fearfully, mouth agape, his heart beating too rapidly, his hands trembling.

He stared a moment longer at the spot where the figure had disappeared, as though he expected it to reappear without warning. But the woods were merely woods now, dark, quiet, forboding. It was several moments before he could stir himself out of the spell cast by the vision. Finally he shook his head. Had it been an optical illusion, brought on by his own sense of disquiet, by the memory of what he had witnessed within the walled garden? Perhaps. At least it was gone now.

Now, as he approached the outer gardens and the mulch and the spade, fallen where he had dropped it, he thought again of the young woman who had shared two words with him and who had suffered the consequences of their meeting and, in her silence, had kept him safe.

His fingers gripped the handle of the spade so tightly that when his left foot, in a sudden convulsive movement, lifted and pushed against the steel rim, the wood splintered and the spade broke in half. . . .

ᨢᨡ 20 ᨢᨡ

Martin Axtell loathed intensely having to touch the woman. She always smelled of urine and soiled linen. Now, here he was again. Twice in one week. Really! Geoffrey was extracting a high price for the occasional game which he shot on the Bledding Sorrow estates.

Now, to add insult to injury, Geoffrey had not even deigned to put in an appearance. It had been Caldy More who had greeted him at the door, Caldy More who had escorted him up to the private wing, and Caldy More who now stood a safe distance away while he, Martin Axtell, was forced to deal with the thin, sunburned female on the bed.

Now he leaned closer and lightly touched her forehead. It was true, she did appear feverish. But it was also true that the young woman appeared to be quite sunburned.

"I said a *little* sun, Caldy More," he scolded over his shoulder. "She looks as though she has crossed the Sahara."

Receiving no answer, he raised up from his position over the bed and glared directly at the tall, silent woman by the door. "Did you hear me?" he demanded.

"I heard," came the sharp reply.

He continued to look at her a moment longer, saw only what he always saw when he looked at Caldy More, a vengeful, sly, illogical, treacherous, unscrupulous, and self-seeking woman, which was probably why Geoffrey had kept her around all these years. At least she was predictable and consistent.

Then he turned wearily back to the woman on the bed. A wasted specimen, if he ever saw one. Her flaming red cheeks merely accented the hollows of her eyes. Terror seemed to be her only response, and the question of the decade, in Martin Axtell's mind, was why did Geoffrey Bledding insist on keeping her around? It would be such a simple matter to institutionalize her and be rid of her. Which brought him to the even more interesting question of Geoffrey Bledding himself, an heir to a family of sheepherders which had failed to produce one remarkable man in more than seven hundred years. He smiled faintly. Genetically, that, too, was a puzzler.

Martin's face that evening expressed a noble, mildly offended air. If he was going to be summoned up the lane every evening, he at least expected to be received by the master himself. Now he pinched his lips together in abject rejection of all that he saw. It was the lack of respectability that gave him offense. The woman, the tiny upper bedchamber, for that matter, the whole hall needed a severe cleansing with the harshest of disinfectants. Strangers meant germs, and classless strangers meant the most virulent germs of all. He felt degraded, put upon, debased. Also he felt snubbed.

He noticed now that the dark blue eyes on the bed were watching him. He moved slightly to the right. The eyes followed. "Is she awake?" he called back to Caldy More.

"Partially. I haven't given her any medicine since noon."

"Why?"

"She hasn't needed it. She knows I'm angry with her. And she's always quiet when I'm angry."

He raised up now, but not too swiftly, in case he might stir the woman to violence. He found it amusing, Caldy More's insistence that the demented creature was capable of such a rational emotion as remorse. "And why does she think you're angry with her?" he asked, not bothering to hide his amusement.

Caldy More stepped forward as though adroitly she were about to seize her chance. Slowly she took from the pocket of her dress a small, folded piece of paper. "I found this in the garden with her this morning. She refuses to tell me where she got it."

The paper was soiled, gave evidence of having been wadded. Martin took it gingerly between his fingers and shook it open to avoid undue contact. He read the maudlin, second-rate lines written in a strong, bold scrawl, then dropped it quickly on the table beside the bed. "Wordsworth at his worst," he muttered. He glanced again at Caldy More. "So what's the mystery? She probably copied it herself."

Caldy More shook her head. "She's scarcely able to hold a pencil, let alone form words." She shook her head adamantly. "No, someone gave it to her and she refuses to say who."

Martin suddenly had a dazzling and heavenly vision; the young woman was dead, Caldy More was discharged, the adult college was closed, and he and Geoffrey were alone in the Queen's bedchamber. It was a comforting vision, the kind he frequently had when the banality of the moment threatened to overwhelm.

"So what exactly is it, Caldy More, that you want me to do?" he asked wearily, desiring only to flee the stinking little room and the repulsive female presences.

"Examine her," she said bluntly.

"For what?"

"She's hot."

"She's sunburned. The next time you want to extract information from her, find a way to do it in the shade."

Caldy More seemed to accept this for a moment, then she moved closer. "And about the medicine?"

Martin was really on the verge of losing all patience. "And what about the medicine?" he demanded. "I'm summoned when it's too weak, and I'm summoned when it's too strong." He stepped away from the bed to the narrow window in the hope of finding a stray fresh breeze of night air. But the window was shut, nailed closed. He turned back, still feeling that Geoffrey was being grossly unfair. "It's a simple case, Caldy More. But you must make up your mind. She's insane. And there's not a great deal that anyone can do about it. She could be sent to hospital, but as we both know, there is strong, albeit mystifying objection to that logical course of action. So now we have two other alternatives. You can try to handle her as she is, or you can drug her. There are hazards either way. As you know, the drug we have been using is Chlorpromazine. In seven years we have gone from a benign fifteen milligrams a day to a dangerous fifteen hundred milligrams per day. We cannot increase it further or she will become totally immobile and death will be only a matter of time. But the choice is yours, not mine, although I will take no part in an increased dosage. I'm a mere medical man and a tired and hungry one. Now, if you'll excuse me—"

But Caldy More had no intention of excusing him. Quickly she stepped forward, blocking his passage to the door. "But you haven't even looked at her. Mr. Bledding said that—"

Martin interrupted angrily. "If Mr. Bledding is so concerned, why doesn't he put in an appearance?"

"He's busy this evening, giving the final lecture to the art league. He asked me to—" She shifted her ground and gave him a solemn, almost pleading look. "Isn't there something in between? I can't handle her when she's totally drugged, and I can't run the risk of—" She broke off. "She's my responsibility, Dr. Axtell."

"You have my deepest sympathy," he said.

There was a silence. He looked back at the young woman on the bed. Mystifying. Really mystifying. Why did Geoffrey insist on keeping her around? She exhibited no more life than the bed on which she was lying.

Suddenly he had an idea, a bizarre one, but nonetheless one worthy of scientific investigation. Slowly he walked back to the bed. He pulled down the coverlet and, using only his thumb and forefinger to avoid undue contact with her flesh, he unbuttoned the muslin gown and laid her body bare.

He heard her give a sharp intake of air. A moment later he saw a faint trembling pass over her body. In truth there wasn't much there. Her upper torso resembled a young boy's, no sign of those enormous mammaries that men are supposed to enjoy but which he found totally vulgar.

Still he drew a deep breath, then put his idea into words. "Does Mr. Bledding use her sexually in any way?" he asked, point-blank.

The sudden and clamorous silence behind him almost provided him with his answer. He looked back, saw the old woman struggling with her protest. "I—I don't know what you're talking about," she murmured.

"Of course you know," he countered. "You, I suspect, know better than anyone." He saw her hands, slightly raised, now motionless, and under her eyes on the projecting cheekbones showed two brick-red spots.

He needed no words. He had his answer. He continued to stare down at the woman on the bed. So! If in seven hundred years the Bledding family had failed to produce one remarkable man, they were certainly consistent in their ability to produce depravity. No wonder there were such strenuous objections to sending her to the hospital. What tales these walls could tell, he thought, looking up and about him.

On the bed he noticed now that the woman's head was thrown backward, every muscle in the thin body tensed, as though expecting the worst. Signs of human life were beginning to appear in her. One hand moved timidly up to cover a breast. Geoffrey's toy, undrugged since noon, was beginning to stir. He would find no docile and ready release this night.

Suddenly he had a brilliant idea, so brilliant that for a moment he felt temporarily breathless. "It is my medical opinion," Martin now began, but did not finish his sentence and turned away. His face slowly flushed, his eyes closed, while his lips involuntarily smiled. "First, cover her," he ordered with a backward wave of his hand.

For a moment Caldy More hesitated, then he heard her step forward, heard the gown being closed, the coverlet spread into place.

When it was quiet again, he looked back, saw the old woman's cheeks pale now, the pupils of her eyes imperceptibly broadened. He had touched a live nerve. Bledding's nanny knew a great deal.

"It is my medical opinion," he went on, "that for a period of time she should be taken off the drug altogether. We are accomplishing nothing. Perhaps over the years we have wrongly diagnosed her illness. She may be perfectly capable of rehabilitation. Certainly in the name of humanity, I think we should try."

Now he paused a moment, pleased with even the echo of his little speech. Humanity was always a good ploy, especially with a stupid woman like Caldy More.

He noticed that the old woman looked as though her heart had fallen and frozen in trepidation and horror. "No—medicine at all?" she repeated incredulously.

"Why not?" He smiled. "Let's just try it. If I remember correctly, the art league is leaving tomorrow. The new group is not coming in until Monday. The hall will be fairly empty for two days. If it doesn't work, we can always go back to the medicine."

He shrugged now, palms up. "I was just thinking of you, Caldy More. If she is in the slightest way capable of functioning on her own, how much easier your job would be."

At this point he felt firmly assured that he had made the right decision. His only regret was that he would not be here to see it, for at that moment he had decided to spend the weekend in York. It might be very good for Geoffrey to spend two days alone with his "wife." Without the benefit of drugs he would find his toy as sharp as a knife and as incomprehensible as madness.

"Let's try it, Caldy More," he argued softly. "For your sake." His eyebrows lifted in pity. "For hers."

But Caldy More was still undecided. "Mr. Bledding will not—"

"Mr. Bledding left the problem to us," he said pointedly. "Mr. Bledding has always left the problem to us."

She nodded, unable to deny it. For a single instant a taut expression crossed her face as she glanced down at the young woman, who still lay with her head pressed backward as though not at all certain that the threat had passed. "What will she do?" Caldy More whispered, as though projecting the worst possible vision.

Again he shrugged. "Probably nothing. You may find her a most agreeable companion." He waved his hand airily in the direction of the bed. "Once Geoffrey admired her intelligence. Well, it must still be there. Somewhere. Give her a chance."

With some force now he pressed the matter to a close. "Give me what medicine you have left," he ordered. "If you like, it can be our secret. Geoffrey need never know. It will be *our* experiment, yours and mine," he added softly, trying to form an alliance with her.

Caldy More closed her eyes as though overcome by the weight of the decision. "He'll know," she whispered.

Martin thought, *Of course he will know.* "Give me the medicine," he ordered again. "Nothing very much can happen in two days. There will still be a residue of the drug in her system. She will not be a totally free agent. Now, where's the harm?"

He saw her glance fearfully toward the woman on the bed as though she were already mad and raving. There was a moment or two more of indecision, then slowly she went to the closet, unlocked it, and handed him the bottle of white pills.

Her face seemd calm now, but he sensed incredible turbulence within her. "I suggest," he said kindly, taking the drug from her, "that you say nothing to Geoffrey. No need to alarm him unduly, particularly when there may be no reaction at all." He forced himself to take her arm, a solicitous gesture designed to comfort. "It will be our secret. And if we can return to him a whole and healthy wife, how grateful he will be."

He smiled broadly and led her to the door. There he paused and called back over his shoulder to the silent young woman on the bed, "Good night, Mrs. Bledding. Sleep well," as though already she were healed and capable of a normal response.

No further words were spoken. He waited patiently in the corridor while Caldy More locked the door behind them, then followed a respectful distance behind her down the steps to the door which led to the rest of the hall.

Obviously Caldy More was still suffering as though she were committing an evil deed with a free conscience. Once the door was unlocked, Martin stepped through it and looked back to reproach her for her unfounded dread. "Believe me, we're doing the right thing," he soothed. "If we sent her to hospital, they would do precisely what we are doing, take her off all medication in order to establish the extent of her ability to respond."

In the shadows he saw her nod weakly. "What she is now isn't even human," she murmured. "She's never really had a chance."

"And we're going to provide her with one." He nodded solemnly. He made a special effort to bid her a warm good night. "I can find my way from here," he offered. "You fix yourself a cup of hot tea and put your mind at ease."

She called sharply after him. "You'll be available if we need you, Doctor?"

"Of course, of course. A phone call away." He bobbed his head in parting and started through the Great Hall. It was all he could do to keep from smiling. There was an early-morning coach to York. He would be on it. The Dean's Court Hotel had a fine dining room and a good wine cellar. It was located directly across the street from the minster, and he would pass a delightful Saturday and Sunday checking on the restoration going on there.

A sudden feeling of elation took hold of him. In the distance, in one of the study rooms, he heard Geoffrey's voice. As he drew near the door, he stopped. The man was expounding on the beautiful proportions of Bledding Sorrow and its adherence to the principles of Tudor Renaissance architecture.

Martin stepped away. The feeling of elation was growing. Indeed he felt a positive compulsion to laugh aloud. He hurried now down the central corridor as fast as his bulk would permit, clamping a pudgy hand over his mouth.

Once out in the night air, he felt the elation subside, become controllable. Now it was simply a quiet joy and a kind of amazement. How foolish of him not to have guessed before. A man whose hunger is satisfied is capable of turning his back on the finest banquet table. And in all these years he had never guessed that Geoffrey Bledding was satisfying his hunger elsewhere.

Now, as he trotted through the gatehouse arch, he stopped, breathless, and looked back at Bledding Sorrow. The symmetry even at night was beautiful. In a way he regretted his deplorable fondness for Geoffrey, regretted slightly what he had done to him. Now it was a matter of seeing the thing through. The woman had lingered far too long, interrupting both their lives. She was already dead. Now may she rest in peace. He doubted seriously if the Bledding depravity extended to necrophilia. In a few days Geoffrey would seek him out, begging him to take away the wretched creature. Then. . . .

The possibilities left him speechless. He felt suddenly warm. And, my God, he was hungry. He saw in his mind the cold leg of lamb awaiting him at home, saw himself sitting before his fire, sucking its meat and bone. Forces, powerful in their concentration, were bubbling.

Then he moved off into the night, walking steadily with face-jarring strides, toward the images that would satisfy his hunger. . . .

She was warm.

She threw back the cover and tried to find a cool spot on the pillow to soothe her face.

Ann, you're going to be late for your class. Hurry, now! Your father expects you to set a standard.

She rolled onto her side.

When are you going to let someone read your poems, Ann?

She pushed the pillow away, a little amazed at the agility of her movements. She was awake and there were voices, but they were tolerable voices, merely gently prodding ones from the past. She could endure them as long as she could identify them.

You really should try to be more outgoing, Ann. There are some nice young men.

She gazed sideways at the wall of the bedchamber. Peculiar. She'd never noticed before how ugly it was.

Can you tell me your name?

Slowly she rolled onto her back, opened her mouth for air.

You must learn to speak theoretically, Ann, to keep up on interesting conversation at table.

She rubbed her forehead, as though in an attempt to keep the voices separate.

Can you tell me your name?

Cautiously she sat up in bed, almost suspect now of her ability to perform such a simple act. She was aware for the first time in a long time of the presence of her legs, her body, her arms, the stinging burn on her face.

She looks as though she has crossed the Sahara.

Now she swung her legs over the edge of the bed.

The sudden movement almost caused her to lose her balance. But she righted herself.

Can you tell me your name?

She smiled softly. The lonely garden had been inhabited. No vision this time. He'd sat atop the garden wall. Now she lowered her gaze to the floor and watched one foot, now the other as alternately, and taking great care not to fall, she moved with measured step, covered the short distance to the table and the folded piece of paper.

Tell me where you got this. I have all the time in the world, and so do you.

Timidly she stretched out her hand and touched the paper. She saw a sun blazing around her, igniting the air and transforming it into a flaming dust. So near and so luminous the sun appeared that everything in the room seemed to vanish; it alone remained and it painted everything with its own fiery tint. It hurt her eyes. Then slowly out of the brilliance, she saw the specter of the woman again, the same woman she'd first seen in the garden. This time she was sitting on the floor near the table, her legs hidden beneath the folds of her skirts, the bloodstains dried now, their cause still a mystery, one hand moving rapidly over her invisible legs, as though she were still suffering inexplicable discomfort.

At the moment Ann spied her, the woman, too, seemed to become aware of Ann's presence. Now she looked up from her position on the floor, her fair face contorted in a weariness that went beyond mere physical fatigue, an extinction of soul and spirit, that one pale hand continuing to claw at something beneath the long skirts, as though she were on the verge of sharing some terrible secret with Ann.

Quickly Ann drew back, not wanting to see, and in the process almost lost her balance. She clung to the side of the bed, openly begging the woman to leave her alone. But the woman would not and now commenced to drag herself across the floor, moving steadily though laboriously to the side of the bed where Ann was clinging. Out of the clamor of her own terror, Ann heard clearly a high-pitched but wailing voice urging her to run away. She said it again and again, moaning the words, then raising her voice in a continuous scream, always the same command, to run, to run, to run.

Then the sight and sound of the specter could be endured no longer. Desperate with fear, Ann buried her face in the bedclothes, clung to the darkness until the wail subsided, was gradually replaced by a more familiar voice asking, *Can you tell me your name?*

Slowly she looked back toward the spot where she'd last seen the specter of the woman. Gone now. She closed her eyes in relief, a residue of fear still washing over her, blended now with bewilderment. Her other visions were disappearing. Why did this one persist?

No answer, but in the quiet of the bedchamber she heard again the soft, familiar voice of the man in the garden asking, *Can you tell me your name?*

Her hands cold, she held the paper with the poem written on it. She must behave or Caldy More would put her to sleep in the sun.

Can you tell me your name?

Had she told him her name? She couldn't remember. As long as the voices didn't scream at her, as long as she could identify them and keep them separate. . . .

She sat on the edge of the bed, gently fingering the piece of paper. She would do her best. If only they let her, she would try very hard to do her best. She would learn to speak theoretically at table, she would be more outgoing, and she would learn to be punctual.

Had she told him her name?

She couldn't remember.

But she remembered his. . . .

❧ 22 ❧

One learned to be grateful for small blessings. On awakening the following morning, Caldy More was most grateful to the Birmingham Art League. The foolish ladies had managed to keep Mr. Bledding busy until the early hours of the morning. It had been after two o'clock when she'd finally heard his step on the stairs. Poised outside her door, she'd been ready to do battle with him if he had insisted on seeing his wife. But blessedly, he had not even come up to the third floor, but instead had gone directly to his room on the second.

Now, weary herself from the long night's vigil and suffering serious misgivings over Martin Axtell's plan, she dressed, still keeping an ear turned in the direction of the bedchamber next door, confident that at any moment she would hear the first wail or blood-curdling scream of her insane and now totally undrugged charge.

She felt obscurely debased that she, Caldy More, a Christian, had to be subjected to such a spectacle. Still, she had, with an acute unexpectedness, a poignant flash of the young woman in all her wretchedness. It was as though God had assigned both of them to the slow torture of the rack.

Now she smoothed back her long coarse hair and deftly knotted it in a bun. Just in case the woman was violent this morning, it would be better to have her hair out of the way. There was some reassurance in the knowledge that Martin Axtell was only a phone call away. And she knew precisely where in the locked closet she kept the long strips of muslin which, in the past, she had used to restrain the woman.

Still, apprehension was there and growing with every

minute. Quickly she pushed the belt of her dress through the loops and buckled it in front, still listening. Silence. There was a faint odor of coffee, which meant that Mavis Bonebrake was busy in the kitchen. But the rest of the hall was silent.

She now checked herself. Ready. She shut her eyes and remembered irrelevantly the young woman's arrival ten years ago at Bledding Sorrow. Dressed all in pink with long blond hair, she'd come closer to resembling Mr. Bledding's daughter than his wife. Even then Caldy More, with her keen faculty of comprehending everything and feeling its nature in an instant, could have predicted the outcome. Mr. Bledding had bought himself a pet, a human pet, and an American pet at that.

Quietly she closed and locked her door behind her. The corridor was quiet. She drew a deep breath and walked to the bedchamber next door. She was sorry she had forced the young woman to sit in the sun the day before. She shouldn't have done that. But the piece of paper with the strange handwriting had been a mystery, was still a mystery, one that she would have to try to solve today after she had solved everything else. It really wasn't fair, wasn't fair at all. Suddenly she heard something or, more accurately, felt something, a cool breeze, the faintest sensation of air passing by her, as though she were not alone in the dim narrow corridor. Quickly she looked over her shoulder toward the grillwork barrier. There, where the heavy blue velour drapes were hung, she saw clearly the image of a woman, a young woman, lying on her side, her mouth moving uselessly, as though she were trying to form words.

Caldy More froze, unable to decide if she should advance or retreat. Then suddenly the specter started to her feet, drew her legs beneath her, on her knees now, then with a piteous scream, she fell forward, her hands desperately flailing at the air, at anything to break her fall, her apparently useless legs curled beneath her, a glistening of fresh blood seeping out over her skirts.

Abruptly Caldy More averted her face from the terrible scene. And when a moment later she looked back, the woman was gone. Quickly she turned in all directions, a small rapid circle, her eyes searching. But there was nothing, nothing that she could see. She felt chilled now and shuddered slightly, her hands rubbing her arms, her heart accelerating.

But it was over. Within the instant the chill had passed, the corridor was just a corridor again, an enclosed artery buried in the center of the vast hall, windowless, and on this floor doorless, no possible way for a stray breeze to enter and pass through.

She stared a moment longer at the spot where she thought she had seen a woman in agony, then scolded herself sternly, reminded herself that she was fortunate in that she was a woman of common sense and rigid discipline. Otherwise she might be inclined to think that. . . . Nonsense. She shook her head and dismissed all thoughts of ghosts. Such foolishness was for the superficial and hysterical young girls in the kitchen. She, Caldy More, knew better.

But in spite of this stoical resolve, she still glanced over her shoulder once again. Nothing there. Then, with admirable bearing, she proceeded to the door of the upper bedchamber, unlocked it, and closed it quietly behind her. In the archway she stopped.

The young woman lay on the pillow, the burn on her face a pink flush. Her eyes were bright, though more sunken and prone to dwell longer on all they saw. Her face showed neither surprise nor terror. She merely stared back at Caldy More.

Still on her guard, Caldy More held her position in the archway. In the past sudden movement had tended to upset the young woman. Now curiously it was Caldy More who felt shy and uncertain under the calm gaze coming from the bed.

She moved slowly toward her, still on the alert for

the first signs of irrationality. The young woman was watching her closely. Caldy More couldn't decide whether or not she should speak. Yet they couldn't very well just continue to stare at each other. It had been so long since she had addressed her as a human being, so long since she had entered the room without bearing the morning cup of tea and white pills.

Finally and with great effort she straightened her shoulders and said, "Good morning," and hoped that the simple greeting would ease the gnawing self-contempt within her. Gazing down on the young woman, so small and helpless on the bed, she suddenly had a clear vision of what she had been a party to all these years. Not that she had had a choice. She was not a stupid woman or a gullible one. She simply did what was necessary, what was required of her to do.

At that moment, as she waited, wondering precisely how her harmless "Good morning" would be received, she remembered too clearly other mornings when the young woman had been a single, screaming, kicking fist of outrage, when under the duress of her illness she had crawled into the far corner beneath the window, her wide, staring eyes glaring, hate-filled, at anyone who entered the room.

Now, remembering all this, Caldy More stared down with greater suspicion on the apparently docile woman. She looked now merely like a convalescent, almost attractively weak and certainly displaying no symptoms of approaching hysteria.

"How are you feeling this morning?" Caldy More asked, still trying to penetrate the masklike face on the bed.

Still there was silence.

Caldy More felt very much at a loss. She had been expecting one of two reactions: either the old hysteria, the screaming and weeping to which she was accustomed, or a completely normal, responding, and, she hoped, grateful young woman who would chat with her and promise to be good. This new, awake, though silent countenance disturbed her. It was unpredictable, and she knew from experience that the young woman could move with incredible speed to violence.

She tried a third time. "You're not in pain, are you?" she asked, knowing better but thinking somehow the expression of concern would make a difference.

It didn't. Instead the young woman seemed hopelessly intimidated by her presence. In the interim Caldy More glanced about, convinced that at least in the beginning patience was the order of the day. There was always the possibility that in a very real sense of the word the young woman *was* a convalescent or, at least, without the aid of drugs, she was being given a chance to recover from whatever demons had invaded her.

Now, while she was waiting, Caldy More looked about at the small room. For some reason the meanness of the furnishings was painfully obvious. Peculiar, that she had really never noticed it before. It resembled a cell with the barest of furniture.

Again she looked back on the woman. She saw the mussed, slightly soiled coverlet and above that the white shapeless muslin gown, twisted and wrinkled.

Caldy More bowed her head a fraction deeper, in a mingled understanding and shame. What she saw made perfect, though rather hideous sense. The room *was* a cell and the woman was a prisoner. Again she had her second clear vision of what they had been doing to her, of what she, Caldy More, a Christian, had been a party to.

Suddenly she strode to the closet door, unlocked it, and flung it open. Before her on the rack were less than half a dozen dresses, only a meager portion of the wardrobe which had been shipped from America ten years ago. What had become of the rest of them? She couldn't remember. And then she did. Several years ago Mr. Bledding had donated the prettiest ones to the parish church auction.

Now she felt resentment. What right had he to do

such a thing? Yet she, Caldy More, had been a party to it, agreeing with him that the clothes were of absolutely no use hanging in the closet. She closed her eyes for a moment, still keenly aware of the young woman behind her whose clothes had been given away in the name of charity. It was as though she, Caldy More, were the one who had been drugged and was now just awakening to the harsh realities of past deeds.

She shook her head with a sudden vehemence. The silence was awesome then. All the times in the past when she had forced herself to feel nothing for the young woman rose up now and took a terrible toll. She felt her heart race, her hand tremble. She knew if she looked into those wide-open and yet empty eyes, she was lost. As if to ban them, she shut her own and walked decisively from the room, knowing precisely where she was going.

In an unprecedented act of carelessness, she not only left the door unlocked but left it wide open as she hurried down the corridor to her own room, where quickly she gathered up a bowl and pitcher of warm water, one of her own fresh towels, a bar of pine soap, and, on the way out, paused for a moment before her dressing table and scooped up her own tortoiseshell box of neutral powder and a small bottle of lavender perfume.

Thus armed against her sudden and involuntary remembrance of past sins, she scurried back down the corridor and into the upper bedchamber, where she discovered that the young woman still had not moved.

Carefully she placed the objects on the table beside the bed. Then, without a word, although she was keenly aware of the young woman's eyes on her, she went back to the closet and withdrew a simple yellow cotton dress, soiled from years of neglect, but still recognizable as a dress as opposed to the gray shapeless smock which hung on a hook on the back of the door. In the box on the floor she found underclothes and carried them, together with a pair of white slip-on shoes, back to the bed.

Slightly breathless from her burst of activity, she stood now at the foot of the bed and looked back down on the young woman with an almost savage fierceness. "Get up," she ordered.

There was no response. A minute passed, Caldy More smoothing the yellow dress across her arm as though it were a child in need of comfort.

But her mind was elsewhere. "It's gone on long enough," she said further, as though the young woman were completely capable of identifying "it" as well as responding to a prolonged period of time.

But in truth she appeared to be responding to nothing. Her head sank against the pillow, her eyes, fearful now, on some dark spot just beyond Caldy More's face.

Now in a minor agony of indecision, Caldy More altered her approach. "Please," she begged. "No medicine this morning. See?" And in spite of the clothes in her arms, she held her hands out as though to reveal that she was, in a sense, unarmed.

"Please, Mrs. Bledding," she tried again. "You've suffered enough. We all have. There's no reason for it. For better or worse, this is your home." She smiled faintly. "We're stuck with each other. It doesn't have to be—" She broke off and let her unfinished thought drain into the silence.

Still there had been no perceptible reaction coming from the bed. The young woman appeared to be watching her, to be listening intently, but the best that could be said of her was that she was implacable.

Feeling an exhaustion that had its roots in futility, Caldy More shifted slightly, stepped closer to the bed, and placed the various objects of apparel near the woman's feet. There was always the distinct possibility that she *was* insane, that under the duress of a new environment, separated from all she had known and loved, bound to a cold, insensitive, abusive, and unfeeling man, struck by the weight of unbearable guilt at the tragic death of her parents, humiliated and dragged back after two escape attempts, obsessed, drugged, and finally weakened and defeated, that now she had simply relinquished all contact with the outline of that world which most sane people call reality.

As she thought of this, Caldy More's eyes filled with a kind of horror. Perhaps there had been no response because she was incapable of response. She had lost her right to life on a technical flaw. She had simply been in the wrong place at the wrong time. Such a realization was not easy for a woman of Caldy More's refined sensibilities. And there was still that enormously painful awareness that she had had a hand in it, had over the years blindly followed Mr. Bledding's instructions, always Mr. Bledding's wishes, the sun, the moon, the entire cosmos, turning on Mr. Bledding's comfort, Mr. Bledding's well being, Mr. Bledding's bloody desires.

Quite breathless now, not from physical exertion but rather from the insurrection brewing within her, her head whirling, she walked to the window in search of fresh air.

Nailed shut! Now in utter frustration, she pounded uselessly at the window frame as though in an attempt to jar it loose. She remembered the day—she had held the nails, a short time after the London police had brought the young woman back to Bledding Sorrow. Alone and locked up for the first time in the upper bedchamber, the young woman had raised the window and screamed her dead father's name over and over again, attracting the attention of the workmen who were then involved with the restoration of the hall, indeed, attracting the attention of everyone within a country mile who had ears to hear. By the time Caldy More and Mr. Bledding had reached the upper bedchamber, hammer and nails in hand, they had found the young woman slumped at the windowsill, slowly, rhythmically beating her forehead against the floor.

Now Caldy More gripped the same windowsill, staring blankly down into the courtyard below. The

Birmingham Art League was just leaving. She saw the ladies lifting their luggage into the boots of their cars, calling cheerily to one another. And circulating freely among them, she saw the slightly balding head of Geoffrey Bledding, his head bobbing continuously as he received their obvious praise and adoration.

The eyes of the old woman standing at the third-floor window narrowed. How different he was now from the silent, possessed man who crept up the stairs at night, like a fugitive, for a nocturnal visit with his wife.

Suddenly there was movement in the room behind her, the sound of water being poured from a pitcher, a chink of china as a soap dish scraped. She whirled around. Incredibly she saw the young woman standing or, more accurately, leaning against the table, her pitifully thin back to Caldy More, her shoulders trembling slightly from the weight of the water-filled pitcher.

Instinctively Caldy More moved to help. But as she drew near to the table, the young woman looked up at her, her eyes unflinching, a portion of her old defiance returning; and yet now it lay behind something quieter, a reminder to both of them that she was still a human being, not capable of much, but able to wash and dress herself.

Seeing the expression on her face and hopeful that she had interpreted it correctly, Caldy More, in a stringent act of self-discipline, retreated a few steps to the straight-backed chair next to the archway. Grateful that the young woman was at least moving under her own power, doubly grateful that thus far she was quiet and gave not the slighest evidence of derangement or hysteria, Caldy More sat carefully on the chair, a resumption of her old formality in her manner, watching carefully each tentative and awkward movement, struck anew by the incredible thinness of the body which was now bared for the purposes of washing, the white muslin gown in a small circle around her feet.

From where Caldy More sat, her hands locked together in her lap, she could clearly see the loathsome accumulation of bruises on the young woman's body, mute testimony to the number of times that, drugged, she had fallen, lost her balance, collided, unseeing, with a wall, a doorknob, bench, hideous evidence which Caldy More in her new and painful surge of conscience could scarcely bear to view.

She noticed now that every move the young woman made appeared to be sheer labor. The bar of soap in her hand seemed mysteriously to take on the weight of a brick. Once, straining forward in her efforts, she leaned precariously against the table, faltered, then stepped back until she felt the side of the bed against her legs, then sat weakly, the upper half of her body glistening with soap and water, shivering now in her nakedness. Her expression, however, was calm, almost fatalistic, as though she clearly understood the cause and reason for her weakness and that it was simply a matter of moving slowly, of depleting all her resources of available strength, then waiting patiently for the reserves to build up again.

Never had Caldy More witnessed such a tortuous spectacle. Time and time again she ached to go to the young woman's aid, to relieve her of the necessity of such an inhuman battle with stubborn limbs, weak and trembling muscles. But since the young woman never asked for her help, Caldy More, in the mood of a true penitent, held her position on the chair and, as further punishment, forced herself to watch it all until literally she could bear it no longer and closed her eyes and bowed her head into her hands, still seeing, even in her self-imposed blindness, the skeletal form, the scattering of purple bruises, the short, mussed, and butchered hair, trying not to dwell on how much she had contributed to the young woman's agony. And failing.

The discreet sounds of washing ceased. There were various small rustlings. She supposed she was dressing. Once more she forestalled the urge to look up. Each seemed now to understand her role clearly, the one at the bed working laboriously to make herself presentable, the one in the chair waiting, head down, as though for a grand surprise.

Finally, about half an hour later, all sounds ceased. Caldy More felt herself caught in a dilemma. Was it time? Was the young woman ready for inspection? And what would she find when she lifted her head? And would it bear any resemblance to a salvageable human being? And if it didn't, what would she do? And if it did, what would she do?

Feeling now a trembling in her own hands, she slowly opened her eyes and lifted her head. For a moment she saw nothing but the mere specks of light caused by the prolonged absence of vision.

Then slowly the image became clear, and she stared upward at the young woman, her frail frame almost lost in the now oversized yellow dress, but her hair brushed and her eyes hopeful in spite of the dabs of white powder on her still-red cheeks.

Caldy More walked the short distance to where the young woman stood and almost did something very irrational. She almost took the woman in her arms. But she didn't. Even though her eyes were blurred with the most embarrassing tears, she smiled. "Don't you look nice now."

And Mrs. Bledding, apparently not absolutely certain how she should respond to such a kindness and confused by the sight of tears in the eyes that were smiling at her, slowly, tentatively lifted her hand and, in a clear gesture of comfort, lightly touched Caldy More on the arm. . . .

23

By the end of an absolutely lavish breakfast it would not be honest to say that the two women were chattering. More accurately, they were exchanging certain limited words under certain still-suspicious conditions and were beginning to understand the silences between them.

As soon as Caldy More had regained control of her emotions in the upper bedchamber, she had gently taken Mrs. Bledding by the arm and walked carefully beside her down the corridor, offering her support only when the young woman seemed to need it, thinking ahead, in her practical English way, that what Mrs. Bledding needed now was a good breakfast.

In the small, crudely furnished makeshift kitchen off the garden Caldy More had literally hurled herself into the preparation of eggs and sausage and grilled tomatoes, thinking as she worked of the customary breakfast of porridge or oatmeal which she had had to spoon-feed the young woman. And of course the ever-present cup of medicinal tea to ensure the young woman's placidity and cooperation until lunch.

Now there was no tea at all, would be no tea, and in an attempt to convey that unspoken message to Mrs. Bledding, Caldy More prepared hot chocolate in ivory Wedgwood cups, remnants of Mr. Bledding's family treasure.

Throughout the preparation of the meal Mrs. Bledding had not moved from the chair on the far side of the small round table where Caldy More had placed her, a convenient position clearly visible from all points in the kitchen and within easy reach in case the young woman showed any signs of agitation.

But in truth, she scarcely moved except now and then to glance out into the garden. Once or twice Caldy More noticed that she rubbed her eyes in a childlike gesture as though she were having trouble with her vision. But for the most part, all that could be said of her was that she sat unmoving, eager to please.

Now, "More hot chocolate?" Caldy More asked, lifting the small china pot into the air.

Mrs. Bledding hesitated a moment as though she were having trouble in forming a reply. Finally she shook her head and murmured, "No, thank you."

Caldy More studied the contents on the plate opposite her. Less than half gone, but it was a start. At the beginning of the meal she had been fearful that Mrs. Bledding would not be able to hold the fork. But again, with an agony of effort similar to the washing-and-dressing process, the young woman had studied the utensil as though trying to remember its exact and proper use, then she had lifted it and commenced eating. Not smoothly and certainly not gracefully. Bite after bite had fallen back onto her plate without ever reaching her mouth. But with telltale averted eyes, Caldy More had left her alone.

Now they sat opposite each other at the table, one with her hands in her lap, head down, the other staring intently at her. Suddenly Mrs. Bledding raised her eyes and looked directly at Caldy More. "Where did I get this dress?" she asked, her voice low, scarcely audible.

Caldy More swallowed the last sip of hot chocolate. In a way, she could not bear those quizzical eyes. "It's yours," she said gently. "You brought it with you from America."

Mrs. Bledding studied the yellow fabric for a moment, a bewildered expression on her face. One hand moved slowly up to her eyes, again that curious rubbing gesture as though her vision were impaired in some way.

Caldy More continued in a light voice. "You have a closetful of them in your room. All colors. Very pretty really."

Some knowledge, some apprehension was dawning on the young woman's face. "I've—never worn them," she said. "They don't fit—very well."

Caldy More faltered. "You've been ill."

Their eyes met. Caldy More wondered how much she could tell her. How much would be understood? How much *should* be understood? Quickly she reached across the table, not quite touching the young woman's hand. "You're better now, though," she said. "Much better. And we can fix the dresses and even buy new ones if you like."

Mrs. Bledding stared back at her as though having to capture the words one at a time and digest their meaning. For the third time Caldy More noticed the painful manner in which she closed her eyes, then opened them. She looked sharply at her now, and under this close scrutiny Mrs. Bledding faltered and turned away.

"Are your eyes hurting you?" Caldy More asked bluntly.

The young woman did not respond. She looked backward over her shoulder toward the garden, opening her eyes directly on the sun-splashed window, then again quickly closing them.

Caldy More looked for a moment as if she could not let the matter be so easily dismissed. She felt a strong urge to give the woman all the care and attention that she had denied her in the past. But she waited on patiently, without any great alarm, her memories gradually giving place to hopes and visions of the future, hopes so intricate that she failed to hear the footsteps outside the door. The first indication that someone was about to join them was the sudden flash of alarm on Mrs. Bledding's face as she glanced quickly away from the window toward the kitchen door.

Caldy More saw her start to her feet as though to run.

"Sit still, please, Mrs. Bledding," she soothed. "No need for alarm. It's just—"

Then the door opened and Geoffrey Bledding appeared. He stopped in the doorway, his eyes falling first on the young woman at the table, a clear look of disapproval on his face. Without looking at Caldy More, he said, "How many times must I tell you? I want her out in the garden when I come in for breakfast."

For just a moment Caldy More struggled with the panic within her, then rose to the occasion. "We're running a little late," she said lightly. "If you'll sit down, I'll fix—"

Then she caught a glimpse of the young woman's face. The wide hollow eyes were focused in recognizable terror on the man in the doorway. A discernible tremor seemed to be passing through her. The red on her cheeks deepened. She seemed as though she were about to say something, but her obvious fear rendered her speechless. Her head bowed. She seemed near tears.

Still Geoffrey Bledding held his position, his face stern. "Why is she still here?" he demanded. "She's always gone by—"

"I told you, we're running late."

For the first time he looked directly at Caldy More. "Was Martin Axtell here last night?"

Caldy More nodded.

"Did he—"

"He did. Everything's under control, Mr. Bledding. No need to worry yourself." For a moment Caldy More felt overcome by tension. Her attention was torn between the crumpled young woman at the window and the glowering countenance of the man in the doorway.

Struggling to present an air of normalcy, she again offered, "If you'd care to sit down, I'll be happy to—"

But apparently Mr. Bledding didn't care to do anything but explore the reasons for this break in his routine. "Why is she dressed like that?" he demanded suddenly, pointing his finger toward the woman at the window.

"Why not?" countered Caldy More lightly. "They are her clothes. She has a right—"

Suddenly there was a little upward movement from the head by the window, as though she had partially recovered. She half turned.

Quickly now Caldy More stepped between them. "Please, Mr. Bledding, either sit down and have your breakfast, or—"

"No! I want her out of here."

"She's not ready." Her heart beating rapidly, Caldy More confronted her master in open defiance. Their eyes held each other for a moment in the rawest sort of confrontation.

Very clearly a battle was being waged, the spoils of which sat by the window in an oversized yellow dress. Caldy More tried again. "She's just finishing her breakfast, Mr. Bledding. She won't contaminate you, I can promise you that. She's feeling quite well this morning, behaving herself beautifully, as you can see. Now, please—"

But the man merely stepped back from the door, his eyes riveted in clear revulsion on the silent woman. Now, as though he were punishing Caldy More, he announced rather imperiously, "I'll take my breakfast in the dining room."

She nodded. "If you wish—"

"I don't wish, but obviously I have no choice."

Suddenly Caldy More stepped forward, pleading openly, sorry that the young woman was hearing everything. "She's your wife, Mr. Bledding," she whispered. "In the name of God, take pity."

"I have no wife," he said simply, and turned and walked rigidly toward the door. He called back once, "I'll be in my office all day and prefer not to be disturbed." He looked back at her before he closed the door, an ominous accusatory glance. "She's your responsibility, Caldy More. Take care that you know what you are doing."

Then he slammed the door and locked it and left Caldy More alone, tremendously occupied with the rising outrage within her. She did not turn back to the woman at first, but continued to glare at the closed door, longing to run after him and give back to him this "responsibility." She pressed a hand against her breast as though to still her rage. Well, there were ways of getting back at him, and she intended to exploit every one of them.

Her head rose then. She looked back toward the window. The young woman sat rather stiffly now, still staring out into the garden as though somehow she had come to grips with her fear. Only when Caldy More walked to her side did she see the tears.

"There, please don't, Mrs. Bledding," she whispered. "You mustn't pay any attention." She started to put her arm around the frail shoulders, but didn't. Instead she changed her tone as though to dismiss the entire incident. "Would you like to go out into the garden now?" she asked.

With the exception of the tears on Ann's face, there was not the slightest change in her expression. Her eyes were glazed, nothing anywhere to suggest the slightest evidence of life or will.

Caldy More found her meekness almost as disconcerting as her tears. "You don't have to go if you don't want to," she explained. "It's going to be different. I promise. You'll see."

But even as she was talking, the young woman stood up and walked to the back door. There she stopped and stood obediently before the closed door as though she knew it would not open until keys were produced.

But the door was not locked and Caldy More urged her to open it.

Again she noticed how slowly the woman responded, as though her thought processes depended on the clear reception of every word. Then slowly she turned the knob and, without looking back, murmured, "Thank you for breakfast."

A few moments later Caldy More looked out of the window and saw the young woman sitting on the stone bench, sitting erect, almost primly, her head turned toward the bottom of the garden, as though she were looking intently for something.

Caldy More eyed her now with a certain pride. At least a start had been made. And while the resurrection was far from complete, it was enough. For now.

Poor Mr. Bledding. It was this thought that provoked a smothered chuckle and gave her the impetus to move rapidly, almost lightheartedly into her morning chores. . . .

24

And Jamie was there, perched on his wall, safe behind the protective boughs of the copper beech. Actually he had been there only a few moments when the young woman had appeared in the kitchen doorway.

His morning had started early and had been busy, carrying down endless baggage from the third-floor dormitory for the Birmingham Art League. Then he had foolishly offered to drive seven of the ladies into Bledding Village so they could make connections for a noon train to London; foolish because seven passengers did not warrant the expense of operating his coach, which was designed for forty-eight passengers. He would have to watch that in the future or the summer would be totally without profit.

But Mr. Bledding had asked and he had obliged. Then, too, it had given him an opportunity to check on his coach, to see that it was in good running order after several days of idleness. He had enjoyed the feel of the steering wheel in his hands again, the sudden rush of pleasure as he had sat in the driver's seat, gazing out and down through the vast expanse of glass on the small automobiles.

Then he had hurried back to Bledding Sorrow, had dashed up to his room, where he had quickly selected a gift for the morning, and had only just climbed into his position on the wall when the young woman had appeared at the back door, curiously unescorted this morning, for he could not see Caldy More anywhere in sight.

At first glance he saw that something was different about her. The dress, for one thing, yellow this morning instead of the customary gray. The day was brilliant,

steeped in azure, with a warm westerly breeze. Not hot
yet, but it would be by noon. He remembered guiltily
the scene from the day before. That was why he had
brought no paper this morning, but rather the small
volume itself. Perhaps he could read to her. At least
there would be no evidence that way, no reason for the
old woman to scold and intimidate.

Again he had that unaccountable feeling of excitement, as though, for no reason that he could understand, this was the one place in the entire world where
he wanted to be, had to be, for that matter.

The night before, in the privacy of his room, he had
tried again to come to grips with his feelings, had tried
anew to understand what precisely had drawn him here,
to Bledding Sorrow in general, to the garden wall and
the mysterious young woman in particular.

There had been no answers, none, at least, that he
had recognized as plausible. In spite of its surface complexity, it was a simple matter. He had to see her again;
he had to know who she was and how she had come to
be here. Somehow he had to make contact with her, to
try until he succeeded to penetrate her loneliness, her
obvious despair.

Beyond that there were no answers, no solutions, and
worse, no alternate courses of action. He felt peculiarly
ill himself, not physically ill certainly, but still helpless,
a mere pawn in a game he'd never played before. And
at the moment of greatest confusion he'd caught one
brilliantly clear glimpse of his role here, of what was
expected of him, of what he had to do. It made no
sense, but since he had no choice, sense and reason
seemed weak and unimportant tools.

Suddenly he looked up. She was closer now, but not
close enough, sitting on the bench, merely looking
toward the end of the garden. It was the difference in
her that held his attention. She seemed more in control
this morning. Her steps to the bench had been slow but
steady, her head erect, the curious flopping yellow dress
now tucked neatly about her knees in a display of

modesty which in the past had been totally lacking. As he gazed down through the leaves of the tree, he finally determined what it was that struck him as strange. Extremes! It was as though she had passed from one extreme to the other, of exhibiting little or no physical control to almost total rigidity, the set angle of her head, the way her hands locked together in her lap.

He considered calling to her, but decided to wait a moment, to give her a chance to come forward of her own volition.

Watching her was totally fascinating. He began to see subtle new dimensions in her face. There was about her a total and painful self-consciousness. He had not noticed it before. She looked like a child on her best behavior, not out of any respect for the decorum itself, but rather because behaving made life easier. Still there were those assertive eyes, rather incongruous in that everything else about her suggested profound inexperience.

Still he was pleased, more than pleased, his excitement rising swiftly. In her new self-awareness he felt less a desire to protect and a greater desire to know. Everything! Who she was. How she came to be here. Why she was cut off from all human companionship.

Now, suddenly, he saw her glance over her shoulder toward the back door as though she, too, might be interested in the number of eyes watching her. Then she was standing, holding herself very erect, her head slightly turned back toward him. He smiled at the obvious improvement in her physical condition. She bore not the slightest resemblance to the helpless, stumbling, uncertain creature he'd first seen in the garden. She was in control, and at the same time she seemed to have sufficient self-possession to know that at any moment she was in danger of losing that control.

Now, as she began slowly moving toward the end of the garden, he felt the excitement within him rise to almost unbearable proportions. He was a truthful man with himself, almost incapable of deceiving himself.

Yet, at this point, no matter how hard he tried, he could not find the reason for his incredible agitation. He vaguely conceived a theory that he felt pity for her. Yet in truth he saw nothing to pity now in the erect and lovely countenance approaching him, barefoot, almost gracefully across the small expanse of lawn.

She was even with him now, her eyes searching upward through the foliage of the tree. Then she found him. Her eyes froze for a moment, locked on his face, as though she really hadn't expected to find him. From his position he could not read any other expression on her face, although once she did look back over her shoulder, as though concerned with the limits of her new freedom.

Then, apparently satisfied, she stepped over the gravel path, moving carefully through the rose bushes until she stood directly beneath him where he sat on the wall.

No words spoken yet by either of them. Then, "Good morning, Ann," he said, amazed to hear how subdued and timid his voice sounded.

In a rapid glance she scanned him, the muscles of her cheek contracted on the right side of her face. "What do you want?" she asked, in a rapid breathless voice. Suddenly, without waiting for him to reply, she whispered, "Go away. Please go away," not looking at him now, her fear clearly visible.

When he heard the tone of her voice, he tried to reassure her. "I won't hurt you," he soothed. "Just to talk. What harm can come of that?" Then unfortunately he remembered the punishment she had endured the day before on his behalf. He started to say something further, but changed his mind.

She lowered her eyes and listened as though beseeching him in some way or other to make her believe differently.

He repeated again, "No harm in just talking," and would have gone on, but at the sound of his voice, as at a pang of physical pain, her lips stiffened again and again the muscles of her right cheek worked.

"Please go away," she begged again, and tried to make her way back to the path, but tottered and clung to the wall for support.

Hearing her speak, he suddenly realized that she was American. A puzzling complication. What was an American woman doing. . . ? But then he saw her sink slowly down until she was sitting at the base of the wall, the old weakness returning. She tried several times to speak again, but apparently could not.

He waited, deciding now to let her take the lead, hoping in some way it would put her at ease. In the interim of silence her fear seemed to be subsiding. She continued to sit near the base of the wall, her head resting gently against brick, her bare legs and feet curled demurely to one side.

Finally she said quietly, "You were here yesterday," and he couldn't tell if it was a question or a statement of fact.

"Yes," he replied. "Don't you remember? I gave you a poem." He went on in a subdued tone. "The old woman made you sit in the sun." He paused, studying carefully the top of the fair head beneath him. "I'm sorry," he whispered.

Now she looked up at him briefly, the blue eyes almost calm within their dark hollow circles. "I didn't tell," she murmured. "I don't know your name."

Jamie smiled. He was certain he had told her, but he told her again. "My name is James," he said, "James Pask. Can you remember it?"

Still looking up, she slowly nodded. The blessing of a faint smile crossed her face, an agreeable light. "James Pask," she repeated, and again glanced inquiringly and uneasily about.

Suddenly he despised his position high above her and longed to jump down beside her, to sit with her at the base of the wall and share her risks. "Do you expect the old woman to come back soon?" he asked.

She shook her head. "I don't know. She was in the kitchen a moment ago. If she's still there, she can see.

. . ." Her voice faltered. In a childlike tone she added, "She was nice this morning. She gave me this." And she held out the yellow dress for his inspection.

Jamie suddenly blushed, not as grown men blush, slightly, without being themselves aware of it, but as boys blush, feeling that they are ridiculous in their shyness. Still her upturned face begged for a reply and he gave it. "It's very pretty," he murmured.

She smoothed the dress down, brushed a spot near her knee. "I have others," she said, not bragging, but more in amazement, as though she had only recently been made aware of the others.

Now she looked up at him as though in confusion. "Do you live in the village?" she asked, apparently still bewildered by his presence on the wall.

He shook his head. "No, I live here at Bledding Sorrow, just as you do."

She seemed to think on this a moment, then softly disagreed. "I don't live here," she said, looking again toward the back door. The delicate features clouded; she drew her knees up and rested her head on them. "I lived here once, but I don't anymore."

"Where do you live now?" Jamie asked, prodding gently.

"In a room," she replied, her voice as light as the breeze which ruffled her hair.

"And where is this room?" he asked.

"A long way away." Her voice drifted vaguely off as though imitating the distance to her room.

He was listening carefully, yet there was still a struggle in his heart between the desire to crawl down the tree and walk away and forget everything he had seen and heard, and jump down the other side and lift her up and walk with her to the stone bench, where they could sit like civilized people and talk.

Instead he did nothing, but held his position on the wall and tried not to think on the thoughts swarming through his head. She seemed more at ease now, the small fair head resting lightly on her knees. He realized that it was the innocence of her expression, together with her delicate beauty, that made her special charm. But what always struck him in her as something unlooked for was the expression of her eyes, soft and serene some of the time, darting and frightened at other times, as though she had not quite learned to live with the constant hazards that surrounded her.

"Ann?" he asked now, growing brave. "Are you Mrs. Bledding?"

Suddenly she looked up at him. He saw at once the panic in her face, like the sun going behind a cloud. He said quickly, "I shouldn't have asked that. I'm. . . ."

But she continued to look up at him, her face no longer stern. Her eyes revealed a certain calmness, but he imagined that in her calmness there was a note of deliberate composure.

"Do you live in the village?" she asked again, apparently moving safely away from his previous question.

"No," he repeated. "I live here at Bledding Sorrow."

Whether it was that she had heard his words or that she didn't want to hear them, she made a sort of stumble upward, twice reached out to the wall for support, and twice failed and crumpled weakly again back to earth.

Jamie prayed silently, *Oh, God, don't let her go yet,* and at the same time, feeling the need for movement of his own, shifted his position atop the wall, preserving his balance with his hands, almost wishing that he would slip and fall down beside her.

She continued to sit in a limp position against the base of the wall, the yellow dress smudged from her recent efforts. Now she appeared subdued and dejected.

Jamie settled on the wall and asked softly, "Do you ever leave this garden?"

No answer. He noticed her fingers sifting lightly through the loose stones in the garden. It was her only movement. Apparently her external as well as her internal composure was fragile and easily shaken.

Again he felt responsible. "Please look at me," he begged. "I'm sorry if I. . . ."

And then she did look up and for the first time he saw tears on her face. The sight took a dreadful toll. "Please," he begged, "don't cry."

Suddenly he remembered the thin blue volume inside his coat pocket. Quickly he withdrew it and held it out for her inspection. "Look!" he urged. "Look what I've brought this morning. Not just one poem but a whole book of them."

While her response was not immediate, it was clear. Slowly she looked up toward the volume in his hand. She made no attempt to brush the tears away. It was as though they had started and stopped of their own volition.

Jamie held the book down for her. He had considered once only reading it to her, but now it seemed important that she touch it, hold it, establish its reality.

She did not reach up for it immediately, but again glanced hesitantly toward the back door, as though at any moment someone would appear and she would have to account for herself.

"Go on, take it," Jamie urged.

Then slowly she reached up, a smile on her face. "Is it—yours?"

He nodded, delighted by the change within her. "But you may borrow it if you wish. I brought it for you."

She took the book and stared at it inquiringly, as though it were a once-familiar object. He saw her hand lightly brush across its cover.

He caught himself smiling with her. "Poetry," he said foolishly. "Wordsworth. Do you know him?"

But she continued to look at the book without speaking and sat slowly back down on the ground, taking the book with her, as though it were the most extraordinary object in the world.

He gave her all the time she needed, delighted with her obvious delight. Once she looked back up at him, and into the expression of her face there passed a shade of embarrassment. With a slight inclination of her head she said, "I was a student once," and her voice was quiet and soft and composed, as though she wanted him to know she was neither stupid nor insane.

"Did you enjoy school?" he asked tentatively.

She nodded quickly. "Oh, yes, very much." She blushed. "The book is good." And again he heard that slightly demented tone in her voice as though her mind were struggling for balance as laboriously as her body.

"Books *are* good," he agreed. "I'll bring you more if you wish. I have several in my room."

Suddenly she looked directly up at him and laughed openly. "My father used to say. . . . " But the laugh died and the words with it, and for a moment she resembled a child's windup toy that had inexplicably lost its power. Then abruptly it was over, as though a black curtain had flapped down in her brain. The laugh was gone, the thought dismissed, the memory pushed safely back. Rather vaguely she lowered her head, one hand gently massaging her forehead, the other hand still gripping the book.

Quickly Jamie rushed in with words in an attempt to fill the vacuum before it overpowered her. "I'm sure you were a good student," he said.

She smiled at his praise and let the memory go. She shrugged. "Maybe once," she whispered, "but not now."

"Why not now?" he asked, watching her closely.

She shook her head. "I'm stupid now." She flushed slightly and hugged the book to her. She seemed to be making an effort to control herself. "Caldy More said that I'm. . . ." But again she faltered as though a new memory of despair had washed over her. When she looked up at him, there was nothing but dread on her face. "I don't want to ever. . . ." Again words failed her.

He felt crushed by the sadness in her face. "Don't want to what, Ann?" he urged.

She appeared to grow thoughtful. Something drew her eyes back to the book. Again she clasped it to her as though she intended never to let it go. With her head down she whispered, "I don't want to get you into trouble."

He felt overwhelmed. A complicated emotion, part anger, part sorrow, part desire, rose within him. "Don't worry," he soothed. "I'll tell Caldy More myself."

She responded with a look of shock. "You mustn't," she warned. "She'll tell *him* and they'll send you away."

"Nonsense," he countered. "I've only loaned you a book. What harm is there in that?"

But she looked down and took her dread with her as though to say that *she* knew the danger in their meeting even if he didn't.

He continued to watch her closely. There was something cruel in her fear, as though it were based on the strongest of substance, the look and manner of experience.

Then he saw her rising to her knees again. She held the book a moment longer, then reluctanly raised it in the air toward him. "You'd better take it back," she said.

Suddenly at that moment the rear door of the hall opened. Caldy More appeared. Ann gave a nervous jerk of her head; a wild suffering expression spread on her face. She drew a sharp breath and looked up, terrified, into Jamie's eyes.

There was no way he could take the book without being seen by the woman at the door. "Sit back down," he whispered. "Put the book behind you." He could see the incredible fear in her face as she hung, as though paralyzed in a half-raised position.

"Sit back down," he urged again, raising his voice slightly in an attempt to cut through her fear.

Slowly she obeyed, her knees giving way; her right arm slipped the book behind her while her eyes continued to focus on the woman at the back door.

"It'll be all right," he soothed.

The woman at the back door had not moved. With one hand raised in order to shield her eyes from the sun, she appeared to be surveying the garden, neither haste nor urgency in her manner.

Suddenly Jamie whispered, "Go to her, Ann. Meet her before she starts down. I'll come tomorrow. I promise."

For a moment he feared that she was too terrified to hear his words, let alone respond to them. But slowly she stirred and, using the wall for support, raised herself to her feet. There was still the problem of the book, which rested on its side at the base of the wall. He would have to come back for it later. There was no time now. Then he saw the two women walking toward each other, destined to meet about midway in the vicinity of the stone bench.

He saw Caldy More smile, saw her reach out warmly and put her arm around Ann's shoulder. Words were exchanged; he couldn't tell what. Stealthily he rearranged the boughs of the tree, drawing a particularly leafy one lower, the better to secure his position. He could not see Ann's face, had no way of knowing how she was responding to the moment of tension. His heart ached for what he was putting her through. Whatever tensions were already existent in her life, it was clear that he was only adding to them.

Then the brief conversation on the path was over, and the two women began walking toward the kitchen door. Ann's head was bowed. He could not tell if she had been threatened in any way. Her step seemed steady. It was only the submissive angle of her head that caused him alarm.

As they disappeared through the back door, he dared to relax, drew a deep breath, and felt a sharp resentment at the recent, brief encounter. In spite of all the hesitancy in the young woman, he knew that she could be reached, knew also that she gave evidence of inhuman abuse, knew further that nothing in the world would prevent him from returning to the wall the following day.

Suddenly he saw the back door open again, saw Caldy More step rapidly out into the sun. Quickly he drew the bough down over him where he had permitted it to flutter loose during his moment of relaxation.

What in the hell did she. . . ? He watched closely as she came forward to the center of the garden, her tall angular frame moving now with purpose as though she knew precisely where she was going.

He drew back even further until he was scarcely sitting on the wall at all, but rather clinging to it, his legs hanging off the other side, one arm clasping the trunk of the tree.

Still Caldy More drew nearer. She stopped now on the path less than five feet from where he sat. Her dark plain dress rose like a cloud about her under a gentle breath of wind. One hand hung listlessly at her side while the other lifted as though to assist her searching eyes.

And just when he was certain that she was about to look up, she spied what apparently she had been looking for. Carefully she tiptoed into the flower bed and with the effort of age reached over near the base of the wall and retrieved the book.

All was lost. Of that he was certain. Obviously the old woman had in some manner forced a confession out of Ann, or perhaps Ann, in her deep desire to have the book, had sent her back for it, forgetting in an irrational moment that he might still be on the wall.

Now he saw Caldy More step back to the path, taking the book with her, brushing the soil off its binding where it had rested in the dirt, her tall thin stooping figure struggling to right itself after the extreme reach to the garden wall.

He considered speaking first. It would have given him a portion of satisfaction not to be found out and called down like a misbehaving schoolboy.

But he held his silence, leaned his head against the trunk of the tree, and waited for the harsh voice to accuse him, to threaten him, to intimidate, as obviously she had done with Ann.

But after several moments he saw her still standing

on the path beneath him, one hand traveling inquiringly over the surface of the book, her thin neck bent in close examination of binding, contents, everything.

A moment later, as though her curiosity had been satisfied, she straightened up, adjusted the waistband of her dress, tucked the book beneath her arm, and with only a slight turn of her head, said, "Good morning, Mr. Pask. . . ."

❦❦ 25 ❦❦

It was after midnight.

Jamie lay on his bed. He was reading, but not thinking of what he was reading, and stopped now and then
to listen to the quiet of the almost totally empty hall.
The events of the day ran disconnectedly in his imagination. *So! She knew!* Those three words had lodged in
his mind all afternoon.

As he had worked with old Peter Endicott in the
outer gardens, planting six new willows around the
white marble birdbath, he'd said those words to himself over and over again. *So! She knew!* And each time
that he had said them he'd looked up from his work,
expecting to see a messenger summoning him to Geoffrey Bledding's office.

But no summons had come, and he'd spent the afternoon listening to old Endicott grumble about Prince
Charles and Princess Anne and the entire royal family
as though they were his own children and he were
somehow responsible.

At four o'clock, sitting in the basement dining room,
having tea with Mrs. Bonebrake, hearing about sexual
exploits that would make a rugby player blush, he'd
again said the words to himself. *So! She knew!* And
again he'd looked up at the sound of every footstep on
the stairs, convinced that now the summons was coming.

But it had never come. And even later when he had
shared a plate of Scotch eggs with Mrs. Bonebrake—the
rest of the staff gone, having been given the night
off—he had still said the words to himself, as though
newly amazed. And his astonishment had grown to
even greater proportions when he'd helped clean up
their few dishes, had turned down an invitation to join

259

Mrs. Bonebrake in the village pub, and still the summons had not come.

He had walked about in the courtyard by himself in the dark as though readily making himself available for the summons when it *did* come. He had even sat in his coach for more than an hour, key in the ignition, hands on the steering wheel, as though his dismissal were a fact.

Now he lay on his bed, reading, not seeing the words, but still thinking, *So! She knew!* He was fully dressed, as though it were still not too late for the summons to come.

Now he took up his book again, an American Western of cowboys and Indians, a world remote from Bledding Sorrow, from all of England, for that matter. But his eyes would neither follow nor comprehend the words. He raised his head and sank into thought. *So! She knew!*

Then why had she not reported it? Obviously the isolation of the young American woman was very important to someone, and he had penetrated that isolation.

Suddenly, and for no clear reason, he saw in his imagination her pale, small bare feet, unused, tender feet enduring gravel in order to reach the wall.

He closed the book. It was hopeless. He rolled to his side. Would it ever be possible for them to meet face to face without fear of discovery? Would it ever be possible for him to walk beside those delicate feet, understand even a portion of the journey they had taken?

At that moment, as though surmounting all obstacles, the wind sent the shutter screeching. It clanked against the side of the hall as though about to be torn off. In his nervous tension and the visions that filled his imagination, he could find no respite.

"Damn it!" he cursed, vainly trying to give a stern expression to his face. Clutching at the side of the bed, he struggled up and moved rapidly toward the door.

But in the corridor he stopped. To his left, just beyond the grillwork barrier and heavy drapes, he heard
voices. Though he could not now remember his destination, it seemed unimportant. He realized that the
muted conversation beyond the barrier had brought him
close to her. Now he stood absolutely quiet.

As best he could tell, it was an argument of some
sort, similar in nature to the one he'd heard before. A
man's voice commanded, "Open the door."

And a woman's, Caldy More's, he recognized instantly, saying, "No!"

There was a moment's silence. Then the man again,
Bledding, he assumed, speaking in a low, taut voice,
"You are overstepping your boundary."

"I'm not," came the protest. "You said she was my
responsibility, and I intend to—"

"Open the door!" The man's voice now was clearly
menacing, as though he were confronting a deadly
enemy. Jamie, still listening on the other side, was
struck by the wildness in both voices, as though they
were strangers, confronting each other in a strange
situation.

The woman now softened, clearly pleading, "She's
awake, Mr. Bledding, wide awake, has been all day.
I don't think you would find her as—"

"Why hasn't she had her medicine?"

There was a pause, then the woman's voice again,
almost deliberately high pitched, as though trying to
shift blame of some sort. "It was Martin Axtell's suggestion. He said the required dosage was no longer safe,
said that—"

"Damn Martin Axtell," came the man's voice again,
not in any sort of open fury, but rather all the more
terrible in its incredible control. He went on. "I'll speak
to Axtell on Monday, but for now, open the door."

Jamie closed his eyes, the better to interpret this new
silence. There was the sound of steps, of someone moving back away from a threat, then a whispered voice

scarcely recognizable as female. "I beg you, Mr. Bledding. Have pity. She's—"

Suddenly there was a resounding slap, a woman's harsh quick scream, a struggle, the woman, all vestige of composure gone, weeping. "You have no right—"

"Go to your room, Caldy More. This is none of your concern."

The silence persisted except for the heavy breathing of the woman, who apparently stood only a few feet beyond the drape. Then Jamie heard a key in a lock, heard a door open.

There were new sounds now, a distant soft pleading, a scuffle, a chair being overturned, something heavy like a bed being scraped across the floor, then another blow, then a second, then a third, then a fourth, each punctuated by a soft gasp of pain.

Listening, Jamie felt light-headed. While he was devoid of total understanding, he knew that something terrible was taking place, and he was powerless to stop it.

At that point everything fell silent. His head bent forward, an expression of intense concentration on his face. For a moment longer he stood motionless, hearing nothing. Then, into the silence, came the tortured sound of a woman weeping uncontrollably. It seemed to come from near the floor as though she had fallen and could not rise. He knelt quickly down near the base of the grillwork barrier. "Caldy More?" he whispered. "Is that you?"

There was one sharp inhalation of air, and then the weeping stopped. Someplace in the distance the soft moans continued, but there was still no response from the near figure, but a faint sniffling as though the woman were trying hard to control her tears.

Now Jamie begged, "What happened?" He tried to reach through the bars of the grillwork, but they were so narrowly set together that he was stopped at the forearm. Now, as his frustration grew, he called again, "Caldy More? Please. What happened?"

Suddenly her voice came from the other side, as stern

and unbending as though it had never known the softening effect of tears. "Go back to your room, Mr. Pask,"
she ordered.

"No," he protested, "not until—"

"There's nothing you can do, nothing anyone can
do. Go back to your room."

"Please, Caldy More," he begged, "I must know. . . ."

There was a rustle of movement as though the
woman were rising to her feet with great difficulty. Her
voice when she spoke again sounded strangled in her
throat. "She's his wife," was what she said, with a
finality mixed with horror. Then he heard a nearer door
open and close, and the corridor beyond the grillwork
barrier was totally silent.

Still Jamie knelt in his foolish position, trying again
to reach through the bars as though he thought in the
last few moments they might have weakened and grown
wider. Finally he sat helplessly on the floor, his forehead damp with effort, with frustration.

With his eyes closed, he did not at first see it, see
the peculiar illumination which sprang from no visible
source and seemed to pass through the grillwork barrier and hover over him for a moment.

The first indication he had of something out of the
ordinary was an intense sensation of heat, as though
he were standing too near an open fire. As the sensation grew into actual discomfort, he opened his eyes,
saw directly before him, in the center of the blaze of
light and heat, the clear outline of a man, the same
specter he'd seen earlier in the garden.

Abruptly he lowered his head and rubbed his eyes.
But when he looked up again, the specter was still
there, now moving toward him, his body, wrapped in
the black cape, appearing strangely liquid in the center
of the light, his head invisible again, perhaps bowed
sharply down in the confines of the hood.

Now he stood less than five feet from Jamie, his hand
raised in greater urgency, the same gesture that Jamie
had seen in the garden, as though the man were urging

him to leave. Now he saw the faceless hood moving slowly back and forth, a clear gesture of negation, warning him of something. Three times he lifted his hand, and three times the black featureless hood moved back and forth.

In spite of his fear, Jamie had a great desire to know and to understand. He started to his feet, then pressed backward against the grillwork barrier. The apparition was now moving away, though clearly visible, the light surrounding him growing even more brilliant, increasing in intensity until he could no longer look at the specter, his eyes watering under the assault of light and heat.

Suddenly he raised his arm across his face in a shield-like position, his mind struggling to digest what he had seen. And in that instant the brilliance faded, the specter disappeared, the heat subsided. He lowered his arm and found himself gasping for breath, his eyes foolishly focused on a flat expanse of plain, drab wall.

He felt weak, still felt in memory the sensation of heat on his face. He bowed his head and massaged the ache in his temples. Was he losing his mind? What he had seen or thought he had seen was madness. And what he had heard or thought he had heard earlier coming from beyond the grillwork barrier, that, too, was madness.

Now he shook his head, struggling for control.

And when, a moment later, the softest, the most pitiful of moans reached his ears, he looked questioningly up at the ceiling, feeling a severe disintegration taking place within him, as though he could clearly see beyond the barrier, beyond the closed door, and into the torture chamber itself.

For a minute he continued to gaze at the hideous projection of his mind. And when the moans came again, louder this time, in deeper agony, his eyes filled with tears, his gaunt face constricted, and he ground his knuckles into the floor until there was no feeling, only blood from the scraped flesh dotted with small, embedded splinters. . . .

~◦(26)◦~

The Newcastle Genealogy Society arrived at eight thirty
on Monday morning bringing rain. Martin Axtell had
to fight his way through the damp confusion of the
courtyard. The early-morning and highly urgent phone
call from Caldy More had pleased him, more than
pleased him. He had been expecting it. What did not
please him was the rain and this new, motley parade
of laughing, chattering, inferior humanity cluttering the
courtyard and central corridor with its endless baggage
and repulsive odor of wet flesh.

Umbrella aloft, he made his way through the chaos,
moving toward Caldy More, who stood waiting for him
at the door. Once he heard her shout over the confusion. "This way, Dr. Axtell, hurry, please."

As if he didn't know. Now a large gaudily dressed
woman, armed with cardboard charts of some sort,
blocked the door. He stepped back to avoid contact
with her, then pushed quickly past, still endeavoring to
follow Caldy More's wildly waving hand.

As he made his way down the corridor, he shook the
rain from his umbrella and paused for a moment in
front of Geoffrey's open office door. Arthur Firth was
there, the weasely little man who lived with the black
woman in Feather Cottage at the edge of the village.
After eavesdropping for a few minutes, Martin determined that the two men were discussing snakes.

Now Martin sent his eyes heavenward. The place was
a circus, a bloody circus. Only as he turned to go did
Geoffrey deign to speak to him. "I want to see you
when you've finished, Martin," he called out, his voice
slightly ominous as though he were displeased.

Martin smiled cordially and shook the rain out of

his mac. "And I, you, Geoffrey," he said, wanting the weasel, Firth, to hear the familiarity in his voice as he addressed the warden of Bledding Sorrow.

Then that damn foolish Caldy More was there, pulling at his arm, openly beginning, "Please, Dr. Axtell. I tried to reach you all day yesterday. Now, hurry."

The central corridor was a perilous journey, all horribly disgusting. Stella Trinder was here, Geoffrey's secretary, trying to read off the room assignments. As far as Martin could tell, not a living soul was listening to her. And he spied the new coachman, leaning rather sullenly against the wall. Not a bad-looking specimen, rugged-looking, yet gaunt, a most attractive combination. Martin stared at him in passing. For some reason the man looked exhausted, in a most anxious frame of mind.

Martin was still close enough to the man to speak and considered doing so. He was really very attractive in a primitive sort of way, working class obviously, but in a region as remote as Bledding Sorrow one learned to make do.

But then Caldy More was calling to him again, urging him to keep up, and he knew he'd get no rest until he had seen the insane woman, had heard about every minute detail of her latest rampage. No matter. The coachman would be here all summer. There was plenty of time.

Now he followed the stern angular woman into the Great Hall, where the noise and confusion diminished somewhat and he was able to see clearly the size and scope of her agitation. "What in the name of God is the rush?" he demanded, stopping for breath and leaning heavily against a near table.

She came to a halt about ten feet in front of him, looking as though her nerves were being strained tighter and tighter on some sort of peg. Her voice was low, rigidly in control. "It's serious, Dr. Axtell. I beg you to hurry. I tried to reach you all day yesterday. You said you would be available. Where. . . .?"

He drew himself up. "I *do* have a private life beyond this madhouse, Caldy More," he said archly. He gazed at her without saying anything more, and in spite of the shadow in which she was standing, he saw the expression on her face. It was a look of fear, which he had never seen on that hard countenance before.

Softening somewhat, he stepped toward her. "I take it she did not have a good weekend?"

She made no answer and in her face he saw conflict.

"What happened?" he asked, trying to appear as her humble servant.

She shook her head as though unable to find words. "Please hurry," she begged, and clutching at the keys in her hand, she found the right one for the private wing, pushed it open, and implored him to follow.

So! Apparently the events of the weekend had been serious enough to shatter the previously unshatterable Caldy More. Obviously the young wife had gone totally berserk, had reverted effortlessly to her old psychotic ways, as Martin knew she would. As he trudged up the stairs behind Caldy More, he thought with a certain hard-won satisfaction that perhaps now Geoffrey would listen to him, heed his advice, and send the woman to a hospital, where she clearly belonged. In the London area would be best, far removed from Bledding Sorrow, a sanatarium perhaps where patients entered and from which they did not emerge. He knew of such a place, had worked there once in his younger days when the helplessly insane had held a fascination for him. It had been a delicious time. So many drugged and complacent partners and small locked cubicles ensuring privacy. A marvelous garden of—

"Please, Dr. Axtell!"

Caldy More's voice cut through his memory, the power of which had caused him to halt in his climb to the third floor.

"Coming, Caldy More," he called up the steps, scolding himself again for not guessing sooner why Geoffrey had insisted for years on keeping the young woman here.

The drugged insane had no peers as far as truly provocative sexual partners were concerned. Alive yet totally malleable, awake yet incapable of registering protest, acquiescent except perhaps for their eyes, they could be effortlessly manipulated for the greatest gratification.

As he climbed breathlessly to the third floor, he found his thoughts physically reviving. At the moment when he was approaching Caldy More outside the locked bedchamber, he noticed the fear on her face increasing. With joy he thought, *It must have been one hell of a weekend.* And while she was unlocking the door, he vowed to himself not to drug the young woman no matter how madly she raged. He would leave her as he found her, violent, screaming, kicking, as an object lesson for Geoffrey, at least until an ambulance could come and take her away.

Then the door was opened. He squared his shoulders, confident of what he would find in the room, and went inside. . . .

~∞(27)∞~

There were forty-five students, male and female, of varying ages, in the Newcastle Genealogy Society, and with only token help from two of the younger men Jamie carried all the luggage up to the third-floor dormitory. In a way, he was grateful for the physical labor. It kept him busy, kept his mind off his throbbing hand and the ominous arrival of Dr. Axtell.

He lost count of the number of times he went up and down the three flights of stairs, his mind working as actively as his body, trying to come to grips with all he had seen and overheard. In the future he would move more boldly. For her sake as well as his. His life had been hard, but never had he been subjected to or forced to witness such blatant cruelty. With the help of Caldy More, and rightly or wrongly he now sensed in her an ally, he would understand all by nightfall, or else he would take the barriers and locked doors by storm and demand explanation.

These slightly illogical and melodramatic thoughts, together with the necessity now and then to be cordial to the stranger of the moment, so engrossed him that about an hour later he was somewhat surprised to find the mountain of luggage cleared from the central corridor.

Because he had nothing to do, his thoughts moved instantaneously to the upper bed chamber. He glanced at his watch. It lacked ten minutes of being eleven o'clock, and still the doctor had not come down. Now he paced restlessly in the corridor, loathing the confinement of rain.

The effects of his recent strenuous activity had worn off, leaving him with only a profound sense of unrest.

About fifteen feet away was Bledding's office. The door was open. Inside he heard voices. It was not his intention to eavesdrop, but he couldn't help overhearing. Then, too, he wanted very much to see Bledding, not so much to talk with him, for he had nothing to say, but rather simply to study the man's face, see if he could find any trace of the voice which he had overheard in the upper corridor, the cold, unbending, almost serene voice of a man capable of inflicting incredible pain.

Now, from the sound of the voices coming from inside the office, he guessed that the deputy warden, Arthur Firth, was still with him. As well as Jamie could tell, they were discussing snakes, Firth's thin, high-pitched voice rising in some agitation. "Well, why are they bringing adders? We are not equipped with a laboratory."

"I know, I know," soothed Bledding. "Still, they are a prestigious group, very active even in London circles. If we treat them right, they are capable of serving us as well."

There was a pause. Jamie stepped closer to the door, head down. A moment later he heard Arthur Firth sigh wearily. "I'll need professional help and advice. They must be cared for in the proper manner or they could be quite a hazard. You realize that, don't you?"

Apparently Bledding nodded. Then he continued in his soothing manner, neither the voice nor the attitude bearing the slightest resemblance to the unbridled cruelty Jamie had overheard the night before in the upper corridor. "I don't know what I would do without you, Arthur," he said simply and with obvious sincerity. "I only hope that I don't put such heavy burdens on you that you are forced to look for another position."

There was a soft modest laugh. "I like it here, Geoffrey. It's quiet and out of the way. I'm more than willing to be of assistance as long as you will have me. It's just that I know nothing of snakes except to avoid them."

Both men laughed heartily at the weak joke. There

was a sudden scraping of a chair against the floor. Then Bledding spoke again, obviously trying to bring the conversation to a close. "I think the crypt would be best. Thin mesh wire cages of some sort. Check with old Endicott. He's good with a hammer."

Arthur Firth muttered something in agreement. Too late Jamie realized that the men were heading toward the door. He had no choice but to confront them in the doorway as though he had just arrived. This he did, making a show of rolling down his sleeves, trying to arrange his face into an expression of blank good humor.

"Luggage dispersed," he announced, overly loud.

Surprise washed over their faces at the sudden intrusion. Arthur Firth drew back as though under attack.

Bledding held his ground, although he stood staring at Jamie, as though he were suspect of the sudden appearance. Then, "Very good," he murmured. "I appreciate your help."

Jamie watched him intently. "Is there anything else, Mr. Bledding?" he asked now, still blocking the door.

For a moment Bledding seemed confused. He raised his forefinger as though asking for patience until his mind cleared. "As a matter of fact, there is," he said finally. "The Genealogy Society would like to go to Sledmere tomorrow. The Christophers have very kindly offered to open their family books. Would it be possible—"

Jamie agreed, the picture of cooperation. "No trouble, Mr. Bledding. I know the house. What time?"

Again there was that momentary confusion in the man's face. Finally Bledding said, "About one, I should imagine. I'll confirm it for you later. You might bring the coach to the gatehouse and load there. If that's convenient, of course."

Jamie nodded. In a way he could not bear those vague skittish eyes. Neither could he understand the realization that he had seen nothing in the man's face to match or support what he had overheard in the upper corridor. This was no demon standing before him, merely a harried and overworked warden, considering simultaneously the welfare of his students as well as his staff.

"Very well," Jamie concluded, now more than ready to end the conversation. He bobbed his head and stepped backward into the corridor.

Suddenly, to his left, coming at full steam, as it were, from the direction of the family wing, he saw a very red-faced, clearly distraught Martin Axtell. The man was alone and discernibly angry. With each step he stabbed at the floor with his umbrella, dragging his mac behind him, his eyes slightly bulging in his anger.

"Geoffrey!" he bellowed while he was still a distance away.

Jamie stepped farther back in order to avoid a collision. He saw Bledding peer around the corner of the door. Still Martin Axtell came at a thundering pace, his expression stern, his anger almost out of control. When he was only about ten feet away, he shouted at the top of his lungs, "Are you making a bid for the prisoner's dock? You won't like it; I can assure you of that. But let me warn you—"

Quickly Geoffrey tried to hush him up. And when he saw that he couldn't, he cleared the office and sent Arthur Firth running while Jamie withdrew to the stairs which led to the basement dining room. He descended about six steps, then stopped, out of sight but still within hearing distance.

The old doctor continued his diatribe as loud as ever, as though his sense of outrage could no longer be contained. "Certain things I will accept responsibility for, Geoffrey," he shouted now. "Certain other things, I will not. I don't know what you thought you were accomplishing up there, but let me tell you—"

Then the door was closed. For a moment he heard Axtell's voice, muted but still audible. Then that, too, ceased as apparently Bledding convinced him of the necessity for quiet. Slowly Jamie climbed back to the top of the stairs. He heard nothing now. The central corridor was deserted. Arthur Firth had disappeared. In the distance near the top of the hall he heard the laughter of the Newcastle Genealogy Society. Below him in the basement he heard the clatter of preparation for the noon meal. He found himself looking for Caldy More, but she, too, was no place in sight. Rain or no, he considered running out to the garden wall. But he knew better, knew he would find the garden empty.

Instead he took the steps to the third floor three at a time, pushed his way through the room-hopping, chattering students, moving rapidly toward the quiet at the end of the hall. He passed his own door and came to a stop at the grillwork barrier. His hands grasped the bars as though he intended to pull them down. Carefully he listened.

Nothing. No sound at all beyond the heavy drapes. He felt shut out, cut off, felt clearly that something terrible had happened and he was not privy to any of the details. He bowed his head and seized the bars again, then turned abruptly and went into his room.

He sat at the foot of the bed and peered down into the rain-soaked outer gardens. Again he felt the splintering effect of his thoughts. It was none of his concern. It was his only concern. Injustices had been committed. Still, she was another man's wife. She was as sane and rational as he was. She was clearly ill. He should never have come here at all. It was the only place in all of England where he was supposed to be. There was nothing he could do. Someone had to do something.

In thinking on all this, Jamie leaned closer to the window, saw below him the central promenade, where, on that first night, he had witnessed the couple in close embrace. He remembered it now as clearly as though it had just happened.

Suddenly he leaned closer to the window. Through the veil of rain he thought he saw them again. There!

About halfway down the promenade. Clearly two figures. He cursed the rain-splattered window that partially obscured his vision and pressed closer still, blinking his eyes rapidly in an attempt to clear them.

At first he thought they were statues, but they were standing a distance removed from the avenues of statuary. And on closer examination, he saw it was not the lovers this time, not, at least, as he had first seen them in the garden. This time it was the black-hooded specter again. And in his arms he was carrying a woman. She appeared to be faint in his arms, her head and hands hanging limply down, her legs. . . .

Suddenly Jamie pressed closer to the window. The distortion of rain and fog on the glass continued to obscure his vision, but he thought he saw in the wet dusk two rivulets of blood seeping out from beneath her long skirts.

For a moment he could not drag his eyes away from the horror. But then suddenly a movement from the faceless black hood again attracted his attention, the same gesture of warning, tinged now, or so it seemed to him, with unbearable sadness.

Because he was standing so close to the window, Jamie's breath fogged the glass surface, further impeding his vision. With the sleeve of his jacket he tried to wipe it clear. And a moment later the wind shifted and hurled a solid sheet of rain against the hall, and for several minutes he saw nothing but gray wetness.

When the wind shifted again and the rain subsided, they were gone. He searched the gardens below as far as he could see from his limited angle and again cursed the rain and his faulty vision and everything that he could not understand.

He closed his eyes against the vivid memory. The fact that he could not share his feelings, his suspicions with anyone only exacerbated his despair. If he had just stayed in Manchester, or if he had never seen the young woman in the first place.

But he had seen her, and now he suspected that she

needed him, and there was no way he could go to her. He continued to stare down at the rain.

There was nothing to do but endure his misery. And wait. . . .

⚜ 28 ⚜

Martin Axtell paced the tiny office, five steps in one direction, three in the other. He knew precisely what was the matter. He was afraid, had been clearly frightened by what he had found in the upper bedchamber. He loathed officers of the law with their arrogant ways and endless prying questions. He had taken one look at the woman on the bed and his mind had raced ahead to a hideous projection: homicide, wife beaten to death, inquiry, the local physician called to testify, the past resurrected and laid out for all the snooping eyes of Yorkshire, Geoffrey imprisoned, Martin Axtell labeled, perhaps even London headlines, HOMOSEXUAL DOCTOR PLAYS PART IN WIFE MURDER.

Now he shuddered audibly and turned to face the rather sullen man behind the desk. He saw not a trace of conscience on the bland face. Geoffrey seemed more concerned that Martin might start shouting again, as though shouting were a much greater crime than the one he had almost committed this weekend.

Martin stared gloomily back at him. His race was over. Now it was time for hard straight talk. "Do you have any idea what you almost did?" he asked, standing before the desk, confronting Geoffrey directly.

Bledding offered a weak excuse. "She was quite out of control. She had to be subdued."

"She is scarcely recognizable as a human being."

"It was for her own good."

"Of course."

A silence.

He saw Geoffrey shuffle through the messed papers on his desk. "Well, is she all right?" he asked.

"I can't say, Geoffrey. There was little I could do."

"You're a doctor, aren't you?"

"Just that. No more."

Their eyes met for a moment. No sound, but a floor-board or two that creaked as Martin paced.

At last Bledding spoke again. "What do you advise?"

"That you stay away from her. Completely."

"She's my wife."

"Yes, and they'll take that into stern consideration at your trial."

Bledding stared up at him. "Trial? She's not—"

"No, but I don't know why she insists on surviving."

Then finally, wearily, Geoffrey buried his face in his hands. From behind this barrier he muttered, "Then place her in an asylum. I'm sick of her."

"That would have been a good idea a few days ago. Not now."

"Why not now?"

For a moment Martin felt his patience dwindling. "Our courts frown on battered women, Geoffrey. Counselors have an annoying habit of asking the most embarrassing questions. Unpleasant charges could be leveled against you. The involvement of the National Trust in your affairs would make it even worse. You could lose everything."

For the first time Martin was certain that his words had penetrated. Geoffrey looked quite shocked, an expression that slid into a grave melancholia.

Before such a devastating look Martin softened. He leaned across the desk. "I know what course to take even if you don't."

Geoffrey stared down at the carpet. Almost pitifully he murmured, "Then, tell me. Obviously I need help."

Good words. At least they were a start. Martin commenced pacing again, no longer in anger, the woman upstairs all but forgotten in his now extremely pleasant projection of a future in which Geoffrey Bledding needed him.

"Stay away from her," he began, "stay completely away from her. You must face within yourself the knowledge that you want to kill her, and will, if given enough chances." He looked over his shoulder to see if the man was listening. He was. Buoyed by the close attention, he went on. "Let her heal. At the end of the summer, when you have a semblance of privacy again, I know a small asylum outside London. It is conducted in an intelligent and enlightened manner. I should not recommend a public institution. Commitments can be traced. It would not be good for you or Bledding Sorrow."

Slowly Goffrey stood and walked to the far wall. Aimlessly he ran his hand over a leather-bound set of volumes. He appeared to be digesting Martin's advice. "Stay away from her, you say?" he repeated. "You mean, move out?"

Martin nodded. "It would be a good idea. Leave her to Caldy More. But you must not go near her. Is that clear?"

Geoffrey nodded. He looked vaguely about the small office. "I could move a sofa in here."

Martin winced at the thought of the master of Bledding Sorrow sleeping on a sofa. He grew expansive and generous. "There's plenty of room at my house. A five-minute walk would put you here every morning at eight thirty." He stepped toward the man at the bookcase. "Let me look after your needs," he murmured. "I know them well enough." He was so close now that he might have touched him. He noticed that the hand caressing the books trembled slightly. He noticed further that the fingers were long and white and delicately tapered. Now he ached for physical contact, but he knew he dare not push too fast too soon. He viewed Geoffrey as a shy virgin who would have to be led subtly to his bed.

"Let me help you, Geoffrey," he whispered, clasping his hands behind his back in order to keep them under control. "I would hate to see a man of your caliber in prison." He shook his head softly. "What a waste, what a terrible waste. And all because of a cheap American wife who tricked you into marriage, then drove you to distraction."

At this close range Martin found himself fixating on the fine blond hair, the way it curled against the nape of the neck, the shell of an ear, the mouth, the lips slightly parted in the throes of personal agony.

Abruptly Martin moved away back to the desk, his rate of breathing labored, knowing that if he lingered a moment longer, he would be forced to touch, to fondle, to embrace.

Now in an expansive mood, he invited, "Come to dinner tonight, Geoffrey, and we'll discuss it further, No need to decide now, and absolutely no need to let matters depress you. The wretched woman is still alive, will probably outlive all of us. What we must concern ourselves with now is you, your well-being. You understand, of course."

For a long time Geoffrey did not stir, did not respond in any way. Again Martin sensed in the man a new vulnerability, which pleased him enormously. It was good to see him faltering, standing helpless, clearly in need of strong supportive arms. "Geoffrey?" he prompted gently. "Are you all right?"

Slowly the man turned. His face was positively ashen, as though he had his first clear glimpse of where his uncontrollable temper might have led him, might yet lead him if he wasn't careful. "Yes, I'm fine, Martin," he said. He smiled weakly, beautifully. "But I'm afraid you must decide my fate. Apparently I'm incapable."

Martin nodded, scarcely able to contain himself. In addition to the new vulnerability, he saw something else even better, a sense of resignation, a letting go of the female upstairs who had caused them both such grief.

"No more talk, then," Martin soothed. "Tonight? Around eight. Good wine. Good food. Just the two of us?"

Geoffrey nooded. "I'm grateful."

Martin lifted his hand in warm salute. A few moments later he was walking across the courtyard in a steady downpour, his umbrella closed uselessly at his side, his mac swung over his shoulder, planning the menu, envisioning the table, the fire, the bed, feeling nothing but a sense of accomplishment, a growing excitement. Something was about to happen. In a way, he was grateful to the cursed, battered woman.

Then he increased his step. He longed to be alone with his own thoughts. As in any courtship, fantasy and anticipation were at least half the mystery, half the delight. . . .

❦ 29 ❧

The rain persisted throughout the whole long day, and during all that time Jamie did not stir from the foot of his bed. He felt the need neither for food nor for human companionship, but instead sat by the window and watched the light change, the rain increase, and in truth saw neither light nor rain, saw instead a blond bowed head, small, incredibly white bare feet, a finely chiseled face, and dark blue eyes, heard her soft, terrified voice, the way sentences were formed laboriously and incomplete, both heard and saw her crouched at the bottom of the wall, holding the book as though she intended never to let it go, then letting go at last in order to keep *him* safe.

He stared down into the garden, then lowered his head, his heart beating, as if he had just stepped back from the brink of a cliff. The most predominant sensation was an incomprehensible sense of helplessness, of not having firm control, indeed any control at all over his own fate and destiny. Now for the first time he felt the chill dampness seeping through the window. He bowed his head again, his clasped hands falling limply between his legs, a pitiful figure, obscurely flattened, a man who at the moment of greatest need for clear vision had gone suddenly blind.

Then softly he heard a knock at his door. He glanced at his watch. Half past eight. For the first time he realized that he had sat the whole afternoon in his room.

Then the knock came again, accompanied by a faint call. "Mr. Pask, are you there?"

He looked toward the door as though trying to see through it. No one had ever knocked on his door before. It occurred to him that his prolonged absence might have been noted, that there were additional jobs that needed doing, although he couldn't imagine what.

The knock came a third time. "Mr. Pask, if you're in, please. . . ."

The voice sounded female and faint. One of the serving girls no doubt, sent to fetch him for God knew what purpose.

Annoyed, he went to the door and opened it a crack. To his complete surprise, he saw, standing on the other side, a very drawn Caldy More.

His senses quickened. He opened the door wider. Here, standing before him, was the one person who could give him information. He stepped back. "Caldy More. Come in, please."

But she shook her head and moved back from the door as though embarrassed. She seemed unable or unwilling to look him directly in the face, but kept her eyes down and riveted on her tightly clasped hands. "Will you come with me? Please?" she asked, and quickly bent her flushed face even lower.

"Where?" he asked.

But she shook her head, as though unable to speak.

He saw or thought he saw traces of tears on her cheeks. Now, not wanting to add to her distress, whatever its nature, he grabbed his jacket from the back of the chair and, without further questions, joined her in the corridor, closing the door behind him.

Instantly she took the lead, walking a good four or five paces ahead of him. She led the way through the twisting third-floor dormitory and down the steps, never once turning back with a word of explanation. Jamie considered speaking to her, but changed his mind. Caldy More was a woman whose silences did not beg to be entered, but rather respected.

Only once did he see her even begin to hesitate, and that was when she passed the closed door and darkened office of Geoffrey Bledding .Then it was not a hesitation so much as a subtle veering toward the far wall, a slight turn of her head as though she were afraid that at any moment the door might swing open and the man himself appear.

But once past that hazard, he saw her draw herself up and increase her speed, still obviously pensive, still determined. From the direction of the study room he heard a male voice expounding on the joys of discovering one's ancestors. "To find out who we are, we must discover who we were," Jamie heard, and the man said something else, but they were moving out of the range of hearing now and into the darkened Great Hall.

It was not until they were standing before the locked door which led to the private wing that he realized with a start where they might be going. As he watched her fumble with the keys, he dared for the first time to speak. "Caldy More, please tell me where—"

But she brushed him aside, sternly shaking her head as though words were not permitted. The door open, she stepped back and motioned him through with another quick jerk of her head.

Resignedly he followed her directions and found himself in a close, narrow anteroom. Ahead and to the right was an open door which appeared to lead to a small sitting room. To the left was a narrow and winding flight of steps, clearly a servant's access in the days when Bledding Sorrow had functioned as a private home.

In some awe and with increasing anxiety, he looked about at the mean surroundings. It was as though the world had suddenly gone gray and brown, all shadows with no visible light sources. Then he was following her again up the stairs, out of necessity this time, for the narrow passageway did not permit two abreast.

The ascent was steep. Several times he saw her reach out for the walls for support. During the climb he tried to get his bearings. They were in the private wing, clearly moving toward the top of the hall. If his estimations were correct, they should emerge into a long corridor at the end of which he would see heavy drapes and a grillwork barrier.

And he did. Breathless from the climb, they both paused at the top of the steps. Two bare bulbs lighted the passage. At the end of the corridor he saw the heavy drapes and knew that beyond them was the barrier and beyond that his room. They had gone in a wide circle, half the distance of the hall, down, then up again.

Caldy More turned and looked at him then. Even in that dim light he saw a confirmation of tears. Looking directly at him, she said, "You have a right to know that I am jeopardizing both our positions by bringing you here."

He waited a moment to see if she would say anything further, then noticed that she seemed to be waiting for his response. He nodded. "I understand."

She led the way down the corridor, talking as she walked, a welcome change from her prolonged silence. "I probably have no right to involve you," she began. She reached up and touched her forehead as though words were difficult. When now her glance met his, it seemed that she saw right through him and understood all. "Thank you for being kind to her," she said simply. She looked down. "*I* have not always been, and for that I'm deeply regretful." This was said as though there were no contradiction possible.

Then, as if she sensed his frustration about being kept waiting, she said, "There's much I should tell you, much I will tell you if you're interested, but now. . . ."

Now she stopped before the first closed door. He sensed within her a new defeat, as though she despised herself.

He reached out with a gesture of comfort, and as quickly she pulled away. Her head bowed and she murmured, as though angry, "She deserves kindness. She's done nothing to warrant. . . ." Again her voice broke.

With greater urgency Jamie begged, "Please open the door, Caldy More."

She looked up, her face brightening. "She asked for you. I would never have bothered you, but she ask—" She seemed as if she would like to say something else, but his stance of brisk waiting made her move past him, key in hand, and unlock the door.

She beckoned. With utmost quietness he stepped across the threshold. It was so still. Never had he heard such a silence before, as though the room were unoccupied. He trod cautiously behind her through a small barren antechamber, moving toward the light beyond the archway. She lowered her head again and indicated that he was to move past her.

Then he stood in the bedchamber itself. His eyes moved quickly over the spartan furnishings, coming at last to rest on the bed. His breath stopped. His head lifted as though invisible hands had clutched his throat. His face was like a crumbling wall. The terrible outrage in his soul was reflected in his eyes.

It was not a human face that rested on the pillow, but rather a purple swollen pulp of featureless flesh. Her eyes were closed, bluish protuberances, recognizable as eyes only by the thin fair brows above them. One unsutured cut above the left eye gaped like a tiny mouth, and a dried rivulet of blood cut jaggedly down the side of her left cheek. Her chin was lifted slightly, the swollen lips parted as though she were having difficulty in breathing. Smaller lacerations dotted the side of her jawbone, and on her thin arched throat he saw individual purple bruises as though a strong hand had held her fast. Everywhere he looked he saw a new source of agony, the tousled blood-matted hair, the single long scratch down the right side of her nose, the hideous raw scraped plane on her right temple glistening with fresh blood, as though she had been hurled to the floor, the thin outline beneath the coverlet lying perfectly still, as though any movement, no matter how slight, would cause new and unbearable discomfort.

With an acute abruptness he lowered his head. He

had seen fights, had once seen a man beaten senseless, but he had never seen anything like this. His chest rose as if he were out of breath; his eyes on her again. Someone was moving behind him, whispering foolishly, "I tried to stop him, but he locked the—"

Suddenly he made an angry gesture of his hand as though he didn't want to hear more. He continued to look down on her, something breaking within him, finding no way to share her agony or relieve her suffering. Uncertain what he should do, he stepped toward the bed and spoke to her. "Ann?" he whispered.

The head did not move. But one small hand resting at her side on top of the cover stirred, lifting, hung for a moment, then moved toward the sound of his voice.

Someone was arranging a chair behind him. He drew it closer to the edge of the bed and with great tenderness reached forward and took the hand, felt it press against his own broad palm.

Caldy More whispered as though pleased, "She knows you. She remembers—"

He heard the normally stern female voice break. At the same time he tightened his grip on the small hand, his eyes closed, fighting for control. Again that overwhelming sense of helplessness swept over him. There was nothing he could do. Without willing it, and certainly not wanting it, he saw a vision of the beating itself, saw her cringing before a terrifying specter, scrambling for safety only to be pulled forward again, on her knees before him, a hand holding her throat while the other hand delivered blow after blow, no escape, no respite, no choice but to endure.

Slowly he leaned forward and pressed his hands, still enclosing hers, against his forehead. At that moment she stirred; the battered head on the pillow tried to lift; the swollen lips parted and in the process cracked and bled.

Quickly Caldy More stepped forward with a clean napkin and dabbed at the blood running down her chin. In an obvious attempt to keep the young woman quiet, she picked up the thin volume of poetry from the table beside the bed. She handed it to Jamie, whispering, "Read. You gave it to her. It'll soothe her and bring her pleasure."

Jamie took the book and tried not to remember the sunny garden, the delight on her face as she had held the book. With one hand still holding hers, he adjusted the book with his free hand, turned to a random page, and commenced reading. With his eyes unfocused, the words danced on the page, but he closed them a moment to clear them, then continued reading.

The effect was immediate. Almost at once he felt in her a secession of fear. Her head lay back, the swollen features relaxing. The only evidence that she was conscious and listening was her hand in his, which did not merely rest there, but instead gripped his palm with weak but discernible pressure, as though she had to maintain that one connecting link or else he might vanish.

At some point during his reading he was aware of Caldy More slipping out of the room. Then he was aware of nothing but the words on the page, the sound of his own voice, the weak but continuous pressure of her hand in his. He lost track of time. The bare bulb overhead burned steadily throughout the night.

He must have dozed, for suddenly he was aroused from the fog of half sleep by the sensation of a new presence in the room. Still caught in the limbo between wakefulness and sleep, he looked down and saw the specter of a woman sitting on the floor near the side of the bed. And she, in turn, looked up at him, an expression of pain and urgency on her fair face. She sat awkwardly, her legs invisible beneath her, obscured by the folds of her long gown. Twice he saw her try to rise, and twice she failed, falling back each time, her agony increasing, tears now streaming down her cheeks, her head bowed in exhaustion.

Was he dreaming? In spite of that possibility, he longed to go to her aid, to lift her up from her pitiable position on the floor. But at the exact instant that he stretched out his hand in assistance, she drew back, her face lifted, her voice clearly audible now, a continuous moan out of which evolved the warning, "Take her away, take her away before it is too late."

Again he tried to reach out and touch her, and again she warned, "Take her away," an unearthly voice, as though an echo, resounding now through his brain, as though coming from a great distance, a barrier between them which would keep them forever separated.

Still in the dream, he heard himself trying to call to her, but his voice was obliterated by a sudden scream. He turned his head sharply to see where this new source of agony was coming from. And when he looked back, the woman was gone, and in her place on the floor were two blood-red spots, still freshly gleaming.

Suddenly he awakened, shifted himself from the uncomfortable position into which he had lapsed, and searched the room, again overwhelmed by the sensation that he was not alone, that in addition to Ann now asleep on the bed, there were other presences in the room, felt but not seen, other wills, other agonies.

He sat up now and rubbed the back of his neck. It wasn't until he saw the first light of dawn beyond the narrow barred window that he realized he had been with her all night. At some point the pressure from her hand had diminished. Still he sat beside her, holding the book in his lap. He tried to dismiss the hideous dream from his mind. There were other, more pressing matters.

Now he gazed wearily down on the bruised face and tried to understand only a portion of what she had endured. He reached over and gently touched her hair and vowed to himself that she would have better days.

He would see to it. He would see to it. . . .

⌬ 30 ⌬

The Newcastle Genealogy Society went someplace almost every day. The coach was in constant use. Jamie did not mind. On the contrary, he needed occupation and distraction quite apart from the evenings he spent in the small upper chamber, so as to refresh and rest himself from the violent emotions that continued to agitate him.

Then, too, daytime passage through Bledding Sorrow and entry to the private wing was hazardous. It was true that now Geoffrey Bledding spent every evening with Martin Axtell and did not return until after midnight. But still Caldy More had told Jamie after that first night that she could not permit him to visit in daylight. It was too great a gamble. For all of them.

Of course he understood. She *was* another man's wife, and certainly legally, and perhaps ethically and morally, Jamie had no right to see her at all. But these thoughts plagued him only during the daytime. At night, after the drive of the day was over, after Geoffrey Bledding had departed the hall for the evening, after the stealthy journey down the steps, the soft knock on the private door, and the quick climb up the narrow steps that led to her room, he always drew a breath of guilty relief. Safe. One night at a time. That was all he asked for.

And in truth, the sight of her each evening almost seemed like a confirmation of that intention, the last questioning of the unquestionable. He merely had to see her every day of his life, and then he would decide never to see her again.

He thought of her constantly during the coach journey of the day. But he didn't think about her in words,

289

rather in images. He saw eyes, the line of hair over a temple, a sleeping face, an outstretched hand. She was healing fast with the resiliency of the young, the purple swelling gone, only the deepest lacerations remaining.

He knew all about her now, for Caldy More had told him everything. During the first days when Ann's injuries were still fresh and severe, he had sat with her and read to her until she had fallen asleep. Then he had spent the rest of the evening with Caldy More, sharing a cup of tea, hearing different aspects of the incredible story; the American college where she had first met Bledding, the marriage, the arrival in England of the child bride, the death of her parents, the increased dosage of drugs over the years.

He had heard it all, and after each evening's recitation Jamie did not merely feel that he had had enough; what was of far greater importance was his growing sense of wonderment that she had survived at all, that and his ever-increasing need to see her again.

Now, about two weeks later—the Genealogy Society had departed and the Transport Restoration League had arrived—Jamie stood outside the grillwork barrier waiting for the prearranged signal from Caldy More that the coast was clear, that it was safe for him to start down the steps and up the other side, where she would meet him at the door.

It was almost nine o'clock. He had been waiting for half an hour and still no word. His impatience grew. The night before, he had left Ann sitting up in bed, her face almost healed, her timidity diminishing with his nightly visits, had heard her whispered confession that the nearer it came time for his visit, the more excited she became.

Now he stood on his side of the grillwork barrier, waiting, listening for Caldy More's step. It was agonizing to know that Ann was so close on the other side, yet clearly beyond his reach. As he waited, he studied the grillwork. It seemed to be held in place by four strong bolts at each corner. It would be a simple matter, with a wrench and screwdriver, to loosen two of the bolts, pull the barrier back, slip through, and restore it to its normal position. In the tool box in his coach he had a wrench and screwdriver. It would be a simple matter.

Suddenly he heard footsteps beyond the barrier. He leaned forward, pressing his face against the bars, ready and fully expecting to hear Caldy More's whispered, "It's all right now."

Instead he heard her say, "Not tonight. Something's happening."

And in the next moment he heard the footsteps moving away. Alarmed, he grasped the bars with both hands, "Caldy More?" he whispered. "What is it?"

The footsteps returned. He could hear her voice grow taut. "Go away," she whispered again. "It's not safe. Please go away."

He clung to the bars for a moment, then called again, more frantically, "Caldy More? What's happening?"

But there was no reply this time, only the sound of receding footsteps. His frustration and anxiety mounting, he considered making the journey anyway, of presenting himself at the family door and demanding an explanation. He'd thought that by now Caldy More was a clear ally. Had she betrayed him? Still he clung to the bars, trying to comprehend this unaccountable break in what had become habit. Ann was waiting for him, expecting him. He could not and would not disappoint her. For the first time he comprehended the intense passion which now filled his whole life. If something serious was happening, he felt that he had a right to know.

But still he waited, some strong, persistent wisp of conscience reminding him that she *was* another man's wife, although the thought appalled him.

The waiting grew intolerable. Again he studied the system of bolts which held the barrier in place. In a way, it might be better for him to stay here. With her room less than twenty feet away, he could hear clearly everyone who came and went. But in truth, the upper corridor was quiet. The general commotion seemed to be coming from the lower part of the private wing, doors opening and closing, a man or men's voices raised in conversation.

Slowly he sank down to the floor. He really didn't give a damn what went on in the rest of the hall. His only concern was for the small door which led to her bedroom.

He looked about him. Then the din of his thoughts began again. He had no right. . . . He had every right. . . . She was another man's wife. . . . She was a solitary child. . . . Her presence physically affected him. . . . She was only an invalid in need of solace. . . . It was impossible to go on concealing things from Geoffrey Bledding. . . . It was inconceivable that they not go on. . . .

Suddenly a hot flush came over his face. His eyes moved swiftly to the two bolts on the left, as though they had spoken to him. It would be such a simple matter. . . .

Then he was on his feet and running down the hall to the stairs and down the stairs to the central corridor, dodging transport students with every step, intent only on reaching the front door, the courtyard, the road, the pasture, his coach, the tool box, then the wrench and screwdriver.

All this accomplished, the two tools in hand, he started back down the dark road. As he approached the gatehouse arch, he heard voices coming across the courtyard, heading toward the road. Quickly he drew back into shadows.

A moment later two male figures appeared, both carrying heavy pieces of luggage. For a minute, as his eyes tried to penetrate the darkness, he thought they were two students. Then, as they drew even with him, he saw clearly the larger man with his arm around his companion's shoulder, urging him to "Breathe deeply, Geoffrey. It's a rare air, a free air. Feel it?"

But the other man said nothing and walked steadily

ahead, leaning away from the weight of his luggage and toward the arm that embraced him.

Jamie watched them until they disappeared into darkness. Then quickly he ran back into the hall. He was just starting up the stairs when he encountered a very flushed and agitated Caldy More coming down. He drew her to one side of the steps. "What happened?" he demanded.

She shrugged, her face as red and perspiring as he had ever seen it. "He left," she declared, still clearly struggling with her own amazement. "He simply packed his bags and left."

"Where?"

Again she shrugged. "He said it was best if he stayed with Martin Axtell for a time. He said. . . ." She stopped and pulled farther to one side to permit two students to pass on the steps. She smiled and nodded to them, waited until they were out of sight, then resumed talking, her voice lowered, though still rushed. "I don't understand," she went on. "Martin was with him, helped him pack his things. I tried to get him to talk to me, but he seemed angry. All he said was that Martin had talked him into the wisdom of moving out for a while, that he would be back every morning at eight and stay until after dinner, and that I was to tell no one of his leaving. He said it was only temporary, until other arrangements could be completed."

She made a curious swift pursing of her mouth, accompanied by a shake of her head. "He's never done anything like this before. I don't understand."

Neither did Jamie. He looked down on her, concerned. "Did he. . . ?"

She shook her head, anticipating his question. "He didn't go near her, didn't even inquire about her, hasn't even recognized her existence since the night of the beating. He said he was leaving things in my hands." Now she stood with her eyes fiercely fixed on the banister beside her. "It's totally without precedent," she murmured. "It was bad enough having him here.

But now it's worse having him gone." She looked up at him, beseeching. "How will we possibly know when he's going to. . . ?"

"Return?" Jamie completed the question for her. In spite of his confusion at recent events, he smiled and tightened his grip on the tools in his hand. "Come on," he ordered.

But Caldy More protested. "She's waiting for you. I looked in on her before I came for you, and she's certain that you're not. . . ."

Jamie was already several steps ahead of her. "I'll get there quicker my way than yours. Come along now, and hurry."

Then it was his turn to lead the way back up the stairs to the third-floor dormitory. Once or twice it was necessary to stop and chat briefly with a student. With the instinct of culprits, both Jamie and Caldy More seemed to sense the need for normal appearances. To have raced through the corridor as his emotions suggested would have accomplished nothing except a Pied Piper trail of curious and slightly bored students.

So they stopped and chatted, inquired about the quality of dinner that evening, gave directions several times to the village pub about two miles away, and finally turned the last corner, which led to Jamie's room and the grillwork barrier.

Caldy More, still bewildered, protested every step of the way. "I left all the doors unlocked," she pleaded. "We're wasting time."

Not until Jamie held up the wrench and reached for the highest bolt did she perceive what he was going to do. She gasped. "No! You can't. He said he would be back. He'll see it and know—"

"I'm not going to take it down, Caldy More," he snapped. "I'm just going to remove these two bolts."

She bowed her head. His voice had been too stern. He hesitated, then stepped back and laid his hand on her shoulder comfortingly. "This way I can slip in *and* out. To all appearances it will look as it has always looked. But if he should come back unexpected and start up to her room, then I *would* be trapped. This is what you might call a fire exit. Nothing more."

He had hoped by his brief gesture and assurance to take the first step toward easing her fear. But apparently she'd lived too long under the stern domination of Geoffrey Bledding. All the while that he worked, her eyes were aflame and she continuously threw apprehensive glances back down the corridor as though the master might appear at any moment and catch them in the act. Even when he had successfully loosened the barrier on one side and pulled it back wide enough for the passage of one person, still she hesitated.

Quickly, easily, he slipped through as though to demonstrate for her how it was done. Ahead of him by about ten feet he saw Ann's door, the temple which in the past he had reached only after a fifteen-minute sprint through the most hazardous of territory. Now how simple it was. In a matter of seconds he could enter where he was not supposed to be or retreat to the legitimacy of his room, with no one the wiser.

All this he tried to convey to Caldy More in so many words. But it was only when he reached through and took her hand and personally guided her across the barrier, pulled the iron grille back into place and readjusted the drapes that she even halfway relented.

"Look," he urged, pointing to the barrier. "Can you tell that anything is amiss?"

Reluctantly she shook her head.

"When I return, I'll reinsert the bolts, and it will be as Bledding installed it. Nothing changed."

But still she wasn't convinced. Not until Jamie offered wearily, "I'll take full responsibility. If we're ever discovered, you knew nothing about it."

At last she nodded. Her eyes then made the brief passage from where they stood to Ann's door. "It *would* be easier," she conceded.

Relieved, he smiled. "Then, let's hurry. You said yourself she was waiting."

What control Jamie had felt himself gaining now slipped away as he entered the small bedchamber. She was sitting up in bed. She looked at him, with an intense earnestness and supplication, and with a declaration so unmistakable that words were needless.

"I'm sorry I'm late, he murmured. He slowly reached out his hand and touched hers. Their eyes remained on each other's faces. She seemed to him the most beautiful creature he had ever seen.

In the moment before she spoke, he imagined himself taking her in his arms, felt clearly in his imagination the whole close substance of her body, her fragility, her tenderness.

He pushed the image gently away and fed instead on her whispered words. "I was afraid that you wouldn't come."

The words were barely audible, but they silenced Jamie. She had missed him, she needed him. An agonized look, as though he were enduring the most incredible torture, passed over his face. Once he glanced over his shoulder and saw Caldy More still standing in the archway with great cow eyes.

Then she left, and Jamie sat on the edge of the bed and allowed himself to get hopelessly lost in the depths of Ann's face.

With no words spoken and feeling only a peace he had never felt before, he sat with her until she slipped down beneath the covers and, still clutching his hand, fell easily into sleep. . . .

~~∞⟨ 31 ⟩∞~~

At midsummer Bledding Sorrow was at its busiest and loveliest. Denied the dramatic frontal view of most stately homes and Great Houses with their sweeping lawns and shimmering fountains, Bledding Sorrow, over the centuries, had learned to live with its rather ugly and certainly hazardous proximity to the main road. Beyond the sloping courtyard and gatehouse arch there was little anyone could do except struggle for survival as they tried to enter the sixteenth-century road which now was trying futilely to cope with twentieth-century traffic.

By way of compensation, Bledding Sorrow, under the gruff and slightly alcoholic guidance of old Peter Endicott, had created a horticultural paradise to the rear of the hall.

Counted as one of the loveliest gardens in all of England, in mid-July it was a dazzling sight of late-blooming roses, asters, larkspur, delphinium, lilies of all sorts, trailing fuchsias, foxglove, early-blooming chrysanthemums, stock, daisies, bleeding hearts; in short, if it bloomed and had color, it could be found in the gardens of Bledding Sorrow.

Interspersed with the floral displays were the topiary trees, pyramids of conical-shaped green, squat fat shrubs, and, framing the entire spectacle, a leafy fringe of light chartreuse willows. Then, adding to the enchantment, at certain intervals, in semicircles of beauty were the statues, full-size and magnificent reproductions of rural working men and women, some captured so perfectly at the job of the moment that from a distance they looked wholly real.

It was a place of incredible and magical beauty,

floral odors mingling with the good smells of sun and earth, a paradise for photographers, for anyone who drew nourishment from the miraculous fertility and variety of nature.

But to the left of the hall, in the small walled private garden, a miracle of greater proportions had occurred. The mistress of Bledding Sorrow had enjoyed a resurrection certainly as great as that of Lazarus. Every morning she could be found tending her flowers as ambitiously if not as expertly as Peter Endicott tended his. She bore little resemblance to the crumpled ill woman who had wandered directionless about the garden only a few weeks earlier. This new woman stood erect, the attractive fabric of new dresses—courtesy of Caldy More—nestling with special softness around her neck, her smooth bare arms turning golden in the sun. Her eyes sparkled and her lips could not keep from smiling at her awareness of her new attractiveness.

Now she stooped and bent with graceful ease, her hands moving over the flowers, plucking the dead blossoms and casting them aside, talking aloud to the new buds, urging them to grow. Almost every room in the family wing now contained bowls of her flowers. And she always saved the choicest for James Pask, blushing a little as she presented them to him, still not absolutely certain what her feelings should be toward this tall, gaunt man who had brought her back from the dead and whose approach could cause inside her the most incredible turbulence of feeling.

In her return to the living, she had, unfortunately, brought with her a clear awareness of who she was, what she was, where she was, and how she came to be there. She knew she was a wife, but she also knew that she never saw her husband. No one ever mentioned him. In fact Caldy More seemed to go out of her way to avoid the subject. Now Ann was beginning to see how easily it would be to forget him completely, as though he had never existed.

James came daily to visit her, whenever he could get away from his coaching duties. And she found herself living in a state of prolonged and intense anticipation, hoping, praying to catch a glimpse of his strong face. Sometimes she caught herself so urgently wishing for his presence that she felt tears in her eyes and her hands would tremble, and she would have to make herself sit very still until the longing passed for fear that Caldy More would see her and think the old illness was returning when she had sat for hours, weeping and trembling for no reason.

She was grateful that all her old specters, all the old horrors and visions which used to plague her were now gone. On thinking this, she looked quickly around, as though to confirm that which she fervently hoped was true.

Suddenly, as though to prove her wrong, she saw, coming from the exact center of the grassy plot, the specter of the hideous woman, evolving again, swirling slowly out of the blaze of sunlight. Again the woman was awkwardly crumpled on the grass, continuously reaching toward the hem of her skirt, her face twisted into angles of pain.

Ann drew quickly back, taking refuge for a moment on the stone bench, telling herself over and over again that what she was seeing was not real, had no basis in reality, but was merely the remnant of her old sickness. On this false note of self-comfort, she dared to look back. But the woman was still there, something terribly wrong with her, now dragging herself across the lawn, her thin, high-pitched voice again taking shape out of the silence, crying pleading, begging for Ann to run away.

Now she was less than three feet from the stone bench, the mysterious deadweight of her body dragging after her, reaching out with one hand, the urgent entreaty on her face as clear as Ann had ever seen it.

Again Ann resisted, denied what she saw and what she was hearing, and quickly hid her face in her hands, hoping, praying that when she looked back, the terrible woman would be gone.

And she was. The grass was merely grass again, and the only sounds were distant birdcalls, insects buzzing in near roses, and the faint rumbling of traffic coming from the road in front of Bledding Sorrow.

Weakened, still shaken, Ann sat very rigidly on the bench, trying to hold herself together. She must not let Caldy More see her like this. She must convince them all and herself as well that she was whole again, rational, fit, no longer plagued by visions and specters that were visible to no one else.

Thus holding herself in check, she resumed her walk, an apparently calm exterior, but still feeling a strange discomfort in the ghostly woman's continuous presence, a sense of foreboding, the certain knowledge that she was alone, yet not alone.

Now, as she moved down the garden path, she scanned the flowers and the high red brick wall behind them. She seemed to be making an effort to control herself as she moved forward in a self-possessed resolute manner. Suddenly she bent her head low as though trying hard not to look at the confinement of the wall, trying equally as hard not to remember why she was imprisoned behind it. Others came and went, James, Caldy More. But she remained fixed, moving only on a path preordained by someone else.

Still, the thought of total freedom was a frightening one. It had been so long since she had seen any human face other than those who were familiar to her. Of late and by listening carefully, she had heard voices in the outer gardens. On occasion she had pressed close to the wall, trying to overhear what was being said, and in those moments she had become again agonizingly shy, imagining herself in a position that required response and fearful that her old silence would return. And the daily medicine. And the nightly horrors.

Now, thinking on these things, she felt her heart

beating far faster than the slow walk down the path warranted. At the end of the garden she took refuge in her favorite spot, the place where she had first seen him perched on the wall. How long ago? Time still seemed lost in a mist.

Now she pressed against the wall and tried to reach up. Short, by too many feet. If only it had occurred to the copper beech tree to grow on *this* side of the wall. She stretched again.

Softly she heard a familiar voice behind her. "I'm afraid you need help," he said.

She turned quickly and saw him standing at the center of the green lawn in a blaze of sun, his hands thrust into his pockets, a smile on his face so beautiful as to defy description.

She had not even a hope of looking normal. Flustered, yet pleased, she did well to straighten her dress, which had become twisted in the process of reaching up. Now, as she saw him start toward her, she ducked her head to hide her embarrassment. Then they stood less than five feet apart, both clearly moved by what they saw.

Jamie asked, "Would you like to see over the wall?"

She gave him an imperceptible nod and seemed to hesitate. But then she saw him standing close beside her, his hands cupped and laced before him, indicating that she was to put her foot in the support and hoist herself up.

She shook her head and drew back, the old timidity washing over her. "I can't."

"Of course you can," he countered, his dark eyes catching hers in a swift sideways glance.

Then he was urging her again. "Come on. Step in, and I'll lift you the rest of the way. The gardens are lovely now. You should see them."

She stared at the cupped hands before her as if she could think of no further reason to refuse. Then slowly she stepped forward, lifted her foot, hesitantly placed her hands on his shoulders, and in an effortless gesture he lifted her to the top of the wall.

Quickly she adjusted herself on the precarious perch, felt the wind blowing her hair a little stronger. Suddenly she looked back down on him, saw his arms still raised toward her as though to help steady her. For a moment, in the warmth and pleasure of his face, she forgot what it was she was supposed to view from the top of the wall.

She smiled and her smile was reflected by him. Rather huskily he reminded her, "The gardens. Look at the gardens."

She obeyed him and lifted her head and for the first time in several long years saw a horizon that was not red brick. Her conception of space was somewhat distorted by her long confinement. She felt at first as though the wind and openness would devour her. As she clutched at the wall, she felt him moving closer, holding onto her legs, as though he understood what she was experiencing, reminding her that he was there and she was not to be afraid.

And she wasn't. Now fully adjusted to a limitless world, she allowed her eyes to scan slowly the incredibly beautiful panorama before her. Every place she looked was a new and greater delight. Her eyes flashed with appreciation as she took it all in, the flowers, the topiary trees, and, more beautiful than anything else, the distant fringe of willows, beyond which lay an even more vast horizon, as broad as the world.

Suddenly she gave a start. Her face clouded. She gasped. "There are people."

But he held fast to her legs, laughing softly. "No. Look again. They're not moving, are they?"

In spite of her dismay, she obeyed him, her eyes fastening now on the peculiar gray people who seemed frozen at their jobs.

"They're statues," he said from the ground. "Would you like to see them up close?"

She looked down on him. "You mean, leave the garden?"

"Why not? We can go one of two ways. Either over the wall now or later through the hall."

He seemed so confident. She wished she could share that confidence. "I'm not supposed to. . . ."

"To what?" he demanded. "This is your home. You have a right to do anything you please."

Still unconvinced and growing nervous on her high perch, she whispered, "What if someone sees?"

"Then, let them."

Her hands were trembling. The thought of walking freely with him beside her was an overpowering one. Still, there were the old risks, the old hazards. She had been shut away and punished for a purpose. What if that purpose still existed? What if her jailor caught her and there was new punishment. She couldn't endure that. Not now.

Apparently he saw the torment on her face, for quickly he reached up, held out his arms, clearly indicating that she was to come to him.

As she leaned forward, he lifted her toward him, more than lifted, held her close. In the sudden and transparent stillness of the day the smallest sounds were audible; a bee buzzing in near roses, the slight wind rustling the leaves of the copper beech. But she was aware of nothing but the sensation of his arms around her, her feet not even touching the ground as yet, held suspended by the force of his arms, his head bent close to hers.

It seemed an eternity, though in reality it was no more than four or five seconds, merely a man helping a woman off a wall. Nothing more.

When she felt earth beneath her feet again, she stepped back, her heart racing. She could not bear to look at him and it was while her eyes were down that she heard him suggest in a voice that was itself quite breathless, "Then we will walk tonight. You'll feel safer then. Tonight I'll show you the gardens."

Her mouth slightly opened, she nodded, certain that night would never come. Strange and mysterious feelings continued to plague her. Now she felt only the need to move away from him. Yet at the instant of this thought, as he took her hand to assist her back to the path, she wanted more than anything to feel his arms around her again.

In a shaking voice she asked, "Are you sure it will be all right?"

He nodded his assurance and continued to hold her hand the length of the garden and into the small kitchen.

Although nothing was pursuing them and there was nothing to run away from, and they could not possibly have found anything very exciting on that garden wall, they hurried into the kitchen, past Caldy More working at the stove, on their way to separate destinations with stricken, though radiant faces. . . .

❦ 32 ❧

Contrary to Ann's absolute conviction, night *did* come. At supper she learned that Caldy More had been apprised of the plan, that Jamie had reassured her that no one stirred in Bledding Sorrow past one in the morning, that he would come for Ann at that time, lead her through the grillwork barrier and down the central staircase. Apparently he had promised further that he would limit this excursion to the gardens themselves and would have Ann safely back within the hour.

Caldy More told her all this over their simple dinner, as though she were trying to convince herself of the safety and prudence of the plan. Ann heard her out, saying nothing, simply listening and seeing finally that strange sad glint of remorse in the old woman's eyes, as though now, for some reason, she was incapable of denying Ann anything.

Dinner over, they washed their few dishes together, then Caldy More suggested with growing excitement that since the evening promised to be a long one, Ann should go to her room and rest awhile. She would join her there later and help her dress.

Ann thought the suggestion strange. She had not needed help in dressing for some time now. But she did as she was told, climbed the narrow flight of stairs, her mind and heart racing ahead to the moment of his arrival, her first journey beyond the confines of this prison.

Now, sitting alone on the edge of her bed, far too excited even to consider resting, she looked about her and, with a wave of pleasure, realized how much her life had changed within the last few weeks. The door was no longer locked at any time and generally stood propped open as now, a glorious ease in comings and goings, Caldy More popping in continuously with small gifts; a new piece of fabric from the village, a hand mirror, a fine brush, a handful of ribbons.

At first, when Ann had been recuperating, she had been terribly apprehensive about the old woman's behavior. The ancient eyes, which now shone with a peculiar brilliance, had once been the predominant features of Ann's nightmares. She still didn't understand everything and frequently exhausted herself trying in some way to account for her own resurrection. And ultimately understanding didn't seem all that important. She was alive, had recaptured a portion of her dignity. She knew where she was and who she was and sometimes even had the courage to think of home and all she had lost there.

Now she left the bed and paced restlessly. At one o'clock, he had said. She had no watch or clock, no possible way to chart the passage of time. Beyond the small barred window she saw night. It must be late, or it could be early. Perhaps he wouldn't come, or perhaps he would, and the thought of both these possibilities struck her as so awesome that, without dwelling on them for a moment, she went back to the bed and sat again, her hands laced rigidly in her lap.

Suddenly she moaned softly. There was nothing very unusual about it. Its deepest implications merely represented a hunger and a need that had never been satisfied. She looked about the room now with frightened eyes. If only she could understand everything, anything. Her life, carefully and lovingly plotted for nineteen years, had then gone hopelessly awry. How long it had been since any voice, any action or response had made the slightest sense to her.

She folded her hands again, trying to bring herself to a semblance of control. She was here, something had conspired to lead her to this small dismal upper

bedchamber, some force—she could not guess what—
had almost anihilated her, but had decided at the last
minute that it needed her further and so had granted
her this reprieve. Now she sat motionless, one hand
not responding to the pressure from the other.

Suddenly she knew that she was not in the room
alone. In the last few minutes she had been joined by
another presence. Slowly she turned her head in all
directions. There! The specter of the woman was there
beneath the window, sitting on the floor, again continuously pulling at her legs, obscured as always by the
long folds of her skirts.

But this time Ann saw something more, saw clearly
blood on the woman's hand, fresh blood or so it seemed,
some terrible wound beneath her skirts now freshly
bleeding.

In a spasm of terror, Ann wrenched her head to one
side, softly begging the vision to go away, to leave her
alone, when suddenly, without warning, the woman
was moving toward her, one bloodied hand outstretched
as though warning Ann, coming closer, closer.

No, she mustn't permit it. She was seeing nothing
because nothing was there, nothing was in the room
with her. She was quite alone. With her eyes tightly
closed, she told herself over and over again that nothing was there, nothing was coming close to her. It was
all in her imagination.

And when, a few moments later, she looked down
toward the floor, the woman was gone.

So intense was her concentration that she failed to
hear Caldy More coming down the corridor. Not until
the old woman was standing in the archway, scolding
her for looking as though she had been talking with
ghosts, did Ann look up. Then she saw her, the old
eyes glittering again with that peculiar brightness, holding in her arms a lovely new full-length gown of the
softest of blue.

Ann thought quickly, it was guilt again, the cornu-
copia from which spilled an endless supply of kind-

nesses. She was sorry about Caldy More's guilt and tempted for a moment to tell her it wasn't necessary, that both of them had merely played their parts.

But she said nothing and bestowed a grateful smile on Caldy More and the dress, a very pretty dress, a little old-fashioned with full skirt, tapered sleeves, and round neck.

And Caldy More said the same thing she always said when she presented Ann with a new dress. "I found the material in the village and thought it would look nice on you." Now Caldy More blushed with pleasure as she placed the gown on the bed. "There were finishing touches," she explained. "I thought it would look pretty for tonight."

Again Ann nodded, her hand brushing lightly over the soft fabric. To her embarrassment, she noticed that her hand was visibly trembling. Caldy More saw it too and moved the dress to one side and sat down beside her, her voice urgent and full of concern. "It's just a walk," she soothed.

Even more embarrassed by her close scrutiny, Ann ducked her head and nodded. "He's. . . ."

"He's a very thoughtful man, that's all. He's taken an interest in you. Nothing to be afraid of." She patted the small trembling hand. "Enjoy the gardens. Enjoy his company. That's all that matters."

Then there passed a tiny light in Ann's eyes, something singularly like a flash of defiance. "I'll dress," she said simply.

And Caldy More grinned broadly and nodded, as though dressing were the most sensible thing she could do.

Throughout the entire grooming process the irrepressible feeling of excitement grew. Caldy More made countless trips to her own room, returning each time with a new gift, a new treasure; lavender water, rose soap, her own dressing gown so that the new dress could be spared until the last moment. Under the steady and skillful assault of Caldy More's hand, Ann felt the fear and anxiety receding. As the room filled with the good smells of soap and sachet, she gave herself wholly to the transformation, making a suggestion of her own now and then, but largely deferring to Caldy More's judgment in almost all matters.

Finally, after more than an hour of preening, shaping, fluffing, and straightening, Ann stood in the center of the room and turned slowly so that Caldy More might admire her creation. For a moment, seeing the old woman's face, Ann was afraid the sight was disagreeable to her. Then Ann saw her reach inside her sleeve for her handkerchief and pat her forehead as though the effort had left her perspiring. But on closer examination, Ann saw that the offending moisture came not from her forehead but rather from the corners of her eyes.

In an attempt to break the tension, Ann smiled and suggested, "That bad?"

Quickly Caldy More shook her head. Their eyes met. "Just the prettiest I've ever seen anywhere."

This was so simply said and so sweet was the truthful and candid expression of her face that Ann went to her and put her arms around her, and for a moment the two women stood in the center of the room in a close embrace.

Then Caldy More insisted that Ann come with her to her own room, where, behind the closet door, there was a pier glass. A moment later Ann stood before the image of a woman she had never seen before, a woman beautifully gowned in blue the color of summer sky, calm, serene eyes, the faintest smile about her lips, a certain shyness, and shimmering fair hair.

While Ann was studying the image in the glass, Caldy More stepped back to a dresser drawer and withdrew a lovely white lace shawl. Without a word she came up behind Ann and draped it around her shoulders. "There's a chill in the night air," she said. "It will be cool in the gardens."

Ann looked up, graciously accepting this last gift.

"Then I'm ready," she announced, smiling at Caldy More in the reflection of the mirror.

Caldy More agreed. She glanced at her watch. "He'll be here soon," she whispered.

Seeing the intense excitement on her face, Ann followed her out of the room and into the corridor, thinking that at any moment the old weakness would return, the blue gown would disappear, and she would become again the thing she feared most in the world.

But she continued to walk erect, clutching the shawl about her shoulders, ready to do what she had to do.

She felt as though some external force were moving her, and she was grateful, for she felt her excitement and anticipation so intensely that she doubted seriously if she could ever have moved herself. . . .

ᦞᧉᥞᥞ᥿ 33 ᦞ᧞᧞᧞

Jamie was unaccountably ill at ease. He had showered and shaved and now stood, fully dressed, at the window of his room, looking down into the gardens. Throughout the whole long day he had looked forward to the evening. But now that it was here, a remote apprehension began to slip over him. He was suddenly and acutely aware of his role as stranger. Everything that had taken place at Bledding Sorrow had been going on for years. Now, who was he to think that he could step in and set it right again?

The fact remained. Geoffrey Bledding had a wife, and in a few short minutes he, James Pask, would be walking with that wife in a secluded garden, under a cover of darkness. Now he stared fixedly down into that darkness. He remembered, curiously, his first night at Bledding Sorrow, the night he had seen the mysterious lovers. Then he had been merely a witness. Now he would be a participant. This thought caused an increase in his anxiety.

As well as he could make out, it was a case of two wrongs. With absolute conviction, he was certain that what he had witnessed and learned about past events was wrong. Still, the woman was a wife, and this rather splendid but old-fashioned idea presented itself continuously to his mind, and he was absolutely powerless to change it, to alter in any way the boundaries and privileges of such a designation. The direction in which he was going was as wrong as Geoffrey Bledding's offenses.

Still, she moved him, stirred him, she entered his mind continuously, obsessively. Only that morning in the garden he had allowed himself the first touch, had

311

lifted her off the wall and held her close on purpose, as though to test his own reaction. And his muscles, nerves, blood, everything had failed that test miserably. The only thing that had brought him to his senses had been the realization of daylight, that they were clearly visible from any number of windows in the private wing.

Now he had set for himself the impossible task of walking alone with her in a setting as conducive to certain strong emotions as any he had ever seen. She would be entrusted to him; she would be his responsibility.

He shook his head and, looking up now at the stars, wished that the night was over. He turned away from the window, still seeing her eyes, like no other eyes in the world. He experienced the sensations of a man sleepwalking. He knew he was approaching the edge of a cliff and he knew he must wake up and recover in time to save himself. He understood fully the battle ahead of him, its outlines, dimensions, costs. What he did not understand was his clear concept of having already lost it.

He glanced at his watch. One o'clock. The hall was quiet, the students sleeping. As a defense against his splintered thoughts, he arranged on his face an expression of cool formality.

There were boundaries beyond which a civilized man would not pass. This resolution finally adopted, he went out of the door, scowling at the refinements of life that kept him separate from animals. . . .

❦ 34 ❧

No words were spoken during the long passage through the hall. Jamie had called for her precisely at one o'clock, had taken note of her new and incredible loveliness, but had said nothing about it. He had merely motioned her forward, had held back the grillwork barrier to allow for her passage, had endured the sentimental cow eyes and last-minute whispered advice from Caldy More. Then, still not speaking, he had replaced the barrier and had led the way down the steps to the central corridor, moving ahead of her all the time, taking note of but refusing to respond to the obvious fear and apprehension in her face. Whether she desired the evening or not, he could not say. At every turn he disciplined his eyes to stay away from her.

Now he paused at the bottom of the steps and allowed her to catch up with him. And when he did look directly up at her, he saw a burning blush spread over her face.

But still no words were spoken, and when she was even with him, he turned away from the bewilderment in her eyes and continued to lead her through the semidarkened central corridor toward the front door.

Once out into the night, when it was no longer possible to see her so clearly, he tried to relax and walk more easily beside her. Out of the corner of his eye he saw her clutching the shawl about her shoulders, head down, her eyes obviously focused on the hazardous cobblestones.

He felt very much at a loss. He was certain that she was confused by his attitude. He longed to talk to her, to explain the battle raging within him. But there were hazards everywhere, even in the harmless sideway glances he was stealing. He saw clearly her hair, loose, falling softly about her neck, the white shawl around her shoulders, the very becoming dress. She did not once look up at him, but continued to walk obediently beside him, around the hall, moving steadily toward the broad rear gardens.

Finally, "It's a pleasant evening," he said.

Her head bowed a fraction deeper as though in a mingled understanding and shame.

"Are you warm enough?" he asked further.

She spoke to the ground. "Yes."

He glanced ahead and saw the beginning of the promenade. "Would you like to walk there?" he asked, pointing toward the long avenue.

She nodded. "If you wish."

"It's not my wish," he said, his voice registering a force much greater than he actually felt. "We're doing this for you, remember?"

He saw her draw back slightly, as though hurt by his tone. He tried to explain. "What I meant was that I'm here every day. It's nothing new for me. This is your evening. I only wanted to—"

Suddenly and without warning, she walked ahead of him, ignoring the central promenade, cutting past him directly across the grass which led to an avenue of statues. He followed after her, saw her lift the shawl and put it over her head as though a new chill had invaded her against which there was little or no protection.

He felt angry with himself for having spoken so sharply to her. Now he walked a few feet behind her, his eyes fixed on her. The dress moved gracefully about her, and her neck and shoulders were shining where the moonlight touched them.

He forced himself to look away and concentrated for a moment on the seclusion of the garden.

In his distracted state, his eyes played tricks on him. He thought he saw movement beyond the topiary trees. The moon, freed for a moment from the banked clouds of the night sky, shone with sharp illumination on that particular area and he thought he saw two figures standing in close embrace just beyond the winged figure.

His head lifted in alarm that they were not alone. Fearful that they would be discovered, he considered signaling to Ann, suggesting that they withdraw to a safer place. But in that moment the banked clouds spread, obliterating the moon, casting the entire gardens into darkness.

He continued to stare at the spot a distance away, now seeing nothing. Slowly he convinced himself that they *were* alone, that perhaps his own chaotic inner feelings had been the cause of the apparitions, either that, or shadows, or the statues themselves, or perhaps even his memory of those earlier lovers whose identity he had never learned.

Again he cast a searching glance in the direction of the topiary trees. There was no one else, only the two of them and the line of frozen statues. Then Ann made a little movement and he looked back at her. She had merely readjusted the shawl, drawing it closer around her neck, as though she were now painfully cold.

The silence was terrible. He knew she was miserable, knew that the evening which had been planned with such excitement had gone tragically sour. He longed, ached to talk to her, to take her arm and feel her moving gently against him, to show her, as though they both were discovering it together, the rose gardens, the statues, the winged figure at the center of the promenade. The need to be close to her was like an incredible thirst. Now he shivered, not from cold, but from the sudden acceleration of his pulse. It was while he was still turned away that he heard a sound which painfully resembled the beginning of soft weeping. He looked quickly back. "Please, Ann," he begged. "Perhaps we shouldn't have come. I don't mean to—"

But she shook her head with a sudden vehemence. He tried to give her time to recover, and it was during this interval that he found all further resistance impossible. He went to her and gently lifted her face, his hand lingering on the side of her cheek. And then, as if by an instinctive gesture, her hand reached shyly up and rested on his. In the process the shawl fell back and caught on her shoulders.

He could not move his hand and he could not keep his eyes from hers. There was gratitude in them and all the old sadness and a grave concern, as though she knew she was hurting him.

But predominant in her eyes was a look of waiting, still timid, but waiting. Their hands moved first, interlaced. Then Jamie stepped forward and took her in his arms. Their mouths met, gently at first, as though testing. She seemed to press against him. Then her arms came around him and pressed him closer, and within the moment all resolutions vanished, passed into oblivion as completely as though they had never existed. He felt strangely both imprisoned and released. He lowered his head and looked at her. Then they kissed again as he drew her yet closer, strained her passionately to him, and she responded, as though it had never occurred to her not to respond.

The third embrace contained nothing of gentleness or timidity. The mutual need for total closeness was excruciating. Her arms flung around him as as if she would bind him to her for eternity, a movement so feverish that in the process her shawl slipped backward from her shoulders and fell to earth.

Jamie was aware only of the slightest brushing across his arm. Their coming together had been so simple, as though all the events in their lives had led them to this moment. Even at the end of the kiss there were still no words. He saw her clearly in the night, her face upraised, traces of moisture from her recent tears of hurt, her eyes fixed on him, no longer surprised or lost.

He grasped her hands and pressed them to his heart. Then, without knowing precisely why he was doing it or where he was taking her, he bent over and lifted her in his arms. Her long dress caught in the press of their bodies. She lay back as though she had fainted, her head rolling softly against his chest.

Then he carried her off into the night, down the promenade, toward the carved bench on which he had sat alone on the first night of his arrival at Bledding Sorrow.

All the ordinary conditions of life, without which one can form no conception of anything, had ceased to exist. He lost all sense of himself. For a long time they merely sat on the bench. He wanted her. But something, some instinct told him, not here, not now. That would come later, at another time, another place. So he only held her. Then later she slipped down to the ground and rested her head on his knee, still no words, her body pressed firmly against his leg, holding his hand, then squeezing it with extraordinary violence as though to test its substance, its constancy.

It was after three o'clock when he finally lifted her to her feet, pressed her close for a final embrace, feeling within her the same peace he felt within himself, as though they both knew the ultimate closeness would come later, that there was no need for haste, that this temporary postponement would only make it sweeter when it did come.

As they started back down the promenade, he spied the fallen shawl and picked it up and placed it around her shoulders.

She smiled. "I didn't know I'd lost it."

And a few moments later, when he pushed open the front door and led her through it, their attitudes changed completely. Once again a cool formality sprang up between them. It even seemed wrong that he hold her hand, and so he led the way, keeping a distance ahead of her, stopping now and then for her to catch up, and bidding her good night finally at the grillwork barrier, seeing on the other side Caldy More in her nightdress, her wrinkled face alive with eagerness, waiting to receive her.

As he restored the bolts to the barrier, he heard only

Caldy More's voice, a hissed, aspirate, and urgent inquiry into the nature of the evening. Apparently Ann said nothing, for a moment later he heard Caldy More whisper, "Well, you're tired. We'll talk tomorrow."

Then he heard both doors close, then heard nothing.

Slowly he turned back to his own room. It was late. Or early. He should be tired. But he wasn't. He stretched out on his bed, fully dressed, and continued to see her face before him, sometimes bewildered or in agony, then saw it smiling, looking up at him, waiting, gloriously expectant. He saw old Caldy More, flushed and overwrought, clearly a conspirator with them. And he saw Geoffrey Bledding, too, his resolute and assured face looking down on him, angry now and accusing.

All these faces came in and went out of his vision, bringing confusion to his already tortured mind. He had not intended to touch her. Perhaps it would never go beyond this evening in the garden. When he was away from her, such possibilities were viable. But he could not stay away from her, and the next time or perhaps the next it would happen. He closed his eyes and rolled onto his side.

All he knew and felt was that what was happening could not be altered. He could flee here tomorrow, perhaps get as far as York, and something would drag him back. Thinking on this, he felt first grief, then joy. Yet that grief and joy were alike beyond the ordinary conditions of life; they were openings, as it were, in that ordinary life through which there came glimpses of something sublime. And in the contemplation of this sublime something he felt his soul exalted to inconceivable heights, while prudence and civility lagged behind, unable to keep up.

Shortly before sleep came, he prayed, childishly, as he had prayed as a boy. "Keep us safe." And even while he was praying, he saw her face. Her heart seemed breaking and he looked at her with sympathy and continued to pray. And every time he was brought back from the prayer by her face, and as her suffering increased, so did his own until at last he fell into a kind of terror.

And as the conflict went on, both these conditions became more intense. Between forgetting her completely and imagining in his mind the act of binding her to him forever, he tossed restlessly on the bed, taking on himself the weight of her suffering as well as his own feeling of helplessness.

Sometime near dawn, greatly fatigued yet still unable to sleep, he found himself reproaching God, blaming Him for his agonies. And in the next breath he begged for forgiveness and mercy.

Most of all, mercy. . . .

ᨄᦢ 35 ᨇᦢ

Ann was not faring so well either. She was grateful that Caldy More had not insisted on talking. She had no words, felt as mute and silent now as at the height of her illness. The evening had left her in a curious contradictory state of emotion. The initial excitement of the dressing and grooming process had been cruelly blunted by his cool, distant behavior. At first she had thought she had angered him in some way, had perhaps imposed on him. The invitation to walk in the gardens had been casually offered. Perhaps he had never intended for her to accept.

Then, when he'd spoken so sharply to her about their destination, she had felt clearly all the rejection of a lifetime welling up within her. She'd not intended to weep. It had been a foolish thing to do. She had thought, wrongly, that her weeping days were over.

But then he'd come to her, and although she wasn't usually so adept at such observations, she'd understood at once the reason for his coolness. He had been as frightened as she.

Now she lay on the bed, by the light of a single burned-down candle, gazing at the ceiling and the ever-changing shadows there, vividly picturing his face, his eyes, the sensation of his lips.

Suddenly the shadows on the ceiling wavered. Other shadows from the far side swooped to meet them. With fresh swiftness they darted forward, wavered, mingled, and all was darkness.

Within the moment she thought, *Death*, and such horror came on her that for a long while she could not realize where she was or that simply a candle had burned itself out, and her hands could not bring themselves to find another candle and another match. She continued to lie in darkness long before she was ready for darkness, and to escape from her panic, she turned on her side and tried to sleep.

She must have lost consciousness because she was awakened a short time later by the horrible nightmare which had recurred several times in her dreams while she was still ill. She saw on the floor beside her bed the same woman.

Now she was moaning, her body terribly distorted, her hands continuously clutching at the blood-red moisture which saturated the hem of her gown. She looked directly at Ann now. Out of her agony came the words, "Go away. Please go away."

She appeared to be trying to rise to her feet, but something prohibited her from doing this and she fell back time and time again, pain increasing, the long fair hair now thrown in disarray, her face twisted and contorted, and, as she always did in this nightmare—it was what made it so horrible—she saw the woman try to rise up in her agony, saw her hand outstretched as though she were begging Ann to help her, one thin white hand clawing at the bedclothes.

She awoke in a sweat and looked silently about the darkened room.

The only sound audible was her own terrified breathing. . . .

❦ 36 ❧

Every night, in the slanted evening shadows within the small walled garden, Ann waited for Jamie. Bledding Sorrow had settled into its summer routine. Students came and went by the scores. The Transport Society gave way to the York Poetry Society. And they in turn made room for the Commonsense Psychology Group from Leeds. Following them came the Tree and Natural Environment people from the Lake District. And the dormitory rooms were always filled, the central corridor and basement dining room bustling.

Within the private wing a routine of sorts had also been established. Every morning at eight o'clock Caldy More hurried to meet Geoffrey Bledding at the front door, to confer with him about a variety of subjects, and at the last minute to give him a report, if he was interested, on the health of his wife, although not once did he express a desire to see her. He seemed more than content living with Martin Axtell and totally preoccupied with the hectic summer schedule and frantic comings and goings within the hall itself.

Then Caldy More would hurry back to the small private kitchen, where usually Ann would have breakfast prepared and waiting for her, the two women enjoying a closeness they had never known before, passing the daylight hours gossiping and sewing and tending their garden, long intervals of quiet and peace, Ann clearly waiting for the evening, when Jamie would appear for dinner with interesting and frequently amusing accounts of the day's coach trip. He took every evening meal with them now, returning from the day's drive, washing up, then hurrying through the grillwork barrier and joining them in the small kitchen.

After dinner the three of them would sit for a discreet time together. Then Caldy More always excused herself, claiming some job that needed doing. And Ann and Jamie, on their own, would wait for the cover of darkness and slip out again through the grillwork barrier, taking now mischievous delight in dodging the students, growing brave, exploring well beyond the confines of the rear gardens, walking on occasion to the edge of the village itself, always stopping off in the pasture so that Ann could admire the handsome coach and extract again from Jamie the promise that one day he would take her somewhere in it.

After that first evening's walk their physical passion seemed to subside. Beyond the superficial closeness of an embrace or a kiss or the entirely comforting sensation of hands touching, they seemed content during this interval to share in other ways. They threw themselves, as it were, heart and soul into the pleasurable task of committing each other to memory. With an almost scrupulous conscientiousness they assigned to each other "turns to talk," and as they opened one to the other the dimensions of their private souls, a bond of incredible intimacy sprang up between them. At times in the evening, sitting at table, they resembled an old married couple, anticipating each other's wants and needs, playing off each other like two perfectly tuned instruments.

For Ann he was simply the brightest star in the firmament. It was inconceivable to her that such happiness would not last forever.

Now, waiting at dusk in the walled garden on an evening in early August, she found herself standing before that place on the wall where she had first seen him, a holy place, the temple of her new religion.

So intent now was her concentration that she did not hear him coming across the grass. But then suddenly she sensed his presence and turned and found him only a few feet behind her and ran to him and into his arms, which were always open and ready to receive her.

He held her close for a moment, his hand pressing against the back of her head. And after the embrace she nestled snugly beneath his arm.

He grinned down on her, a slightly mischievous light in his eye. "Can you keep a secret?" he whispered.

She nodded, not trusting herself to speak, so great was her happiness.

Again he warned her in mock seriousness, "You mustn't tell Caldy More. She'd only worry."

"I won't," she promised. "What?"

He leaned closer and whispered, "Tonight a ride in the coach."

She looked at him a moment, not certain whether he was teasing or not. He had promised before, but for some reason had always put it off.

When he nodded again to dispel her doubts, she threw her arms around his neck and he clasped her to him and lifted her up until her feet left the ground, then commenced whirling with her, her face buried in the warm familiar contours of his neck, twirling around and around, the rest of her body airborne, both of them laughing, breathlessly laughing until Caldy More called to them from the door, scolding them for behaving like dim-witted children, advising them to come and eat dinner before it got cold. . . .

Why Jamie had selected this particular evening for a coach ride he wasn't absolutely certain. It was true, she had begged him often enough. But it had always seemed too great a risk, too obvious a hazard. The absence of the coach at night could be noticed by anyone and reported. He would have to account. And there was always the remote possibility of an accident. The narrow roads and lanes of Yorkshire were filled with madmen who drove with an appalling egocentricity, as though their automobiles were the only ones within the entire East Riding. Daily Jamie had to watch out for them, and nightly he returned to Bledding Sorrow with palms aching from gripping the wheel.

So while he had long ago ceased to worry about his moral responsibility to Ann, he now seemed totally preoccupied with her physical well-being. It was as if, having been denied freedom of movement for so long, she literally hurled herself into life. On their evening walks she frequently ran ahead of him, scrambled down ravines, then up again, balancing herself on fallen logs across narrow streams, finding a challenge in everything and running to meet that challenge, as though it had never entered her mind that she could lose, could fall, could slip. It was as though she were totally blind to the hazards around her and saw, either by choice or conviction, only a safe, gentle and supportive nature. While he found such an attitude charming, he also felt an increase in his responsibility.

But this afternoon, when he had been driving back to Bledding Sorrow with the Tree and Natural Environment people, after a day of touring local gardens, they had stopped at a place of such incredible beauty that he had thought of her and how much she would enjoy it, and he had longed to share it with her and had vowed to bring her back this very evening.

It was a spot about ten miles away called Sutton Bank, an incredibly high-rising plateau, the road climbing at a sharp angle upward to a point several hundred feet above the floor of the Yorkshire plains. During World War Two glider pilots had used it for training purposes, easing their small powerless craft off the edge and into the force of upsweeping wind.

Now it was deserted except for tourists and nature lovers. The primary attraction from the high point was, of course, the view, a panorama so vast and dazzling that it almost seemed as though one could look from world's end to world's end. From that great height the fields and scattered farmhouses and herds of sheep and cattle looked manageable, an assumption of order that Jamie had found incredibly satisfying. The livestock were mere dots of black and white, the farmhouses thimble-size structures of patient brown, the fields so meticulous and even they looked as though they had been laid out by a master draftsman, and enclosing the entire spectacle, a vast inverted blue bowl softened by drifting white clouds.

Now, at dinner, thinking on all this, he looked over at Ann and saw again on her face a curious, suppressed, almost rigid little smile like that of a child just barely able to contain a secret. And he did not nudge her this time, for now he felt on his own face the same foolish expression. Only by concentrating intently on the food on his plate and by drawing Caldy More into a gossipy discussion of the scandalous cook, Mrs. Bonebrake, was he able to pass the meal with a semblance of control, all the while covering for Ann when she smiled at the wrong places and merely played with the food on her plate, her normally good appetite blunted by the excitement of the evening.

Then there was the agony of coffee and dessert and the washing-up process, and finally, blessedly Caldy

More muttered something about two weeks' ironing and withdrew to the small laundry room off the kitchen.

Jamie and Ann exchanged a look of breaking patience. Then Ann was running ahead of him out of the room and up the narrow steps to the third-floor dormitory, moving at breakneck speed toward the grillwork barrier, which by now she knew all too well how to manipulate herself, ignoring Jamie's shouts for her to stop and get a sweater, apparently ignoring everything but the need for night air, for the sensation of movement and freedom.

It occurred to him as he raced after her down the corridor that she had never even inquired where they were going. Obviously destination was not as important as the anticipation of the trip itself. And by the time he reached the grillwork barrier she was through it, leaving him the task of restoring the bolts so that nothing would look amiss. By the time he reached the central staircase he saw her below on the second-floor landing, caution abandoned, moving steadily through a group of students as though she had a perfect right to be there, impervious to their curious backward glances.

He increased his speed and drew a deep breath of relief when he saw Bledding's office dark and locked. Still, she had taken, was taking enormous risks, and in a slight surge of anger, he increased his step even more and moved out into the late-dusk evening just in time to see her rounding the gatehouse arch, apparently running toward the high pasture and the waiting coach.

She was leaning against the locked coach door, trying to catch her breath, when he finally caught up with her. For a moment he was unable to speak, the air in his lungs depleted after the long sprint.

Finally he looked sternly down on her. "You should have waited," he panted. "You should have let me go ahead. What if someone had seen us?"

Her eyes were brilliant with excitement. "Where are we going?" she begged.

"Did you hear what I said to you?"

She nodded, not really chastised, more an attitude of humoring him. "No one saw us," she said meekly.

"They might have."

"But they didn't."

It was a hopeless cause. No matter how hard he tried to look sternly at her, he felt only joy at her obvious joy and an excitement almost as great as her own.

In order to have the satisfaction of the last word, he kissed her lightly on the forehead and warned, "Next time, wait for me. Promise?"

She promised. At least she nodded her head, then stood excitedly back while he unlocked the door. She blushed when he bowed low and, with mock grandeur, murmured, "Madame, your coach," and with a great sweep of his arm indicated that she was to step up.

Nothing would do but that she try every seat in the coach, all forty-eight of them. As he guided the cumbersome vehicle out of the pasture, his concentration was divided between the hazardous road ahead and the delighted exclamations coming from behind him as she slid in and out of one seat, then another.

As he turned onto the narrow main road, he called back to her, "Find one and settle. It's dangerous. Ann, please, you must—"

Suddenly, out of the corner of his vision, coming from the blind spot of the gatehouse arch, he saw a small automobile careen crazily onto the main road. He slammed on the breaks and gripped the wheel; the abrupt stop hurled Ann violently forward. The coach slid onto the soft shoulder, narrowly avoiding a direct collision, its right tires only inches away from the yawning ravine opposite the hall.

The small car proceeded on down the road, apparently impervious to its near calamity. Quickly Jamie set the emergency brake and hurried to Ann where she had fallen down the steps and against the door. He lifted her up, his face full of concern. "Are you all right?"

Obviously sobered by the near accident, she nodded and clung to him for a moment, then obediently slipped into a near seat. "I'm sorry," she murmured. "It was my fault."

Jamie took his seat behind the wheel and looked apprehensively out through the wide expanse of windshield. "Let's get out of here before someone sees us," he muttered.

With the release of the emergency brake and a slight grinding of gears, he pulled the enormous coach back onto the road and away from the perilous edge.

Ann, still clearly shaken, asked, "Who do you suppose it was—in the car, I mean?"

He shrugged. "From their speed, I'd say it was a staff member in a hurry to get home. As I said, it doesn't matter. No harm."

And so saying, he settled the coach into a safe speed and disciplined his eyes to stay away from the rearview mirror and consoled himself with thoughts of the evening ahead.

For the duration of the ten-mile trip Ann said nothing, gave no indication of her mood, and sat quietly as though she were afraid of distracting him.

Not until he was in the process of coaxing the coach up the steep incline which led to Sutton Bank did she give any indication of movement at all. Then he felt her sit excitedly up, felt her finger brushing lightly over the back of his shoulders.

Finally at the summit, he parked the coach on a safe, even stretch of land across the road and, taking her by the hand, led her to the edge of the precipice, seeing her face by moonlight, the warm August wind blowing her hair, a look of questioning amazement in her eyes.

"Sutton Bank," he explained gently. But that's all he said, for suddenly she pressed against him, nestled in under the security of his arm as though the vision were too vast, too overpowering, as though such a wealth of space after so long a confinement frightened her. He could feel her trembling through the thin cotton dress and pulled her closer.

"No need to be afraid," he whispered.

The animation left her face. She lowered her head and looked around uneasily at the sheer descent. "I'm not afraid," she said, though she clung to him as though if he let her go, she would surely fall.

Something about her fragility and the obvious scar tissue of her fear moved him enormously. He led her to a spot about fifty yards away where the incline was gradual, where over the years people had trampled out a discernible footpath to the bottom of the cliff. Playfully he suggested that they climb to the bottom of the bluff, then climb back again, just to see if they could do it.

She hesitated only a moment, then took the challenge, led the way slipping and sliding down the steep incline, he following after her, delighted with her sense of abandonment, both of them shouting and laughing at each other, grabbing for grasses, protruding roots, rocks, each other, anything to break their fall.

It was a steep descent and an even more grueling ascent. More than an hour later they clawed their way back up to the summit again, breathless, dirty, overheated in the close August evening, but still laughing at their triumph, as proud as though they had scaled Everest. Exhausted and warm, Ann loosened the buttons on her dress and lay back on the soft grass.

Jamie sat close by, watching her. He knew she was looking up at him, could see by moonlight her face glistening with perspiration. "It was a fine climb," she whispered. "Thank you for bringing me."

He could not take his eyes off her, her position on the grass, her arms flung over her head, the faintest smile on her lips. For a moment he thought he would not move, but then he did, bending over her, their mouths meeting with a violence that shocked both. He covered her with kisses. His hand touched her hair, caressed it, felt her head through its softness as her body arched toward him.

Her hands gripped him convulsively, as though she knew at the precise moment he knew. Her head lay back in his arms as he swept her up and carried her into a grove of trees a short distance away. Clothes shed in a matter of seconds, they returned to each other, gloriously naked and unencumbered. They stood for a moment, assessing mutual beauty, then in the tenderest of gestures she put her arms around his neck, and he went with her to ground, the union complete, although it was a curious moment of passion, no immediate acceleration, but merely a quiet coming together, as though after the hunger of a long and mutual frustration both were content simply to lie as one.

Only later did his hands commence further exploration, his lips closing around her breasts, her whole body lifting upward as though in an effort to receive all of him.

Then, passion. Then muscles tensed, nerves alert, all sensate points alive, rhythm increasing, blood racing, mouths open to accommodate the ecstasy toward which they were building. Then his hands held her head still as he covered her cries with kisses until the pleasurable agony subsided, and they both lay quiet, as spent and exhausted as though they would never move again.

A few moments later he rolled to one side, relieving her of his weight. But she merely followed after him. He held her close, the sweetest possession of his life.

He started to speak. "I—"

But she covered his lips as if to hush him.

They remained in each other's arms, unspeaking for almost an hour. Then, as if by mutual consent, they rose and, in the dressing process, discovered with great pride that their love had left scars. Around her shoulders and at the base of her throat were tiny purple marks, and on his back were three small scratches, barely letting blood, but all the same she soothed them with her tongue.

It was after four in the morning when they returned to Bledding Sorrow. She waited at the pasture gate while he parked and secured the coach. Then, together, moving stealthily through the Great Hall so as not to disturb the sleeping students, they made their way to her upper bedchamber, where again they tried to feed a hunger so deep they both knew it would never be satisfied completely; glorious explorations, testing the design of the human body to its ultimate capacity, still awake, though totally spent, at dawn, lying quietly in each other's arms, staring upward at the vaulted arches, listening carefully and sadly, as though it were the most dismal sound in the world, to the first morning crowing of a rooster. . . .

∼◦《 38 》◦∼

Geoffrey Bledding, with the same somewhat solemn expression with which he conducted his staff meetings, sat in his darkened office at four A.M., his hands locked tightly before him on the desk, his eyes staring fixedly straight ahead.

First of all, the phone call from Arthur Firth had disturbed him, the man babbling on about how the coach had almost run him to ground. What the coach had been doing out in the evening, Geoffrey had no idea. Since Bledding Sorrow and the National Trust were paying for the outrageously priced petrol, he did not appreciate James Pask taking private excursions.

And second, what had Arthur Firth been doing at the hall so late? Generally the man kept an eagle eye on the clock and was halfway out the door by the time the six o'clock bell ceased ringing. Undoubtedly the man had a good excuse. There were several as yet unsolved problems regarding the arrival of the Manchester Herpetologists and their adders next week.

Suddenly and quite wearily Geoffrey bowed his head into his hands. Martin Axtell was right. Bledding Sorrow had become a circus. Still, he must remember to question Firth *and* James Pask. Good excuse or not, in his present state of mind Geoffrey was suspicious of everything. Everything.

And third, there was the matter of Martin Axtell. The present arrangement could not go on much longer. The man's veiled innuendos and constant and fluttering domesticity were about to drive Geoffrey to distraction.

Then last night the party— "Just a few close friends from York to cheer you up," Martin had said. Friends! Tawdry, aging queens, for the most part, limp-wristed,

333

a whole roomful of Martin Axtells and a few drab women, the pawns who made them respectable in society's eyes. Abruptly and sharply he shook his head as though to banish the memory.

He had endured it until about one o'clock in the morning. Then he had left and had walked up the hill to Bledding Sorrow. He longed, ached, suffered to come home. And this *was* his home. He raised his eyes now in the faint light and looked pitifully around him. He longed to serve the hall as lord and master with respectful dignity and would have if only fate had given him a chance.

Now he ran his hands through his disheveled hair, his brows scowling, his eyes gleaming with a proud and angry light. First he had allowed himself to be driven to the small cramped private wing, and then he had permitted himself to be driven totally from his own home. *I can't hide myself,* he thought, and with that manner peculiar to him from childhood, as of a man who has nothing to be ashamed of, he left his chair and strode confidently about the room.

It was decided then. He would come home. It was obvious he was needed. Apparently in his nightly absences a form of disintegration was taking place; the coach being driven about at all hours, Arthur Firth coming and going whenever the mood pleased him, and God alone knew what else, to say nothing of his own suffering.

He glanced about, his thoughts, his emotions stumbling over the word "suffering." What the world did not realize was that a man with dull eyes could feel as acutely as anyone else.

Suddenly, without warning, he recalled the specters which had so tormented him before he had moved in with Martin. Merely thinking on such matters caused him to look sharply up, as though he were again under attack. In the stillness of the early morning he thought he heard something, a thin, high-pitched cry of a woman. He listened a moment longer, both hands clutching at the desk. *Dear God, don't let them return,* he prayed. *I have done nothing. Whatever happened here before, it was not my doing.*

But even with his eyes closed, his mind engrossed in his prayer, he could still hear her, the woman screaming, an unbroken wail of agony.

Abruptly he closed his eyes, sweat rolling down the sides of his face. In a torment of pain, he pushed backward in the chair, unable to bear it. And blessedly a moment later the sound was gone. He looked about in the stillness, breathing heavily as though he'd run a great distance. Reason returned. The wind. It had been merely the wind echoing through the entrance front with its projecting bays.

Suddenly he clenched his fists, told himself again sternly that it had been the wind, only the wind, always the wind. Nothing more.

He was tired now from his sleepless night. Still, he found a certain satisfaction in resolution. And regarding his wife, he would simply stay away from her. From the beginning the relationship had been impoverished. At first it had been an interesting experiment; his ego had enjoyed the attention of both the father and the daughter. But in this respect Caldy More had been right. He should have left her where he had found her. On American soil.

Now he could not divorce her. He would not bring that scandal down on his family name. He would simply leave her alone, and after the summer session was over and the hall and the village had settled into winter's quiet, he would discreetly have her committed to Martin's London asylum. No one would miss her; very few even knew of her presence. The entire matter could be executed with the greatest dispatch, the honor of the family name preserved and his own sanity and well-being vastly improved.

Thinking on all this made him feel better. He could now face the day. It was never a very good idea to let someone else take control of one's life. Centuries of

Bledding genes and blood had led him to this conclusion. Now, with fresh force, he felt conscious of himself from the springy motions of his legs to the movement of his lungs as he breathed. Apparently for a period of time he had lost his will, but now he had found it again, and in the silence of early morning he felt more like a Bledding than he had felt for a long time. It was a good feeling, a feeling of rightness, of control, of clear superiority, of resolution.

He could feel it so clearly it must be visible. And in a surge of excitement, the kind of which he had not experienced for a long time, he went to the door and started out.

Then suddenly he heard movement down the corridor. He fell quickly back. Holding the door open a crack, he peered closely in order to identify the early-morning traffic, a carousing student perhaps, a kitchen aide arriving early.

As the footsteps drew nearer, he adjusted the door to a hairline crack, just enough for him to perceive and identify two figures. One he recognized immediately, the tall, gaunt, now incredibly mussed figure of the coachman. And the woman, twining about him as though he were the support, she the vine? Bledding's eyes stared, unfocused. His breath stopped.

His wife!

At first he wasn't certain. Not even when they passed directly in front of the door was he absolutely certain. Only when they started up the stairs and she raised her eyes to the coachman did the full impact of recognition sweep over him.

Suddenly it felt as though the office were closing in on him, the walls literally pushing against him. He continued to watch until they disappeared up the stairs. His hands felt damp. Incredible heat was coming from somewhere. When they were safely out of earshot, he closed the door and leaned against it. Then he paced, turned, returned to the door, pacing again, tossing about like a sick man, coughed and, when he could not yet clear his throat, coughed again, the pain of humiliation rising.

Sometimes when his breathing permitted, he gasped, "Oh, my God." Sometimes when he was choking, he muttered angrily, "Slut!" His thoughts were of all sorts of things, the husband cuckolded, deceived, dishonored, the coachman trespassing, Caldy More, the ally, cuckolded, deceived, dishonored, but the end of all his thoughts was the same. Death. Death, the inevitable end.

Now he saw nothing but death or the advance of death in everything. Darkness had fallen on him. He sat down, then got up, then sat down again, outraged, humiliated, dishonored, cuckolded. He looked toward the closed door from under his brow. Dishonored, cuckolded, cuckolded, dishonored. The steady assault of those two words was dreadful.

He pinched his eyes shut, his feverish head struggling to stay erect. He grasped the desk and clutched it and clung to it with all his strength. . . .

❧ 39 ❧

Caldy More awakened early from habit. But she stayed in her bed. No one would be wanting breakfast right away. Of that she was certain. She had heard the lovers returning; almost dawn it had been. She knew further because she had good ears and because she had been listening that Ann had shared her bed for the remainder of the night, what little had been left of it.

And what matter? Caldy More stretched beneath the sheets, luxuriating in the easeful awakening. She felt remarkably unencumbered. The old morality, the old piety was gone. Lacking heavenly scales, she had felt the need to balance earthly ones, and after ten years of purgatory, during which time she, Caldy More, had aided and abetted Satan himself, the young woman was due an interval of bliss. There would be no judgment coming from Caldy More. Judgment was for God, and she felt very ungodlike this morning, felt sixteen and foolishly giggly as though her own life had had a rebirth. How long it had been since she had rolled about in bed like a young girl. Usually on the instant of awakening, her feet would hit the floor and she would hurl herself, duty-bound, into the rigid schedule, the awesome responsibilities, the grim early-morning meeting with Mr. Bledding.

Suddenly she sat bolt upright in bed. A glance at her watch told her seven forty-five. He was always punctual. She must be, too, or he would surely suspect something.

The delightful interval over, she flew into activity now, pulling her clothes on, quietly resentful in a way that her carefree life had been so short-lived, but hur-

338

rying all the same out of habit, an ingrained need, a birthright almost, a fear of angering the master.

As she tiptoed past the lovers' door, she contemplated calling to them. James was still there; she was certain of it. He had his own coaching duties later that morning. But then she decided against it. There was time, and she would give it to them. Customarily coach trips left about ten A.M. She would call them after her meeting with Mr. Bledding. Moments were precious. Still, they had to keep up the appearance of normalcy, or the scandal would break about their heads.

Now she hurried past their door, almost capable of feeling their ecstasy, her mood alternating between dread at seeing Mr. Bledding and delight for the two in each other's arms, feeling herself quite another woman, utterly unlike anything she had ever been before.

At precisely eight o'clock she stood in the open doorway, looking out over the cobblestone courtyard, slightly damp from morning dew, her eyes searching the main road for a glimpse of the familiar, slightly bowed figure of Geoffrey Bledding. He was nowhere in sight. Feeling a chill on her arms, she stepped directly out into the morning sun, still searching in the customary direction. But there was nothing, no sight of the man at all. Curious. He was always punctual.

She stood a moment longer, trying to perceive a reason for his unprecedented tardiness. Unfortunately where Mr. Bledding was concerned, the excuse of simple human frailty was not adequate. And because of this, she felt her apprehension rising, found herself turning nervously at each sound.

Two young serving girls from the village now appeared, walking briskly across the courtyard, their faces swollen and sleepy. They smiled and nodded their good mornings, and Caldy More started to inquire whether or not they had seen Mr. Bledding on the road. But then she changed her mind. The simpleminded girls would take the harmless inquiry and turn it into a major item for kitchen gossip. So she held her tongue and waited until they were safely past, then again resumed her search of the gatehouse arch, her eyes inspecting each shadow, confident that at any moment the man would materialize.

Suddenly, from behind her, she heard the two girls calling to her from the long central corridor. She looked back. One said sleepily, "Mr. Bledding sent us to fetch you," she said. "He wants to see you in his office."

The other added with just a hint of a smile, " 'Immediately,' he said. His very words."

Caldy More blinked at the two young faces, her eyes like deep wells of light fixed on them. Apprehension was growing. She felt that all the muscles of her face were quivering. "Thank you very much," she said, and indicated with a bob of her head that the girls were dismissed. She waited until they had disappeared down the steps to the basement dining room, then she closed her eyes, struggling for a moment of self-control. He must have arrived early. How early? And why early? Suddenly she shivered in the morning chill. Then she straightened her back and walked steadily down the central corridor.

The office door was closed. She lifted a hand to knock and at that precise moment heard him call, "Come in, Caldy More."

She hesitated a moment, trying in those brief words to read his mood, to interpret his tone of voice. Then slowly she pushed the door open and went in.

The tiny windowless room was dark. For a moment, after the blaze of sun, she saw nothing. Then she saw him in outline sitting behind his desk. Reflexively her hand went for the light switch.

"No! Don't turn it on," he ordered.

She tried to make her voice normal, her concern sincere. "Are you all right, Mr. Bledding?"

He did not respond except to say, "Close the door!"

She did as she was told and the darkness increased, and her anxiety along with it. In a way, the darkness was a blessing. She was certain her face would have betrayed her. Now she made an attempt at lightness. "I was waiting for you," she began, "where I always wait. I was beginning to worry that—"

"I came early."

She nodded yes, agreeing with the obvious. When he gave no indication that he would explain either his early arrival or the darkness, she inquired again, "Are you sure you're all—"

"I'll be moving back tonight, Caldy More," he said, his voice now unmistakably cold.

But now Caldy More's concern was not for how he was speaking, but rather for what he was saying. "Moving back?" she repeated. "Why?"

His voice rose. "I have a right, don't I? Are you challenging my right?"

"No, of course not," she murmured. "It's just something of a surprise. That's all."

"Yes, I'm sure it is."

In the cover of dark she found it impossible to read his face. Now his voice sounded calm, exceedingly calm, too calm. She recalled with growing terror the old scenes, the nightly visitations, the drugs. She would not be a party to it, not now. With a faint voice she asked, "And—what about—your—"

"My wife?" His voice cut through hers as though he had been expecting the question. "I'll stay away from her and I expect her to extend me the same courtesy. I do not want to lay eyes on her again. Ever! Is that clear?"

Caldy More nodded. "Clear, yes, but perhaps difficult. She moves about now with free—"

"She won't be with us for much longer," he interjected. "I'm sure you can keep us separate for a few weeks."

Again Caldy More faltered. "I—don't understand. Where will she be?"

"It's not your place to understand, Caldy More. It's your place to follow orders."

Caldy More stood quite still, holding herself erect,

anger rising. "I'm afraid I must disagree with you, Mr. Bledding. You thrust on me a responsibility that I did not want. I accepted it anyway, and now I feel that I have a right to—"

"You have no rights," he shouted. "You are now and always have been in my employ. Nothing more. Do you understand?"

She nodded and drew rapidly back to the door. Something was wrong, terribly wrong. His voice, tone, attitude were cold and unrelenting. She wanted only to leave his presence. But as she reached for the door, he stopped her.

His voice now was restrained, as though he were making a conscious effort to control himself. "I'd appreciate it if you'd send two of the girls to Martin Axtell's for my things. Give him the message that I'll phone him later. I'd further appreciate it if you'd prepare my rooms. I'm sure you understand."

She nodded, although in truth she understood nothing except that an overwhelming sense of foreboding was beginning to invade her. She waited a moment to see if he would say anything further, and when he didn't, she murmured something about looking after everything, then hurriedly opened the door and closed it behind her.

For a moment, standing in the brightness of the central corridor, with the students hurrying about her on their way to breakfast, she had the curious feeling that perhaps she had imagined the encounter. But then she knew better, knew that there were incredible trials ahead of her, knew above all else that there were two upstairs who must receive this news immediately.

She moved closer to the wall in order to avoid the steady flow of human traffic. Their laughing, chattering voices sounded amplified in her ears. Perhaps she should just leave. But where would she go? What would she do? And what would happen to Ann?

She recalled his veiled threat. "She won't be with us for much longer."

Then suddenly she was running, pushing her way through the onslaught of students. She did not understand what was happening, but she felt that it was something beyond her, even unalterable.

Still, she had to try....

❧ 40 ❧

On August 21 the Manchester Herpetologist Society arrived with scant luggage except for the two large wicker baskets which came separately in a small white lorry.

The entire staff, or at least those who were free and curious, watched while four handlers, with extreme care, lifted the two wicker baskets and carried them hurriedly directly down to the crypt.

Geoffrey Bledding stood to one side with Arthur Firth, witnessing the operation. Now and then he glanced apprehensively toward the front door of the hall, waiting for the momentary return of Mr. Cumstey, president of the society, who had gone ahead to check the facilities which had been prepared in the crypt.

A few moments later the man appeared in the doorway, a short, thick lame gentleman with a clubfoot, in his shirt sleeves now, his face red and perspiring from the long climb up. "Bledding!" he shouted, motioning him forward with his cane, summoning the master of Bledding Sorrow as though he were little more than hired help.

Arthur Firth whispered nervously, "He looks mad as hell."

And Geoffrey responded acidly, "Of course, what else?" Then he lifted his head, his warden smile firmly in place, and called cheerily, "Coming," and loathed himself and his circumstances with every step.

Now Mr. Cumstey leaned heavily on his cane, one hip thrust outward, slowly, ponderously shaking his thick head. "Most unsatisfactory, Mr. Bledding," he scolded. "Most unsatisfactory. They need light as keenly as we do and sun. The crypt is damp and dark. We can

344

scarcely see them down there, let alone study their habits."

Geoffrey tried to draw a deep breath. "I—we—thought you might bring them up for the purposes of study, then take them back—"

"Aha!" exclaimed Mr. Cumstey. "That is precisely the failing of public opinion. They view the poor creatures as something evil, something to be avoided, hidden away, and in the process their ignorance multiplies, and—"

Geoffrey interrupted the lecture with a firm reminder. "They *are* dangerous, Mr. Cumstey, lethal in fact—"

"Not if you know how to handle them, not if you respect them," the man countered, "which is precisely the purpose of this conference, to bring the adder up out of the Dark Ages and into the light of the twentieth century."

Geoffrey looked wearily behind him and motioned for Arthur Firth to join them. "Tell Mr. Firth what you want, Mr. Cumstey, and he will see that you get it. For now I would suggest that we leave them where they are. I do have the staff to consider."

But Mr. Cumstey's lyricism would not be abated. "Have you ever seen them in the sun, Mr. Bledding? They are dazzling, truly beautiful—"

"I'm sure they are." Geoffrey nodded. "And we'll try to arrange that they have sun. For now I must insist that they—"

Cumstey bobbed his head up and down as he finished the statement: "—stay where there are. Yes, I know." He tapped his cane against his clubfoot impatiently as though weary of dealing with the ignorance of the world. He called to several of his associates standing nearby, and the group of men headed back down the central corridor, obviously on their way to the crypt, their heads bobbing back and forth, clearly commiserating with one another.

The courtyard was empty now except for Geoffrey and Firth and a few of the young serving girls from the kitchen, who still stood with their arms clasped about their bodies, pinched expressions of revulsion in their faces, as though they had been able to see clearly into the wicker baskets.

Geoffrey called out to them, "It's all right, girls, you can go along to your chores."

One warned weakly, "You keep them bloody things locked up, you hear, Mr. Bledding?"

He assured them that he would. Suddenly, out of the corner of his eye, he saw the coachman, James Pask, standing in the doorway.

The man raised his hand in salute and called out, "Luggage distributed, Mr. Bledding. Anything else?"

Geoffrey looked closely at him, searching the gaunt face for signs of remorse or guilt. Nothing. Nothing that Geoffrey could discern. "No, that's all for now, Mr. Pask. Thank you."

He continued to watch coldly as the man turned and went back into the hall. Arthur Firth watched with him and commented, "A strange one, that one."

But Geoffrey said nothing. He turned his back on Arthur Firth and went directly to his office. There he closed and locked the door and sat alone in the dark. . . .

ᦒᦷᦲ 41 ᦺᦷᦱ

Ann and James, of course, had found the news of Geoffrey Bledding's return distressing. For a few days they moved very cautiously, wearing expressions of resigned sadness, staying completely away from each other during the daylight hours, removing the grillwork barrier only after midnight.

But when they discovered that Bledding apparently intended to keep his promise and stay completely away from her, they grew brave, although courage had little to do with it. The simple truth was that both had fallen ill, the greatest of illnesses, a mutual and intense love which rendered them helpless and left them totally vulnerable.

They shared their meals now in the small upper bedchamber, regretful of the extra work they were causing Caldy More but unable to keep their eyes from each other. There was gratitude in their expressions and sadness as though they each knew he was hurting the other, sometimes infinitely timid, other times frantic and brutal. They moved as if in a most rarefied air, each holding the sweetest possession he had ever known.

Occasionally Jamie felt they should be more cautious, but the feeling never lasted long. Reassured as he was both by Caldy More and Ann and by his own urgent need to see her every possible moment, he found that with the exception of those hours spent on the coach, his entire world was Ann's room and now and then, when it was safe, the small walled garden.

Since Bledding's return they had never ventured beyond the confines of the private wing. Again, neither felt the slightest deprivation. They were all they needed, had ever needed, would ever need.

The success of the arrangement was due in large part to Caldy More, who had quickly and efficiently established dual routines. Bledding's hours were early to midmorning, and during this time Ann and Jamie simply stayed on the third floor and out of sight. As soon as he left, they were free to come down and roam at will, for he never returned until late at night. Caldy More always reported to them on the man's mood, which seemed as subdued and glacial and therefore as normal as ever.

So as long as Caldy More was there to direct traffic, there was no reason why the arrangement shouldn't work. To Ann and Jamie, Geoffrey Bledding was little more than a distant footstep on the staircase, a half-empty cup of tea, a crust of toast.

There was one problem. With the summer season and Jamie's employment drawing to a close, what would they do then? On occasion, during July's ripeness, when summer had seemed an endless season, James had considered the problem and dismissed it. He was living in too close proximity to her ever to consider life without her. Still, of late, with the new early-morning and late-evening nip in the air, he had been reminded of the season's end and thus the natural end to what, quite simply, had been the most glorious interval of his life.

His ideas had changed since his arrival at Bledding Sorrow. For the first time in his life it was impossible for him to think in terms of right and wrong. It was out of the question to consider such incomprehensible happiness as wrong. And it was also out of the question to consider Ann's circumstances as he had first seen them at the beginning of the summer as right. Now the glowing, witty, and passionately alive young woman bore no resemblance to that pathetic, bowed, terrified, and drugged creature he had first seen from his perch on the garden wall. So, for the most part, right and wrong were moot points.

Compounding his problem was the realization that

Ann, no matter how beloved, would be of no help to him in this decision. She had surrendered herself up to him utterly and simply looked to him to decide her fate, ready to submit to anything.

So what they would do and where they would go in less than two weeks was an enormous and unresolved question. His ambitious plans to succeed as an independent coachman had retreated into the background, and, feeling that he had got out of that circle of activity in which everything was definite, he had given himself entirely to his passion, and that passion was binding him more and more closely to her. He no longer thought of her as another man's wife. She was his, had perhaps always been his, was the source of all his light and life. If the future was troublesome and full of hazards with her, there was no future at all without her. It was that simple. And that complex.

One afternoon a few days after the arrival of the Herpetologist Society, and James having no coaching duties, Ann and he walked in the garden at noon.

Caldy More had assured them it was safe. "Mr. Bledding"—she smiled—"has problems in the crypt." Without taking time to explain, she had prepared a light lunch for them, then hurried off to a dreaded conference with Mrs. Bonebrake concerning the week's menu.

Left to their own devices, Jamie and Ann finished eating, then went out into the garden. They walked without speaking to the end of the path, to their sacred spot, the place where they had first met under the unhappiest of circumstances.

Ann stared at the high wall, then laid her hands on his shoulders and looked for a long while at him with a profound, passionate, and at the same time searching look, as though she were studying his face to make up for the time she had not seen him. She said simply, "Thank you."

There was such tenderness and warmth in what she said that Jamie clasped her to him with terrible need.

At the end of the embrace he looked down on her. Under his close scrutiny, she seemed to bow her head a fraction deeper. He lifted her face while her slender fingers moved swiftly around his hand. He asked solemnly, "When I leave here, will you come with me?"

She looked up at him, her eyes wide, clearly comprehending the invitation. She smiled, then laughed, with that deep sweet laugh which was one of her greatest charms. "I don't have much choice, do I?" Then her face clouded, the laugh died quickly. She brushed her lips across the tips of his fingers. "I don't want to be a bother," she whispered.

The light died away in her eyes and a different smile, a consciousness of something, he did not know what, and of quiet melancholy came over her face. "What if he follows us?" she asked. "Where will we go? Twice before I tried to run away. He—" Suddenly she stopped as though she could not go on. She laid her head on his sleeve.

He tried to comfort her. "It'll be over soon," he reassured her. "I know places where he will never find you."

She shook her head with sudden conviction. "You don't know him. This time he'll come looking for *you*. I don't want. . . ."

She looked up at him. He bent over and again clasped her to him, trying to hide his emotions. "We'll find a way," he promised. "As you said a moment ago, we have no choice." He had recovered himself and lifted his head. "Leave it to me. We'll go north. Scotland, perhaps. He may look for a while, but then he'll give up."

She continued to look at him. With incredible sadness, she mourned, "We can never marry."

A word occurred to him. Divorce. It would be difficult, but not impossible, his testimony against Bledding's concerning Ann's mistreatment. Perhaps later when they were safely away, he would discuss it with her.

But for the moment he soothed her with a whispered pledge: "We're married now." His brow furrowed as he stared down on her. "You are my wife," he vowed. "My only wife."

All at once blissful attention.

Again he embraced her, and in the moment before their lips met, he caught a glimpse of her face.

She looked luminous and serene, as though she were listening to the stirrings of new life within her. . . .

✠ 42 ✠

Mr. Cumstey was impossible. Every day for three days he had accosted Geoffrey Bledding, scolding him for the thoughtless and inadequate accommodations in the crypt. Now, after yet another heated encounter with the herpetologist, Geoffrey went to his office and stood again in the dark, with difficulty remembering where he was and who he was.

He continued to feel disgraced and humiliated. He was little more than a paid servant in his own house, obliged to accommodate, required to serve.

Now, adding to and compounding the deep and apparently unhealable wounds incurred by his brutal exposure to an inferior and demanding public was the classic face of the man with horns, the cuckold, the husband betrayed.

Suddenly he felt James Pask's elevation and his own debasement. This sense of his own humiliation before a man of inferior station made up a large part of his misery. It was not the loss of his wife that was causing the agitation. It was his own degradation, the shameful memory of seeing the two of them slip in that night, his awareness—and he had checked—of the loosened bolts on the grillwork barrier, his vision of the two of them slipping back and forth, the betrayal, the humiliation.

While he had never before thought of the American woman as being mistress of Bledding Sorrow, now he saw her clearly in the role. He found the thought a perverse comfort, for it enabled him to see her falling from a much greater height, from a sacred position once occupied by his mother, by his grandmother, a backward-stretching line of stern, worthy, and disciplined ladies.

Now he sat at his desk, still in the dark, like one distraught, clasping his hands and laying his head on them. His thoughts were as dark as the room. Images, memories, ideas of the strongest description followed one another with extraordinary rapidity and vividness. Still, he wanted more. He wanted to catch them in the midst of their passion, to see for himself, and he wanted to punish them. Punishment, as always, was a comforting thought.

Abruptly he left his desk and went to the door. He peered cautiously out and saw students hurrying to the basement dining room for lunch. He stood still, as though he himself were a culprit, and kept repeating stray words from some chain of thought, trying to check the rising flood of fresh images. He listened and heard in a strange mad whisper certain words repeated: "I am humiliated, degraded, debased. . . ."

He moved a hand up to his mouth and pressed in an attempt to keep the words in. When the students had passed by and the corridor was empty, he started out. Then suddenly he withdrew again. There were additional footsteps coming from the direction of the Great Hall. With held breath, he waited as the footsteps drew closer. Quietly he closed the door all the way and kept his hand on the doorknob. Directly outside his office the footsteps stopped.

For several moments his head bent forward, an expression of intense concentration on his face. With staring eyes, he leaned against the door, waiting, listening.

Then softly he heard a knock, heard Caldy More's voice. "Are you there, Mr. Bledding?"

He stood motionless, silent.

She knocked again. "Mr. Bledding?"

Still no answer. She knocked a third time, then apparently gave up, obviously convinced that he had gone down to lunch with the others. Good. Better! With their protectorate and ally absent, the two in the private wing might grow careless.

He waited a moment longer until he heard the clack

of her heels on the basement steps. Then quickly he slipped out of the office and hurried through the empty rooms, moving steadily toward the family wing. Each step was a curious contradiction, a pleasurable yet agonizing effort. He was seeking relief from his suffering by searching out the source of the suffering itself. He wanted to see them; he wanted a clear and indelible vision of what he was judging, blaming, hating.

As he approached the door that led to the private wing, he felt something akin to hardly disguised glee. Carefully he tried the door. Unlocked, as he knew it would be. Obviously there was no longer any need to contain a deranged wife. Obviously the wife had recovered.

He let himself in, then stood for a moment, listening. No voices to give him direction. Then he would be his own map, would follow his instincts. The upper bedchamber at noon was unlikely. Their passions, unchecked by night, would place few or no demands on them during the day. It was his estimation that, luxuriating under a false sense of freedom, they would be sitting openly at table or walking in the garden. Whichever, he was now ready to confront them in their disgrace.

He moved along the small corridor to the kitchen, now making no attempt to disguise his footsteps. But the kitchen was empty. His eyes, drawn with distress, looked about the table at the remnants of a meal for two. Even so simple a sight caused fresh humiliation. The bitterness and shame threatened to overwhelm him.

Then suddenly he looked out of the window into the garden. And drew back. He saw them then, standing as one near the far wall, the man smiling, the woman staring up at him, her arms moving around his neck, the kiss itself prolonged, hands flattened as though their bodies were enjoying memories of greater knowledge, sharper sensations.

He watched it all with a curiously flat expression, his mouth open slightly, watched beyond the kiss as they continued to press tightly together, their arms intertwined.

Then he had no further reason to stay. His limbs felt peculiarly weary. The image of betrayal had been sufficiently burned into his mind. It was enough even for him to recover his poise. He felt strangely relaxed now, as an unjustly accused man who finds proof of his innocence would. The humiliation was there, but eased. Not the slightest regret.

He stepped away from the window, his recent agitation manifested only by a slight trembling in his hands. Obviously they felt safe, at home in the garden, for they had not displayed even the slightest hint of guilt.

Now he walked steadily back to the door and closed it quietly behind him. He stared for a moment at the whirling colors of the Oriental carpet beneath his feet, concentrated on it the mass of desires which demanded satisfaction. He had other responsibilities. He would not degrade himself further by lurking outside their sin. He had the students to think about, the strident complaints of Mr. Cumstey. . . .

Suddenly it was as though a violent shock of electricity had passed over him. He raised up from his concentration on the carpet. The weariness in his limbs that he had felt a moment before had suddenly gone. His expression was calm, almost fatalistic as his inspiration came very quickly and easily. He had been told, so he knew it was true, that the adders needed air in a confined walled space. The private garden was a confined walled space. Apparently the two lovers felt at home in the high walled garden. That thought, too, joined the conspiracy. A careless accident, surely a tragic one. Absolved of all guilt. Revenged. A chance that it might not work. But a greater chance that it would.

His sense of humiliation was diminishing. With his characteristic decision, without further hesitation, he went back to his office and closed and locked the door.

Sitting behind his desk, he was struck by the definiteness and ease with which the plan evolved. Shortly before dawn the following morning, before anyone stirred, the thoughtful warden of Bledding Sorrow would go to the crypt and fetch the wicker baskets and carry them to the private garden and turn the captives loose. Restless and angry after their long confinement, they would undoubtedly seek shelter in the damp shadows of the far garden wall. There they would flex and coil and burrow deep into the fallen leaves, unnoticed until, sensing vibrations from the ground, they would. . . .

His breath caught, his eyes closed, his awareness of the potential of the plan cut deep. Of course, there was a chance that it might not work, but a greater chance that it would.

Now he looked calmly about the room. He felt natural, restored. He seemed about to speak to someone, to spring forward, to explode. Then, without warning, his hand thrust forward toward the lamp.

It was absurd that he should sit in darkness.

He needed light. . . .

❧ 43 ❧

Ann stirred. Dawn. Perhaps later. She raised up in bed and tried to judge the time of morning by the slanting angles of sun pouring in through the barred window.

For a moment, on awakening, her eyes shifted from the spilling sun to the window itself. It suddenly occurred to her that her time with the barred window was limited, that one day soon she would never have to look at it again.

With a rush of happiness, she nestled deeper into the bed. Her hands fanned out over the spot where he had recently lain beside her. At times like this, when she was alone, her ever-increasing happiness frightened her. Sometimes, half asleep, she uttered what she now felt more intensely in her heart than at any other time in her life.

What if it were to end? What would I do?

Paradoxically her deep love, steadily growing more intense, did its work and seemed to tease her now with thoughts of conclusion. There was no position in which she was unconscious of his existence, not a limb, not a part of her body that did not ache and cause her an agony of desire. Even the memories of him awakened in her the same intense excitement as the man himself. It was as though all her life were merged into this one feeling, this love.

Now she sat up in bed and gazed before her with the same concentrated expression in her eyes. It was beyond dawn—she was certain of it—a midmorning sun. Perhaps he was already in the kitchen having coffee with Caldy More while she, lying in bed late, was missing precious moments with him.

The thought of seeing him coming so fast on the

heels of the thought of losing him provoked in her an insoluble dilemma. He was always so near, and she knew he was near, yet when she was alone, he seemed so far away, a figure so distant that at times she couldn't even quite bring herself to believe he was real. These chaotic feelings were now even stronger than ever, and even less than before did she feel capable of comprehending their meaning.

The only cure, as she knew from experience, was to dress and go and find him, seek his hands, the gentle weight of his arm around her shoulder, the dark reassuring warmth of his eyes. That was the only balm capable of banishing old fears, old terrors.

Then she was out of bed in a blur of activity, slipping on a dress, running a brush hastily through her hair, reverting, under the pressure of the moment, to her old habit of no shoes, running at last, barefoot, down the long corridor, not calling his name aloud, but certainly thinking it with each step, an obsessive determination to find him, look again on his face, seek his assurance that nothing would ever separate them.

Suddenly, midway down the corridor, she stopped. Something was stirring behind her. She whirled around and focused her eyes on the open door of the upper bedchamber. There, just emerging in a blaze of light, she saw the spectral image of the woman again, dragging herself forward, one thin bloodied hand raised in Ann's direction, crawling pitiably, her mysteriously useless legs nothing more than dead appendages beneath the long skirts.

Ann shuddered and pressed backward against the damp wall. Why didn't the woman leave her alone? Why had all her other specters and terrors vanished save this one? But at the moment she was asking herself these questions, the woman inched forward, her face contorted, that one small hand clearly beckoning now, as though she were urging Ann to stay.

Then there was a low moan as though some incredible pain had threatened to overwhelm her. Then she was moving again, dragging herself forward down the long corridor, clearly entreating now, her mouth open, communicating but not with words, rather with feelings, unspoken warnings, powerful signals, now openly begging Ann to return to the upper bedchamber.

Again Ann pushed backward against the wall, her head moving from side to side, confused, not wanting to add to the woman's agony, but unable in any way to understand or oblige her. And as her bewilderment and terror increased, the woman dragged herself even closer, so close now that she reached out and touched Ann. And the feel of that hand, so cold, sensations which defied description, caused Ann to back away. She could not stay. She would not stay, not when there was a possibility that *he* was waiting for her.

So she turned her back on the woman and closed her eyes to the puzzling entreaty.

She took the narrow staircase in a dead run and fairly burst forth into the kitchen, where a rather startled Caldy More looked up. As Ann stopped in the doorway for breath, her eyes had already searched the kitchen and found it wanting. Rather breathlessly now she asked, "Where is he?"

Caldy More shrugged and turned back to the sink, where she was washing dishes. "He's gone to service the coach and check on the schedule for the rest of the week," she explained, as though it were something Ann should have known. Suddenly Caldy More looked back over her shoulder, fatigue and perhaps a little anger in her face. "You should have waited until I came for you," she scolded. "This is very difficult, but you can make it easier by cooperating." Then she turned back to the hissing water and soapy foam and left Ann to digest her disappointment.

Now, slowly, Ann walked toward the table at the center of the room, carefully studying the obvious remains of his breakfast. She tried to speak above the clatter of dishes at the sink. "Did he say when he would be back?" she asked.

"When he's finished, I would imagine," Caldy More said without looking up.

Between the emptiness of the kitchen and Caldy More's short temper Ann faltered. For a moment she had a glimpse of the future without him, all hope, all promise lay razed. She sat heavily in the chair next to his empty one, feeling beneath her bare feet a fine layer of grit on the floor. Her hand reached timidly out for a half-filled coffee cup, his, she imagined. Gently she ran a finger around the rim of the cup where his lips had rested. It was as though her old illness were returning. She felt infinitely isolated, alone, an ominous stinging behind the bridge of her nose, hideous memories of the days when she had sat alone, weeping for no reason.

Suddenly, as though to push the illness away, she buried her face in her hands and tried desperately to regain control. A moment later she felt a hand, gentle but firm, on her shoulder and heard Caldy More's voice, soothing this time, apologizing. "I'm sorry," she murmured. "He'll be back soon." Her voice brightened. "Why don't you have breakfast and wait for him in the garden? He likes to find you in the garden. He's told me so."

Ann lifted her eyes, the tears almost under control. She shook her head, trying very hard to understand her feelings. "Are you ever afraid, for no reason, Caldy More?"

The woman sat down beside her and covered Ann's hand with her own. "When I was young, yes. But it passes. All the terrible things that you think might happen never do, and you get so busy trying to fight off all the terrible things that you never even dreamed would happen that, somehow, you just get weary and give it all up as a bad job and do the best you can."

Ann looked imploringly into her eyes. It was not a particularly lovely view of life. Again she shook her head. Her own bleak mood at the moment could not be dissipated. Half humorously, half seriously she said,

"I think it's safer being unhappy. At least when you're unhappy, you have nothing to lose."

Caldy More scoffed at that. "And what exactly is it that you are going to lose? Whether you like it or not, I suspect that Mr. James Pask is yours for as long as you want him. He talks of you continuously. He's even making plans. Did you know that?"

Ann nodded, but still the strange feeling invaded her, a dread, a doubt of everything.

Now, as though to help to dispel Ann's glumness, Caldy More bustled about the kitchen, fetching fresh coffee cups and a platter of breakfast rolls, talking all the time. "In fact, I've been meaning to speak to you about that. If you're leaving next week with him, we have packing to do." Her face was close now and suddenly stern. "And I don't even want to know where you are going. I've forbidden James to tell me and now I'll forbid you. When questioned," she added sternly, "I want to be able to say honestly, *'I don't know.'*"

Her strong emphasis on the three words amused Ann, and the faint sadness in her eyes moved her. She reached up suddenly and caught the woman just as she was turning away. She clasped her hand and said simply, "I'll miss you."

The show of affection had a disastrous effect on Caldy More. Her lined face contorted as though she were in pain. The silence between them was awkward, as though they had both been crushed by the simple display of feeling and by their mutually shared weight of memory.

As Caldy More's lips began to quiver, Ann rose, and the next minute they were in each other's arms. The embrace was warm but over quickly. Caldy More, obviously unaccustomed to such an open display of emotion, quickly fled the room and left Ann alone to digest the sweetness of the moment, to try as best she could to conquer the black mood which continued to threaten her.

Glancing about her now, she said no to the silent

emptiness of the kitchen and chose instead the high blue sky and fresh morning air of the garden.

He would come back soon. It was only a matter of time. She pushed open the back door and stepped, barefoot, onto the soft dew-wet grass. He liked to find her in the garden. Caldy More had told her so. Then that's where he would find her. She looked intently about her, locked in with her own thoughts. She saw in her mind the thin figure in the gray smock dress. She remembered clearly the honeysuckle man, the rose-bush family, and the old white kitchen cat. Suddenly she shuddered. That world was over and she would say good-bye to it as firmly as she would say good-bye to barred windows and high brick walls.

She walked carefully now down the garden path, feeling a new sense of restrained excitement, her thoughts whispering together, retreating, then advancing again as she dared to think ahead to her life with him. In all honesty, she could not imagine it. What would happen if he ceased to love her? Was there anyplace on earth where they could go without fear of being found? Would she be a burden to him?

Abruptly, as though to outrun the barrage of un-answerable questions, she ran to the end of the garden and leaned heavily against that spot on the wall where she'd first seen him. Her breath was failing her, the blood rushing to her heart. Oh, how she needed him, now, at this moment. She sighed and her face, sud-denly taking a hard expression, looked as if it were turned to stone, affecting composure. She must be patient, must conquer the fear. There was nothing to be afraid of. Clutching her chilled hands, she began pressing them to her face.

It was while her eyes were still closed that she heard the woman again, knew without looking that she had followed her out into the garden. Now the specter was screaming at her, a new depth and degree of urgency that Ann had never heard before.

And when she removed her hands from her face, she

saw the woman, as she knew she would, lying helplessly on the grassy lawn a short distance away, both hands now extended, begging, the pale face all but obscured by the mussed fair hair, her eyes wide in unspoken and unseen terror.

Ann was on the verge of speaking to her, of trying to discover the cause of her fear when suddenly she heard a new sound.

Softly, around her feet, she heard a subdued stirring. She lifted her head. With her hands hanging exhausted at her side now, she looked down. There was another soft rustle, the fallen leaves around the base of the wall in constant agitation. She caught only a glimpse of shimmering brown. Then the base of the wall where she stood was alive with movement.

Suddenly all about her there was a whir and hiss of uncoiling. Her hands moved out as though for protection. As the small sleek heads emerged from the blanket of leaves, she screamed. At the moment she moved, she saw clearly their silver-liquid tongues striking at her feet. She screamed again and fell backward. The pain itself was not nearly as great as the apprehension of pain, merely small pinpricks in each foot, as though she had inadvertently stumbled into a thornbush.

But she saw them clearly now, and that was the horror, two, three, four, five of them coiling and uncoiling, lifting their heads, striking again and again at her feet. In a paroxysm of terror, she dragged herself back to the path, then lifted her head and cried for help. As they slithered closer, she screamed again and tried to move farther back. But now the pressure from the weight of her body caused the tiny pinpricks in each foot to explode into a fiery heat. Her head fell backward, her face strained in its exertion as the flames climbed up both legs. She screamed again, an awful scream which never paused and became still more awful, as though she had reached the utmost limit of terror. Gasping for breath, she tried again to drag herself farther away from the wall. But her feet and legs were completely useless now. Numbness had set in. They simply followed after her like dead appendages.

Death rose clearly and vividly before her mind. She tried to scream again, but the air caught in her lungs. Helpless now, she had no choice but to lie back, to gaze for as long as she could on the high blue cloudless sky.

A moment later a mist shrouded everything. She tried to raise her head, but could not. The numbness was spreading.

Then she thought again that life might still be happy, and how desperately she loved him, and how fearfully her heart was beating. . . .

❦ 44 ❧

Jamie did not know if it was late or early. To his unfocused eyes the bare bulb overhead outside her door seemed to be burning brightly. It must be late. He could hear through her door Dr. Axtell and the others moving about, washing, saying something. The hours passed somehow despite the wild-voiced cry inside his head.

Wearily he leaned against the wall, slid down, and sat flat on the floor, his head resting on his knees. The whole long nightmare of the day rushed over him. He sighed and flung his head back and began to feel afraid he could not bear it, that he would burst into tears or run away. Such agony was it for him, and still it was not over.

From the depths of his brain he could still see her, saw himself returning earlier this morning, casually, from servicing the coach, only to find the central corridor in an uproar, people rushing about every which way. He remembered how twice he had tried to stop certain staff members, seeking information, but they had brushed him off as though their own hysteria prohibited lucid speech. Then he had followed the traffic to the private wing and had found a most incredible sight, people lining the narrow hall, craning forward for a glimpse of something, Caldy More weeping uncontrollably at the kitchen table, the cook, old Mrs. Bonebrake, bent over trying to comfort her, and in the garden several men with long hooked sticks poking about through the fallen leaves, and—here his heart almost stopped—near the far wall a small cluster of people bent over a fallen figure with fair hair.

Now he closed his eyes and ground his forehead

365

into his knee. He had arrived in time to cradle her head in his lap and restrain her arms, while Dr. Axtell, without benefit of anesthetic, had cut open both her ankles and applied tourniquets in an attempt to bleed the poison out of her system. Blessedly she had lost consciousness. Now he wished he could do the same.

But still the minutes passed by and the hours and still more hours, and his misery and horror grew and were more and more intense. Without allowing himself even to think of what was to come, of how it would end, he had in his imagination braced himself to bear up and to keep a tight rein on his feelings. He had been forced merely to watch as two strangers had lifted her up and carried her, still unconscious, to the upper bedchamber. He had followed after them, ignoring Geoffrey Bledding's cold dismissal, had watched, helpless, as the man had shut the door in his face, that same door behind which now the source of all his light and happiness lay, perhaps dying, certainly suffering, for throughout the whole long day he had endured her moans.

Suddenly now that same door opened and Caldy More appeared. There were tears in her eyes and her hands were shaking. Seeing Jamie, she knelt before him and embraced him. "She's alive," she whispered, "just alive."

He saw her flushed and overwrought face, her gray hair in disorder. He was about to speak to her when he heard Geoffrey Bledding and Martin Axtell inside the bedchamber talking quietly.

Quickly Caldy More rose to her feet and motioned for him to come with her to her room. He stood up, too, but shook his head, clearly indicating that he intended to stay where he was. They had no right to shut him out. Again Caldy More motioned for him to follow after her quickly.

But again he shook his head and held his ground, his eyes riveted hopefully on the partially open door. In the next moment the two men appeared, Dr. Axtell looking worn and weary, the front of his white coat smeared with drying blood. Following behind him came Bledding, his face drawn and white. Axtell was speaking with growing anxiety, something about they could not move her but needed help. And Bledding was listening, head down.

As they emerged into the corridor and caught sight of Jamie, all talk ceased. Bledding stepped forward, clearly taking control, his face as remote as ever in spite of his pallor. "I thought I told you to go about your business, Mr. Pask," he said.

Jamie hesitated only a moment before his cold authority. "I was only wondering how she—"

"How she is is none of your concern," Bledding interrupted. "These are unhappy circumstances, but they are family matters." He looked sharply about as though suddenly realizing where they were. His voice rose. "And this is the family wing, a private wing. It is closed to all members of the staff."

As his anger increased, threatening his control, Axtell stepped forward and placed a light but restraining hand on his arm. In a conciliatory manner he urged Pask, "Run along now. I'm sure you have duties. The woman is doing as well as can be expected under the circumstances." He smiled. "I'll be with her all night. She'll be in good hands."

But still Jamie held his ground. He had to see her; he had a right to see her. For a long moment the tableau held, the two men, Bledding and Axtell, standing as though they were blocking the door, Jamie clearly confronting them, and a short distance away Caldy More, leaning on her own door, clearly terrified.

Finally Jamie drew back a little. He was in error. He had no right, none at all, at least none he could explain to them or anyone else except perhaps Ann. At the thought of her, he bowed his head, his eyes clouded, his lower jaw trembling. Not trusting himself to speak further, he turned and started, out of habit, toward the grillwork barrier.

As he drew even with Caldy More, she suddenly stepped forward, her eyes bright, her voice unnaturally loud. "Did you wish to see me, Mr. Pask?" she inquired. She did not speak further, but lifting her head, she simply gazed at him with her speaking eyes.

He stopped. The realization of what he had almost done was instantaneously converted into a shocked alarm. Another moment and it would have been too late. He was clearly aware of the two men behind him, waiting and watching.

Finally he mumbled, "Just wanted to say how sorry I was, and —"

Caldy More rushed in to help. She took him by the arm and turned him in the proper direction toward the stairs at the end of the corridor. She murmured, "Thank you," and told him good night. She did not raise her head, but gave the smallest nod.

Then he was moving again, trying to walk steadily and erect past the two men, who were still watching him closely, sullen, intense interest on Bledding's face, mild amusement on Axtell's. He glanced about at Bledding. Those cold eyes and thin lips seemed to be saying, "Where are your pretensions now?"

Jamie hurried on down the corridor, no one speaking behind him, no sound at all except for the measured tread of his own footsteps. When at last he was out of their sight and on the stairs, he heard muffled comment, heard Bledding call to Caldy More to fix them a light meal, then she was to go to bed. Jamie considered waiting for her in the kitchen, then decided against it. It was too risky for her as well as for him. Yet with Axtell in the room all night there was no hope of seeing Ann. He did not fully realize it because it was too terrible for him to realize his actual position as an outsider, and he shut down and locked and sealed in his heart that secret place where his feelings lie. He could not deal with them and still function. And he had work to do.

He hurried on down the stairs and out into the Great

Hall. In a way, action helped, the sense of his own movement. Although his face was white and set, the awareness of a destination helped to keep his mind off the realization that if her life was over, his was over. He kept saying to himself, *I must do something. I must act.* And a kind of anger at his helplessness swept over him, a wild determination to make some gesture that would show he could strike out against the dark clouds that enveloped him.

Although it was after midnight, in the central corridor he found small clusters of students still standing about, talking in muted tones. And sitting on the bottom step of the broad staircase, his head down, surrounded by three other men, he saw Mr. Cumstey.

Suddenly Jamie lunged forward, his eyes fiercely fixed on the man who had brought him to such grief. The others fell back as he approached as though sensing his anger. Grabbing the man by his shoulders, he lifted him into the air and pinned him against the banister, his hand drawn back in a fist.

Mr. Cumstey's watery blue eyes grew wide under the assault. His hands flailed about in useless motions, his mouth opening and closing as though his fear had suddenly rendered him speechless.

Effortlessly Jamie held him with one hand. He was aware of a sudden stir of excitement behind him as the others drew near. But his anger was not directed at them. Here was the one, the pudgy little clubfooted man, cringing in fear before him.

Now, as his fist lifted higher, Mr. Cumstey tried to struggle loose. "No, Mr. Pask, please don't, please," he begged.

"Why did you do it?" Jamie demanded. "Surely you knew that was a garden, that people walked there."

The man shuddered, still struggling, jabbering something. His eyes rolled backward, leaving two white ovals. Saliva ran from the corner of his mouth. He shook his head and closed his eyes as though struggling for control. "I didn't do it, Mr. Pask," he gasped. "I swear on all that's holy, I didn't do it."

Jamie stared at him, his fist still raised. "Then who?" he demanded. "It had to be you or one of your people."

"No, I swear it," the man shouted. "We left those baskets in the crypt. We weren't happy about the arrangement, but, my God, man, we know better than to—"

Suddenly he broke off and slumped against the banister, weeping openly. In some bewilderment, Jamie watched him. He released his hold on him and the man slumped heavily to the floor. He turned now and confronted the small audience of strained faces behind him. Again he demanded, "Then who?"

They shook their heads in various firm denials. One man said, "That's what we were trying to figure out."

Another inquired urgently, "How is she?"

Jamie looked at the faces, all blurring together now. He stepped away from the fallen man and all inquiry, unable to force his mind beyond the simple question, "Then who?"

They had no answer for him. Mr. Cumstey was now struggling for control and failing, his arms flung over his head. "I can—only—suggest"—he sobbed—"that it was someone who did not know adders." Suddenly he looked up, his face ravaged. "Please, Mr. Pask, you must believe me. I would never—"

Then another spasm of grief washed over him and he buckled again. Jamie watched him until he could watch no longer. Then he stepped back. He felt caged, helpless, locked in and shut out all at the same time. The question inside his head would not relent. "Then who?"

He spun around and ran down the corridor and out into the night air. He did not stop until he reached the gatehouse arch. Then he looked back up toward her room. The tears were silent but hot. They burned his face.

He focused on the dim light of the upper bedchamber as though it were a beacon, the only source of light in his world. He prayed to God without ceasing. And every time that he felt he had been brought back from a moment of oblivion, the same unanswered question reached his ears. "Then who?" And he fell into a strange terror too powerful for prayer.

As the moments passed, both these conditions became more intense because of her sufferings and his feeling of helplessness before them. Unable to bear it any longer, he ran off toward the high pasture and the comfort of his coach.

But the question merely followed after him.

Then who? *Who?*

❧⟨ 45 ⟩❧

Martin Axtell poured the last of the wine and looked across the table at Geoffrey Bledding. "Then who?" he asked again. "If she dies, that question will be of paramount importance."

Bledding looked up, his face pale. "Will she die?"

Martin shrugged and meticulously arranged a slice of cheddar on a biscuit. "With venom, you never know." He chewed slowly and spoke around the food in his mouth. "For your sake, I hope she doesn't." He sipped at his wine. "You haven't answered my question. Do you have any idea who—"

Suddenly Bledding pushed angrily back from the table. "Why do you insist on asking that question?"

Martin matched his anger, his voice rising. "Because if she dies, the authorities will ask it and keep asking it until they have their answer." He looked sternly at Bledding for a moment, then his expression softened. He shook his head sadly. "You should have stayed with me, Geoffrey. I could have helped you. Now. . . ." Again he shrugged and popped the last morsel of cheese into his mouth.

He looked about at the small antechamber, a most unappetizing place to eat, particularly with the woman lying in the next room, drops of her blood still splattered across his white coat. Still, a man had to have food. It would be a long night, possibly a grim one.

Now he glanced up at Geoffrey, who was pacing back and forth before the small table, the food on his plate untouched. Martin had never seen him so distracted. "Sit," he soothed. "Eat. There are always ways." He smiled in the dim light, pleased now with the look of hope on Geoffrey's face.

Bledding sat tentatively on the edge of his chair. Martin grew expansive. He stood up and circled the table until he was standing directly before Geoffrey. "First," he began, "I would suggest that we do everything in our power to keep her alive. That may mean calling for help tomorrow. A surgical team from York. I can arrange it. She can't be moved. It would only cause the poison to spread farther." He smiled pointedly. "The concerned husband must do everything in his power. As I said, I can arrange it."

Geoffrey looked slowly up at him. "And then?" he whispered.

"Then if she survives, it will simply go down as accidental snakebite. The authorities will leave us alone." He stepped closer. "And at the first possible opportunity you will send her to the asylum outside London." He shook his head sadly. "The trauma of the accident plus her already questionable mental stability will be far too much for her. No one will contest the decision. She will be a recognizable invalid."

His hand reached out and touched Geoffrey's hair, a soothing gesture. "You really should have done it years ago. When will you learn to listen to Martin?" His voice had grown quite husky, his hand smoothing, smoothing.

Geoffrey looked up into his face, submitting to the caress. "And—if she dies?" he asked.

Martin touched his lips now as though to hush such a despicable question. "If she dies," he whispered, "you were with me. All night." He stepped closer until he was standing between Geoffrey's legs, applying subtle pressure with his knee to the man's groin. *"All night,"* he repeated, smiling softly.

Again Geoffrey lifted his head, made no attempt to pull away. Gratitude replaced the agonized expression on his face. Then he lifted Martin's hand and kissed it, and the hand, with a weak movement of the fingers, responded to the kiss.

Martin felt glorified by such a radiance of happiness

that he could not bear it. Suddenly he felt himself borne back to a world of unlimited possibilities. He clasped Bledding to him, then disrupted the embrace, scolding gently, "Enough. For now." He felt unutterably happy. The man was his at last, clearly his. "You sit here and rest," he urged. "Try to eat. I'll go look at the patient."

Geoffrey's agonized and swollen face was fixed intently on him, a tress of hair clinging to his moist brow. He turned again to Martin and sought his eyes. With no words spoken, he conveyed a message of total gratitude. And total submission.

Martin accepted both. For one of the fewer than three or four times in his entire life he felt desperately, completely happy. . . .

A pall hung over Bledding Sorrow. The following morning a cold rain swept in, adding to the deep gloom. The routine of the hall had been totally disrupted. Breakfast was served in the basement dining room, but there was no one there to eat it.

At ten A.M. a small white lorry pulled into the courtyard. A few moments later four men carefully and quickly carried two large wicker baskets up from the crypt. They stored them in the back of the lorry, locked the doors, and the vehicle sped off into the rain.

Caldy More watched it all, as near to total disintegration as she had ever been in her life, yet somehow maintaining an appearance of outward strength and calm. Only her red and swollen eyes betrayed the grief she felt inside.

At eleven A.M. she stepped out into the rain to greet a large blue van with a flashing red light atop and awesome surgical equipment stored carefully in the back. The surgeon, a tall thin man, his hands encased in gray kid gloves, strode purposefully toward the front of the hall. He was followed by two nurses, young women with curiously hard and unchanging expressions on their faces.

Caldy More ushered them without speaking through the hall to the door of the family wing, where Martin Axtell and Geoffrey Bledding greeted them and took them the rest of the way.

Less than twenty minutes later Geoffrey Bledding told her that the decision had been made, the diagnosis unanimous. The poison, localized in her ankles, was slowly spreading to the rest of her system.

Amputation. Of both feet.

Still Caldy More held the disintegration at arm's length. She followed every order, every command, moving as quickly, as efficiently as the expressionless nurses themselves, fetching stacks of white sheets, draping them about in the small antechamber, converting it into a makeshift surgery, moving back to make way for the large oak table which two men brought up from downstairs, covering the table herself with a large piece of green plastic, then another white sheet, voluntarily stepping aside as the equipment was brought up and arranged, the sterilizer full of instruments, the oxygen, the anesthetic, the containers of extra blood. Still and throughout the entire procedure she held the disintegration at arm's length.

Not until all was at ready, the surgeon and Dr. Axtell and the nurses scrubbed and clothed in white gowns with masks over their faces, the extra illumination turned on and focused on the white-sheeted table, Ann carried still unconscious to the operating area, a sheet placed over her midsection, her feet, pitifully swollen, butchered, infected, discolored, scarely resembling feet at all, arranged a distance apart and slightly elevated, a black rubber mask placed over her face, not until this moment did Caldy More give in to the disintegration.

She threw one last burning look about the room, then she fled the torture chamber on uncertain legs, feeling a great desire to cry out, her hands reaching ahead as though there were hazards all about, hot air from another world blowing over her, some terrible outrage in her soul manifesting itself in her churning stomach. She made it to her own room, to the sink on the far wall. There she bent over and vomited.

She felt in the pocket of her dress and found a handkerchief and pressed it against her lips, then knelt a brief moment before the sink and leaned her forehead against the cool porcelain.

Softly, behind her, she heard the quiet opening of the door. But she did not turn. In a moment a hand lay on her back.

She heard him speak. "I—had to come." And around and through his words she heard the cries of a drowning man.

Then she looked up. He stood before her as wet, as soaked through as though he *had* drowned. Obviously he had tried to walk off his grief in the rain and had failed. He bore not the slightest resemblance to the James Pask she had met at the beginning of the summer. This man standing before her now, his hands hanging helplessly at his sides, looked consummately defeated, looked as though something had crushed him to extinction. She could not rid her eyes of him, of the terrible interrogation in them.

His head bowed. He took two or three involuntary steps away from her. Then again he stopped. He looked pitiably about the room, gazing steadily for a moment at the wall beyond which the surgery was taking place. His eyes were full of tears and his look was unbearably naked.

Caldy More could not watch him any longer. Her head sank lower. She barely caught his words as he whispered, "I will look after her. I will take care of her...."

⌬ 47 ⌬

It was three days after the surgery before James had a chance to see Ann. Security around her room had been close, constant comings and goings of the surgeon, the nurses, Dr. Axtell, always someone in her room or standing outside in the corridor, blocking him out, shutting him away.

He passed this time like a zombie, wandering through the gardens, lurking outside the grillwork barrier, waiting for the first signal from Caldy More. Two or three times every day old Mrs. Bonebrake brought him a tray of food and sat with him in his room and insisted that he eat something. Apparently she knew, had known for some time what had happened that summer at Bledding Sorrow.

"I may not know much," she boasted, "but I know men, and the sight and sound and smell of one in love. So! Eat!"

And Jamie had eaten. A little. Enough to ward off the icy chill in his blood, a feeling of loss, a very physical feeling of something concluding.

Then early in the morning of the fourth day, as he lay stretched out on the pallet he had made at the base of the grillwork barrier, the closest he could get to her without being discovered, he heard a frantic whisper coming to him through the barrier and beyond the drape.

Suddenly he sat up and bent his head against the ironwork. "Is that you, Caldy More?" he whispered.

"They've left. Come quick," she said. "Hurry. Please hurry."

Within the instant he was on his feet, his trembling fingers struggling with the bolts, fumbling hastily at the procedure he'd worked effortlessly hundreds of times before. Finally, in a surge of anger, he jerked the barrier back with such force that bits of plaster pulled loose and fell about his feet.

On the other side he found Caldy More. "Only a minute, please," she begged. "The doctor and nurses just left, but Mr. Bledding and Axtell will be back. Only a moment, and then I must talk to you."

Her eyes blazed on him. She was making a visible effort to control herself. Even in his own agitated state he saw an unprecedented urgency in her expression.

"Go, then," she whispered, stepping back and giving him clear access to the closed door of the upper bedchamber.

As a man dying of thirst approaches a natural spring, James took the door running. Inside the small antechamber there was the strong odor of anesthetic. He stopped for a moment as the pungent smell burned his nose. Against the far wall he saw a large oak table pushed to one side, a piece of green plastic folded neatly on top, a larger stack of sheets beside it. Behind all his rage and sense of loss was the knowledge of what she had endured, had yet to endure. Cruelly there flashed across his mind an image of Ann running the night they had gone to Sutton Bank, the delirium with which those small feet had devoured the terrain, Ann leaping, Ann teasing him to catch up, Ann standing on tiptoe to embrace him.

She shook his head. It was beyond words now, a matter of will. His demeanor was intense, almost tragic. Something in him faltered, then strengthened, and he walked softly through the arch and into her room.

He stood both frozen and incredulous, in no way prepared for what he saw. He closed his eyes a moment, fearful that he would pass out. He gripped the side of the arch, only vaguely aware of Caldy More standing behind him, grasping his arm, as though she were trying to transmit a portion of her strength to him.

Then he forced his eyes back to the bed, to the small

fragile figure lying there, her head without benefit of pillow, resting awkwardly on the bed, her face as pale as though she were dead, the fair hair hopelessly matted and twisted, her arm extended rigidly and strapped to a board, long tubes attached to upturned bottles draining red into her veins, her body so thin it scarcely stopping at the knees, bandages taking over and culmade indentations beneath the sheet, the sheet itself minating in the white-swathed stumps which rested, elevated, on twin pillows.

Countless times his eyes made the same torturous trip, recording everything, always stopping at last on the lack, the absence, the vacuum, the emptiness, as though some terrible perversion in his soul were forcing his concentration, refusing to let him see what *was* there and forcing him to concentrate on the mutilation.

He saw deeper still, could sense the suffering in her central being that had nothing to do with physical pain, but rather a silence, an emotional extinction. The body would recover. The soul might not.

Now he moved toward the bed and there was more horror in the quietness. Her eyes were closed, her lips dry and parted slightly. She gave no indication that she was even aware of his presence.

He looked back questioningly at Caldy More. "Is she still asleep?"

She nodded grimly and dabbed at her eyes with her handkerchief. "They're keeping her sedated again," she whispered. "I've been forbidden to go near her." Suddenly the old woman broke into open tears. The dam had given completely away, her supply of native-born strength depleted. She sank into a near chair sobbing uncontrollably.

For a moment Jamie was torn between the silent woman on the bed and the disintegrating one behind him. But as Caldy More lifted her face and warned him through her tears, "It will come to no good. They're going to send her away." Jamie walked back to where she sat and knelt before her.

He tried repeatedly to draw her hands away from her face so that he could hear what she was saying, but the tears, dammed too long, and the deep sorrow could not be abated.

It was several moments later when, still sobbing, her breath now catching in spasms, Caldy More looked at him, the warning and apprehension clearly visible in her eyes despite the tears. "It will come to no good," she repeated brokenly. "They intend to keep her drugged and send her to an asylum outside London."

Suddenly she grasped his hands and pulled him to her as though she wanted him to understand precisely what she was saying. "They are going to send her away. Do you understand? They are going to get rid of her." Fresh sobs came fast on the heels of old ones, the woman's face a blur of wetness. She sat up now, staring at him, her shoulders heaving. "Take her away," she ordered. "Take her away. Tonight. If there is any justice in heaven, you will be forgiven. Take her away tonight. Take her as far away as you can travel, but take her away."

The old woman's voice had fallen low and ominous. The tears had subsided somewhat as though mere grief didn't stand a chance when pitted against her monstrous plan. "I'll help," she whispered, leaning so close Jamie could feel her breath on his face. "It can be done late tonight. Mrs. Bonebrake will help, too. She's told me she would. She'll serve Mr. Bledding and Axtell dinner late. Just the two of them. She'll keep them busy. When it's time, you come for her and take her away." The tears returned. "It's her only chance"—she wept— "her only chance."

As she bowed down again, giving in to her grief, Jamie looked about, confused and bewildered by what he had heard. He looked quickly back toward the bed. "Can she be safely moved?" he asked, the plan mounting in his head. "Caldy More, can she be safely moved?" he repeated more urgently.

The woman nodded. "She was awake last night,

spoke to me, asked for you." She wiped a sodden handkerchief across her face and gestured toward the tubes and upended bottles. "That's the last of the blood. The surgeon gave strict orders that she be put on solid food today." She shook her head vehemently. "But they won't do it and they won't let me do it. It's their plan to keep her weak and helpless. Oh, for God's sake, take her away, Jamie." Softly she reached out and placed her hands on both sides of his face, forcing him to look at her. "See it through," she begged, "take her away. For her sake."

Suddenly, from a great depth, a sharp feeling rose up within him. "For *my* sake," he corrected softly. "For my sake, I'll take her away."

A flood of relief covered Caldy More's face. She closed her eyes and looked heavenward as though in silent prayer. Jamie walked slowly back to the bed and looked down on the pale face, the closed eyes. With great tenderness he bent over and kissed her lips. In his new resolve the ache was diminishing. Gently he brushed his fingers over her face. She stirred slightly, her cheek pressing against his hand, as though she were aware of his presence. Again and with less apprehension he glanced toward the white-swathed stumps resting on the pillows. Falling on his knees before the bed, he touched her hand, kissed it. He would be her heart, her eyes, her hands, and her feet.

Suddenly Caldy More was at the window looking down. "The lorry just left," she warned. "They'll be back up in a minute. Hurry now. They mustn't find you here."

He took a long last look at Ann, bent over again and kissed her lightly on the forehead, then followed after Caldy More. He slipped through the grillwork barrier, inserted the last bolt, then listened carefully from the other side. A few moments later he heard men's voices coming down the corridor.

He heard Bledding call out sharply, "Caldy More,

what are you doing? We've warned you. Stay away from her."

Caldy More didn't reply. Apparently she simply walked off down the corridor. He heard her footsteps receding in the distance.

A moment later he heard Axtell soothing. "Don't be so hard on her, Geoffrey. She'll begin to suspect. You really must learn to leave everything to me."

Then Jamie heard a door open and close. He stood frozen a moment, unable to digest the realization that they were in the room with her.

Finally he held himself in check. The day would pass. Night would come.

For now he had work to do. . . .

⊸⧫《 48 》⧫⊷

It was after midnight and still raining.

Jamie stood at the top of the broad central staircase in shadows, listening to the activity below. The hall was deserted. The Herpetologist Society had drifted off during the week; shocked and apologetic, they had canceled their conference and fled.

What Jamie was listening to now was old Mrs. Bonebrake. The woman had outdone herself, had prepared a sumptuous feast of roast beef and Yorkshire pudding, appealing with an unerring instinct to Martin Axtell's insatiable appetite. The late-night meal was being served in Geoffrey Bledding's small office. The plan was under way. The grillwork barrier had been pushed back. Jamie was to wait for a signal from Caldy More that Ann was ready, then he, in turn, was to signal Mrs. Bonebrake by dropping a white handkerchief down the stairwell. She would see it and would shortly insist that the office door be closed as the chill was spoiling the food. In these few minutes Jamie was to carry Ann down the staircase and out to the safety of his coach.

Now, as he waited in darkness, looking down at the light below, he felt an inner trembling. There was no need. Everything had been worked out to the smallest detail. He had packed his own belongings and had stored them in the boot of the coach that afternoon. And Caldy More had slipped stealthily out with an armload of warm blankets and pillows and had made a most comfortable pallet on the floor of the coach directly by the door so that at all times Jamie could merely glance down and see Ann. Caldy More had even salvaged the piece of green plastic used in surgery for

Ann's protection against the rain. It had been decided among the three of them, Jamie and Caldy More and Mrs. Bonebrake, that it was far too hazardous to bring the coach to the gatehouse arch. The roar of the motor could easily be heard. Jamie would have to carry her to the high pasture, then drive the coach past Bledding Sorrow and through the village to the motorway which led to Manchester.

It would work. It would have to work. Now nervously he walked to the top of the stairs and looked down. He heard Martin Axtell laughing heartily, clearly enjoying himself. Bledding apparently was maintaining his usual silent mask.

He stepped back into the shadows and looked the other way down the corridor, past the grillwork barrier. Suddenly he saw Caldy More step out into the dim light and wave to him. He felt a faint exultation and moved swiftly down the corridor and into the upper bedchamber, where Ann lay on the bed, swathed in blankets, completely encased in the green plastic covering, only her head showing.

Caldy More's face was flushed with excitement as she led him to the bed. "Axtell gave her an injection. She's still drugged," she whispered. "Perhaps it's best, at least for a while."

Jamie nodded and quickly lifted her into his arms. She was so light. He thought, *I could carry her forever*.

Caldy More followed after him. "Be careful of her legs," she warned as he guided her through the door. At the grillwork barrier he stopped and glanced back.

The old woman looked up at him, a look that was almost dry, as if she had foreseen the farewell and had prepared herself for it. "Look after her," she whispered. "Look after yourself." Then quickly she stepped forward and gave him the white handkerchief for the signal and almost sternly urged him, "Hurry along now."

Jamie took the handkerchief and hesitated a moment longer. What could he say? There were no words, only a smile with a depth of feeling behind it. Then he tighened his hold on his precious cargo and hurried down the corridor.

At the top of the staircase he looked down. The door was still open. He could hear their voices. Carefully he leaned over and dropped the handkerchief down the stairwell. He waited. Ann stirred, moaned softly. He leaned over her face, trying to check the sound.

A few moments later he saw Mrs. Bonebrake retrieve the handkerchief, and several minutes after that he heard her scolding the men for allowing the food to get cold. There was a pause. He heard the door close.

Then he was running as fast as he dared, clutching her to him, taking the steps two at a time, the voices behind the closed door growing louder as he descended to the central corridor.

He did not hesitate, but increased his step, breathing heavily now, not from exertion but from tension. Keeping his eye on the closed door, he rushed past it and greeted the cool, rain-filled night air with an explosion of speed, shielding her face from the rain with his head, running steadily across the courtyard and through the gatehouse arch, up the road, longing, aching for the first glimpse of his coach and freedom.

As he approached the high pasture, he broke speed. His lungs felt as though they were about to burst. Her head rose lightly from his chest and for a moment he thought she might be awake. But she wasn't. Another soft moan escaped her lips and he realized with a twinge of despair that in spite of the drug, she must be feeling some discomfort.

"It's all right," he soothed. "It's all right." Quickly he threw open the door of the coach and placed her gently on the pallet. Her head rolled from side to side for a moment, her face contorted, then she was quiet, unaware that they were gloriously free. He tucked the blankets firmly around her. In a dim light which had no recognizable source he studied her face. He was filled with an incredible happiness.

Then quickly he slipped behind the wheel of the coach and inserted the key. The enormous engine turned, growled, vibrated. He adjusted the windshield wipers, cleared the broad expanse of glass, pulled the gears into place, released the brake, pressed his foot against the accelerator, and in darkness guided the coach to the pasture gate and the steep incline beyond.

He felt for a moment a brief period of repose, as in a room when the last candle burns out. He did not, as he had done at other times, recall the whole train of thought. He fell back at once into the feeling which had guided him, and he found that feeling in his soul even stronger and more definite than before.

He had nothing to fear.

His life was beside him. . . .

Geoffrey was annoyed by the old woman's fluttering attentions. Unprecedented. He knew all too well that the hag hated him as much as he hated her. Still, Martin was enjoying it, and he owed Martin a great deal.

So he sat throughout the heavy meal saying little or nothing, feeling a restlessness he could not wholly account for. For one thing, he was worried. It was *his* head on the block, not Martin's, if anything went wrong. They shouldn't have left her alone, although in truth he was grateful to be out of the stuffy, smelly room. He found her mutilation hideous, the stumps resting on pillows. How Martin could even bear to touch her he didn't know. She was a monstrosity now, fit only to be locked away from human eyes.

Then Mrs. Bonebrake was there again, forcing more food on him. As she reached across the table with a platter heavily laden with roast beef, he could see her armpits, see long hairs protruding from beneath the sleeves of her dress.

The sight of this and the smell of food caused him to gag. "No more," he said sternly, pushing back from the table.

Martin looked up, surprised, and scolded him. "My goodness, aren't we gloomy tonight?" He smiled in mock sternness. "And this good woman has gone to such trouble." He lifted his glass, as he had lifted it countless times before. "A toast to the chef *par excellence*," he slurred.

Mrs. Bonebrake giggled giddily. *"Par excellence*, me arse," she replied, "and all me efforts going stone cold." She pointed sharply toward the open door. "No wonder Mr. Bledding lost his appetite."

Abruptly she closed the door, slammed it, a further disturbance which jarred Geoffrey unduly. "Leave it open," he ordered.

"Not on me life," she protested, standing before the closed door now in open defiance. "I worked half the day on the meal before you," she pouted. "I'll not have it ruined by the chill that creeps down that staircase. Three things a meal must be," she now intoned. "One, cooked properly, two, served properly, and three, eaten properly. It may not bother you, Mr. Bledding," she concluded adamantly, "but it bothers me."

Martin broke into applause. "Truly spoken by a dedicated chef," he commended. He winked massively at Geoffrey. "The most temperamental animal in the world, really, a good chef," he whispered broadly. "You should know. You've been around me long enough. Now, eat, man." Suddenly he speared another enormous piece of meat and placed it on Geoffrey's plate. He looked sad. "Who knows when such a morsel as that will come your way again?"

Geoffrey bowed his head. He could not fight both of them. So he tried to oblige, for Martin's sake, because he owed Martin a great deal. Still the food stuck in his throat. He could not swallow. He could smell the woman standing behind him blocking the door, an unappetizing odor of body heat mingling with the smell of beef. As he lifted his knife again and cut into the meat, a thin rivulet of blood seeped across his plate. He watched it spread, a red artery growing wider. His eyes watered, his wretchedness increasing. He felt himself becoming physically ill. The small room, so close now with the door shut and the smell of human bodies and too much food, was overpowering.

Martin looked closely at him and smiled a subtle and affectionate smile. "I say, are you all right? You look positively white."

Geoffrey, half closing his eyes, looked straight before him and did not answer. Now he saw, in his mind's eye, her feet before amputation, discolored, swollen, yellow pus coating the open wounds where Martin had tried to drain out the poison.

Suddenly he stood, his hand clamped over his mouth. He saw Mrs. Bonebrake, alarmed, move to one side and throw open the door. Then he was running. He was aware of Martin calling after him, but he couldn't stop. The hot rancid fragments of undigested food rose in his throat. He swallowed them back and ran through the open front door and out into the refreshing chill of the rainy night.

He made it as far as the gatehouse arch. Then all the tension, fear, and anxiety conspired against him. He leaned over and vomited. For a moment he was afraid he would lose consciousness. He felt dizzy. Spittle drooled from his open lips, the smell of his sickness compounding the nausea within him.

Mists shrouded everything. The physical upheaval had caused his eyes to water. His head ached. There was a constant ringing inside his ears. Weakly he moved away to the far side of the gatehouse arch, clinging to the cool wet bricks, still trying to free his mind of the hideous events of the last few days. He had wanted her death, not this. What if the asylum outside London refused to take her? What if she somehow convinced them of her sanity and they returned her to him, a mutilated horror who would require constant and lifelong care?

Now he leaned heavily against the bricks, his head still spinning, trying, in spite of his illness, to understand how and why it had started, how he had brought himself to this point, to this horrifying circumstance, this nightmare of suspicion and fear.

He had needed an outlet, a release, even though it had been an artificial one. After all, she was his wife. He had had certain rights and she had had certain duties. Using the phallus had done her no harm, and of late he had begun to feel increasing activity stirring in his groin, as though at any moment his damnable impotency were on the verge of being cured.

His sixteenth-century ancestor, a Bledding like himself, had for a while been cursed with impotency. A few years ago a London historian working for the National Trust, poring through family papers, had found a passage in a diary and had shown it to Geoffrey with great amusement. "This limp toad"—so it had been phrased—"that hangs between my legs."

Suddenly he shook his head. He didn't want to think about it. It was over. In a way, he was now wedded, out of obligation, to Martin Axtell.

He shuddered heavily and pressed closer to the bricks. Suddenly the silence of the night wavered. A rumbling. He looked up. It was coming from the high pasture, or so it seemed. He listened. A powerful motor accelerating. He did not understand. Quickly, and for no reason, he glanced up toward the light of the upper bedchamber. There, silhouetted behind the bars, he saw the figure of a woman. Caldy More. Again he looked closely, sensing something wrong. What was her interest in the cold rainy night, and more important, what was she doing in the upper bedchamber after both he and Martin had expressly forbidden her to go near the woman?

Now the roar increased. He listened closely, his head heavy with images and memories. The coach! It was the coach approaching the pasture gate, someone leaving, stealthily, under cover of night. For a moment it was only an incidental and somewhat ludicrous puzzle. Then, what if. . . ?"

Suddenly understanding flickered out of his nightmare, filling his heart with terror. The sense of his own humiliation before the coachman made up only a small part of his misery. They were escaping! He glanced quickly back up toward the window as though to confirm his suspicion. Caldy More was still there, watching. They were escaping, and she had helped them, had perhaps even instructed them where to go, where to find the proper authorities.

As he stood in the shadows of the gatehouse arch, his fear and suspicion changed rapidly to rage. No! It could not end like this. He would lose everything. He could not endure the prisoner's dock or worse, confinement behind bars.

Suddenly, irrationally, he ran out onto the darkened road. Through the dim mist of rain he saw something coming from the top of the hill, a great lumbering machine, motor growling, moving rapidly with increasing speed through the dark.

No! He mustn't permit it. He could not endure a trial, people laughing at him, shrieking, snickering, talking, everything taken from him, the woman testifying, being carried into the courtroom, her mutilation openly displayed as proof, Caldy More confirming, even Martin perhaps turning against him, as Geoffrey was certain he would, under pressure.

Now, beneath his feet, he felt vibrations, wheels accelerating, picking up speed on the incline. The roar in his head matched the roar of the approaching coach. He wanted to stop up his ears, but could not. Wildly he looked about him. There, just inside the gatehouse arch, he spied an automobile, belonging perhaps to one of the girls in the kitchen. Without thinking or caring whose it was, but knowing precisely what he intended to do, he ran, stumbling, toward it, threw open the door, and slid behind the wheel.

His panic was increasing, though blending now with a kind of excitement as he found keys in the ignition. Fate was on his side. Within the moment he felt the motor turn over and then he was backing out and around, angling the automobile directly toward the blind spot of the gatehouse arch.

He must not let them escape. He must not compound all his other mistakes with this one last and perhaps fatal inability to act. Summoning all his will now, he accelerated, the car shot forward, clearing the arch, careening wildly out onto the road in pursuit of the coach. He was prepared and willing to run them down if necessary, to force the coach off the road. *They must not escape. They must not escape.* That refrain increased inside his head as the car moved rapidly forward.

He was gaining on them, the speed of the car increasing, moving parallel now with the coach, his hands gripping the wheel, reason gone, only one single-minded goal, driving him down the winding, twisted, rain-slick road, and that was the destruction of the coach and whoever might be in it.

Now the road narrowed. The night was black. He bent forward over the wheel in order to see better, still pressing his foot against the accelerator, speed increasing, even with the coach now. The strain showed clearly on his face, the wide-set eyes now focused rigidly on the enormous hulk on the right.

Timing was all, the right moment, the right rate of speed. *Now!* Suddenly he jerked the wheel sharply to the right, heard a grinding of metal as steel met steel. And in that moment the coach, as though wishing to avoid a collision, veered toward the edge of the road.

Once more Geoffrey looked up. As far as he could tell, the coach was out of control but still moving forward. With all his might he pressed the accelerator down until it was touching the floorboard. Now he could see the outline of the man behind the wheel, struggling, his body angled away from the direction in which the coach was heading.

In one final enormous effort Geoffrey drew even with the front of the coach and again jerked the wheel of his car sharply to the right, deliberately forcing the coach closer to the edge of the ravine. Suddenly, behind him, he saw a blaze of headlights in the rearview mirror, gigantic twin eyes blinding him. There was the screech of a horn, a hiss of air brakes, the monstrous tires fighting for traction on the rain-slick road as the coach swerved dangerously toward the edge of the deep ravine.

Blinded, Geoffrey jerked the car back into the center of the road. At the same moment he felt the rush of air as the coach careened past him, still veering peril-

ously close to the edge of the steep ravine. The right
wheels caught on the soft shoulder. It continued moving for a moment at a high rate of speed, balanced now
on two wheels, clearly out of control.

Suddenly Geoffrey slammed on his brakes, pulled
the car over to the safe left shoulder, incapable even
of thinking anymore, aware of nothing, for nothing
else made any difference. Quickly he stumbled out from
behind the steering wheel, watching.

A feeling such as he had never known before rose
up within him. He did not take his eyes off the raised
wheels, the huge thing balancing tentatively on the side
of the ravine, still moving forward, air brakes whining
uselessly now, the smell of petrol, of burning rubber,
the coach literally suspended in midair on the side of
the precipice, as though for just a moment fate de-
bated which way to send it.

Then, with a roar, it fell, turning completely over,
then over again and still again, small explosions here
and there which were almost lost in the crash itself, a
never-ending din of steel crumpling, glass shattering, a
high-pitched whine of jammed gears, an awe-inspiring
descent of incredible violence until at last it struck bottom, shrouded in darkness and silence except for escaping steam, and even that was shortly over. Then,
nothing.

Geoffrey staggered forward to the side of the road,
looking down. It was done! A faint smile crossed his
face. It was done! He had won. He continued to stand
as though paralyzed, then a wild joy seized him. He
was free, his honor avenged. Then softly there was a
wind at his back, and it seemed to be pushing him forward. A disturbing thought occurred to him. What if
they weren't dead? What if, somehow, one or the other
or both had survived the crash?

Once more he looked down into the ravine. Nothing
was clearly visible, although he smelled smoke. He
listened fearfully. Had he heard something? A cry?
Still the wind pushed at his back. There! He heard it

again. But no one could survive what he had just witnessed. Then, what was it?

Suddenly he started down. He had to see for himself. He had to be certain. It would be awhile before the others at Bledding Sorrow realized he was gone and came after him. He had time. And he had to see, to make certain.

He took a step, then two, reaching out on either side for handfuls of foliage that would help him down the steep descent. A few steps later and he was in total darkness. Brambles caught at his trousers, as though trying to prevent him from descending deeper. Listen! What was that? His whole body now began to tremble. Now, midway down, he could see the outline of the enormous coach, its blunt nose buried in the earth.

Abruptly he stopped. He didn't want to go any farther. He'd seen enough. No one could survive that wreck. He tried to take a step backward, but his foot slipped and he slid forward, his hands reaching out frantically on either side. He could see the escaping steam now and when he tried very hard, he could make out something that looked like the outline of a human body stretched out on the ground.

With all his might he tore himself away. The ground was wet, and the mud had sucked in his shoes. There was no traction. He kept slipping back down, falling nearer and nearer the wreckage.

Breathless now, he gave one enormous wrenching upward, grasping for grasses, branches, anything to assist him out of that pit of hell. Then suddenly he heard it again, the faintest of cries, growing louder now. He turned and looked back over his shoulder. A single cry escaped from his lips. There, hovering over the wreckage of the coach, he saw clearly two specters, evolving out of the smoke and escaping steam.

For a moment the breath caught in his throat and he could not breathe. He experienced the most acute spasm of terror he had ever known. Then he saw clearly the figures moving toward him, hideous, familiar figures, the specter in the black hooded cape and the woman with blood-red skirts.

He cried aloud in his agony, a single, earth-shattering "No!" But still they came, hovering directly over him now, forcing him back to earth until he was lying flat on his back, saliva running in a thin stream down his chin, his eyes distended in fear.

He cried out again pitiably, "What do you want? Leave me alone!" But suddenly the specters descended, closed in on him, pinning him to earth, his arms and shoulders where their hands first touched him chilled now as though he were dead. His face had become fixed and he could not move his mouth. He tried twice to cry out, but no sound left his lips. Then again he felt the two cold hands on his shoulders, saw clearly the woman's face, her eyes questioning, threatening, then slowly turning toward the wreckage of the coach.

He had no choice. He could not move. He lay still, his head pressed backward against the earth. Then, sternly, the black hooded figure on his right directed his attention toward the smoke and steam. It had become so quiet. He raised his head in an attempt to do as he had been told. And in that moment he saw, evolving out of the vapors, a room, liquid-appearing at first as though underwater, then gradually assuming shape and substance, a room he clearly recognized, the small upper bedchamber of Bledding Sorrow.

Again he tried to wrench free from the horrible apparition, but the specters on either side continued to hold him fast. He had no choice but to follow the ordeal to its conclusion. He looked up again. The room before him was drawing nearer now, so close that he was on the threshold, surrounded on all sides, as though it intended to devour him. The whole darkness of the vast and tragic night was alive, and the specters seemed to be watching him. The silence had become so great that the ground resounded each time his heart beat, the specters on either side still forcing his attention to the small upper bedchamber before him.

He followed the direction of their concentration with dread, with resignation. He saw the door to the bed-chamber being slowly opened. A sound of deep breathing, the same as that of sleep, began to rise from the room. He saw clearly the Elizabethan arches, the flickering fireplace, and a woman lying on the bed.

Suddenly his jaws clenched with anguish, motionless now, as out of the shadows stepped his ancestor, the sixteenth-century Geoffrey Bledding. He saw clearly as the man moved toward the sleeping woman, tried to close his eyes as he saw his ancestor leaning over her, a vicious face belonging to a monster who seemed to have ten arms, all working in demonic unison, stripping off her nightdress, thrusting her arms behind her and binding them rigidly with a length of hemp rope, encasing her body in fiercely drawn bondage, and knotting it finally about her legs.

Already Geoffrey had seen enough and again tried to wrench free from the horrible reenactment. But the specters on either side continued to hold him fast, forcing his attention.

Then he saw his ancestor stand back as though to view his handiwork. He seemed to take pleasure in the lady's passionate but useless strainings, her pitiable cries for mercy. Then suddenly the small upper bedchamber was quiet. The stillness shimmered in the firelight. A cold wind occasionally rattled at the window. But that was the only sound. The madman took his place behind the door as still as death, as though seeing his honor avenged were his only need, like an intolerable thirst that had to be assuaged.

The lady grew equally as still, as though she knew that at last she had come to an end of her own making, as though she knew that the coachman would come and that they were both doomed.

Geoffrey was panting now, his fear almost smothering him. He longed not to see what was coming and twice he tried to avert his face, and twice the specters with their hands as cold as death forced him back, forced his attention on the scene in the upper bed-chamber.

It seemed an eternity, though in reality it was no more than a few seconds. Apparently the lady heard his footsteps first because she was accustomed to listening for them. Outside the door they stopped. For a moment there was silence again, as though some instinct had warned the coachman. But within moments Geoffrey saw the massive oaken door give, swing open a few inches.

Suddenly he saw the lady try to rise up from her bondage as though to warn the coachman. And then there was no more silence. The coachman took one step farther into the room. And the mad eyes of Geoffrey's ancestor, fixed on him from the shadows behind the door, lifted in triumph, the man himself stepped out behind him and, holding an ax by the blade, raised the broad wooden handle and brought it squarely down across the top of the coachman's head. The man fell forward, unconscious, across the floor.

At that moment, unable to endure any more, but still pinned against the earth, Geoffrey cried aloud, "No more, please." But the specters smothered his cries and again forced his attention back to the scene before him. Helpless, he watched as his ancestor flew then into a rage of activity. Quickly he stripped the coachman and bound him in the same fashion as he had bound the lady. Then he dragged him roughly across the floor and placed him beside her, both helpless now, completely bound and at his mercy.

A few moments later the coachman stirred, tried to raise himself as though he were not yet aware of his own helpless position. But it was the last motion he was to make in that world. For suddenly Geoffrey saw his ancestor pull the coachman roughly over, place one rigid foot against his back, slowly raise the ax up into the air, and bring it down with one stunning blow, decapitating the coachman with such force that the head went spinning across the floor, spewing blood in all directions, while the body itself lay twitching for several minutes, now a less feverish lover.

At the exact moment of the blow Geoffrey lost consciousness. He could not bear to watch any longer. But a moment later he felt the specters on either side shaking him, his arms and hands so cold now he could scarcely feel them. He was whimpering like a child, openly begging them to leave him alone. But there was more, and again they forced his attention back to the small bedchamber, to the sight of his ancestor standing now over the lady, holding her lover's head by the hair, forcing her to look at it, placing it finally on her breast.

Geoffrey lay in a misery of cold and terror. The world as he knew it had disappeared. In every direction that he looked he saw blood or the threat of blood, heard an unending scream while a bitter wind, a piercing wind penetrated to the very marrow of his bones.

Now he watched as the lady nestled her cheek against the blood-moist hair, as though she were scarcely aware of the feverish activity around her legs. And in truth she was whispering to her lover's head when he saw his ancestor raise the ax again in the air, a whirling, hissing sound as he brought it down once, then twice. He saw the lady's head jolt backward against the floor, saw her hands lift, claw for a moment at their bondage, then fall limp at her sides.

The full impact of what had happened came to him only when he looked up and saw his ancestor standing over her, holding a severed foot in each hand, shouting down on her over and over again that now she could not even follow her lover's ghost into purgatory. A few moments later, as the blood ran from her body, unabated, her head rolled to one side and she was still.

Across this waste the wind continued to blow, increasing in speed now. Geoffrey closed his eyes, unable to look further, no matter what they did to him. On either side he was still aware of the specters, staring at him now, as silent as the frozen air, as the frozen ground on which he lay. They continued to stare at him; they made no move; they made no sound.

Then, through terror-filled eyes, he saw them as they began to move forward to a position directly in front of him, as though with one unexpressed accord to make him witness to the end. Slowly the male specter pushed back the hooded cape. There where his head should have been was a jagged cavity, the severed tendons of his neck extending upward like pieces of frozen iron. And on the other side the woman, in her turn, slowly lifted her skirts, revealing the torn stumps, arteries hanging loose, her feet severed, fresh blood streaming from the empty sockets.

At that moment Geoffrey screamed. Freed from them at last, he stumbled upward, intent only on escaping from the grisly scene. Every few paces he fell, for his shoes would not grip the mud, and each time he fell, the specters turned and watched him.

He continued running, sliding, falling, picking himself up until his breath went and he came to a halt near the top of the ravine, unable to move farther and scarcely able to breathe. And this time the specters did not stay to look at him, but moved quickly back down the incline, hovering protectively over the wreckage of the coach, disappearing finally into the vapors and steam and smoke.

From where Geoffrey had last fallen he saw the road, but there was nothing where he stared but long rain-soaked miles and the terrible silence and the cold. He looked backward in the direction from which he had come, but the wreckage was no longer in sight, and he could not remember the direction of Bledding Sorrow.

Indeed he ran in one direction only to stop and think frantically, *This is not the way*. And at once he began to run in the opposite direction. He could not get warm. He could not free his mind from the horrible scene he had just witnessed. He slipped and slipped again and went sliding down a small hollow and feverishly clawed his way back to the road and finally fell exhausted, terrorized, his body curled around in a half turn. He lay crumpled by the side of the road, tasting dirt in his open mouth, the night dark, rocking him on its surface, memories passing over him like streaks of mists over water.

Then suddenly, blessedly he saw lights as from a car, heard footsteps running toward him, heard a woman's continuous scream, finally saw a shapeless figure bending over him, heard Martin's voice. "Are you all right? Geoffrey, are you. . . ?"

Slowly he raised up, willingly giving in to the support of the man beside him. Through the darkness he saw Caldy More, her face agonized, bringing her continuous screams with her.

Let her scream, he thought. It was over now. Martin was here. Martin would take care of him. And again he leaned eagerly into the comfort of the man beside him, giving in willingly to his every command, allowed him to place him gently in the front seat of the near car, welcomed his soothing, "It's all right now, it's all right."

And Geoffrey knew that it was, in spite of Caldy More's cries. He saw her now at the edge of the road, looking down toward the wreckage of the coach, both hands grasping the sides of her head as though trying bodily to contain the horrible realization of what had happened. In her hysteria, apparently disregarding personal safety, she started down the treacherous incline.

Suddenly Martin shouted, "No!" and scrambled the few feet down after her, dragging her back to the road. "It's not safe," he cried, trying to shake her out of her hysteria. "There may be explosions." And Mavis Bonebrake was there, panting, continuously murmuring, "My gawd, my gawd."

Again, screaming pitiably, Caldy More tried to break loose. And again arms reached out to restrain her. Martin scolded, "Good Lord, woman, are you mad?

The thing could go like a bomb." Quickly he looked over his shoulder and shouted to Mrs. Bonebrake, "Drive back to Bledding Sorrow and call. We need help." He jerked Caldy More flat onto the ground and shouted again to the heavy retreating figure, "Call York. The idiots in Bledding won't know what to do. Call York."

Mrs. Bonebrake nodded and hurried off on her mission. Now Caldy More lay crumpled on the wet earth, weeping uncontrollably. In the interim Martin returned to the car, in which Geoffrey was sitting. He asked softly, "What happened?"

With a frightened expression Geoffrey glanced toward the top of the hill as though attempting to recreate the accident. He shook his head as though his first impulse was to say nothing at all. But with an obvious effort to control himself, he murmured, "It— was coming down the hill, too fast. . . ." He shifted in the seat, then stood up hesitantly, as though his words represented the incarnation of that brute force which had inevitably controlled him. Suddenly he stopped short and looked directly down at Caldy More. "Was Mr. Pask alone?" he asked.

But either Caldy More failed to hear the question or didn't want to answer. Instead she dragged herself a few feet away from where they were standing and continued to moan softly, her eyes fixed on the black depths of the ravine.

Suddenly, coming from the direction of the village, they saw a single light, a bicycle obviously, pedaling steadily toward them up the road. A few moments later a young boy, about sixteen, with red hair and mud-encrusted boots and the arrogant, confident, and slightly sullen look of the young, drew near. On the front of his bicycle was strapped a bulging canvas bag and a rifle was slung over his shoulder, clearly a poacher, a brave lad who had been hunting illegally on the Bledding estate under a cover of darkness.

Apparently he was unaware or unconcerned that the

master himself stood only a few feet away. Quickly he unstrapped the flashlight from the bars of his bicycle and ran to the edge of the ravine. "Blimey, what a crash," he exclaimed. "Heard it all the way to the village, I did," he added, more in excitement than terror. He glanced toward Martin Axtell and recognized him. "Want me to take a look, sir?" he offered, as though the thrill of the moment were so great that he'd take a closer look anyway whether Martin desired it or not.

But Martin approved. "There's a good lad," he urged. "Be careful, and don't touch anything. Just call up if there's anyone. . . ."

The boy, already starting down, grinned back at him. "Alive, sir? There's nothing human alive down there. I can promise you that."

Then, as though he could no longer contain his excitement, he slid down the slope, the light from his flashlight bouncing eerily off the underbrush, descending even deeper to the bottom of the ravine, where now the illumination from the flashlight, a single small eye, swung in limited circles across the coach, its crushed, blunt nose buried in earth, its hulking rear suspended in midair, the tires still spinning, steam escaping, smoke spreading.

The little knot of people at the top of the road stared intently down. Even Caldy More raised weakly up on one arm, her face ravaged and her eyes fixed on the tiny bouncing light. No one spoke. They merely waited and watched in a state of suspended animation.

Suddenly the light moved around to the area at the front of the coach. It held still for a moment. No longer casting distorted shadows, it now appeared to be frozen as though focusing rigidly on something. Then abruptly it went out. Once again the area at the bottom of the ravine was plunged into total darkness.

Caldy More gasped, a sharp intake of breath. Martin paced restlessly, shouted down, "Hallo. You all right?"

No answer.

Geoffrey continued to stand a distance apart, as though to separate himself from what was going on. Except for the slight quiver of his lips and the moisture in his eyes that made them lighter, his smile, in the darkness, was almost calm.

Now, again, Martin shouted down the ravine, "Hallo? Are you there?"

Still no answer. It was several long moments before they heard the sound of the boy's footsteps, weaker now, faltering as though he were having difficulty standing erect. He was on his hands and knees as he climbed to the top of the road, his face white, drained of all color. He appeared to be close to fainting, for once he struggled to his feet, he fell forward again, shaking his head back and forth, a low sound escaping from his lips.

They watched, helpless, as he stumbled off into the night, apparently unable to speak at all except for mindless mutterings. . . .

ᏬᏬᏋ(**50**)ᏋᏬᏬ

By the broadest of standards, the accident was a grim
one. It was almost dawn when the emergency vehicles
arrived from York. By then a fair-sized crowd had
gathered, clogging the road in both directions, making
rescue operations difficult if not impossible.

In truth, it mattered little, for there was nothing to
rescue. Even the inspectors from York, grown somewhat jaded by the daily carnage on the giant motorway, took one look at the scene at the bottom of the
ravine and had to pull back for a moment. They worked
throughout the early hours of the morning in teams,
spelling one another, climbing for relief to the top of the
ravine with trembling hands and white faces.

The young woman had been thrown clear, although
the impact of the crash had reopened her fresh ampu-
tations. Cause of death: internal injuries and loss of
blood.

The coachman, less fortunate, had been thrown forward by the force of the violent descent. His head had
shattered the wide front windshield while the lower
half of his body had apparently caught on the steering
wheel. The splintered glass, in guillotine fashion, had
severed his head from his body. The decapitated head
had rolled a few feet to where the woman lay; her one
outflung arm appeared to be beckoning it to come
closer.

It was late in the evening before the wreckage was
totally cleared. The inspectors from York questioned
Geoffrey Bledding at length. He told them, in close
concert with Martin Axtell, that his wife, fresh from
radical surgery, had grown suddenly, dangerously feverish. They had tried to contact the surgeon in York and,

failing, had decided it would be most prudent to take her immediately to the hospital. The coach was selected because it was the vehicle which most resembled an ambulance, enabling her to lie prone in relative comfort. Martin and Geoffrey were to have followed in the automobile.

No one contested the story. Why should they? What was the purpose? The two were dead. It was over.

The inspectors nodded their heads sympathetically and wrote their reports. Cause of accident: a rain-slick road, a coach, under the duress of a crisis, traveling at an unsafe rate of speed over hazardous terrain. It was all so inevitable.

No charges were filed. . . .

Epilogue

It is the coldest of Novembers.

Bledding Sorrow is closed now. Geoffrey and Martin Axtell are in the south of France, preferring the Mediterranean sun to the chill damp English winter.

Caldy More is something of a recluse. She lives alone in a small cottage in a remote corner of the Bledding Sorrow estate. She walks to the village now and then, and people see her and try to engage her in conversation. But she says nothing and shakes her head and moves quickly away.

The rest of the staff has scattered, each to his own particular destiny. The Elizabethan jewel of a house is boarded and shuttered. A caretaker provided by the National Trust lives there alone and patrols nightly.

Winter will pass, as it always passes in England, public opinion to the contrary. Spring will come, and Bledding Sorrow will be opened and aired, and the students will fill the third-floor dormitory rooms, and the tourists will flock in greater numbers to see its unparalleled treasures and to listen for the lady's cries. Because of the tragic accident, the legend will enjoy a tremendous rebirth, and Bledding Sorrow will flourish.

But nothing will happen. Not for a while. It may take a hundred years or longer for the right forces to converge again.

And then. . . .

I cannot help but like Oblivion better
Than being a human heart and human creature,
But I can wait for her, her gentle mist
And those sweet seas that deepen are my destiny
And must come even if not soon.

—STEVIE SMITH

Shanna

A woman with surging desires
of the spirit, the flesh,
and the heart . . .

Ruark

A man burning to possess her
in vengeance and
in ecstasy . . .

Shanna

A romance of passion
beyond wildest dreams!

Kathleen E. Woodiwiss

The author of the bestselling epics THE FLAME AND
THE FLOWER and THE WOLF AND THE DOVE has
written a breathtaking saga that moves with rapturous aban-
don to London, the Caribbean, and Virginia—an unforget-
table novel that will stir the hearts of millions across the
country, throughout the world.

AVON 31641 $3.95

Permanent deluxe edition

SHANNA 4-77